Also by AC Benus

The Secret Melville Series
Seven filmscripts based on the sea novels of Herman Melville
ebook: ISBN 9781953389022; paperback: ISBN 9781953389039

Mojo
A modern reimagining of Petronius' ancient novel Satyricon *set in Trump's America of conmen, the conned, the ultra-rich, the sexy and the downright silly. "A laugh riot!"*
ebook: ISBN 9781734561074; paperback: ISBN 9781734561050

One Hundred and Fifty-Five Sonnets for Tony
A bold testament to love
ebook: ISBN 9781953389114; paperback: ISBN 9781953389107; hardback: ISBN 9781953389121

Demon Dream
Redemption and shared humanity shine in this retelling of a medieval Japanese legend
ebook: ISBN 9781953389138; paperback: ISBN 9781953389145

Mikhail Kraminsky, and other poems
Two collections of early poems exploring the pain of youth and being closeted
ebook: ISBN 9781953389152; paperback: ISBN 9781953389169

First Love: Poems for Ross
For everyone's first love; both bitter and sweet
ebook: ISBN 9781734561081; paperback: ISBN 9781734561098

Also by AC Benus

Hymenaios, or The Marriage of the God of Marriage
A Classical style myth in 2,600 lines of Blank Verse
ebook: ISBN 9781953389091; paperback: ISBN 9781953389084

Summer 2020 – Hell in a Handbasket
A contender for the Pulitzer Prize in poetry, 2021, this collection grapples with the year of pandemic, racial justice and environmental crisis
ebook: ISBN 9781953389015; paperback: ISBN 9781953389008

The Thousandth Regiment
A Translation of and Commentary on Hans Ehrenbaum-Degele's First World War Poems "Das tausendste Regiment"
ebook: ISBN 1657220583; paperback: ISBN 9781657220584

A Man in a Room and other poems
Verse following the year when the poet was 21 years old
ebook: ISBN 97817345103; paperback: ISBN 978173456107

The Easiest Thing in the World, and other poems
Marking the third anniversary of the Pulse Nightclub terror attack
ebook: ISBN 9781734561029; paperback: ISBN 9781734561036

Rima Fragmenta, or Fragments of a Rift
Fifty Sonnet for Kevin
ebook: ISBN 9781734561005; paperback: ISBN 9781734561012

Carême in Brighton

a novel – AC Benus

an AC Benus Impression
San Francisco

ISBN 978-1-953389-21-3 (ebook)
ISBN 978-1-953389-17-6 (paperback)
ISBN 978-1-953389-20-6 (hardback)

CARÊME IN BRIGHTON: A NOVEL.

Although some characters in this novel are based on actual personages, their representations in this book are entirely fictional.

Cover photos:
Backrground: Pixaby.com – Darkmoon Art
Knife: Pixaby.com – Lindsey Home

Part Titles:
Sugar work *pièces montées* from Carême's 1815 *Le pâtissier pittoresque*

Chapter Vignettes:
Artwork from Carême's 1828 *Le cuisinier parisien;*
Images of a set of Maison Odiot *attelets* in the author's collection

Library of Congress Control Number: 2022902936

"The human mind should hold itself independent of the little trials and vicissitudes of everyday life; for it should repose in the strenght of its diginity; and the truly immortal gift of the Diety should rise superior to the petty caprices and oppressions of man."

Lady Sydney Morgan
(*Saint Clair*, 1803)

Table of Contents

Table of Contents (Cont.)

Producing a cold, murderous atmosphere, not a soul who lived through 1816 would ever forget it as "the year without a summer."

The bad weather served as allegory for notoriously uncertain times. Napoleon may have been taken down by the Allies the year before at Waterloo, but little feeling of relief accompanied it within the mind of the Everyman. For the ordinary people, there were no rainbows in the sky to promise a liberated and stable world, as God's vow to Noah had been, but a return to oppression and brutalism. The status-quo-enforcing Congress of Vienna had seen to that.

No, instead of the assurance of forgiving portents, after the tumultuous flood of twenty years of war, there was nothing but an ominous, starvation-engendering vault of air overhead. It was such that with the constant chill and damp, the people felt as if they were on the verge of a shiver that would not come; of one they could not shake.

It rained in Paris as two men sat in the Hôtel Galliffet.

"These are dark, very dangerous times," Prince Talleyrand was saying monotone while tapping his foot. "Dark and potentially explosive."

The Grand Chamberlain of France – the Nation's highest Minister of State – carried every one of his sixty-two years as crease lines around the large blue eyes that peered from his otherwise alabaster face.

He was a survivor and more than wily enough to occupy towering positions in each of the consecutive Administrations of France. First under Louis XVI, then the Revolutionary Government, the Terror, and the Directoire. But it was *over* Napoleon's Empire he held the power that allowed Talleyrand to fenagle 'continuity' and remain the leverage behind the incoming Louis XVIII. It was shrewd, ever-calm, eternally unflappable Charles-Maurice de Talleyrand-Périgord who was in control.

The far-younger man sitting across from the Chamberlain in Talleyrand's private office was pivotal to his plotting possible deviations for the course of history. Theirs was one final, pre-mission conference before the agent was dispatched overseas.

As for the would-be provocateur, he had met with Talleyrand any number of times but never felt comfortable subjected to the minister's unflinching gaze. It was made all the worse by the fact the man hardly ever regarded a person with anything but half-raised eyelids. The stare never parted from anyone beholden to the Prince Chamberlain, and that was nearly everyone.

The younger of the two said, "Leaving Paris will be bittersweet, but I shall not miss this strange July with its smog, produced by all the coal-fuelled parlour fires choking the city."

Disinterested, the minister replied, "It's human nature. Every one of us scrambles for just a bit of warm and comfort."

"Yes, it's true. But I will be loath to remove myself from our city, as she's the beating gastronomic heart of Europe. I do not want to miss any important innovations while I'm playing the exile."

With bone-dry wit, the Chamberlain retorted, "Take some of your passion to Brighton. I'm sure they need it there, amongst their damnably greasy mutton chops and turnips."

Behind his thin smile, all joking aside, he gloated silently about his accomplishment. He'd groomed in the man before him now an asset so deeply covert, not even the professional's closest of colleagues knew of any connection to the powerful minister of international affairs.

But the Prince wasn't shy of reminding the other of his allegiance to Talleyrand. "As you go about your mission, *Monsieur,* I trust you will bear in mind who plucked you from obscurity and placed you where good fortune could best discover your talent. Talents, I'm assured, worthy of the great name now attached to you."

For the one sticking his neck out for France, the snake-like hiss of implicit threat rattled in his ears. Hypnotic and dark, the effect was like that of a mouse under a cobra's spell. *"Oui, Seigneur.* I shall not forget the power you have wielded and may yet wield."

The blow was struck. "And do not worry while you are absent – your Agathé and Marie, left behind in Paris, will be under my constant watch and supervision." He grinned. "They'll never leave my sight."

The other man chilled. He walked a tightrope, and although motivated by a deep-seated patriotism, he was never allowed to forget he acted under compulsion. "Thank you."

"Well"—the Chamberlain cleared his throat—"leaving thoughts of Paris behind, I can tell you the same rain and saturated conditions, the same coal-choked smog plagues London. In addition, the tripling of the price of fuel there is only adding to the cause of the English revolutionaries. The stench of revolt – of a coming forced change – is in the air. The place is a tinderbox where the people merely wait for a spark to detonate."

"If such an explosion comes, then the *Roast Beefs* will feel their empire reduced to match an armless France."

"Right you are, *Monsieur.* And it is well under way. Graffiti slogans appear overnight all over the city, for even on the walls of Carlton House – the Royal residence – it is painted: 'Bread or the Regent's Head!' And this fat George is pelted with stones, mobbed and jeered wherever his carriage dares to go in public, even on the day he slipped on his rented crown to open their Lordly Parliament."

"Is this then why," the agent enquired, "the Regent spends so much time by the sea, in Brighton?"

"Presumably, for its action fit a coward who runs from the reality of his starving people to live like Genghis Khan in his country retreat, swaddled in all manner of exotic luxury."

The other scoffed. "And such a man is credited with defeating our mighty Napoléon. Preposterous!"

"Yes, my friend, and we know it's not over yet. Even a dying stag can gore its hunter to death."

"At least I hope to be away from unhealthy air at the English seaside."

"Speaking of which, you and your associate's travel arrangements have all been made. You will leave by private coach this afternoon for Calais. Once you have settled into your new positions, your coded intelligence reports will get from Brighton to Paris via secret fishing-boat handoffs. Use the designated drop-off location and times, but never be seen doing it."

"Oui, Seigneur."

"You will be my eyes and ears in the English court, so report everything you hear, even if you think it's inconsequential. All intelligence can lead to leverage of the most appalling variety."

"Every detail . . . ?"

The Prince sighed, annoyed. "Once again, *Monsieur,* I cannot overstate the importance of your intelligence-gathering role in addition to your primary objective. Report all, even that which seems mundane, for one small element from you may fit as a key to unlock the import of another strand of information I've received from others."

"Yes, Prince. And my associate is not to know of any of this?"

Talleyrand grinned. "Of course not."

"And not to receive any blame should my ultimate task go awry, and the plot be uncovered—"

"Again, of course not. That is assuming you do not *force* any unforeseen out-comes."

Thus, once more, the elder spy-master's covert threat was overtly understood by the younger man.

The Grand Chamberlain rose, extending a hand to be grasped.

The operative stood and shook it.

"Remember," said Talleyrand, "Whitehall's empire is cracking under the weight of independence movements growing in Dublin, Edinburgh and Cardiff. Soon, these capitals will declare their sacred sovereignty over the inactive and costly bureaucracy of England. So, *bonne chance, Monsieur. Au revoir!"*

The younger man let go his hand, barely able to mutter, *"S'il doit être."*

PART I

Summer 1816

Chaumière sur un Rocher

Chapter 1: Settling In & Second-Hand Pies

Whenever Cornelius Hook was tasked with something he thought beneath his station, he went about it with a taciturn chip on his shoulder.

His chore today was showing a newly arrived Frenchman around the Pavilion, but as he led the way, rattling off statistics, the Private Secretary's mind wandered. A portly middle-aged man himself, he was not so sure the excited gossip preceding Carême's arrival had been worth all the hot air it generated. After all, as a Royal retainer of a certain dignity – albeit a nobility mostly reinforced amongst his peers by the gold braid of his uniform – the secretary was left to wonder what was so strikingly 'Romantic' about a tall, well-built foreigner with fine features, a chiselled nose, dark wavy hair and a Byronesque stance . . . ? And surely, this *celebrated* chef's paltry thirty or so years of life on Earth put him at a considerable ways-of-the-world disadvantage.

Antonin Carême, for his part, tired and road-weary, dutifully followed the Regent's personal lackey in a bit of a daze. Talleyrand's descriptions of George's seaside villa had failed to do justice to the house's remarkable interior.

"The Pavilion is a work in progress," intoned the officious Hook as they mounted the North Staircase. They were moving from the main level of the retreat – the ground floor – to the upper, or Chamber Floor. "You will find several areas analogous to Rome under construction."

Fatigued as he was, the beauty of the three windows of the stair landing struck Carême the moment Hook stepped out of his line of sight. Natural light came through panes of satin glass overpainted with full-length portraits of Chinese Immortals – two goddesses on either side of Guan Yu, the god of war with martial flags rising behind his shoulders. Their size was incredible, for the windows went from the landing's floor, up fifteen feet, ending in arches close to the stair hall's ceiling. The room's walls were a luxurious pink, grisailled in shades of indigo with foliage and exquisite birds in the fashion of Chinese blue and white porcelain; and the space was centrally lit by a soffit-enclosed skylight.

"So, I'm sorry," concluded the Private Secretary.

Carême nearly ran into him. *"Pardon?"*

Miffed at being ignored, Hook repeated, "I said, I'm sorry you will find your stay with us inconvenient. Noise; dust; smell of wet plaster."

"It's no hindrance to me, *Monsieur*. Perhaps I will appreciate watching the final form of the Pavilion take shape."

"Yes." The Regent's secretary turned and continued to lead the men's way to the Chamber Floor, muttering, "If you stay that long."

What Cornelius Hook could not have known is how serious Carême had been. A chef and pastry artist, the Frenchman's interest in all things architectural was innate, and Prince George's country home was proving to be a feast for the senses; tired as they were, everywhere the cook cast his eyes, new delights awaited.

More appeared, for at the top of the stairs, they passed through a pair of open doors into a very large room.

"This," announced the functionary, "is the villa's North Chamber Gallery. There is another attached to the South Staircase. You will find all the principal spaces of the Pavilion are symmetrical."

Dark indigo walls rose to another soffited skylight. The decoration consisted of bamboo trellises painted between the four doors leading to the bedroom suites. Atop a golden carpet sat bamboo furniture to invite casual lounging, and the sofa across from the fireplace had a table pulled up to it perfect for meals. Cushions and upholstery were uniformly done in blue silk.

The secretary drew Carême's attention to one of the portals. "This," he chanted as if before the holy tabernacle, "is the Regent's suite of private apartments."

He then strode to an identical door on the opposite side of the Gallery. He opened it. "And these are my lodgings – directly across from the Prince."

The men went inside. Carême's trunk, and his various smaller bags, sat in the middle of the floor, in front of Hook's bed.

"His Highness thought this would be the best place for you to live."

Now the chef had uncovered one of the roots of the lackey's hostility towards him. Placing his hand on the trunk, he said, *"Non; non.* This will not do. Kindly have my things moved to the chef's room in the Servants' Hall. I will be content there."

Failing to placate Cornelius Hook, the Prince's secretary looked more incensed than ever. "You negate this honour . . . . You"—a new, malicious light came into the Englishman's eyes— *"prefer* to be in the servants' wing, no doubt closer to your . . . your . . . compatriot."

Carême sighed, knowing what he had to say would fail to do him no good. *"Monsieur* Hook, you will forgive me, but I am tired from the long journey. In addition, I am not used to trying to express myself in a foreign tongue, which for me is English. I do hope we have not started off on the wrong hoof, as they say. I will make amends if we have."

The functionary sneered; he was at a crossroads. Cornelius could accept the chef's invitation to a peaceful coexistence, or— "In the first place, it's 'foot.' Off on the wrong *foot.* And secondly, I am not a man used to being asked by Royal staff members to accommodate their inadequacies. This, I trust, you will understand."

Tired, it is true, but not easily intimidated, Carême stepped up to the man. He altered his methodology, as being direct had led him to a roadblock.

"Mr. Secretary, I would like to ask you: What size meal does our employer, the Prince, usually take for dinner?"

Hook blinked. "Well, that is dependent on the number of guests at the Pavilion at any one time. If for himself and one or two family members, then generally the Prince will be served a soup, two entrees, a roast, two side dishes and a pudding."

Carême was aghast, suddenly questioning his entire *raison d'être* for being there. *"Monsieur,* I am not accustomed to laying any dinner service for less than two soups and four *entrées."*

"Well"—the secretary exhibited a bit of hesitation—"it should be noted the Regent is watching his weight, as the whole Nation watches it anyway. And, *they've* only ever seen it expand!"

Carême was dismayed, not only at the information, but at what he perceived as Hook's disloyalty. He'd have to be cautious around this one.

"D'accord. Now, concerning my position in the household, I wish to be where I, as *chef de cuisine,* belong – in the servants' quarters. Please see to it my belongings are moved there. And then, you, may continue to rest your head here, at the Prince's beck and call, *non?"*

Having extinguished the functionary's fires – for now – Carême gestured for Hook to continue his tour.

A few minutes later, they'd retraced their steps down the North Staircase and had travelled halfway along the Central Corridor, when Carême noticed something and stopped them.

On a large table against the pink and blue wall sat an architectural model under glass.

"Ah, yes," explained the secretary, "this is Mr. Nash's vision for the completed Pavilion."

It was fantastical: the variety of shapes and forms of the roofscape were done in liberal-handed interpretations of the best of Mogul architecture, and yet the overall impression retained the charming whimsy of a child's playhouse.

"This," Hook said, pointing straight down in the middle, "is the central onion dome over the Salon; the room right behind us." The man then motioned to the far ends of the building model. Here, two identical blocks anchored the extremities of the Pavilion and were capped with enormous curving tent rooves. "The one on the right will be the Music Room – the ballroom, in essence – and the other on the left is the Banqueting Room. The shells of both have been built, but His Highness diverted all construction efforts to completing the dining space first, in your honour."

Carême's eyes were still going over the minute details of the model. The dominant Indian features were traced out and completed with fascinating detailing relating more to European gothic than anything Eastern. The hybrid design was captivating.

"You know," the secretary continued low, "I hope you will conduct yourself in a manner befitting your situation in a large household."

"What do you mean?" Carême stood upright.

"I mean, I hope you'll 'be cricket,' as we say, and not try to outshine the rest of the Pavilion staff."

"You are saying I should remember my place?"

"Indeed."

"Then I will remember the Regent engaged me to bring the Pavilion up to Continental – or, as your countrymen say, 'European' – standards for Royal residences."

The functionary snarked, "Engaged at exorbitant prices."

"What I earn should not be any concern of yours, but my success should. For my artistic triumphs here will benefit all – my rising tide will elevate even your presumably already high reputation, *monsieur* Hook."

The secretary was oddly gratified. If this was the attitude the Frenchman was going to exhibit in England, then his time here was bound to be short. The man pasted on a bland smile, gesturing. "Shall we?"

The lackey led them towards a pair of unpromising mirrored panels. Under the landing of the South Staircase, they were full-height, unadorned and gave the impression of being low, which they were not. Sounds of construction and workman-voices increased the closer they got, and Carême suspected the Private Secretary was ushering them through discreet servant doors.

Nothing could have been further from the truth, and the chef's willpower alone kept him from gasping. For they passed into an enormous room; at least sixty feet to the opposite wall from where they stood. The central portion was some forty-foot-square, and rose to an arched ceiling of that height or more, resting on triangular pendentives. Between these flaring supports needed to transition a square base into a circular dome, large openings in the wall allowed for clerestory windows. Sunlight poured in on a construction scene where men on towering scaffolds executed geometric stuccowork on the lower half of the ceiling. More plasterers travailed on laying and smoothing the acres of wall space.

As it stood, every detail of the architecture was white, and Carême felt as if one of his monumental sugar models had come to life.

"This," the secretary announced as he started to breeze through it, "is the Banqueting Room. I trust it will serve your needs, when complete."

Carême as a consummate courtier could smell when an arch remark came his way, so ignored it.

In truth, although known for his large-scale catering – including baking the wedding cake for Bonaparte's second marriage – the fruits of his labours had yet to be showcased in a grander, purpose-built dining room than this one promised to be.

Through another set of doors catty-corner from where they'd entered, Hook showed the chef into a long intermediary space. Deep counters lined the side walls, providing copious storage below. The worksurfaces above were spacious enough to hold the serving trays of an entire army. Although, where they entered, a set of French doors led outside, the room was mostly lit by a continuous skylight down the centre.

"In here is the Decking Room. A staging area for the dishes, glasses, food, linens, and on and on. Everything that goes in or out of the dining room."

"But, *pardon,*" asked Carême, "if the Banqueting Room is unfinished—"

"The family take dinner in the Salon most afternoons. But if there are many guests, then either the Blue– or Yellow Drawing Room can be set for up to thirty-five place settings."

"Covers; but, *d'accord*. This is good information."

Leaving the Decking Room, the pair entered a neat and tidy service corridor. There were pretty Chinese-design blue and white Delft tiles from the floor to a wainscot.

Turning left, and proceeding down a good run of the Central Service Corridor, the secretary turned left once more through a pair of open wooden doors.

Carême's senses were instantly bombarded with the familiar: the smells of fresh produce and meat being prepared for cooking; of wood smoke and the heavy feel of charcoal fumes. There were also voices of professional cooks coordinating their intricately timed work with one another.

"And here," the functionary proclaimed, "is the Great Kitchen. His Highness rushed this room to completion specifically for your arrival. You should find nothing lacking."

And indeed, visually Carême saw before him a work-space of nearly perfect arrangement, and what a space! Thirty-five feet wide, and at least forty-foot long, four iron columns – cast and painted to resemble bamboo – supported a central smoke trap in the ceiling. Entirely windowed in glass, ventilation and natural light was in abundance. The placement of the slender pillars neatly divided the space into separate work zones: roasting on one long wall; cooking ranges on the other; and symmetrical preparation tables and an oval steam table down the centre.

Not merely a 'kitchen' in the basic sense of the word, here was a temple – nay, a cathedral – to cuisine. 'Europe' contained no rival, and it was ready for his command.

Carême caught the functionary eyeing his chefly wonder. Trying on Hook's bland smile for himself, he replied, "It will do."

They were distracted.

Kitchen staff slowly halted their activities one by one to watch the unfolding 'scene,' for a flurry of heated voices were advancing towards the two men's position.

In the vanguard of the charge was François Distré; several of the eyes amongst the crowd noting how confidently the mid-twenties man conducted himself.

"Chef Carême," he announced, "talk to this . . . this, head waiter—"

"I am not the head waiter." Gris Thorndyke defended himself. "I mean, I am not a *waiter* at all, as I told you, but the Chief Footman."

"Not in that costume." François gestured dismissively to the servant's uniform.

For indeed, the otherwise prime-of-life man appeared juvenile in his white stockings, black satin knee britches and red-liveried cutaway coat, tortured in gold braid.

"In France," Distré insisted, "we have done away with such humiliating suits in favour of proper dining-room attire."

The chef got an unexpectedly candid inspection of the troops under his command, for cap- and apron-wearing undercooks stood with folded, idle arms.

And to Carême's dismay, he saw a few women among the cooks' ranks, one of whom stood next to a guffawing man with the end of a pencil-thin cigar sticking out from under his cap. More junior staff stood in small groups, including a younger, teenage clot of undercooks who openly laughed with raised knees and shoulder-grabs onto their 'mates' to keep from thrashing around on the floor in giggles. One particular fair-haired youth seemed to be their leader, as he had an extra sparkle in his eye. Next to these tittering, older-teen slouches gathered the kitchen's youngest workers – spit-jacks stayed with sweep-up boys, and scullery maids with wash-up girls.

"François—" Carême started but was cut off.

"And what about you"—Thorndyke thrust a finger in François' chest—"what's a *may-tra doh tell* anyway? Maybe *you're* the waiter disguised under a fancy, made-up title."

The Chief Footman gestured to another gentleman of the group. "That sounds like the job of Head Table Decker, John Lightfoot."

"He sets the table," insisted François, "but I help him do it to accommodate the food placement plans Carême creates, and do it with the Chef's authority."

Mr. Lightfoot spoke up in François' defence. "I'm supportive of Monsewer Distray's help. Another pair of hands and eyes are always welcome, especially if the Chef has specific arrangements in mind."

Gris was gobsmacked. "There have never been any kitchen expeditors in England before and we've managed just fine."

François scoffed. *"You* think."

The Private Secretary tried to interject, "Now, men—"

"English standards are just as high as French."

François snorted. "Ha! The state of the culinary and serving Arts are far more advanced in France than England; everybody knows that. Anyone who's honest."

Carême placed a calming hand on his *maître d'hôtel's* arm. For in point of fact, the twenty-five-year-old François – born in 1791 – was a true child of the Terror and exhibited his generation's particular combination of zeal and restraint, once the need for restraint had been shown to them. "I believe we have gone off on a tangent. What was the original topic of this 'discussion'?"

"Suits," Thorndyke said. "How our footman uniform needs to be replaced."

"Why?" asked the astounded secretary, fingering a bit of his own braid.

"Every dining room in France," François explained with far more calm, "is served by men in street attire, as they are no less citizens than those sitting at table. Republican suits, Carême, was our topic, and how the Regent's home needs to join the 19th century."

The chef could see François' point. The britches and red coats appeared very *ancien régeime* to Carême's modern sensibilities.

"Just off the boat," griped Thorndyke, "and already wants to mess about and change things!"

François restrained himself.

"Ah! Just the person we need." Hook motioned towards a dour man fast approaching the group. Once he was close enough, the secretary did the introductions. "Chef Carême, may I present Donald Bland, Financial Comptroller of His Highness' kitchens, Brighton."

Gris dove in with both feet. "Yes – these 'Republican Suits' for me and my men will cost money; money Mr. Bland may not have—"

"Just a moment, Mr. Thorndyke," the newly arrived functionary said. "We will settle this in my office, but for now, we are taking the Chef's time before he has a proper lay of the land." Bland snapped his fingers and pointed at the leader of the roustabouts. "He'll show you the various support spaces."

In another moment, the Comptroller had ushered the arguing parties to his office and told the rest of the kitchen staff to "Be about your duties!"

Carême turned; he was face to face with the boy's smiling blue eyes. "What is your name?"

The young man whipped off his cap, smile gone – replaced by a multi-hued blush. "Thomas Daniels, sir."

"Age and rank?"

"Undercook; soon to be eighteen, Chef."

"Bon. Après vous."

The boy modestly stood there; mouth slightly agape.

Carême gestured. "I said, please lead the way."

"Yes, Chef." The undercook brushed aside the edge of his apron to stick his crumpled cap dangling from his rear pocket.

They entered the blue-tiled Central Service Corridor, heading back towards the Decking Room, but turned left into a spur corridor.

Thomas pointed to glass doors at the end. "That's the main servant entry, and the Pastry- and Cold Kitchens are off this hallway."

He ducked through the door closest to the exterior entry.

"This is the Cold Kitchen, or the Confectionary."

The room met Carême's expectations. There was good, natural light, the walls were tiled up to the ceiling in plain, cream-coloured rectangles, and numerous tables and cooling shelves were capped in white marble.

The chef stepped to the cooler. He lifted the lid and spied a perfectly clear, crystalline five-pound weight of ice.

"Bon," Carême said. "And there is more, *non?"*

"Oh, shure – tonnes more. There's an ice house buried under the southwest corner of the grounds, and with the winter we had this year, she's full to the brim."

A steady supply was necessary if Carême was to make the expected ice creams, gelatine-set dishes and his famous, colourfully layered *suédois*.

As they moved on with the tour, exiting the Cold Kitchen through another door, Carême couldn't help noticing how tempting the boy's cap looked in its current position.

Thomas, perhaps sensing this, became chatty. "I hope you are finding everything to your liking." He shed an apple-cheeked grin on the chef.

Carême gathered his thoughts. "The size, layout, light and ventilation of the Great Kitchen is unexpectedly well done."

"She's all down due to your predecessor, Chef Weltje, a Dutchman. He had some clever notions which turned into solutions."

"Like what?"

"Well – as you mentioned, ventilation. Weltje wanted the clerestory windows to open and close quickly, and be operated by anybody with a free hand. So, the architect built hidden rods in the walls with cranks down in the corners. He can solve any problem."

"The Regent's architect?"

"Yes, sir. And Chef Weltje saw that everything was in place for your arrival. Rumour has it the copper range hoods and the hundreds of pots and pans cost six thousand Pounds. Enough to buy a very large mansion outright, for shure."

Despite the boy's warmth and charm – artless as it was – Carême felt obliged to begin Master Daniels' education. "When referring to a kitchen's complement of 'pots and pans,' you should say *batterie de cuisine*. That way, everybody knows exactly what you mean. Proper French terms keep all things precise."

"Yes, Chef." The lad's expression betrayed his confident words.

"I mean, a *roux* is a *roux,* ever and always. But a translated 'brown butter paste,' or 'butter and browned flour base,' or many hundreds of other descriptions waste time and leave one guessing whether a *roux* is actually meant."

"I see your point, *monsieur Carême.* I will get better."

And here, this teenage youth's sincerity for improvement, touched Carême. Cooking was a hard life needing commitment first and foremost.

Thomas had guided them into a large and homey room. "This is the Staff Dining Hall."

They walked across it, left straight through the other narrow end and into another corridor. As the pair strode past several shut doors, Thomas said, "These are the offices of various Pavilion staff."

"Is one for my use?"

"Not here, no," Thomas replied, glancing over his shoulder. "You have a glass office off of the Great Kitchen."

"D'accord. Very well."

"The Kitchen Comptroller moved himself in there after Chef Weltje's departure, but he's packing up now – and not happy about it either."

This was useful intelligence to Carême. It might make it into his first report to Talleyrand.

In the Delft-tiled corridor once more, heading back towards the Great Kitchen, Thomas turned right and walked through an open door. "This," he told Carême, "is the Household Kitchen."

Carême noted it was also large, neat and tidy, and again lit by its own skylight.

They went straight through it, into a space of equal size. "This is the Steaming Kitchen, sir." He pointed to a corner where huge copper boilers were polished to gleaming perfection. "There's the station for syrups and sugar works, Chef."

This room had windows and a door to the outside. Young Master Daniels led Carême into a colonnaded open space. "The Kitchen Court, sir. And over there"—Thomas gestured to the far left where the walkway pillars came to an end—

"she's the Kitchen Stables. Right now, there are only a few cows and goats we keep for the milk."

This gratified Carême, for it was much easier to keep a few well-fed Holsteins than to risk procuring a variable product on the open market – especially the cream.

They were not alone in the court; two of the undercooks, a man and woman, were smoking leaning against the wall.

As Thomas ducked back into the Steaming Kitchen, he told Carême in soft tones, "That's James and Audrey Keenan, Irish cooks."

If Carême had been displeased to discover women undercooks in his kitchen, he was shocked to learn that some were also *married* to each other!

Saying nothing while Thomas led them back through the Household Kitchen, Carême's head was filled with notions of how eccentric this England was. Little did he know he'd just seen the tip of the iceberg.

Straight across the Central Service Corridor, Thomas conducted the chef into another open court.

An octagonal tower of bricks rose nine or ten stories in the air. Carême was astonished.

"This is the Water Tower," Thomas explained. "Well water is filtered as she's pumped to a tank at the top, and then filtered again with charcoal as she's piped into each kitchen with regulated pressure. You will find the Pavilion's water is always soft, sweet and fresh."

"That's ideal for baking," the chef found himself mumbling.

Thomas chuckled. "Speaking of which, step this way."

From the Water Tower Court, the pair passed through a door into a brick-lined room.

"This is the Pastry Kitchen."

There were spotless wooden tables, dough troughs and proofing racks, enough baking capacity to feed a small city. Carême was pleased.

"And then, Chef"—the young man exited through an internal door—"we have the Pastry Larder."

The storage space was shelved all around, and good smells abounded from containers of spice, blue-paper-wrapped sugar cones, boxes of Irish moss, food colours, and a hundred items stacked, arranged and coded for quick use.

Next to this room was a larger one with glass-doored cabinets on each side. "In here," Thomas said, "Chef Weltje archived his sugar work centrepieces."

"His *pièces montées?*"

"Yes. He left 'em here to inspire future artistic efforts at the Pavilion."

Carême opened a door to take a closer look. He saw a sugar work rustic folly with green fencing around it. Carême tried not to sound dismissive as he asked, "And you? What do you think of the details; of the colouring?"

Thomas didn't know and shrugged like a small boy put on the spot.

"I think," clarified Carême, "the modelling is sub-par, and there is a total lack of delicacy in the colours. The green, for instance, is much too strong."

Inappropriately, perhaps, Thomas Daniels laughed, his eyes though, kept gazing in wonder. "I can imagine what old Dutchman Weltje would say to you. But I'd tell you, he was also a pastry chef, just like *Monsieur.*"

Carême felt slighted. Line-order cooks who grew to be *chefs des cuisines* derided bakers grown to the same positions, even though the generalists couldn't produce a brioche to save their lives. "I can only hope pastry chefs are treated with more respect in England than they are in France."

The chef's attempt to let the boy know he'd just insulted his boss failed.

Instead of feeling humbled, Thomas felt emboldened. With a jocular stance, he told the handsome Frenchman, "People must tell you you look more like a poet than a cook."

Carême was taken aback. "Your 'Byron'?"

Eyebrows flared above his radiant smile. "Him too, but I was thinking of Shelley.

> *"Thus shall icy hearts be heated,*
> *Freed complete from their frozen rills,*
> *For ne'er will Spring be defeated,*
> *'Spite the hoarfrost-wilt daffodils."*

Being compared to a writer suited Carême's artist self-perception, but them again, what was the chef supposed to do with this boy's overly familiar nature?

Several minutes later, Thomas had taken the Frenchman to the glass-walled office where the Kitchen Comptroller stood, packing papers and ledgers into a rectangular basket.

He knocked and immediately opened the door, startling Donald Bland. "What is it?"

"I've finished giving the chef a tour—"

"Fine. Come in, Carême."

Thomas was all smiles. "But, sir—"

"Boy"—the Comptroller got needlessly assertive—"get back to your duties."

"But—"

Bland yelled, "Do as you're told!"

Carême, complacently watching this unguarded exchange, had an unbidden notion crash upon him. He saw on Thomas the sad deflating of his naturally ebullient character. The young man's jokester happiness had been crushed in the way only one with a personal connection can inflict on another.

This was more intelligence, albeit of a matter he might keep to himself.

Carême closed the door behind him.

Bland pushed the basket aside, and then made Carême sit as if a guest. The moneyman plopped down in his seat behind the desk, all elbows and intimidation.

"Well," he said, half-bored, "how was your tour? Ours is a facility of a quality you are probably not used to"—he paused, seeking out a suitably dismissive term—"over *there.*"

"The arrangements appear satisfactory. But the proof will only come once these Kitchens are tested executing one of my large dinners, say with thirty-two or more *entrées.*"

Carême could instantly see the *cost* of such a dinner pinged the Comptroller's banker-heart.

"And then"—Carême had an enquiry of his own—"what resolution did you find for the clothes question?"

Bland was belittling; haughty. "The footmen shall stay dressed as they are, as is the tradition, in red jackets and black knee-britches."

Carême let the subject go, knowing it was far from settled.

The functionary pulled a fat ledger from the top of his basket. "Now we must get down to some business. This," he said, opening the tome to a marked page, "is the Book of Entitlements. Each Royal Kitchen has one; it says how much extra money each servant in the operation of the food preparation is entitled to at the end of the year."

"Bonuses."

"Crudely put, yes."

"And these *entitlements,* work how?"

"The excess food and drink from His Highness' table are sold to agents around Brighton. I keep the records here." The man's finger slid over a row of figures. "Take our German Sous-chef, Friederich Bauda, for example. Last year he was entitled to the income from twenty loins of veal at 15 Shillings each; twenty pounds of butter at 1-Shilling-10-Pence a pound; and 19 Pounds in 'used' liquor sales. This came to 35 Pounds extra income for him – or the equivalent of the yearly wage of a Royal footman."

Carême was astounded, but shrewd. He knew the true game afoot. "And Herr Bauda must run around to the local chop houses with these joints of veal?"

Bland blinked. "Well . . . no. I . . . I take care of the money. The system is like that of 'a lay' on a commercial ship. Each crewmember who signs the Articles of a voyage is entitled to a percentage of the final sales of the cargo, but it is recorded as equivalents in the books – Crewmember 1 gets fifteen combs; Crewmember 2 gets 20 hand mirrors, *et cetera.*"

"And who in this kitchen," queried the chef with undue calm, "has direct oversight of the sales? Who handles the money *for* the staff until they get paid off at the end of the year?"

The Comptroller blushed in anger. He slowly rose to his feet, hands flat on the desk. "I do. And if you are . . . are . . . suggesting—"

There was a knock at the door. François was on the other side, lining up Sous-chef Bauda and all the head undercooks in charge of various crews.

Bland stormed to the door, opened it and went out briefly, barking, "Carême will be with you shortly!"

By the time he headed back into the office, Carême had serenely assumed his proper station – in *his* chair, behind *his* desk.

Bland controlled himself; what choice did he have? "So, will you sign the Book?"

"*Non.* This system is . . . how do you say it? *Arcane.*"

Miffed he had to say the word himself, Bland repeated, "Arcane."

"*Oui* – so, no. François and I, we will not be signing it."

"But, with your celebrity's name, and the amounts we'll get for second-hand pies made by you, the entitlement pool will grow very large."

"And all the 'second-hand pies' I make, François will sell so that he and I can split the money."

"But, but," the functionary sputtered, "you're taking cash away from the Entitlement Pool; out of the hands of your fellow chefs and colleagues."

"Out of the hands of middlemen, yes." Carême slammed the book shut, shoving it towards the Comptroller. "At the end of the year, I shall present my own bonuses to deserving staff. They will not suffer."

Bland appeared to hate the Frenchman. Gathering up his things – includeing the ledger – he stormed off.

Carême sat a moment more and thought he might have trouble with that one.

Many hours later, the time fast approaching one in the morning, Carême sat in his quarters writing his first coded Intelligence Report to Talleyrand. As the desk was situated in front of a window, he occasionally glanced at movement atop the Pavilion's water tower. While watching the gilt dragon weathervane swivel in the wind, he once more wondered how much information to hold in reserve against the all-powerful Grand Chamberlain of France.

He picked up his pen.

1 kj39de 2 ke3 mwl4nf. 3 8 om3c 9 10 kmw3ck lnd3mge8snv ynd9 un2 qpl4m8xjtzl wfvu 1 agnh 7 ngvd8f 3 dsw4cx 2 lkmb8ch. Gm9cuvyrpb, 8 it8k 3 bethgn7dcpmq 6 xzw8mvntdlh 3 10 opflbn8kwf nr7g blj3jn. 1 wumk4jmx 5 hb4k 3 xze, hv fjc4ex 3

Le voyage a été pénible. De la boue et une bruine continuelle nous ont accompagnés tout le long du chemin de Calais à Douvres. Maintenant, la côte de l'Angleterre est recouverte d'un brouillard sans soleil. L'humidité du bord de mer, si proche de

The journey was arduous. Mud and continual drizzle accompanied us all the way from Calais to Dover. Now the English coast is blanketed by sunless fog. The damp of the seashore, being so close to the villa, aggravates my condition, and the Pavilion itself is run as an undisciplined mess. Here the sound of constant hammering is accompanied by the acrid smell of paint. The cooking facilities are complete, but the staff seem organized as if it were 1716 and not 1816. Unbelievably, but there is a man and wife working in the kitchen as undercooks! This will suffice to show the lack of proper order in which these *selles de rosbif* wallow.

But, enough. We will have our first dinner service tomorrow, and I'll keep my ears open for important information. So far, my access has been limited to functionaries – men born to 'merit' through accidental titles and not risen to their positions through honest work – or, those who are called 'stuffed shirts' in this country. I've had the distinct displeasure of navigating the self-appointed turf of the Regent's Personal Secretary and the Financial Comptroller of the Pavilion's kitchens. Needless to say, both men's manoeuvring will be irrelevant as soon as I gain access to the Prince himself . . . .

Carême had to stop. He pulled his sketchbook over to hide his spy missive because François had just knocked gently on the inter-connecting door between their rooms.

The younger man entered without waiting for a reply.

The chef needn't have worried, for François acted oblivious to Carême and his current activities. Instead, he paced the floor.

"*Incroyable!* These . . . these backward cretins do not know what a *maître d'hôtel* is or what one is expected to do for his chef."

Carême's tone was soothing. "*Villon,* the dust has yet to settle. We are learning about them; they are learning about us. It is a process that must play out in its own time."

"I suppose you are right, as always. But still—"

"François, come here."

The impassioned young man ceased his roundabout motions. Carême had turned his chair and was inviting François to rest in a familiar position. He went to his mentor and sat on the floor, resting his back between the man's legs.

Carême smoothed François' hair. "We are foreigners in a foreign land. We need time to settle in here. And what an exotic place this Brighton is."

"The Pavilion is a strange building. I've already been exploring."

The chef chuckled; he knew François would have investigated their environs by this point. "And what have you uncovered?"

François began to feel the effects of Carême's touch. He spoke more tenderly. "I've been up on the roof and looked at the iron framing for the unbuilt onion dome. I've been to the top of the water tower and looked at the view. I've found hidden stairs and discovered the upper floor of this building is like a maze."

"You always did like to explore. You showed me interesting places at the Château Valençay every time we cooked there."

François laughed. "And you launched an expedition against every nook and cranny of the musty old library of the Château. Too bad you didn't find the Menon thesis on court cooking on its shelves."

"Yes, that was a disappointment. But, never mind; we did uncover rare old volumes of poetry there . . . ones that turned out to be important – personally – to you and me—"

François reached behind and took Carême's hand. "You don't regret it, do you?"

"Regret what?"

"Making me your protégé."

Carême chuckled again, this time due to warm nostalgia. "It seems like only yesterday I pulled you away from Chef Laguipierre at the Élysée Palace."

François said, full of true Gallic sincerity – brooding and dark – "I owe everything to you. I strive every day to implement your teachings to the best of my abilities."

Carême turned him around and descended on François' lips. "I have no regrets, *Villon.*"

Chapter 2: An Introduction & Reunion

The structure of eating for family and servants was very different: 'below-stairs' ate three square meals, but had to work these sit-down affairs between the up-stairs' five daily repasts.

From the perspective of the entitled, they'd rouse to a room already warmed by a fire built in the dark by silent hands. Then – per their habituated wake-up times – a valet or lady's maid would appear with cocoa to imbibed in bed. Naturally, this was a private 'meal.'

Next was a buffet-style breakfast for anytime they'd care to get up. Such gatherings were public.

'Tea' could follow at noon, and was taken in chambers either alone or with one or two intimate family members or friends. Then they would have to change and get ready.

Dinner was at 3 or 4, depending on the time of the year. As the main spread of the day, its commencement had to be flexible to ensure sufficient daylight by which to eat. It also proved to be as public a spectacle as a horse race. Not only the food was on display for every eye to consume.

The final meal of the gentry's day was again taken in seclusion, with just a few, close persons gathered near. For at 8 or 9, supper would be sent up.

Faced with the prospects of having to eat among strangers in the Staff Dining Hall, the expatriate Frenchmen had struck upon another solution, one co-opting the lordly concept of 'private' repasts.

On the first full day they were there, François rose well before the crack of dawn; had risen before a tiptoeing girl sent to light the man's fire found the maitre-d' and chef together in Carême's chambers.

The young man had lit a lamp and gone down to the Pastry Kitchen. As if a house maid himself, François carefully set the dry oak kindling and fuel into one of the bake ovens. Fanning it, making sure the flame caught, he mapped out the Frenchmen's breakfast for their premier day of labour under the Pavilion's fanciful rooves.

The beehive warming, he went about another task in this room, gathering eggs and butter, and a bowl for the flour and sugar. He washed his hands up to the naked elbows and then set about making sugared brioche – double buns – in a limited edition of six. The two men could snack upon these throughout the day.

The brioche tins greased and filled, he set the baking tray close to his heating oven, stoked the fuel some more, and then went upstairs to bathe and change. As the far-too cold water for July bit into his skin, he knew this day would be full of challenges.

Dressed in one of his 'Democratic' suits to proclaim he lived and died a Citizen of the French Nation, he slipped out of his room. While doing so, he saw a light under Carême's door and knew his mentor was planning the day's dishes; he'd be down soon.

So, François hurried on his way. He passed by the Household Kitchen, seeing it rousing itself with oatmeal and other stodgy 'English' fare, but the young man had decided not to jostle for cooking space, as he was an outsider, in there. Instead, he lit two of the wall sconces above the centre of the twenty-foot-long range, for he'd cook in the splendid isolation of the Great Kitchen. Picking up a curfew, he selected a few choice coals from yesterday's roasting fire, which had been nursed overnight under the pan's cover. These would be all he needed, so François set them in his range position, and added a new twig or two before he dashed off to pop his rolls in the oven.

Carême arrived and went to his office. Very calmly, François set a skillet atop his range coals to heat up, got a bowl, salt, pepper and six eggs. These he beat with a good slug of cream and took to the pan. A dollop of sizzling butter later, the eggs went into the skillet, and the men's omelette was under way.

By now, the spit-jack boys were there to rekindle the roasting fires, so he asked one to go fetch his brioche buns from the oven.

By the time the lad got back with the six glistening rolls, François had plated his omelette, and washed and dried his pan.

A second boy arrived from the larder just then with what the maitre-d' had asked him to fetch. So, the two small pots of apricot and peach preserves went on the tray with the omelette and sweet rolls.

He let himself into the office and sat down.

Carême – who had an excellent view of it from his desk – glanced at the huge kitchen clock.

François served himself and started eating, crumbs falling a bit as he enthu-siastically said, "As the city market is just the other side of Castle Square from us, I'll run over there sometime today and review the quality of the meat and seafood."

Carême was busy with papers. "Good. Survey the selection of produce as well. The Royal Household is still on an *ancien régime* model, and I understand most fruit and vegetables are grown by the kitchen gardens at Kew and Kensington Palaces. I will have to speak to the Kitchen Comptroller about the details; we may need some things from the public suppliers."

François nodded. "Yes, Chef. But we can know nothing until the day's *carte de menu* is written." And then slyly, while tearing and munching shreds of his bun, he added, "That Comptroller is an unpleasant man, no? Too much power—"

"Too much power corrupts, yes." Carême did not want to talk of him. His paperwork was finally complete, and he placed it between the boards of a portfolio. Now he ate, and did so quickly.

However, small bites between smiles told François he'd met the master's exacting expectations. Although it was only a *petit-déjeuner*, a little validation stoked the fires of François' self-confidence for the full day of work ahead. He was also gratified to fuel his mentor, the man . . . he—

The thought was interrupted by rough knocking. The Private Secretary said cryptically through the glass, "It's time."

The Frenchmen stood, making sure their attire was prim and proper.

A few minutes later, the Regent's personal assistant led Carême and François through a green-baize door into the *chinois* opulence of the Central Corridor. Carême had his portfolio tucked under his arm, and the new-arrivals appeared much better than in their grubby travelling clothes of the day before. Comfortable, they were both consequently more confident.

François had not seen the Central Corridor before, and fought hard not to express his astonishment. The sturdy pink of the walls with their overpainting of trellises and arbour bamboo reminded him instantly of the fanciful and subtle colours Carême used on his *pièces montées* – or, his sugar work showstopping centrepieces. François instantly realized Carême was in his element.

As they walked below the painted glass skylight and fantastical silk lantern chandelier along the middle of this passageway, commotion caught the men's attention. For just then, a youthful couple in stepping-out attire came from the door leading from the Blue Drawing Room. The young woman had high, coiffured hair – a tortured fight against the naturally ebullient nature of her flaxen finger curls – and wore a cream overcoat seemingly too warm for the alleged summer day; it was also too detailed for the fishing shores of Brighton. The handsome man, on the other hand, wore a far-more practical grey jacket with a cinched waist and wide lapels for changes in the weather. The pair were engaged in lively conversation, which suddenly stopped as the lithe mistress addressed her trailing lady's maid. "If we can avoid that beastly rain from starting again, Brigitte, we shall stroll outside for at least an hour."

"Oui, Madame."

While the women were thus distracted, the separate parties of three suddenly grew large as one.

They weren't more than a foot into circumnavigating their contrasting directions, when the overly dressed lady halted in her tracks.

"Goodness gracious, me!" the young woman cried with zeal. "You *must* be the celebrated Carême."

"*Oui . . . madame . . . ?*" Carême looked around for an introduction.

"Your hand-someness," the lady assured him, "precedes you."

Flattered, but flat, he replied, *"Merci."*

At this point, the Regent's secretary was forced to 'do the honours,' though he felt it was beneath him. "Princess, may I present Antonin Carême, your father's *latest* French chef. *Monsieur* Carême, Her Royal Highness, Princess Charlotte Augusta of Wales."

Carême bowed, slightly; more than slightly amazed to find this nattering girl of nineteen or so was the English Crown's heir-apparent. *"Princesse, enchantée."*

"How very capital, to meet you here, while—"

Charlotte's giggling reply was cut short by a curt Germanic throat-clearing aimed at the Pavilion functionary.

"Ah, yes," the secretary added, "and Her Highness' Royal Consort, Prince Leopold of Saxe-Coburg."

At the mention of his name, François instantly stiffened with hostility. In his mind, this detestable *Bosche* had been part of the militarily lucky pack of elite nabobs who brought down the far-nobler Napoléon.

Now Leopold smiled, stepping forward and shaking Carême's hand. "We have met before – once."

"Oh, really? And where was that, Your Highness?"

Leopold almost looked loath to mention it. "On the Fields of Vertus, the day you catered the Allies Victory Celebration in France."

"Ay, yes. Now I recall. You were in the entourage of Grand Duke Nicholas of Russia, *non?*"

"Yes. Yes, I was." He smiled. "I owe much to his brother, the Czar, for placing me under the Grand Duke's wing."

"Oui." Carême let the sensual connotations of being 'under the Duke' drop.

"Nevertheless," Leopold said brightly, returning to his rightful position, slightly behind his wife, "you shall find Brighton a wonderful place to explore, abounding in many natural sights within pleasant walking distance of the—"

François stepped in. "Not much time for that, *Monsieur.* We will be *working* in this town, not lazily strolling—"

Carême interjected, "My associate—"

"François Distré, *maître d'hôtel,* Carême's chief assistant." He held Leopold's eyes, forcing the prince to accept a handshake.

He stepped to his left. *"Princesse,* François Distré." He held out his hand, and after a wide-eyed moment of pause – due to the novelty of it all – Charlotte placed her fingers in it. He immediately rotated her palm and kissed her wrist, as one does with married ladies.

Not quite satisfied, he took one more step to bring himself before the pretty lady's maid. "Brigitte, François Distré. *Enchantée, Mademoiselle."*

"Oh, là, là!" the maid exclaimed, giggling as the dashing man took and kissed the top of her unmarried hand.

François was lucky he did not see the seething annoyance flashing across his mentor's face.

But in another instant, all else was forgotten as Charlotte slapped hands in mirth and laughed outright. "What jolly entertainment!"

And yet the fun was not contagious, for Leopold applied a firm touch on her elbow and said, "Good day, gentlemen. We are out for our morning constitutional."

As they walked towards the Reception Hall, and the front door beyond it, Charlotte managed to call back a bright, "Working up an appetite for your first dinner, Carême! Good day, gentlemen."

The secretary gestured to keep the Frenchmen on course, and Carême noted how hungry François' eyes were taking their leave of Brigitte. If the maitre-d' could have gotten away with a wink, the chef knew he would have done it.

The three men continued on to the end of the Corridor and up the North Staircase. As they went, the chef considered the attributes of the Royal Couple. Not the most handsome of girls, Carême's mind was struck with an ancient analogy, for although Cleopatra was praised as a beauty, the portrait busts of her Ptolemaic forefathers establish she came from a long line of ugly men, and therefore, could not have been anything but a womanly version of them. So too, Charlotte with her Hanover homeliness had to compensate with attention-getting coiffures and light-coloured, youthful costume.

Her carriage was noble but occasionally faltered. At such instances, her slouching bespoke a bored disinterest in remaining the centre of everyone's attention. Carême suspected the young woman much preferred her cloistered time alone with Leopold.

The Prince Consort, quite frankly, was facially far above Charlotte's rank, for although 'looks' mostly sort themselves out so that like loveliness mates with its natural equal, there was something about Charlotte's wealth that supplied what her family's inheritance of unsightliness could not. For he, on the other hand, in the tight trousers of an officer's uniform, or the be-slacked looseness of ankle-length, 'walking about' britches, exuded an alluring disinterest in all and sundry's interest in him. Tall, erect, with red-brown hair of a light and untampered wave in it, he made for a striking ornament for the more wallflower frumpiness occasionally seen from Charlotte.

Was theirs a match made in Heaven? Or, perhaps it was one fomented in the belly of Whitehall, that ramshackle centre of Imperial British bureaucracy and spying capacities.

As they entered the North Chamber Gallery, François got lost in thoughts of exploration. He wanted to gain access to the hidden courts providing light to the centre of the house, and see how on earth the architect had devised skylights on *two* adjacent levels. The effect was like magic – it did not seem possible.

Suddenly the Private Secretary stopped in front of the Regent's door, blinking as if it were his first glimpse of Carême's *maître d'hôtel.* "Oh, no. *This* will not do. There is no mistake that His Highness is receiving only Carême in his private chambers."

François' high spirits took a blow, but he expected his mentor would defend—

"*Villon,* it's all right. Go inspect the market, as you wanted, and later you and I will meet in my office to discuss what the Prince wants for dinner today. *Oui?"*

François' spine involuntarily stiffened, taking the unexpected hit as it had, but he nodded, bowed and headed back downstairs.

Carême could see François was hurt – and perhaps he shouldn't have used his personal term of endearment for the young man – but the circumstances were all out of the chef's hands.

Cornelius Hook rapped on the door. An *"Enter"* sounded from within, and the functionary opened the portal for Carême, who went in alone.

The door closed behind him, he gripped his portfolio in anticipation and made his way through the Regent's antechamber. Closed doors to Carême's right led to 'private' space, but open double doors to his left led to light and colour.

When he got to the opening, an impressive sleigh bed in a velvet-draped niche stood across the room opposite him. The luxurious drapery was of a purple so deep it looked blue, and it gathered in swags below a gold dragon-shaped crown at the ceiling.

A bay window on his right steeped the bedchamber in cloudy light from the outside.

Carême stepped into this impressive room and surprisingly found the taskmaster of the British Universe propped amongst far-too many pillows on a sofa. Pulled up to him was a small table from which he'd reach for his chocolate pot to fill his diminutive cup.

This he sipped quickly, seeing the chef and gesturing to an armless seat for Carême to perch upon.

Once he had, the Frenchman was taken aback to observe one socked, Royal foot on a Chinese gout stool.

"You must be the great Carême, about whom we've heard so much."

"I am Antonin Carême, yes, Your Highness." The chef deflected the 'great' designation for now. Instead, he was struck by the dishevelled look of the man in front of him. George lounged in a silk dressing gown that was ridiculously embroidered with an enormous silver and red Order of the Garter cross. Whom was it meant to overawe, his manservant?

The Prince poured himself another cocoa. "How was the crossing? Travelling must have been horrendous, what with the weather being so poor."

"I have found the conditions at Brighton much better, Your Highness." In Carême's mind, this seems a very meagre introduction – he'd be hard pressed to imagine any crowned heads of the Continent opening a conversation with 'How's the weather?'

The chef also admitted to himself that George's appearance was a bit of a distraction, for his sandy hair was unkempt in a way suggesting it was usually covered by a wig. He showed a pudgy face with cupid-bow lips, rather long nose and slightly buggy eyes. He was handsome in a somewhat past-his-prime way, and from Talleyrand the chef knew the Prince was soon to be fifty-five years old.

But the most distracting feature of all was the Royal belly. Its barely covered protuberance informed Carême the man's corset must lay abandoned nearby, and caused the proud Frenchman to feel sure Chef Beauvilliers was never permitted to see Bonaparte so *en petite tenue* – or, in such a state of undress.

Remembering his portfolio, Carême pulled out a drawing. "I have brought illustrations from my book *Le pâtissier pittoresque,* Highness." He set before the Prince a precise architectural rendering of a Chinese-style tea house, which the bored Regent promptly splashed with hot chocolate.

"Very nice" was the extent of the Royal reply.

Carême had hoped to share with his new patron the scope of his own orientalist mind, but now—

"That's fine, and so will anything be you wish to create at the Pavilion. You have *carte blanche, Monsieur."*

"Well"—Carême put his now-soiled rendering away—"we should discuss plans for my first dinner here—"

Carême's business-like tone was cut short by a flippant grunt and sigh. "You'll manage. There are few guests at the Pavilion today, so a small table for ten will be set up in the Red Drawing Room."

Carême did a quick mental calculation: ten covers for a First and Second Table – plus a hot dessert – equalled thirteen total dishes. He could have cooked and served such a simplistic meal in his sleep.

But instead of talking about food, the Prince wanted to gossip. "Tell me," he said slyly, "how is it that France has *two* prime ministers?"

Carême blinked; wasn't it obvious? "Although of the same rank, one Grand Chamberlain is tasked with leading France's international affairs, and one Arch-Chancellor manages the country's domestic concerns."

"Talleyrand and Cambacérès, respectively."

"Yes, Your Highness."

"I know you've worked with both men, so what are they like?"

Since he wanted to chitchat, Carême would regale his master with some court banter. "Naturally, my insight will be along the lines of 'table talk,' but Cambacérès – the domestic minister – was exceedingly frugal during the height of Napoléon's reign, only hosting State Dinners for fifty twice a week, on Tuesdays and Saturdays. While Prince Talleyrand fed at least thirty-six four times a week. Cambacérès preferred men to sit with him, never having more than three or four women at his State Tables."

"Is that so?"

"*Oui.* What is more, he insisted these ladies serve as ornaments to the occasion, with highly embroidered gowns, feathers in hair and diamonds on bracelets."

"I say."

"Have you heard, Highness, of his famous altercation with the *duchesse de La Rochefoucauld?* I ask because it is so well-known in France at the moment."

"I don't believe I have; please tell."

Carême slid to the edge of his seat, sharpening the Prince's anticipation. "At one of these functions, Cambacérès smiled but took offence at the Duchess' tasteful attire, sailing up to her, exclaiming, *'Ah, Madame!* Such a charming *négligé* you have on.' But the woman, famous for her wit, answered on the spot, 'Arch-Chancellor, you must forgive me, for I've only just now come from the side of the Empress and didn't have time to dress *up* for you.'"

The Regent laughed, and Carême could relax, thinking how one harmless anecdote had bought him much of the Prince's good favour.

However, the Regent continued to laugh and pinged the gout in his toes. He turned a bit sour as he asked, "Is it true Cambacérès is a *Mary-Anne?* Which is what the diplomats say."

Carême did not need to know this new-to-him term to comprehend its import, and the chef was taken aback afresh to think Prince George was not delicate in his approach.

Confirming, without being blunt, the chef smiled. "Let us simply say, there was a reason Bonaparte chose *him* to revise the laws, and now the Code allows *amour* to flourish in its entire bouquet."

The Regent mumbled under his breath, "Aunt Yurelle, indeed."

As the potentate had just used the Arch-Chancellor's camp nickname, he was sure George knew more than he let on.

The Prince continued, "Ah, yes – the Napoleonic Code. The German and Italic nations are adopting it too. I suppose we *should,* but here we're saddled with the 'Modern' law reforms of Henry VIII. In other words, a hotch potch of privilege and tradition, written and unwritten, by the Entitled for the Entitled. And nothing will change until the governed force us to include protections for them."

By the Regent's cynical chuckle, Carême understood the stated time of change was to be 'never.'

"Well, then"—Carême tried to guide this *levée* back to its purpose—"for today's dinner, I viewed the cold stores last night and saw a brace of woodcock aged perfectly and ready for a *pâté,* or a savoury pie, as you say."

"Of course; of course." The Regent was not interested. "Do what draws your chefly curiosity. We're confident my guests will relish the flavour of my trust in you."

Carême was disappointed. A courtly servant, such as he, always put himself in jeopardy when forced to guess what his *seigneur* wanted. A moody master was the reason the recently deposed French Emperor burned through thirteen chefs in twelve years.

"And speaking of trust," George added, "that extends to other matters, Carême. Having negotiated your way compunctiously through the households of both Talleyrand and Cambacérès, I know your mum discretion will migrate with you here. The Pavilion is a place as complex as the home of either of France's *two* prime ministers."

To the man's banal grin, Carême replied, "Rest assured, Your Highness, I'm discreet in everything I do." He refrained from smiling himself.

The Prince, indicating a gold clock on the wall, intimated the interview was over. "Enjoy your cooking, and you let us know if you are in need of anything."

"Yes, Your Highness."

Carême stood, bowed his head slightly. He moved away, and then returned, adding, "There is one matter of service that has arisen."

"Oh, yes?"

"My *maître d'hôtel* feels your Royal dining rooms should reflect the current standards on the Continent."

"By all means."

"Specifically – the footmen's uniforms."

"What about them?"

"They shouldn't wear any. They should provide service to you and your guests in appropriate, egalitarian attire."

"Then by all means, let it be so. Whatever is *de rigueur* in Paris, so shall it be in Brighton!" This gave the Prince a belly-laugh, which hurt his gout.

"I'll see then to the proper outfitting of the footmen with the Kitchen Comptroller."

Having obtained assent through a regal nod, Carême bowed once more and quietly left the chamber.

Lost in his own thoughts, the chef exited the Regent's suite and was surprised to find a woman sitting on the bamboo couch of the Chamber Gallery. The sofa table was pulled up to her and set with breakfast.

He was delivering his "Pardon" when he suddenly realized to whom it was addressed. All his cares became instantly forgotten; and his oh-so-professional demeanour, completely set aside.

"Lady Morgan!"

For her part, if she had not known any better, the woman would have sworn the chef's voice rang like a child's. She'd hoped to catch her old friend off guard like this, and delightfully, he'd fallen into her innocent little trap.

"What are you doing here?" the Frenchman asked.

"Having breakfast, and I insist you sit," said the Irish novelist. "Sit and remain with me, dear Carême."

The chef glanced around as if a naughty schoolboy. "Well – only for a moment. There is so much to do." He brought over one of the side chairs and pulled it in tight as he sat opposite Sydney Morgan.

Without asking, she straightaway poured him a cup of tea and made a place for him at the table.

The chef realized Lady Morgan's actions of effortless hosting contrasted with the Regent's never enquiring if he'd like cocoa. *"Merci,"* he said, trying to hide the depths of his gratitude.

"'So much to do' for today's dinner?"

"Yes. There is much to organize by testing," replied the chef. "You will be there, *non?"*

She smiled. "I shall indeed. Will you be following the quaint English custom of serving one dish at a time?"

Carême's response was to sip his tea without replying; he knew his old friend well enough to spot a joke. And she knew his art well enough to comprehend the way diners would eat at one of the chef's meals. "And how is Lord Morgan?"

"He's fit as a fiddle and at the stables right now, seeing about squeezing in a morning ride, if the weather holds. Sometimes I wonder if he doesn't love his horse more than me."

They laughed.

"Charlotte and Leopold too," said the chef, "are out walking."

"And how is François?"

"He is well. He's here with me."

"That's wonderful, and as I would expect; ten years is a long time, longer in fact than my marriage to Lord Morgan. I admire it tremendously. And how are Agathé and Marie?"

Carême set down his cup and saucer. "They are fine; in Paris, you understand." From the chef's point of view, the contemplation of his common-law wife and daughter was a bit of a sore subject. "And how is your new novel doing?"

The woman demurred by sitting back on her seat and grinning. "My *National Tale, O'Donnel?* Thank the stars that since it came out last year the gentlemen of the press have been favourable to it."

"So I have read. Many are calling it your masterpiece; so intriguing in its plot—"

Lady Morgan inadvertently cut her friend off with a good-natured chuckle. "People do like mysteries, so that will not change, but please know the descriptions you might read of *O'Donnel* are from my publishers, not me."

"Descriptions?" Carême sipped his tea.

"Yes"—Sydney Morgan laughed again—"things like: 'A man with a heavy family name, but saddled with a pocketbook light from centuries of free-spending, encounters odd happenings on the estate of a crafty Countess.' Etcetera; etcetera."

"It sounds wonderful to get lost in, but I am sure you have filled it with love and pathos as well. As the fine artist you are, you can have it no other way."

"Thank you, *mon ami.* Artistry or not, fortunately the sales are brisk, so I count me among the lucky."

"Luck," Carême said matter-of-factly, "does not need waste much time promoting the gifted, which you are, Lady Morgan."

This warmed the woman's heart.

"However," the chef continued in a more conspiratorial tone, "I am surprised to find a Republican-leaning Irish novelist billeted in the 'country cottage' of the English ruler."

"Well," she replied smiling again, "the Pavilion is full of the unexpected, so be prepared to encounter all sorts. But – concerning me – I sometimes wonder myself how I came to be a welcome guest here, for far-more damning is my title of 'lady novelist.' That species of creative type is nowadays held as the most spuriously deserving of praise in the land of Defoe and Fielding."

"*Mais, oui.* But a woman would never write *Moll Flanders* or *Tom Jones,* and for good reasons!"

Lady Morgan's reaction was to scoop up Carême's hand. "Oh, how I've missed you, my dear friend."

"I too, *Madame.* We had such . . . adventurous times in Paris."

"That we did. Grand times and times busy tracking down all manner of mysteries and mayhem."

"We made an effective crime-solving pair."

"That we did, and the Pavilion's routine should prove boring in comparison to the gun-powder plot to blow up Napoleon's palace!"

"I can only hope," Carême said wryly.

"And here I find fate has stepped in to bless me once more."

"Oui, Madame – how so?"

"I took the invitation to Brighton as my chance to work on my next book. Not a novel, but a travel monologue of France. I brought all my notes with me from our time together, and now that you are here as well, I can compare the people, places and situations of my memories against your superior knowledge."

Carême appeared ill-at-ease. "I am happy to assist, but . . . . "

The novelist was quick to reassure. "But fear not, Chef. Per our agreement in Paris, and for the reasons only you and I know about, your name will not appear in my *France.* As far as the public at large need understand it, we barely know one another."

"Yes, thank you. It is better not for me personally . . . but, as you know, for others."

She squeezed his fingers. "Yes, I know."

Lady Morgan brightened her voice, letting the land go and patting the top of it. "But you're here for the serious job of creating your art. So far, how are you finding the Pavilion staff?"

Carême sputtered his lips. "They give me those who are married; they give me youths who think standing around and joking is 'work' – those *têtes de linottes.* "

Lady Morgan laughed, translating the term to English. "Chuckleheads. But, you will guide them as you go along; of that, I am sure. And the senior staff, how are they?"

More lip-sputtering arose. "It seems already the Regent's Private Secretary and the Kitchen Comptroller do not like me."

Sydney Morgan hunkered down her tone to warn, "Speaking of which, *mon très cher Carême,* you must be on guard. Not everything is as simple as it appears at the Pavilion. Here, like any centre of concentrated power, the balance of courtly dirt is at play."

Carême was a bit puzzled. *"Le dirt?"*

"Yes. Intelligence; information. In the manner of the way each one might secure a slice of pie, everyone here dishes something on the other. It's a finely tuned stasis maintained by possessing leverage, or so-called dirt, over superior and underlings' heads alike."

Now Carême understood and he thought Lady Morgan exceedingly kind to warn him, although, needlessly. One does not need to warn a shark he swims with sharks.

He was about to thank his friend, when the pair began to hear an odd 'tink; tink' noise. Soon, the tempo both increased and grew jagged. They looked up at the same time to realize it was hail hitting the Gallery skylight.

They chuckled darkly in unison, thinking of all those caught out in it.

The time stood at a quarter of nine, at least via the hands of the regulator clock of the Great Kitchen.

This precision instrument hung above the double doors leading to the Larders, and Kitchen Court beyond. Now, Carême casually observed business transpire below it. For the day was done, and while many members of staff cleaned and put away, the Kitchen Comptroller enticed food-buying agents with dishes set on the counter of the enormous Welsh dresser by the doors.

The chef watched keenly, because he'd just sent François over there with his untouched woodcock *pâté en croûte.*

After the maitre-d' uttered a few syllables concerning the pie's pedigree, the agents tussled in a bidding war to get it – quite forgetting anything the Comptroller had on offer.

François pointed out which of the other dishes had Carême's personal touch upon them, and those too sold fast and furious.

Once all the leftovers were sorted and being carried out into the night air, the moneyman and François came back to the chef's position; the Frenchman counting coins the whole time.

Carême sprung his news upon them. "By the way, the Regent's decision on the matter is this: Footmen shall serve dinners now in their 'natural' attire. The uniforms are out."

François was overjoyed. In his mind, he knew Carême would come through for him. He always had in the past.

The kitchen bean-counter was a mass of seething rage. He skulked away with a murderous glint in his eye.

To Carême, it appeared that François wanted to kiss him, however, the younger Frenchman put a spring in his step, saying before running off, "I'll go tell the footmen to come in their best clothes tomorrow!"

Carême smiled, turning to go to the office, collect his papers and get ready to go up to his chambers for the night.

But his way was blocked – a man who did not belong to the kitchen stood there.

"Chef Carême," he said warmly. "Allow me to introduce myself – William Kitchiner, M.D."

The Doctor struck an unusual figure. Tall and on the spare side, he possessed what the polite referred to as 'a high forehead,' if by high one meant balding up to the middle of his skull. The hair on top and on the sides was light brown, and that included a downright curly set of sideburns. He had darker eyebrows, like the painted-on C's of a doll's face, below which resided gold wire spectacles with pale-blue lenses. His left eye must have been partially sightless, for the thicker glass on this side magnified the appearance of his pupil to nearly twice that of the right.

"How do you do, Doctor Kitchiner? You seem to know who I am already."

The man grinned. "Antonin Carême, the world's most famous chef."

Carême bowed slightly; no use denying it.

"Well, if you will excuse me, I must attend to some paperwork."

The Doctor came close. His voice lowered. "Before you do, there is something I must show you."

Moments later, Kitchiner led Carême through the Central Service Corridor, and then up an unfamiliar set of steps. In an upper floor hallway, Carême glanced to his right while they walked. Through the windows he could see fancifully tinted light come up through the Central Corridor skylight.

They were in the section of the servants' quarters reserved for chamber staff. Kitchiner took them to a modest bedroom with a small window onto the same inner court.

The narrow room was supplied with two beds, which was usual for understaff accommodations, but one bed was made and the other occupied. Small medicine bottles and a lamp stood on a bedside table.

While Kitchiner quietly closed the door behind them, Carême stepped closer and saw a teenage girl was dreaming fitfully through a fever. Without hesitation, he took the cloth soaking in a nearby basin, wrung it out, folded and placed it on the girl's forehead.

In the meantime, the Doctor had been taking her pulse. "This is Luluh Connell, one of the chamber maids. She fell ill this morning, only it's not an illness at all, dear Chef. She's been poisoned."

"*Comment ça?* I mean, how?"

The Doctor held the girl's arm and hand for Carême to inspect. "See this skin discolouration?"

Even in the low light of the room, the chef could make out blotches all over her limbs of a faint, blue colour.

Likewise, Carême noticed each fingernail had a white line across it from cuticle to cuticle.

"These," the Doctor explained, "reveal acute arsenic poisoning."

Glancing into the tormented girl's face, the chef asked, "But who would want to kill her?"

"That, *Monsieur,* is the question. My informants among the Pavilion staff are as dumbfounded as His Highness on the subject. And yet, she hasn't been home – has not left the property – for months. Whoever is doing this, is in the house."

Carême brought his attention fully to the Doctor. "And why draw me into the matter?"

"The young woman with whom Luluh shares this room was able to tell me she thinks Miss Connell is involved with someone who works in the Prince's kitchens, but she does not know who."

"So, you think I should—"

"Keep your eyes and ears open; make some discreet enquiries; and for certain, keep the girl's poisoning a secret. His Highness has heard of your investigation skills, and trusts your delicacy in . . . in, remaining silent."

The courtier in Carême had his hackles raised. A threat hidden in the diplomacy of a compliment is still a threat. "And you, sir?"

"I shall be trying my best to save this girl's life."

"Begging pardon, Doctor, but I was asking who you are to the Prince Regent . . . that he entrusts such delicate missions into your care?"

The Doctor stepped close, but a smile appeared. "I am to his Royal Highness what all of us should be: a dutiful, loyal subject."

Concurrently, lower in the house from the Doctor and Carême's conference, François leaned against the wall in the walkway of the Kitchen Court. Beyond the columns, Thomas Daniels scrubbed the *outside* copper of an enormous ham boiler with sand, water and a cloth.

François Distré had taken it into his head to assign this grunt work, which was far below the undercook's station, as a pre-emptive measure. Both parties involved understood it as such, albeit, Thomas operated without knowing why. Thus seems the fate of most people as they go about their daily lives.

In any event, the darkly brooding François was there – as he'd told the boy – to make sure the work was completed correctly.

James Keenan came out dressed in his street clothes. The stogie usually ornamenting the under-brim of his cap was between his lips, already lit.

In slow deliberation, the Irish cook claimed a column to lean against with his back to François. However, after a little while, he rotated to cast a friendly inspection of the Frenchman. The glowing of his cheroot dangled loosely at the end of his left-hand fingers.

François nodded cool greetings, and James came next to him.

"Smoke?"

The maitre-d' shrugged. "Why not?"

After Keenan pulled a fresh cigar from his inner coat pocket, François bit the tip and spat out one end. He then put it to his lips and beckoned with quick fingers for the older man to come in close. Face to face, smiling Irish blues twinkled against introspective Gallic browns in the men's shared ember-glow.

They parted, and James pulled up a patch of stone wall for himself to lean against. He blew out smoke and gestured with his cheroot left-handed. "Punishing him? That young Master Daniels is a decent cook, and what's more, he's willing to learn."

François drew in an acrid hit of smoke. Keenan had just made him dislike Thomas even more; the boy's fault – unreckoned in the Frenchman's conscious thinking so far – was his uncomfortable resemblance to François at that age.

"I wish my wife would hurry up," said James. "End of day should mean heading home, not standing around and gossiping with the maids." The under-cook's smile was a teasing one now. "That's women, huh?"

François only shrugged and continued to smoke, but thought to himself how James was a natural-born charmer, one not afraid to exploit his physical appeal whenever he could. The man was blithe, an inch or so taller than the *maître d'hôtel,* and a mirror of nature with his good looks and glossy dark hair. François imagined the rogue had left many hearts broken in his wake.

Despite his apparent ineffectualness, the Irishman persisted in his efforts to win François over. He hit upon a new topic. "I saw you've come into conflict with Gris Thorndyke."

François stiffened at the Chief Footman's name.

"Don't worry," the undercook chuckled. "He's a twat, what we'd call a 'while man' – conceited, but not so smart; probably all that gold braid went to his head. In fact"—he lowered his tone to draw in François' confidence—"word is, Gris likes to frequent a certain house of disrepute in Brighton."

François puzzled. "Women, you mean?"

"Not women, Monsewer, but *one* woman old enough to be his mam. She ties him up; she has a pony crop; she's a cruel taskmaster who debases the puny man's haughty spirit."

François smiled. James had just given him courtly leverage to use against his 'enemy,' if he ever needed to.

Keenan kicked away from the wall to stand upright. He laughed. "But, he hates you because you've humiliated him in public, and that he cannot tolerate." The man snubbed out his cigar on the wall, tucking the cool end behind his ear. "So watch where you step. And even, what you eat." James laughed and laughed.

François wondered if the Irishman now thought him beholden for the gift of intelligence James had shared. In any event, François would toss the smooth talker something juicy as compensation later on.

Audrey Keenan appeared in hat and thick shawl from the household door. She joined them with a grin. "What are we talking about, boys?"

"What a tosser Gris Thorndyke is," James said.

She smacked his chest. "Keep your voice down, love. But yes, he is. We all saw the tussle you had with him over the uniforms, and I'm glad you won—"

"Over the nasty *redcoats,*" her husband interjected.

"—Because the wait staff should be dressed like men, not performing monkeys—"

"Or toy soldiers."

"So true." François agreed with them.

Audrey shivered theatrically. "It's the coldest July of my life, especially away from the kitchen fires." She laced her arm through her husband's. "What do you say, love? Should we try to get home before the rain starts again?"

"Yes, Audrey, we better saunter hence. See you in the morning, François."

"Good night," said the Frenchman, feeling a bit warmed to both of them.

"And say," Audrey told him, "you should come to the pub with us one night. You'll enjoy it! And they serve real Irish fare."

"All right; we'll see." François' reaction was charmed but cautious. The company he might enjoy, but towards the prospects of Irish food, he harboured doubts.

The couple departed.

Almost instantly after they'd exited the Court for Castle Square, the skies opened up.

François smoked, coming forward to lean on a column. He glared remorselessly at Thomas getting soaked, shivering in the downpour. The boy continued to polish.

Many hours later, Carême stood at his chamber window looking at the Water Tower. Its clock hands said it was quarter to one in the morning, and the pompous gold leaf on the dragon weathervane got beaten by the rain.

François entered through their adjoining door. He held up a half-filled bottle. "I brought Armagnac."

The men sat at the table with a lamp on it and sipped.

"How did you get this?" Carême enquired.

"It was left over from today's after-dinner service. I saved it from being sold by that Donald Bland."

They enjoyed the burn of the brandy in silence for a moment; it began to relax and unfetter the restraints of the working day.

François chortled darkly. "How amusing it was to meet Charlotte and Leopold off guard like that this morning."

"How much you entertained with your lady's maid act."

François ignored that, preferring to return to the Royal couple. "What an unpromising heir-apparent the British Empire has in that air-head Charlotte. And *Prince* Saxe-Coburg? Leopold looks the right arrogant little fool standing behind the petticoats of power."

"Well . . . ." Carême attempted to gather his thoughts.

"And you saw the way Leopold gloated over the Allies Victory dinner at Épernay, the Russian *Champs-de-Mars.*"

The chef contradicted him. "Or, perhaps, the Prince Consort only mentioned it because that's where he and I had met before."

François understood the cognac was only deepening his personally dark mood and thereby vexing Carême. He elevated his spirits. "I stand corrected."

"Anyway, *Villon,*" said the chef, "bake some *madeleines* for the Princess' breakfast-tea first thing tomorrow."

"Yes, Chef, I will. Tell me, since you met with him this morning, what type of man is the Regent?"

"Honestly, it's difficult to say. He seems to brook no dissension, and yet listens carefully to everything that's said. He appears to have far-reaching plans, but disguising them as whims until the time is right to implement them. I must remind myself to be on guard around him."

"Sounds like a complex master."

"We will see. Oh, and Lady Morgan is at the Pavilion. We had a few moments to catch up today."

This was indeed unexpected news to François, unwanted too, as it further irked his jealousy at not being able to keep Carême all to himself. "How . . . wonderful for you." He drained his glass and refilled it instantly.

François' sentiment was not lost on the chef.

"Yours was not the only unforeseen encounter today," said François.

"Oh?"

"Yes. Tonight I had a smoke with the Irish-couple undercooks, the Keenans."

"Don't remind me"—he grinned—"a man and wife working in *my* kitchen. Anyway, what did they say?"

"Not much, but they were testing me, so I'd advise you not to let them get too close to you. I can smell a scam stuck to them, although what, I'm not quite sure."

"Well, I'll deal with them as *chef de cuisine;* no more. But, considering these English barely speak the language of food, today's dinner went off rather smoothly."

"Indeed," agreed François. "But it was a shame no one even cut into your woodcock *pâté.*"

"By the way, how much did you get for it?"

"Only 2 Pounds and 6 Shillings."

"Only! That's a lot of money."

"Yes, but tomorrow, the food agents will bring more cash. Your presence at the Pavilion caught them by surprise."

Carême re-filled both their glasses. "I have to tell you, after you went to tell the footmen to dress normally for tomorrow, I had an odd encounter."

"With who?"

"One Doctor Kitchiner. He's an operative of the Regent's in some capacity and took me to one of the servants' rooms. A girl is sick – poisoned in the Pavilion."

François sat upright. "Is it serious?"

"Yes. She may still die. And the Doctor – and Prince – have tasked me with investigating it. And I assign you to a special duty."

"Which is what?"

"Observe everyone in the kitchens for signs of the same poisoning: spotty skin or lines across the fingernails. Do it undercover."

François joked "Is there any other way?" before turning serious. "I will do as you say, but it might be hard to find a motive, let alone a culprit, limiting our search to the kitchen staff."

Carême had an 'Ah-ha!' moment; he'd enlist the help of Lady Morgan to gather intel on the rest of the Pavilion staff.

François brought Carême out of his thoughts by touching the chef's hand.

In a calm and stilled motion, the men rose to their feet, embraced and kissed. François relished the feel of Carême's arms around him.

Later, naked, their movements proceeded along the same, unhurried lines. Eventually both lay in bed on their sides, Carême behind.

François' hand went to the back of Carême's head as they made love.

Chapter 3: of Jack Hartell's Heartbreak & Rust-Proof Iron

The new day that had dawned over Brighton was oppressively colourless. However now, as midmorning approached, the skies were simply grey with overcast clouds. They were not as leaden as before.

Carême and Lady Morgan met again after the chef's daily *levée* with Prince George. They found a place where they might spend a few, unobserved minutes exchanging information: the Chapel Royal.

The Irish novelist knew the way and guided the Frenchman to a separate building at the south-east corner of the property. Carême was amazed to get into the stone structure – which struck a rather plain appearance from the outside. He found himself standing in a soaring space of the best taste. Known to him as *Directoire,* it was the style of the 1790s emphasising delicate lines, delicious hues and disciplined Classical proportions. Utterly 'un-oriental,' the Chapel Royal had robin-egg walls with thin plaster pilasters rising thirty feet to a pale yellow barrel vault ceiling. One full-height window in clear glass comprised most of the narrow end at the north.

The pair began strolling to the centre of the open-floored church.

"Before the Regent started construction on the Music and Banqueting Rooms, this was George's entertainment venue."

The chef was aghast. *"Comment ça?"*

"It was raised as a chapel to show the King how 'pious' Prince George can be. But soon after, it became the place he'd throw balls and serve banquets. And look there." She gestured to the thinner side of the room along the south. "He has theatrics given here as well."

Carême spied what she meant. For the balcony across this end of the chapel was arrayed like an opera house's 'Royal Box,' right down to the rich drapery hanging in gold-fringed swags from the up-curve of the barrel vault.

It was an odd feeling for Carême to contemplate how this space, intended to stay quiet and contemplative, was utilized to throw live-for-the-moment parties. Was George intentionally thumbing his nose at convention? Or had he merely blundered his way into an affront to decency? Carême resolved that the answer was 'no' to the mistaken notion. The appropriating of the chamber was too bold an act for it to have been accidental, and no doubt was taken against strong advice from his Counsellors.

However, the two visitors were here for business.

"What have you uncovered?" the chef asked. "Anything good?"

Sydney Morgan began speaking excitedly. "Yes! Let me spill the beans on what I've found out, mostly via my lady's maid talking to the other lady's maids, especially Brigitte, Princess Charlotte's servant-companion." She paused for breath, preparing to get lost on a tangent. "That *mademoiselle* de Saint-Exupéry is so charming! She's pretty, tasteful, well brought-up – talented at the piano too – from what I understand."

All of this praise put Carême in a slightly foul mood, though Lady Morgan did not know why.

She frowned and continued in a more sober manner. "Anyway, back to what I've learned. Word of mouth has it, as the Doctor already told you, Luluh Connell does indeed have an admirer amongst the kitchen staff; and it's one known to be sweet on her. The new intelligence adds that the girl was secretive with who because the lad is 'below her' station."

"But she's a chamber maid."

"Correct. So that makes me consider who in the kitchens fits this 'lowly' description. The answer: one of the young men charged with doing more menial tasks."

"Ah. Very clever of you, Lady Morgan."

"The lad could be risking his neck to filter treats from the table scraps up to her, but I don't know if that has anything to do with her rapid decline."

"Yes." Carême nodded slowly. "It seems unlikely: in fact, *incroyable* to think the young man is trying to kill her, if indeed he is 'sweet' on her."

"True, but stranger things have happened, and you never know until you know. You know?"

The novelist's presentation of vernacular Irish wit had been rather lost on Carême. So too was the woman's laugh now greeting his puzzled scowl.

"There's an old Irish proverb that runs, dig into other people's gardens and expect them to root through yours. I wouldn't be at all surprised, dear Chef, to learn spying for foreign powers is best done in the servants' hall."

She again laughed; and again Carême failed to perceive what was so funny. Truth was, his mind was elsewhere.

Unbeknownst to them, but concurrently, a very different scene was unfolding in the Pavilion's Decking Room, for François had begged use of the facility from the Head Table Decker – with whom he had an amicable working relationship – to deck out the footmen in proper 'Democratic Attire' for serving the day's dinner.

A bit of levity passed through the footmen like an electrical current. It was funny to them to see one another in anything but cutaway coats, white stockings and black britches.

The young men stood in an antsy line as François fitted them one by one. Yesterday evening, he'd gone out and found a town tailor – a French one, naturally

– and now, while the tailor's assistant jotted notes right behind them, the two inspected the troops. They surveyed the young men's best from-home attire and augmented to suit the dignity of the Regent's home.

While Gris Thorndyke scowled and folded his still red-coat-clad arms in the background, François went up to the next in line. He ran his fingers under the lapel of the handsome lad, found some fraying, and told Monsieur Appert, "This one will need a new coat."

"Colour?" the tailor asked.

François frowned in concentration. Then he asked the boy slyly, "Which colour would *you* like?"

The question thoroughly thrilled the footman. "I've always wanted a snuff-coloured jacket – you know, a rich brown."

Distré glanced at Appert, who nodded.

"Then snuff you shall have!"

Setting aside the lad's excited glee, François resumed his inspection. The young man's trousers were acceptable, but his waistcoat was not. "A new vest; yellow satin, I think." He moved up to the boy's neckwear. A ruffled frill, which he'd probably obtained from his father, was both too dingy and old-fashioned to serve.

François ambled to an open trunk of neckgear the tailor had brought. He selected a colourful scarf and returned to his charge.

Standing before him, and personally undoing the old, he removed the frill and fixed the new example in place.

The youth was all smiles feeling the imported silk against his neck.

"There," François said through his own grin. "Now when you feel this luxury formerly only belonging to the Lords caressing you under your chin, hold your head a little higher and remember your station. Be proud to serve Carême's food."

Ignoring the contempt-spiked snigger coming off the Chief Footman, François gave the lad a brotherly double-shouldered slap. "Now take off your old jacket so the tailor can measure you for your new one."

"Thank you, Mister Distray!"

François stepped to the next man in line, but the Kitchen Comptroller came storming over.

"Who," he demanded, "has authorized the hiring of a tailor!"

Feeling both assured and wry at this point, François decided to have some fun. "Carême did, *naturellement.*"

The moneyman puffed up. "Dare I question if the *chef de cuisine* has the unilateral authority to approve outfits for footmen that will run into the hundreds of pounds!"

François applied some fake innocence onto himself. "I only work on Carême's authority, naturally, and he likewise only proceeds on the Regent's authority . . ."

The bean-counter's face tightened, waiting for the now-inevitable hammer blow.

" . . . Which His Highness gave this morning."

"I . . . . I . . . . Oh. I—"

François draped his arm across the functionary's shoulder, false friendship ringing hollow in his voice. "Next time – before barging in where you are not needed – you had better check in with your lord and master first, *n'est-ce pas?*"

Donald Bland broke off the hostile embrace in a near rage. But before he left, the man hailed the Chief Footman. "Mister Thorndyke, I would very much like a word with you, please. In private."

The pair skulked off, each parting with hateful glares for the smiling *maître d'hôtel.*

Just then, Carême entered from the outside through the glass doors.

François hurried instructions to the rest of the footmen. "Pick out the scarves you like, wear them and keep them fresh. Also, wait for the tailors to measure you. You ALL will get brand new work suits!"

The young men, thoroughly won over to Distré's side, shouted "Huzzah!" as a body and nearly stampeded to inspect the selection of neck attire.

By the time François got there, Carême was already sitting at his desk and poring over his layout for the day's dinner. The maitre-d' closed the door behind him.

"Ah, François." The chef stood. "Let's review today's battleplans."

Side by side, the men studied Carême's table setting sketch showing the guest positions and food placement, the latter of which were assigned numbers for coordination twix kitchen, deckers, François and the footmen.

"A round table will be set up today in the Salon. There'll be fourteen covers equally spaced around the edge. The food in the centre will be arranged thus: soups here and centrepiece roasts here. Two large plates placed between each of the roasts and soups will hold the *entrées,* which will total eight."

The arrangement was like a clockface, with soups at the twelve and 6 o'clock positions; centrepiece roasts at three and nine; and the *entrées* at one and two, four and five, and so on.

"Yes, Chef Carême."

"Here's the *carte de menu* the Prince agreed to for today."

Carême handed François a piece of paper, and the *maître d'hôtel* scanned it. Number coded to match the plan, the menu consisted of one clear soup and one vegetable puree, or potage, two fish *relevées* – including fried turbot with lobster sauce – two cold centrepiece 'roasts' and eight *entrées* - like scallops of pheasants with truffles, and individual macaroni pastry shells with brown-butter mushrooms. This completed the First Table.

The second setting had two hot roasts, eight *entremets* – including French-fried potatoes and glazed apple beignets with almonds – and the meal would be rounded off with single-serving coffee flavoured soufflés sent hot to the table straight from the ovens.

In point of fact, a two course meal with a mere sixteen side-dishes was not much of a challenge for the Frenchmen's capacities.

"Oui, mon chef."

"What's the status of the preparations so far?"

"For the cold centrepiece roasts, Sous-chef Bauda has finished the quail chartreuse, which turned out beautifully. Now it chills in the Cold Kitchen, waiting for you to place the final garnishings."

"Excellent." The chef stopped what he was doing and engaged François with a waxy, emotional gaze. "A chartreuse – marvellous old item of the *grande cuisine* – so simple, who would think the unfussy combination of summer cabbage and summer game could produce something so profoundly delicious? But it does." His manner, after a blink, returned to the professional. "And I want you to personally make the pistachio aïoli to go with it."

"Yes, Chef. It's my privilege, and I'll do it exactly as you showed me."

Carême was too busy to smile. "Yes, I know."

There was a knock on the glass. It was Doctor Kitchiner, looking very dour.

The man let himself in and closed the door carefully behind him. "I'm afraid, old boy"—he was addressing the chef—"the girl is dead. The Prince wants answers."

After a protracted moment of silence between the three men, Carême grew resolute. "Well then, there's only one thing to do – confront the staff. Will you join us, Doctor?"

"No. I must attend to the matter of getting the dead's remains, God bless her, out of the Pavilion with no one seeing. I will leave you two of my men though."

Kitchiner gestured through the glass at a pair of clean-shaven and fairly well-dressed fellows lingering by the roasting spits for warmth.

"*Bon.*"

The Great Kitchen, if one just looked at the equipment, appeared like a ghost ship running along without a crew. Saucepans, taken off the boiling embers, were set aside; steam cauldrons bubbling along had their bags of vegetables lifted out; great skewers of roasts – long as a man is tall – stood hurriedly unhooked from their iron stands before the vertical cages of roasting coals. What's more, faucets trickled instead of gushed where numbered pots of the *batterie de cuisine* sat amidst moist sponges and containers of brick dust to scour them clean; brooms, ever-present in the diligent hands of tidy young men to keep refuse off of Carême's floors, leaned higgledy-piggledy where abandoned against doorjambs and preparation tables. But where were their people? The normally attentive-to-a-flaw army of sauce-makers, steamtable fellows, spit-jacks, scullery maids and sweep-up boys?

They were absent from duty, but had been marshalled, face forward, into a single line of inspection down the length of the Great Kitchen. Filed by rank, Sous-chef Bauda anchored the column from the honoured position close to Carême's office. From there, cooks, under-cooks, and every position of preparation and clean-up followed.

The only ones not included were Kitchiner's pair of men, who stood with folded arms – one each at the Great Kitchen's adit and exit – and François, who leaned against the massive warming table right in the centre of the facility, from where he could scan the whole line of staff with an easy head-turn.

Chef Carême, the worthy individual, the supreme general of their culinary forces, strode down the waiting column of cooking soldiers with his hands behind his back, and his chefly knives slung from his belt like sabre and cutlass. The eyes below his white toque cap were Gallic and serious. Speaking, his tone imparted the same deliberate intent.

"Upstairs," he said, pausing for effect, "an hour ago, a young girl of His Highness' chamber maids – a Miss Luluh Connell – only seventeen years of age, died. She, my friends, was poisoned."

François kept his eyes alert, looking for telltale signs of emotion. The line of possible perpetrators was long though, and any reaction Carême's words might cause would be subtle.

The chef continued his pacing. "And furthermore, we have reason to believe one of you gathered here today is mixed up in her death." Carême arrived at the place where a be-capped and innocent looking Thomas Daniels stood. He eyed the boy, adding, "We just want answers."

François watched this exchange intently; too intently it turned out. For farther down the line, the *maître d'hôtel* missed fifteen-year-old Jack Hartell, sweep-up boy, stuff his mouth with something. He missed that while the boy chewed and swallowed awkwardly, the young man's eyes were miserable. That they welled with tears as if their youthful owner's life was over, having just learned the girl he loved was no longer alive.

Carême took up his stroll again. "One of you was involved with Miss Connell, and we would simply like to know who." The chef's progress was halted; he heard an odd sound. Muffled at first, he tried to locate it.

Carême glanced at François, who was hearing it too and scrutinizing the line of people to—

Suddenly, Jack Hartell's teeth began to chatter violently. All the colour had drained from his face. He started gagging, foaming at the mouth uncontrollably.

As Distré, Kitchiner's men and Carême all darted to the boy, Hartell crashed to the floor, knees buckling and sending him toppling to the tiles on his right shoulder. His legs drew up, and in this helpless foetal position, began to convulse.

François and Carême arrived, making Jack's fellow sweep-up boys stand back and give them room.

Carême reached in the boy's mouth, ensuring his tongue wasn't blocking his airway. That assured, the chef inspected the victim's sputum, which now coated his hand – it had a strange, pale sage colour to it.

Meanwhile, François had rifled through the lad's pockets and now held a palmful of broken sugar work fencing. It was a horrible dark green.

"*Villon,* get the mustard powder, now!"

The maitre-d' jumped up to do as instructed. Thomas was within Carême's sights, peeking over the shoulders of Kitchiner's men, so he told him, "Fetch a cup of water."

"Yes, Chef!"

Now Carême stuck his fingers down Jack Hartell's throat – all the way. The boy vomited a horrid mass of barely masticated green candy fragments, yellow stomach acid, and iron-smelling blood.

Again he did it; again the boy's stomach was emptied on the floor.

François was back. He held a cannister.

"Sit here," Carême told him, "and cradle the boy."

François did, pulling the limp Jack Hartell up by sticking his hands beneath the young man's armpits and drawing him close.

Carême tore off the lid of the mustard powder, used his clean left hand and dug into it. In another second, he smeared it on Jack's tongue and all around the inside of the boy's mouth.

Thomas stepped close with the water.

"*Merci,*" Carême said, taking the mug and holding it to Hartell's lips. He poured some in, using his other hand to rub downward on the boy's throat to make him swallow.

Once Jack did, Carême continued administering the mustard powder this way.

After three or four doses, the young man opened his eyes. He was dazed and confused seeing the chef's face so close to his own, but tears started and he pleaded for understanding. "I didn't mean to hurt her . . . to kill her. Oh, God – I loved her—"

"I know; I know," the chef said, comforting him. After saying "It will be all right" and brushing the boy's forehead, Carême stood.

Footmen from the Decking Room had been drawn to the Great Kitchen by all the commotion and now stood outside the circle of staff surrounding the stricken boy.

"You and you"—Carême picked out two footmen—"assist the Doctor's men and carry this boy upstairs so Kitchiner can help."

"Yes, Chef!"

François stood, hefting the lad with him, and handed Jack over to the footmen. They and Kitchiner's men hurried with the sobbing youth through the door to the Central Service Corridor.

Calmly, Carême said, "François, come with me."

Chef and *maître d'hôtel* also exited the kitchen, heading to the pastry suite's display room.

Thinking he recognized the broken pieces of sugar work in the boy's possession, Carême opened the central glass door of the display cabinet. "Help me move it out."

François on one side, Carême on the other, slid Chef Weltje's *pièce montée* forward. Both men glanced at the back. Sure enough, various sections of the green fencing were broken off and missing. "I thought so," said Carême.

They took it all the way out and set it on the table.

After this, François led Carême to the larder. He located and pointed to a shelf of boxes, each with a hand-coloured label bearing the name of the manufacturer and a Royal Warrant, proclaiming the proud contents had been made exclusively for the Regent's use.

Carême pulled out the 'green' container, opened it and inspected the sage-coloured powder inside. *"Mon dieu,"* he uttered slowly, "it's arsenic." He held François' gaze. "It's Paris Green fabric dye and should never have been marked as 'food colour'."

Together, the two collected all the boxes of pre-made food pigment to dispose of immediately. The chef expounded, "Such 'lazy' products will ruin the health of modern man. You know as well as I do what a bounty of natural shades plants provide: if yellow is desired, soak safflower; if red is wanted, crush annatto seeds; if green – the easiest of all – boil spinach. *Mon dieu."*

"What shall we do with Chef Weltje's poisoned confections," François asked. "The temptation is too great for the staff to nibble here and there."

"It's obvious: they must be destroyed. But, for now, lock them up. I'll need His Highness' permission to get rid of them properly."

"Yes, Chef."

By the time the great suite of kitchens were back on course to serve the Pavilion's dinner at 4, and all the ready-made 'food colouring' consigned to a fire François had built in the kitchen's open court, Doctor Kitchiner was lightly rapping on the glass of Carême's office.

The chef waved him in. "How is the boy?"

"Stable. I think he'll live. The others told me how you saved his life. How did you know the mustard powder would countermand the arsenic's toxicity?"

Carême's smile was then a little more than evasive. "Some things a person just picks up along their journeys in life."

The Doctor closed the door and sat himself down. While he took off and cleaned his glasses, he told the chef casually, "I've already spoken to His Highness about the unfolding of events, and how the investigation is over – thanks to you – and I can assure you, he is very pleased."

The spectacles went on again, but this time propped near the tip of his nose. Kitchiner eyed the chef over the top of them, repeating, "Very pleased. What's more, *cher* Chef, he feels he can abide his faith in your good character." Kitchiner sat back in his chair; folded his arms. "And I too feel you are a person who can be trusted."

Carême wasn't sure where this was leading, and so simply nodded once in politeness.

"In any event"—the Doctor brightened his tone—"I am hosting a little gathering at my Club tomorrow night, a private function, and I think you should attend."

"*Oui?*"

"Yes. *Oui.* Nothing elaborate, mind you. In fact, the point of my little get-togethers is to eschew all formality. We assemble as friends; friends who have a mutual interest in food."

Carême already sensed he had no avenue of refusal. "After my duties here are complete?"

"Oh, yes. I'll send a carriage around to collect you at half seven. All right?"

The Doctor stood to go, but paused in his tracks to add, "And, although I'm sure he's delightful company, my invitation does not extend to your - to, that is - François."

Kitchiner left without waiting for any reply.

The maitre-d' uttered a hush-hush "Follow me."

Carême, behind him, and by this time labouring for breath a bit, contemplated the twilight murkiness of these out-of-the-way steps somewhere in the upper registers of the Pavilion.

"It's just a little more." François offered this assurance from out in front. "I know all the workers have gone home for the night."

François turned a corner. The sound arose of a door getting an extra-firm push - then light appeared.

They stepped out amid a rooftop construction zone. A large flat area, which contained various stacks of fresh-cut lumber, and smaller piles of meticulously numbered iron girders, plates and angular supports – and many other components whose function was not obvious to the chef. But Carême's sensibilities to craftmanship were instantly drawn to the fact that each iron support, no matter how large or small, was completely blued against corrosion. Such a display of forethought indicated the protection of the structure of the Pavilion's rooves from rusting was not for George, the Prince Regent, but his descendants two hundred years from now.

François called from up ahead, mounting a temporary set of steps.

By this time, Carême had caught his breath and soon followed. Once he got to the top, he could tell why François' exploratory nature had been pulled up here to begin with.

A work in progress, the old curving roof of the Salon was arched over by self-supporting iron joists. These formed the base for vertical iron members that would support the elaborate onion dome soon to encase and rise soaringly above them.

François clambered higher from the ringed walkway upon which they stood to the wooden construction platform built atop the iron joists. Knowing the chef would join him, he went to the edge and sat down, drawing his knees close to his body.

Once Carême was sitting by his side, both men gazed over the open countryside and gentle incoming waves lapping the seashore. The sun was setting at their backs and casting their shadows undistinguishingly from those of the Pavilion's fanciful silhouette.

After several minutes, Carême told François, "I have to tell you, that odd doctor invited me to a *soirée* tomorrow night."

"At his house?" This was news to François.

"No. He called it his 'Club'."

"But you have your doubts about him and his invitation?"

"Perhaps – however, tomorrow night I shall see."

The maitre-d's body language changed. It was all Carême needed to say to inform François he was not invited. He gazed over the darkening landscape.

"Thank you for bringing me up here." Carême tried to sound wistful. "It makes Brighton seem a world unto itself, away from the actual, dire circumstances of our times."

"Agathé writes from Paris that breadlines are forming. She's heard rumours armed gangs of ex- *Grande Armée* soldiers are secretly banding together to fight Louis XVIII's rule."

"Democratic uprisings are going on in Italy, Russia, Germany – all a sizzling fuse on a bomb sooner or later to go off."

"You forget London. Protests by the hungry, and radical actions, are happening there too." François' heart was not in the conversation. He felt he was in a twilight world himself.

The chef inhaled and raised his eyes from François' profile. He gazed at the structure around him. Compared to the 'rusted' results of the Congress of Vienna, whose designers were not as careful as the Pavilion's architect, the New Europe was being built on a flawed under-structure. The desire to move on to a post-Napoleonic era, but ignoring the hunger for self-government that birthed the French Revolution in the first place, was creating a pretty façade on a rotten framework. It was only a matter of time before the political structure fell.

However, despite all the gloom of the present, Carême wanted to focus on hope for the future – not a grand, re-designed European future, but a small, intimate one for he and François.

"Radical times or not, *Villon,* the life I've chosen, with its malignant chef's lung, means I won't be around for much of a retirement. And yet I want enough time, with you, to pen my all-encompassing cookbook."

François wouldn't look at him.

"It will be *our* legacy—"

"And Prince George, he'll be your publication patron?"

The chef scoffed. "I doubt it. Each time I present my methodically planned meals and sugar work architecture, the Regent is bored and ends all discussion with a permeative 'I'm sure it's fine, Carême. *We* trust you'."

François stared at the shadowy whitecaps rolling in at the beach. In his heart of hearts, all he wanted to do was pledge lifelong devotion and assistance to Carême and his writing ambitions . . . . But, he knew he could not.

Chapter 4, Part One:
Crossed Signals

Twenty-four hours after Carême and François had first set foot on the onion dome substructure, the chef was being rattled in a carriage alone. A foreigner in a foreign land, this was almost his first chance to see the City of Brighton since the day he had arrived at the Pavilion. He sat close to the window and drank in the sights.

At least the clearing skies of the previous night still held sway. What's more, the westerly breeze pushing the clouds out to sea had brought warming temperatures.

Now perched on his coach seat, moving from the grittier streets of working-class Brighton to its genteel circles and squares of upscale townhomes, Carême regarded the warm evening almost as if that sacrosanct moment after a violent shudder. The body is suddenly flushed with warmth, no matter how fleeting the sensation.

This feeling was lost though, for rarely was celebrity far from attending Carême's every move, and quite frankly, the chef was seldom, if ever, alone.

He sat back, letting his eyes tilt up to the cabin's ceiling of black fabric, and tried not to worry. Who and what was this enigmatic 'Doctor' with enough clout to summon Carême away from the Royal marine villa for an evening; what did he want from the Frenchman; and what, if anything, could the chef glean for Talleyrand from this foray to a traditional English gentleman's club?

The carriage turned a corner, and suddenly the vast expanse of a twilight sea was there. Its liberating brace of salt air was immediate, and the vehicle slowed as it promenaded along a grand ocean-front boulevard. Each building here was stand-alone, high in stone facades and balconies, and grand – very grand.

The coach pulled off the promenade, onto a driveway, and wound around to deliver Carême's carriage door to the house's main entry.

A footman in sombre clothes had appeared from within and was waiting. He opened the vehicle door, saying, "Good evening, *Monsieur* Carême. The Doctor is awaiting you."

As this young man had gestured to the entrance, Carême began strolling that way, taking the time first to note every single window of this 'Club' was shut tight against the summer air – unlike the neighbouring houses, whose curtains flirted freely in and out. But not only that, each window of the Doctor's was dark, and this only because white shutters inside the window frames were tightly buttoned up, blocking all light and sense of movement from escaping the premises.

As he walked, he tried to remember the last place he'd visited with this level of security from prying eyes. It would come to him, but for now—

The front door opened. Out stepped Doctor Kitchiner, his eyes beaming from behind his round spectacles.

"My dear Carême! A most hearty welcome."

"*Merci.*"

"Won't you step this way?" Kitchiner led by striding into a spacious-but-plain hall. As he closed the door behind the chef, he asked, "Was the carriage ride all right? No trouble, I take it." He started walking down the hall, away from the street-side of the building.

"Trouble? No. In fact, it was very relaxing to see differing parts of the town."

The pair had come to matching double doors; one on the right, one on the left, no doubt leading to the building's front parlours. But both rooms were closed to view, and Kitchiner sailed right on past.

"Good; good," the Doctor said. "One must step away from the Pavilion to grasp how remarkable a place it truly is. At least once in a while."

This comment deserved a noncommittal smile, so the chef gave it.

Now they'd come to a second set of doors, this time, open. As the Doctor again walked past these, Carême slowed his pace a bit. He peered in, seeing men sitting at long worktables, poring over stacks and stacks of paperwork by lamplight. This was fishy to Carême, for of all the folklore he'd heard, none had suggested Englishmen went to 'the club' to work.

Nearing the terminus of the hall now, a staircase appeared around a corner, but before getting there, Kitchiner stopped next to a doorless frame. Behind it was a five-foot by five-foot windowless 'room'. A lit lamp hung on the back wall.

The Doctor stepped in, motioning for Carême to follow. Kitchiner spoke into a brass mouthpiece. "Top floor, please."

After an awkward pause and grin from the Doctor, Carême was jolted. The floor started moving – moving up. Despite his rigidly enforced sense of Gallic composure, the chef lashed out with both hands onto the walls. "*Mon dieu!*"

"You're perfectly safe. Don't you have lifts in France – American contraption – I should have explained."

Carême relaxed a bit as he saw the shadow of the second floor give way to an open hallway matching the one they'd left below.

"You see, Chef, there's a man stationed at geared pulleys in the cellar. You tell him what floor you want, and he cranks you up or down."

The Doctor laughed good-naturedly as the hall of the third level came into view.

The vertical ride ended on floor five, not in a passageway like the lower levels, but a vestibule with a door on the opposite side.

Following the only way out, the pair once more were thrust into the twilight air, for they stood on a roof – or, at least the flat section of the Club's roof.

Kitchiner showed the way again. "Up here, I can properly begin my tour. Follow me, if you will, please, Chef."

Passing through another nondescript door, Carême was instantly hit by a warmer atmosphere. It was wetter and loamier too – the air of a greenhouse. For indeed, they'd entered the short side of an arbour hugging the length of the property. To the men's left, the lower half of its 45-degree-angled roof was made of glass in wooden frames. Below this access to natural light grew an organized thicket of potted plants. Some vines sprawled on trellises and dropped bright 'fruit' of the most unappealing nature. In fact, to the chef's culinary eye, all of these examples of greenery looked strikingly unfamiliar, and many, downright noxious. Perhaps *medicinal* was the better descriptor.

"For botanical analysis," Kitchiner volunteered from out in front.

And that information corresponded to what Carême saw on the other long wall; for under this section of non-glass roof, a continuous counter ran at sitting height. On it, an occasional lamp was lit and low to define workstations. Where stools pulled up, the remains of the workers' day lay scattered about: microscopes; botany books left open to particular illustrations; and sample herbarium cards with dried plant specimens sewn on.

Once he had arrived at the other narrow end of the space, Kitchiner paused his hand on the lever of a set of double doors.

When Carême got up to him, another enigmatic sparkle from the Doctor's shaded eyes greeted the chef.

"And this," said the man turning the door handle, "is my inner sanctum. Doctor Kitchiner's Cabinet of Curiosities!"

It was an open penthouse, and Carême immediately assessed it was much like the greenhouse they'd just left, only bigger. In fact, much bigger. It was wider, taller and fronted the entire length of the building along the ocean-facing boulevard. The structural layout was the same: the half of roof sloping down from the right was covered with exposed wooden beams, while the rest to the eaves-line on the left was glass.

Under this section were raised platforms with handrails. Each level hosted a myriad of telescopes pointing up to the stars, and spyglasses on tripods looking over the sea.

There must have been a hundred or more in varying types, sizes and materials.

Passing a curtained area off to the right of where they'd entered, the long side of the room under the solid roof was organized in sections. In the middle of which rose a couple of steps up to a personal *bibliothèque*. Bookcases lined two walls up to the start of the roof timbers. The shelves were entirely full, and more so, neat stacks of books littered the floor in front of them. Carême mounted these steps, inviting himself to have a look-around. The centre of this elevated space was dominated by an immense library table. It was large enough for twelve to gather round and confer, and now sat strewn with maps and nautical charts. These doubtlessly pinpointed sundry 'hot spots' around the world.

Along the shallow end of this bookcase area, two further steps mounted up to a smaller platform, in the centre of which stood Kitchiner's desk. The chef thought he'd have a peek, but his arm was stayed by the Doctor's "Tut; tut – sensitive papers," of which eagle-eyed Carême had indeed been intent to view.

From this elevated position, he noticed a piano down on the main floor. He went to this, picking up one of the half-finished compositions scattered atop its closed lid. The score Carême held in his hand was headed: "Bubble and Squeak, or, Fried Beef and Cabbage." The presumable lyrics were scrawled above four bars of music:

*"When 'midst the frying pan, in accents savage,
The Beef rudely makes quarrel with the Cabbage . . . "*

The chef felt the composer's presence over his shoulder, so he quipped, "Very clever to set the words and notes of beef and cabbage, but from my experience of English dishes, something is missing. You might have to resort to the Chinese pentatonic scale to accommodate:

P - O - T - A - T - O."

The men chuckled.

Beyond the piano area – with its four chairs and music stands for impromptu quintets – Carême's eyes drifted to the back of the room. From this distance, it was easy to discern two primary features: a large cooking hearth with its chimney going up and up, through the roof, and the rough-hewn but inviting kitchen table establishing the boundary of Kitchiner's culinary domain from the remainder of the open penthouse.

As they approached this side of the room, the Doctor veered off to the area on the right-hand of the hearth. This part – bordered on one edge by the raised platform of the man's desk – had a large Welsh dresser on the long wall, stocked and displaying enough pewter and china plates to feed two-dozen guests. In the corner beyond this hutch, next to and flued into the hearth chimney, resided a two-burner iron stove upon which sat a five-gallon pot with a spigot near the bottom. Shelves behind this stove contained a remarkable collection of herbs and spice containers, plus colourful but small bottles of liquid – most only half full, but – all tightly corked down.

"This," the Doctor explained with evident pride, "is my sauce kitchen. It's here I do experiments, seeking to invent the perfect steak sauce, vegetable sauce, and all-round utility condiment. Mark my words, dear Chef, one day every house in the Kingdom will have at least one bottle of 'Doctor Kitchiner's Paten'd Zest' for immediate use. No more slaving over a pot when the chop is ready to eat."

The master *chef de cuisine* was more than a little dubious.

As Kitchiner continued on with the tour, he sang out, "Ready-made, shelf-stable food is the future, my friend!"

Carême certainly hoped not.

As the chef was led past the hearth, he noted the classic design, complete with a pair of beehive ovens bricked into the back wall. Hanging from the generously sized mantle were an array of cooking implements, well-blackened from frequent use. And although no fire was lit this evening, off to the side, shiny-new tin meat screens and reflector ovens stood ready to roast choice cuts before an open flame.

Past the hearth, and set at a ninety degree angle to it, a brick range was evenly dented with six gridiron-topped depressions for charcoal cooking. Above them ran a copper hood to draw off the fumes.

Lastly, the Doctor moved around the range, and in the corner opposite the sauce kitchen was tucked a large desk. Again, shelves were mounted on the wall above the workstation, but this time they held lenses. For indeed, the desktop was devoted to optical grinding equipment. Various-sized crystal bars, whose triangular surfaces could be used to test for colour rendering accuracy, were outfitted in a leather case on the writing surface. Other sets of test lenses were there as well – one to confirm ultraviolet light protection, and another to gauge colour blindness correction – amongst others.

From here, Kitchiner turned and mounted steps up to his telescope platforms. Carême followed in wonder, for each level they continued to rise, the optical devices grew larger and larger. From this closer vantage, he could now see the skylight windows were all operable by chains and pulleys. Once open, the business ends of the telescope or spyglass could be thrust out into the unhindering air.

Upon the very top level was an absolutely enormous telescope – the largest Carême had ever seen, for certain – and by it, a small stepladder going through a hatch in the roof.

"This way, Chef."

Carême followed, and soon both men were sitting comfortably on a platform overlooking the sea. The evening air, with the sun just now setting in the west, was warm and redolent of adventure.

The same evening air greeting Carême and Kitchiner filled the Kitchen Court of the Pavilion.

François leaned on the wall, smoking a thin cigar, which had been gifted by James Keenan as he once again waited for his misses. Now the Keenans, in their 'going home' attire, kept the young Frenchman company as they shot the breeze.

"Say, anyway"—James was priming the barrel—"how much do you and your *chum* make peddling his uneaten dishes every week?"

François rolled the tight stogie between his fingers. That was none of the undercook's business.

"It must be hauling you in a pretty penny." James took a drag, the illuminated end of his cigar lighting up smiling eyes he never took off of François.

"The amount in the end," replied the noncommittal maitre-d', "can never properly reward the efforts Carême puts into his creations."

The Irish couple exchanged glances, each daring the other to laugh in their colleague's face.

"And where," asked Audrey, "is the chef this evening? We've all seen the two of you thick as thieves, so why a night on your own – all of a sudden."

"Carême was invited to supper by that – unique – Doctor Kitchiner."

"Ah!" cried James. "Kitchiner, the eccentric; everybody's heard of him, but few seem to know him."

François found that information very interesting.

"Well"—Audrey dug in, her eyes now smiling as well—"no use feeling rejected—"

"Abandoned."

"—By your, your mate, because you're not as 'upper crust' as the good Doctor requires to visit his Club."

"That's right. Carême's new gentleman friend may shut you out, but we won't."

François knew a ribbing when it came his way, but still the feelings of being rejected and lonely were real in him.

All of this was set aside, for coming from the Castle Square side of the Court was Charlotte's young and pretty lady's maid.

As Brigitte drew close, François stood like he wanted to talk to her, but the Frenchwoman eyed the Irish undercooks and began to untie her bonnet as she sailed indoors.

Realizing he was standing now, François felt self-conscious. He snubbed out the stogie, which he'd suddenly soured on, against the stone wall and stowed the rest in his apron pocket.

He decided to rub their faces in it. "So far this week, we've made 8 Pounds and 10 Pence extra selling some of Carême's dishes."

The Keenans were stunned into silence. The quoted sum was equal to their weekly salaries, combined.

At the same time, about a mile away, two very different people sat on a roof-top, engaging in conversation suitable for the setting. For one, they could hear the sea breaking as surf upon the sands of Brighton's most hospitable beach, just across the wide boulevard and five stories down. But also, as the warm evening breeze blew on Kitchiner and Carême's faces, the sun finally touched the western horizon, and the stars emerged before the moon could rise in the east.

"This is the first pleasant day I've seen here," said Carême. "Even now at the start of August, the Pavilion housemaids keep busy lighting fires in the bedrooms at four in the morning."

"Well, at least Brighton is not alone. Such fires are being lit from Moscow to Boston, and back again to Glasgow. In fact, I suppose we are relatively warm here on the South Coast, for my correspondences in Scotland have recorded three inches of snow fell last month."

"In July?"

"Yes."

"Then, no doubt, the crops have failed."

Kitchiner was serious. "Yes. Failed food staples from Naples to Saint Petersburg, and back to us. Only steam-heated grow-houses are producing."

"Thank goodness His Highness' greenhouses have kept me in operation."

The Doctor removed his glasses to clean them. He slowly shook his head. "Nature periodically takes time to remind the human race how puny we are. Here, all the armies of Europe have paraded around for a twenty-year series of wars and slaughter – as if that mattered – when Nature could wage battle on us with instant destruction." The spectacles went back on. "Are you, dear Chef, aware why 1816 will go down as 'the year without a summer'?"

Carême puzzled. "You mean a direct cause?"

"Oh, yes, it's all been due to one single, earthly event. Tambora."

The chef felt awkward in his ignorance. "You will forgive me, but as a front-line cook, I have little time for the News of other—"

"Mount Tambora. In April of last year, she – this volcano in the Dutch East Indies – exploded. Violently, as Pliny the Younger recorded Mount Vesuvius did in 79 A.D. Tambora incinerated thousands of people on the instant she exploded, and sent a shockwave out in all directions. When it got to London, the sound was so great, it cracked windowpanes, and I, out in the street at the time, had to stop and cover my ears."

"Ah, yes!" Light dawned in Carême. "François and I were working in my pastry shop and we heard it too. We thought an Allied bomb had gone off in the *Place de la Concorde,* mere blocks away." Now Carême shook his head. "How difficult it is to imagine the power of a disaster three quarters of the way around the globe touching each of our lives materially."

Kitchiner gestured across the sky. "Materially, yes, even now, because Tambora's eruptions in 1815 sent a mountain-full of ash to the top strata of Earth's clouds. The effects are still being felt as it comes down again to block sunlight and make it rain non-stop."

Carême suddenly equated the natural disaster under discussion to the military disaster of Waterloo. That too had altered the political climate of the world with far-reaching effects for so many.

The chef once more decided to broach who Kitchiner was exactly to the Regent. "The last occasion we had a chance to discuss it, you told me you were but a loyal servant to George, but – if I may be allowed – I still believe there is more to the matter."

Instead of shrugging it off, Kitchiner addressed the request for information head on. "Well, dear Carême, you might say I assist His Highness with more delicate matters."

Like sweep-up boys accidentally poisoning Royal chamber maids; that much the chef already knew.

Carême lowered his voice. "Private ones?"

"Well, those—"

"Or matters of State?

The glasses came off again. "Both, as you have so sagaciously already assessed."

"So, you are – *comme ça* – my official minder?"

"No; no!" His very vehemence belied the good Doctor's objection. "You may merely consider me a friend of the Prince. One set with the task of ensuring your visit to England is an amiable one for all concerned."

Carême accepted this for now. No doubt, more intelligence was required to form a complete picture.

The Doctor gestured over the sea. "You know, when important News is expected from Europe, I bring my spyglass up here to intercept the messages coming from Paris via the Signal Towers. Such a wonder of the modern age, when headlines from overseas capitals can arrive in a matter of hours, not weeks."

"Yes, you mean *le télégraphe,* the system where coded light signals are passed from one relay tower to the next. A French invention, if I am not much mistaken . . . ?"

"Oh, yes – by Claude Chappe. A clever idea, for sure. And by intercepting the signals, my reports knew all about the results of the Congress of Vienna – and our New Europa – before any of the London papers did."

Reports, Carême wondered. Reports to whom?

The Doctor continued at a merry clip. "Perhaps you can tell me: is it true that Talleyrand, when asked how in the Devil he was going to keep France from being carved up by the Allies, said 'By bringing more casseroles!'"

Amused, Carême replied, "I would say that's a bit of lazy translation."

"How so?"

"Shortly before leaving for Vienna, Louis XVIII tired out the Grand Chamberlain with endless requirements. It was then Talleyrand quipped, *'Sire, j'ai plus besoin de casseroles que d'instructions écrites.'* Meaning: 'Sire, I have more need for *saucepans* than written instructions.' He planned on wining and dining French liberty into the minds of the victors as *the* reason France must always exist as she is."

Kitchiner chuckled. "Well, he succeeded. So, cheers to his princely sauce-pans!"

Carême smiled; he was beginning to like this eccentric-yet-gentlemanly man. He had style, which most people sacrifice for success, never knowing resistance to conformity was the first test of character they failed.

Meanwhile, François was alone. The Irish couple had offered their 'Good Nights' a few minutes ago. So now the Frenchman moved up to one of the Kitchen Court's pillars. He leaned against it, brooding on circumstances and the stars just beginning to appear.

Unbeknownst to him, Brigitte – minus bonnet and shawl, and fixing her hair in place – peered around the doorframe from the Pantries and Household Kitchen.

Once she saw François was alone, and ascertained there was no one behind her to witness and gossip, Brigitte stepped up to François' side.

The man remained oblivious to her presence.

She cleared her throat. "A cloudless sky for a change."

François' startled reaction instantly displeased her. Brigitte had caught the withdrawn young man at a disadvantage, and disliked botching his opportunity to pursue *her.*

"Well, I . . . " François stumbled over words. "Yes, it's true." He felt his own awkwardness belie the role he was meant to play. In another moment or two, his wits reassumed their pre-eminence. He re-leaned on his column, this time with arms folded and body positioned to face the lady's maid. "A nice night for romance."

Brigitte was not impressed. Through a bland grin, she replied, "Yes. I suppose."

"It hasn't been warm in so long – at night."

"Yes," she said, glancing back at her escape route. She followed up with more hair preening as she made to go. *"Oh, là, là* – the time. I must—"

François stopped her by taking her hand.

Now Brigitte forgot almost everything else.

He led her back to the more private position of leaning against the wall.

She protested much too weakly. "I really can't stay long, as I have many things to prepare for our journey."

"Which journey?"

"The Princess; she and Leopold will travel home to Claremont House in the morning. It's near to London." The young lady suddenly blushed. "It's their – *my* – last night in Brighton."

This raised a complex reaction in François. He too felt that time was ticking. "But your mistress doesn't need you?"

"This evening, no."

"And that *Bosche,* Leopold?"

She chuckled, revealing something of a shared dislike of the Prince Consort, at least as a matter of principle. "He? He is off this night to a casino, gambling – no doubt – with his wife's income."

François smiled. "Were you employed in Paris before you came here?"

"Oh, yes." Her spirits brightened. "The centre of the world. I was companion maid to the Marquess de Cussy."

François was impressed. She'd named a very noble French family, one as powerful under Napoleon as they had been under Louis XVI.

To the maitre-d's eyes, the girl appeared the same age as François, meaning she too was a child of the Terror. And unrevealed to François' perceptions was just how much Brigitte had suffered under Robespierre's Regime, for her parents, as the head of their minor nobility family, had had their brains lopped off in the *Place de la Concorde,* like so many thousand others.

François sighed with gentle feeling. "I miss Paris, and her food."

Brigitte's soft spot had been found. She began gushing warmly, "Oh, how I miss Carême's pastry shop just off the *Place Vendôme.* The puff pastry tea cakes with the whipped cream and strawberries were my favourite."

"The *puits d'amour.*"

"Yes! *Fountains of love* – so delicious. The one with pastry cream and chopped pistachios, also very good."

"Carême's motivation for taking on a pastry shop was to bring knightly food to the masses. His were democratic reasons."

"Let them eat brioche! Literally."

François laughed. "That is exactly right. Like our best seller there – the large meringue stars. Carême was first to pipe them from a pastry bag with a fancy tip. The kind Marie-Antoinette got were much duller."

"*Oui?* How so!" Her lower lip glossed over in an adorable pout.

"What she ate was plain – spooned and tapped down before baking. Like the buttons of *macaron* today."

"How interesting. So we're eating better than a queen."

"Yes, but unfortunately, Carême just liquidated the business in June. During the retreat of the *Grande Armée* and the Allied occupation, the cost of getting flour and butter – good quality stuff – was much too much for him."

"How sad! You mean *La Pâtisserie Carême* is closed?"

"No; no. It's still open, under the same name and using Carême's recipes."

Her hand fell upon François' lower arm in relief. "Thank goodness. I need something to look forward to back home."

"You have anyone special, back home?"

"*Non.* I do not." She dared not ask him the same.

He placed his hand atop hers, returning to the pastry shop topic. "Carême would have kept the business, but he decided to focus on private cooking again. He needs to restore his finances and pay off the debts the shop carried – it's the reason he accepted the Regent's offer to come here." His fingers moved up her arm to draw her a little closer. "Plus, Carême now has a family to support."

"He does?"

"Yes; a de facto wife and daughter."

For the life of her, Brigitte de Saint-Exupéry could not puzzle out why relaying this information made François appear so emotional. Then she thought it must be a general sentimentality in the handsome young man concerning building a family. This added dimension suddenly flooded her with attraction for the 'sensitive' man.

She said haltingly, as if revealing too much information, "The *troubles* and food crisis in Paris caused by Napoléon's defeat and the Allies' occupation – I know them too well. This is why I left France. So you see"—she kissed him, tenderly—"we are equal refugees to circumstances."

She moved her upper thigh to brush against his crotch.

"I wish," she said softly, "I could take you to my room in the women's wing . . . . And it's too bad tomorrow . . . . I will be—"

François took her hand. He led her calmly along the colonnade and into the Kitchen Stables. They found an empty stall with new-laid straw. Thus in the half-light, they pressed close, kissing wildly while she massaged his member through the fabric of his trousers. Eventually, he turned her to face the wall, lifted her skirts and rutted her. The closer and closer her pleasured grunts, and the feel of her enclosure's response to his presence became, the more his tears fell unwitnessed behind her. By the time they climaxed in unity, François was choking back sobs, just holding onto her shoulders and resting his cheek on her back.

Chapter 4, Part Two:
Kitchiner's Cabinet of Curiosities

Doctor Kitchiner led the way back down, this time choosing the oval staircase next to the lift. He chatted merrily the whole time, but Carême only replied when necessary, for in his mind, he was cataloguing all the observations he'd so far made of this 'Club' – this central base of Doctor Kitchiner's operations.

At the building's main floor – the one above the street level – Kitchiner quit the stairs and showed the way down a grand corridor. Carême knew it was the main level not only by the stucco and delicate paint colours, but by the ceiling height. The *piano nobile* of this structure was about sixteen feet high, creating a very noble sense of space indeed.

At this point, the chef's jovial host glanced at this watch again. "The others are expecting us."

"Others?"

But before the Doctor could reply, he did something unexpected. He pulled up in front of a door and paused. As this highly polished mahogany portal was still far from the front of the house – where, no doubt, the grandest state rooms overlooked the sea – Carême was surprised.

By way of cryptic response to the chef's enquiry, Kitchiner lowered his head and pushed his glasses a bit higher along his nose. "Indeed."

The Doctor opened the door and strode in. But Carême's view remained blocked. In its place, other sensations vied for his attention, for compared to the hallway, this spacious salon was brightly lit. A central chandelier was draped with crystal swags and drew the chef's interest to the ceiling. The room was square, and a reeded medallion fanned out in flawless plaster. Where the perimeter corners left pendentive spaces, a lovely pale-green background supported rondels of frolicking cupids.

Carême heard warm chatter and female laughter. Then the chef was stopped cold in his tracks; he couldn't believe his eyes. At a round table sat the Prince Regent. A lovely lady was seated at his right, while to his left was Princess Charlotte and Lady Morgan. The members of the party were in mid-conversation, and as cozy as could be imagined.

Just at that moment, a matronly woman with a large tureen bundled in through another door; a swing-door from some hidden servant access point. She was all smiles and greeted each of the seated guests as family.

The woman set the soup by the left hand of one of two empty chairs. Kitchiner called out, "Dear Carême, I'd like you to meet Mrs. Elizabeth Lister. She is my good gal Friday, the most in-demand caterer in London, and an advisor to me on all things cookery. *And* – a dear friend."

She made a dim show of protest, but drank in every syllable of praise.

"Mrs. Lister," the Doctor continued, "may I present Antonin Carême, *chef de cuisine* to His Highness' kitchens, Brighton."

"Enchantée, Madame." Carême bowed slightly.

To the sight of which, Lister picked up the hem of her apron and curtsied with a slight giggle. "The pleasure is all mine, Monsewer."

Then her attention turned to the Doctor. "Now, sit. The Mullagatawny's getting cold."

As the two new-arrivers took their places, Mrs. Lister exited the scene to attend to the next menu item.

To Carême's pleasant surprise, he realized there were no servants in the room, and Kitchiner himself unlidded the tureen. The man gestured for Princess Charlotte's soup bowl. It passed from Lady Morgan to the Regent's hands, then to his companion's and on to the Doctor's. He ladled in a portion, and back the filled dish went to its owner.

Motioning for the bowl of the Irish novelist, Kitchiner said, "I believe, Chef, you know everyone here, except perhaps Mrs. Fitzherbert."

"Maria Anne Fitzherbert," the lady supplied her full name.

Carême smiled and nodded at the attractive woman across from him. *"Enchantée, Madame."*

"Likewise," she replied most politely.

To the chef's eyes, this un-titled lady was in her 50s, but vigorous and natural in youthful energy. Her abundant ashen hair was tastefully tied up by a wide blue ribbon. She wore a gown suitable for an informal supper, for the cut was Classical – a scooped neckline – yet up-to-date – with balloon sleeves to encase her upper arms – and in a luxe French silk with the most charming field flowers embroidered on it. Upon the creamy expanse of her ample bosom sat a large diamond-wreathed portrait of the Prince.

The Regent suddenly interjected: "Call her Fitzy; I know I do!"

Princess Charlotte laughed and laughed at this, passing her filled soup bowl to Carême, via Sydney Morgan.

It seemed this night of surprises would keep on giving, for although 'Fitzy' had been mentioned in a dossier on the Regent given him to read by Talleyrand, the report said the Prince and his lover from the 1780s had split long ago. Now the chef speculated news of the break-up could have been merely *official,* and of the type of counterintelligence someone like Kitchiner was in a position to disseminate.

The good Doctor's head turned back as he spoke to the Prince. "Would you kindly play Mum and do the honours?"

"Certainly." The Regent stood, went to the sideboard and picked up a white Bordeaux. "The *Haut-Brion* to start with, Kitchiner?"

"Yes. That would be excellent."

And so, George Augustus, ruler of the British Empire, uncorked and dutifully filled everyone's wine glass.

Not knowing exactly what to think, other than believing neither *Empereur* Bonaparte nor King Louis XVIII could be conceived of doing this, Carême took solace in appreciating the wine chosen was among the best of France. At least he was amongst connoisseurs.

As he rounded the table with the bottle, George indulged in idle chatter. "It's a hinderance on our Age that the wine glasses are so small. We need more than a single-shot size so there's more privacy at table. Here you go, Fitzy. As it is, damn footmen constantly hover over one's shoulder just to top off a glass."

Carême agreed, as he always wanted guests to relax and feel at one with one another, free from the ever-present 'downstairs' ears eavesdropping.

"All right, then"—the Prince plopped the bottle hard on the table-cloth— "just let us keep the wine within reach and serve each other!"

Although crudely stated, Carême could again see George's logic concerning keeping the bottle on the table. Maybe someday this would be standard procedure.

The lid went back on the tureen; everyone had a full bowl of soup and a full glass of wine. "Mrs. Fitzherbert," said the Doctor amiably. "Might you be willing to offer the toast?"

The lady stood with her wine. "To good food, good conversation, and His Royal Highness."

"Cheers" went round the room as George helped his helpmate retake her seat.

"Let's eat!" Kitchiner said with a spoon already in his hand. "The Mullagatawny is perfect for the season."

Before Carême took his first taste, Lady Morgan smiled and drew some of the room's rapt attention away from him. "My husband, Princess Charlotte, informed me you are leaving Brighton?"

"Oh, yes. I am not fond of the travelling rot, but in the morning, we'll start out for home." She ate soup, and then glanced at her father. "It's been a wonderful stay, as always, excepting – of course – the revolting weather." Her attire was again overly youthful and gewgawed. Her yellow hair was forced into an 'up' positioning it never seemed to get accustomed to, and pinned in front with a diamond brooch of three Prince of Wales feathers.

"Well, with any luck," added Mrs. Fitzherbert, "Today's clear skies will follow you all the way back to Surrey."

The Princess snorted. "Bestial weather. So un-English in its nature."

The twenty-year-old's logic evaded everyone.

Lady Morgan was brave. "How so, Your Highness?"

She downed another spoonful before laughing. "It doesn't play fair!"

In the meantime, Carême's palate had adjusted to what he was eating. Only the excess of cayenne pepper perturbed his artistic—

"So tell me, Chef"—the Princess' attentiveness turned full-bore on him—"what is your opinion of English food, in general?"

"Oh, Charlotte," Fitzy tried interjecting, "let the poor man eat."

"No; no," insisted the Princess, "it's something simply *everyone* is dying to know."

Carême mustered his considerable Byronesque charm and replied, "Everything I've been served, Your Highness, has been constituted of the freshest ingredients, and handled in simple yet deft ways to bring out that natural flavour." He smiled upon his host. "And tonight's soup is no exception." The Frenchman diplomatically left the bit about the over-seasoning unmentioned. He didn't have to spoil the meal.

"Oh, Carême," cooed the Regent's mate, "that's wonderfully well put."

"Hear; hear," echoed George, drinking some wine. "A man of taste."

"Speaking of our cuisine and the sup of supper, Chef Carême, have you yet had real English turtle soup? The kind best served with a glass of sherry on the side." Kitchiner had polished off his curried first course and was dabbing his chin with a napkin. "For all intents and purposes, it's our national dish."

Carême shook his head. "I don't believe that I have."

"In that case, I'll ask Mrs. Lister to copy out our procedure for you. You will find it's well worth trying."

Carême took another spoonful. "Give it to François to test out."

Deflated, the good Doctor's voice lowered. "As you wish."

By way of reviving brighter spirits, Mrs. Fitzherbert leaned in and gushed a bit. "You may not know, Lady Morgan, but I am an enthusiastic reader of all your novels."

"Why, thank you. You do me a great honour."

"Oh, I have been your admirer ever since *The Wild Irish Girl* came out. In it, you portray such a sensitive and beautiful unfolding of Irish culture and history."

"Well, I've found so many youth in Ireland today are removed from knowing much about their past, so I thought it's best to 'preach it' as gently as I can in my fiction."

"It works marvellously well. It is, if I may say so, effective because it unfolds as part of the entertainment."

The Regent interrupted. "Chef, how long have you known Lady Morgan?"

After a pause, in deference to Fitzherbert, he replied, "Oh, several years." Then to Morgan, he asked, "When was it you and your husband first came to Paris?"

The lady giggled. "Not to betray my age, but 1810 – but we were, yet to be married then." The Irish author blushed most becomingly.

"We had wonderful and useful adventures then."

To Carême's open and honest words, Doctor Kitchiner and Prince George exchanged a significant look. Perhaps it was akin to a voiceless 'now we are getting someplace.'

But just then, Elizabeth Lister backed through the service door with a large platter and a silver basket of rolls. Her arrival set many in the room to action, for Kitchiner got up and took the empty tureen to the sideboard; Fitzherbert rose and collected the empty soup bowls; and George groaned to his feet to see about the wine.

A beaming Mrs. Lister set her food on the table, again to the host's left for serving, and Carême saw the platter featured not a poached fish, or a roast joint of meat, but a large salad. The central mound of fresh greens was everywhere surrounded by neat piles of other ingredients: dressed cucumber slices; shredded carrots; sliced radishes; rounds of red onion slices; blanched French beans; chopped gherkins; whole cooked sprats. The dish was garnished with watercress, nasturtium flowers and quartered lemons here and there. The aroma was simply wonderful.

"Ah," the Doctor said, joining Mrs. Lister with a hand across her shoulder. "The Salamagundy! It looks momentous."

"Oh, I forgot the dressing and butter for the bread." The caterer trailed off once more.

But unperturbed, the evening's host remained on his feet and began fixing miniature examples of the platter's arrangements on a stack of salad plates he had standing by.

The Regent asked from the sideboard, "What do you think, Chef. How about a *Côteaux du Roy René* for the salad?"

"Most excellent, Your Highness."

While the Prince uncorked and began filling new glasses on the table with the rosé, Elizabeth Lister re-appeared and discreetly placed a sauce tureen of the salad dressing and a dish of butter on either end of the table before quietly quitting the room once more.

To his delight, Carême immediately smelled fresh chervil.

"The traditional dressing for the Salamagundy is a melted butter-water, or what the Italians call a *bagna càuda.*"

When the Prince poured his wine, Carême asked, "Your gout seems to be improving, Your Highness."

"Ah! *Blame* Kitchiner for getting me up and on my feet. He's prescribed me something new – charcoal pills. How he figures these things out, I shall never know. But I shan't wait to know what I'd do without him." The man smiled.

By the time George was re-seated, everyone had a salad plate before them and could eat. The basket of bread and dish of butter circled the table in opposite directions. Once these two had settled again, His Highness picked up his fork and started eating. The rest, with hungry eyes, followed suit.

"Our dear Mrs. Lister," the Doctor was saying to the chef, "is a direct descendant of the famous Lister; the Dutch researcher and M.D., equally famous for his microscope, being personal physician to King William III, and his *book.*"

Carême asked, "Book?"

And Princess Charlotte blurted, "Related by marriage?"

To address the lady first, Kitchiner disabused her of the notion. "No, Your Highness. She's a direct descendant of Lister's." And then to the chef he answered, "His amended and annotated version of the Ancient Roman cookery book known as 'Apicius'."

"Ah!" The Frenchman nodded recognition. He'd seen editions of this rare Classical artifact in the French National Library. However, the Princess was not done.

"Direct?" she asked, astounded. "Then how on earth can she be a *Missus*, Doctor Kitchiner?"

"Simple, my good Lady: Elizabeth Lister, caterer *extraordinaire,* has never been married, but as a presumed 'widow,' it's far easier for a woman of business like her to advance her vocational goals. So, professionally, she's known as *Mrs.* Lister."

Charlotte guffawed. "How strange. I must be naïve concerning the lengths some women will go to—"

"For a woman of talent and ambition," interjected Lady Morgan pointedly, "a slight ruse – or a slight withholding of fact – can benefit her tremendously."

The Princess sighed, picking up her fork. "I suppose." She poked some of her vegetables with a frown. "I'm glad I can be me."

After a pause of just eating, Doctor Kitchiner re-grasped the thread of his conversation with Carême.

"King William was much taken with Lister's *Apicius,* and in fact wrote a book about it."

"The King, *Monsieur?*"

"Yes. It's a charming tome of the type known over here as a table-talk book – full of stories, food lore, and sometimes, recipes. This evening's Salamagundy is from King William's book!"

"Remarkable," chimed Mrs. Fitzherbert. "This is food people ate a hundred years ago?"

"Yes. Exactly so."

"It's so light and delicious."

"I agree, Madame." The good Doctor proudly pushed his glasses up. "Good food has no expiration date – at least not the preparations that make good food."

"Is the salad to your liking?" Lady Morgan asked gently of Carême.

"Very much so, *Madame.* It is, as Mrs. Fitzherbert says, light and fresh; perfectly of the season."

The Regent was up again, re-filling wine glasses.

"I'm so pleased you think so," said Kitchiner. "Tonight's little gathering might be considered a tasting panel. Mrs. Lister and I chair our official 'Committee of Taste' in London."

"For what purpose, Kitchiner?" enquired the Regent.

The Doctor beamed with pride. "We are going to publish our findings in book form. It will contain tips on running a household, present various victual preparations – *properly* instructed – and contain a good deal of personal food-culture observations and philosophy of my own. The Committee is to test each recipe for taste and technique before it is included."

Carême nodded his approval. "A modern approach. Very commendable." The chef noticed Princess Charlotte was evidently not fond of vegetables. She'd hardly done more than move her fork about, looking bored, and in the end, only nibbled on a couple of the less offensive legumes.

"It's one thing I admire," the Doctor continued brightly. "The French treasuring of your culinary past. Why, anyone who's studied over there will know Taillevent's book – the Taillevent chef-knight buried 'neath a stone with sword and cooking pots carved on it. And everyone there learning their craft studies Pierre la Varenne's first truly modern cookbook of the 1650s."

By this time, Carême had watched as Princess Charlotte completely abandoned her salad. Instead, she split a roll in two, slathered extra portions of butter on both sides, and then paused with a scowl. Her survey of the dining table had not returned the presence of a sugar bowl. She ate her roll sullenly.

"Well, Doctor"—the chef restored his attention to his host—"Varenne *is* good to study for background knowledge, but he was not as good a chef as Vincent la Chapelle."

The Doctor radiated good cheer. "I agree whole-heartedly. His *Modern Cook* from the 1730s is unparalleled." He turned quizzical. "Do you, Chef, know his preparation for mackerel—"

"Smoked in fennel fronds and served with a *velouté* of . . . of – *comment c'est, les groseilles à maquereau—*"

"Gooseberries! Yes. That is one of my favourite dishes; it is so straightforward and delicious."

Carême – a professional trained for years in the art of not being taken aback by anything – was wholly amazed. He'd hardly imagined an eccentric English dilettante and he would find overlap in the veneration of a cook long gone, but he had. Unused to the feeling admiration for a contemporary, as it was, Carême now looked upon Kitchiner as someone to be respected – a man of learning and discernment.

"And in London, a publisher has bought the rights to publish a translation of Beauvilliers' *Art Cuisinier*. It will cause a sensation when it comes out—"

"Cooks do go on about their books . . . " Kitchiner's enthusiasm was cut off by the Prince Regent.

"Beauvilliers, who?" asked Mrs. Fitzherbert.

Carême replied. "One of Napoléon's finest and longest-serving chefs. His book – his life's work – appeared in 1814, sadly, only shortly before he died of chef's lung."

"What's that," Charlotte enquired with wide eyes.

The Doctor provided a medical explanation. "A slow poisoning through constant CO inhalation. Carbon monoxide – it gets in the blood instead of oxygen."

"Yes," affirmed Carême. "Most chefs do not escape it and live to old age. I'm to be no exception."

In his mind, the urgency of writing his own legacy *livre de cuisine* – a great one to put all those come before to shame – pressed his consciousness. In the urgency too was the inner physical weakness he could sometimes feel. His clock was ticking.

A tactful acknowledgement, via a wave of pity, circled the table for the great artist among them, but this charge of human connection passed by the Prince unnoted.

"You know, Carême, old boy, I collect memorabilia surrounding your former emperor." George drained his wine glass, adding with a lip-smack, "In fact I have Napoleon's table from Fontainebleau – the one on which he signed his surrender – back in my toilet room at the Pavilion. I'll show it to you sometime."

In rote acknowledgement of his royal employer's favour, Carême bowed his head slightly. "As you wish, Your Highness."

While the Regent had been off on his self-admiring tangent, Lady Morgan stood and re-filled the glasses. She remained standing and offered a toast.

"Please raise your glass and drink: Long life to Carême, and to a bookcase full to the brim with his books."

"Hear; hear," went round the room.

Mrs. Lister arrived, and Lady Morgan helped her gather plates and remove the Salamagundy platter.

At the same time, the evening's sommelier spoke to Carême from the sideboard, where he was fiddling with something. "You're not one to imbibe much of the wine, are you, Chef?"

Carême rarely found himself in situations where he let himself go. "No, Your Highness. It's a lesson I learned from Talleyrand. He said, 'If you make it through a meal on one glass, you will have come far'."

The ladies laughed, including Lister, who was placing a very large compote on the table by the Doctor's plate.

Suddenly, George's arm moved, and there was a pop from a champagne bottle in his hand. "What, if anything, does the Prince de Talleyrand say about the bubbly?"

"Ah"—Carême smiled—"that he says you take, swirl, smell, set down again and enjoy through discussion!"

In the meantime, Lady Morgan had been playing Mum and dishing out the dessert. Carême was unprepared to see the blob placed before him.

He asked the Doctor, very much not knowing, "What is this?"

"It's the new dessert sensation sweeping London at the moment: 'A Trifle'!"

Carême looked once more, but all he could make out was an amalgamation of some manner of cake, red jelly of a sort, *crème anglaise,* and a mound of whipped cream on top. The one thing he for sure recognized was the most offensive – a scattering of variously coloured candy sprinkles.

Kitchiner sat down and explained. "A summer dessert of sponge biscuits soaked in maraschino brandy—"

"My favourite!" the Regent interjected like a schoolboy.

"—Topped with red currant jelly, custard and whipped cream."

Taking up his spoon, Europe's highest paid chef tried it and decided it tasted like it looked. But to his surprise, when he glanced up, no one was searching his features for an opinion. Instead, while they were eating their desserts, a table of contented faces surrounded him, especially that of the young Princess. This brought a moment of happiness. "You know, I'm thoroughly charmed. This supper reminds me of ones so common in France before the Revolution."

Feeling the mood turn slightly dark due to the mention of the French troubles, and indirectly, its bloodshed, Princess Charlotte asked, "And what fate was decided for that kitchen sweep-up boy?"

The Regent, rather cavalierly with spoon in hand, replied, "Thanks to Carême's quick action, and the Doctor's expert tending, he was nursed to stable condition in the Pavilion, and then rushed through a secret court proceeding here in Brighton, convicted and Transported to Australia."

The women were taken aback. Almost as if in one voice, they murmured: "Poor lad."

Kitchiner, clearer of head, explained it to the gathering. "It was the best possible outcome. He killed a girl, not meaning to, but killed her. In a public trial, the judge would be obliged to set the boy as an example for all Royal Household staff members and hang him. But now, once Jack Hartell arrives in Australia, he'll be released on his own recognizance. He can start over again."

Mrs. Fitzherbert shook her head. "Over, maybe, but with no money or family to fall back on—"

The Prince Regent gently laid down the law. "Fitzy, dear, as Kitchiner said, it was all for the best. There is no need to scandalize the Pavilion over the antics of a seventeen-year-old girl, and a fifteen-year-old boy."

"No; quite right." Princess Charlotte was in complete agreement, and on her second bowl of Trifle.

From there, the party ate on in moody silence, not knowing the rain had started once more outside. As for the greatest chef in Europe, he tried a second spoonful and decided the confetti candy on top was actually properly placed after all. For this was a dessert best served to children – *and* served in the Nursery – out of sight.

Kitchiner, perhaps partially reading his mind, asked Carême, "Have you ever heard of baked fruit Charlottes, Chef? Apple Charlotte is the best known."

"No, Doctor Kitchiner, I can't say that I have."

"When the apples come in, I will bake you one." He smiled across the table. "After all, it was invented at Buckingham House, in honour of Princess Charlotte's Grand *ma-ma.*"

"Oh, Doctor," the Princess cried, "you're a *dear!*"

As the rain began to pound in earnest outside, Kitchiner rose within the room's warmth to propose a toast.

"The Pleasures of the Table, dear friends, are of
all Ages, of all Countries – and in spite of any Stoic's words –
reward all equally well with Community of Spirit.
Raise your glass, and say with me: 'Yes, a thousand times;
A thousand years, yes! To good food and good company."

PART II

Autumn 1816

Pavillon des Palmiers

Intelligence Report No. 26

Jj3m l8hew 3 1 j7kmf 3 1 vnj9jwfd,

1 ke5m urc fr9jw pi3gcwx lk4b po gi5jdlii5md ouv. 1 jge5vznwx .ec8h 1iei. qgc sonf fhs8e 3 jn jV7elz vs7ufhbs 3 wk4chfuv hk6nd 7 ofh1e mg ik4dfco 4 1 lkn fcv 1 in-jkgtm5fv, con5 fbx8 3 jhn3ybdcwkt 3 uv7fc.

Cher Doyen de l'école de la Concorde,

Le temps sur cette maudite côte ne s'améliore pas. Les prétendus «mois d'été» ont fait place à un automne déterminé à apporter glace et neige au niveau de la mer dès la mi-septembre, soit dans une quinzaine de jours.

Dear *Doyen de l'école de la Concorde,*

The weather on this damnable coast does not improve. What was alleged to be 'summer months' have now given way to an autumn determined to bring ice and sea-level snow as early as mid-September, or in about a fortnight.

The prolonged rain has made living in this so-called palace nothing but restless, and it's a construction zone where there's little chance to escape out-of-doors. Night and day the hammers fall, the carts roll up with the new iron structure for the roof. And to think of all of this money squandered – paid for by their Parliament taxing the working brothers and sisters of this subjugated 'union' – when it could go to importing wheat from North America to keep the people from wasting away in the streets, but the Lords here do nothing for the common folks.

It is no wonder my sources tell me London is in a precarious position at the moment. More slogans – this time written in pigs' blood – have been scrawled on the Regent's palace. In addition

to the one seen everywhere of 'Bread or the Regent's Head!', a
new one is accompanying it, saying 'String up the Lords by their
Silken Cords!'

However, News of the riots happening in the Capital, and how
the pretty toy soldiers of the 'House Guard' mow down the
hungry wretches in their very rags is entirely supressed. Anyone
with printing equipment is watched by Whitehall's secret police,
and countless others have been rounded up and tortured to
name the Freedom Movement's leaders. God help the working
people of this country if the efforts of Reform fail, for an England
not a Republic in the 19th century will mean Imperial-style
subjugation for many parts of the currently free world. The despised colours of their banner of slavery will never see the sun set
on it.

Maybe we, as planned, can help their overthrow along.

Frankly, it *has* to change. The hypocrisy of the English Lords
telling the Irish, Scotch and Welsh that they live in a 'Constitutional Democracy' is crueller than the lash. These self-same
agents of Whitehall's oppression talk of democracy as if they
were America, but outlaw freedoms, jail and torture as if they
were Russia.

Give me *la belle France* any day!

As for the character of Prince George, he hides from his subjects
– for good reason – in his splendid isolation of fantasy palaces,
but is too familiar with those who serve him directly. In Brighton,
he can sometimes be seen talking to staff members as lowly as
horse grooms or scullery maids, but offers no warmth to his
chamberlains and exchequers. He too seems to operate on the
fear the Lords will betray him instantly, if it will save their own
necks.

Now, I must close, as the appointed time for handing off this
missive approaches. But I will say something of English food, for
of this subject I know you have a natural curiosity. In brief, I can
relay the English have but two sauces – 'Custard' and 'Mustard'.
The first, what we know as *crème anglaise,* is served on top of all
things sweet; the other, on all the rest. I will also say they have a
savage regard for heat: cayenne pepper is generously sprinkled
onto everything, tinging white soups and sauces pink! Since we
have been here, the sluggards in the kitchens have been amazed
by the concept of using white pepper for white food!

The Pavilion functionaries, high ranking ones, are a pack of jackals protecting their jobs before all else. Now that autumn is here, I expect there will be some fights brought to the fore, but I and my associate are up to the chore of keeping them in their place. In short, dear Prince, be assured I am focussed on my mission here; I will achieve the goal you set for me, so please leave Agathé and Marie alone. I still have time!

Regards,

Instituteur Marron Glacé

Chapter 5: The Gasolier Rises & Eavesdropping

The exact dividing line between Summer 1816 and Autumn 1816 was nearly impossible to identify. The gloom of the previous winter hardly had a chance to fade before the tilt of the Earth's axis returned Europe to darkening days and lengthening nights. Furthermore, Nature seemed determined to present much worse. She seemed ready to promise a crueller winter yet to come, one where starvation could hunt across lands apparently slipped back to primeval conditions.

But in the insular, escapist world of the Regent's Pavilion, workers had been pushed to their limits, and through great efforts, the architect's vision for the extreme ends of the marine villa had come to fruition. The stone-stuccoed tent rooves – as enormous as they were – were all buttoned up and dry, waiting with calm for the season's first freezing rain to test their guttering systems against freeze-thaw's notorious prying action. For sooner, rather than later, wandering English couples strolling by the property would cast eyes over to see snow settle on this European Taj Mahal of the vanities, so far out of context, plopped as it was in the centre of brick and coal-dust Brighton.

In any event, the frozen precipitation was still a remote threat on this fair September day. The weather was so unaccountably fine, Lady Morgan had fetched her friend from his kitchen office at midmorning. She knew he'd be free for an hour or so, before his rush to see the day's dinner set out by 3 o'clock. The chef's routine was dependable, so she 'took possession' of Carême when she could.

Now they walked side by side along the Steine, an elevated strip of communal open land the Prince of Wales abutted the east lawn of his Pavilion property against. Still the demesne of the Brighton backbone – the fishermen – their nets were picturesquely run atop wooden racks to dry above the grass.

The singular pair of world-renowned novelist and chef strolled towards the Gardens, a public park of tall oaks and shady benches upon which to sit and listen to the not-so-distant surf roll in.

"You strike me as tired, my dear Carême."

The chef inhaled some fresh air. "No more than one would expect. The Pavilion is a hive of activity, as Charlotte will be arriving today. Tomorrow most of my time will be taken up preparing *pièces montées* for her welcoming dinner."

"Oh, how exciting – your sugar work architecture." She chuckled warmly. "I will never forget what you told Talleyrand a few years ago. You said, *'Prince,* there are three disciplines of architecture: stone, wood and pastry. I excel at the third, most difficult of all.'"

Sydney Morgan laughed again, clutching at his arm. Carême smiled – warmly, too – but honestly, he didn't see anything particularly droll about what he considered a straightforward statement. Being an aerial architect of molten sugar was just as demanding as bringing a pleasure palace to an English fishing town.

They found a lonely wooden bench and sat down in the Gardens.

"Will Lord Morgan be at dinner today in the Blue Drawing Room?"

"Oh, yes. This morning he and a few friends – all men, of course – rode out early to Rottingdean for a picnic."

"Oui? Rotting . . . . "

"Rottingdean. It's a picturesque village a mere jaunt up the coast. I should organize an outing for us up there too, someday. You and me, and François?"

"You are too kind, *Madame.* But it is difficult for both of us to be away from the Pavilion at the same time. Work obligations, you understand."

Lady Morgan diplomatically refrained from asking if more than 'work' was dividing their domestic interests. Instead, she leaned back while raising her face to the sun. Her manner became drenched in nostalgia. "Oh, Carême, do you know what this reminds me of?"

"No. What, *Madame?"*

She sat upright and took his hand like an eager schoolgirl. "Our afternoon teas with *monsieur* Denon! Just Lord Morgan, yourself and I with our host – poring over his fascinating drawings from Napoleon's Egyptian campaign and exploration."

"Ah, yes. They were wonderful, relaxed afternoons."

"His windows would be open to the *rue Saint-Honoré,* with all of its modern noise and hustle, and we'd be so removed from it, looking upon the glories of an ancient civilization never before seen by Western eyes."

"I can tell you," assured the chef, "Dominique-Vivant Denon is planning on publishing all of his surveys as hand-coloured engravings – in extra-large folio format."

Lady Morgan sighed. "I must have one when he does – no matter the expense. How gleeful it makes me feel. He must document his findings for Europe to see."

"And that he shall. After all, France did some good in Egypt."

Sydney Morgan's mood changed. "Good in terms of uncovering the Rosetta Stone, yes. But not good when considered from Bonaparte's war crimes."

"The massacre?"

"Yes," she insisted, "his slaughter of three thousand Muslim soldiers who had already surrendered at Jaffa. Such 'Christian' brutality will haunt Western and Middle-Eastern affairs for generations to come."

"Oui, Madame. There is no covering such actions under the notions of Glory."

"As we'd say in Ireland, a crime is a crime is a crime. There's no avoiding it."

"Bonaparte's order was a radical action, and it has no excuse."

"Exactly. Sometimes I feel the political climate today forgives any radical action, as long as it advances a certain party towards their goal."

Carême had to chuckle a bit. "Are not your novels political, advocating for the solemn cause of Irish Liberty?"

Sydney Morgan paled. "They are and they do *pressure,* dear Chef, but through peaceful means. The leverage my work exerts on the upper classes aside, I remain filled with personal abhorrence that the Republican Movement is willing to seek out violent methods for overthrowing the British Empire's colonization of Eire."

"No doubt you are right." Carême attempted to return the presence of the sunny day back to his friend's consciousness. "And, as for our shared 'old times' in Paris, we puzzled over many an enigma together."

She smiled and clutched his arm once more. "That we did!"

Lost in the happy moment, Carême suddenly remembered the amount of work lying ahead of him. "Oh, my! Tomorrow – such a lot to do. Did you know the Regent gave orders to try and complete the Banqueting Room by this time to-morrow? He wants his welcome home dinner for Charlotte to be the first held there."

"Ah, I see. You are making your *pièces montées* for the completed space."

"*Oui.*"

"How many?"

"There are three sideboards, so one large sculpture for the central buffet, and two smaller ones that will be moved to the table when François sets it up for the Second Course."

"Oh, my dear Carême, I can hardly wait to see them tomorrow. I'm so happy."

So was the Frenchman. He placed a hand atop hers. "You cheer me, Lady Morgan. It is for eyes like yours – eyes that see and appreciate how much work it takes – that I build my edible pavilions of sugar."

The mood was such, Lady Morgan ventured, "You must feel so isolated sometimes; an artist among politicians."

"Well," the chef admitted, "I do have François. We are in a strange adven-ture, in a strange land, *oui* – but we are in it together, despite those who look on us with suspicions."

Sydney Morgan patted her friend's hand, but then withdrew it and cast her glance off towards the sound of the sea. "Suspicions. Yes, that's what it's like to be a . . . in England."

Carême's head twisted a bit. "To be a . . . ?"

She turned and lowered her voice. "An adherent of the Church in Rome."

Carême understood. An underground Catholic in a land where George's father was somehow to be worshiped as a holy man. "Yes, it is," he replied simply. A light suddenly went off in his mind concerning Kitchiner's duties – and the Regent's circle of intimate friends. He asked delicately, "Tell me, is Mrs. Fitzherbert also, a, shall we say, *religious* woman?"

It wasn't delicate enough to keep Lady Morgan from being astounded. After a pause rich with internal debate, she turned candid. "Yes. Yes, she is."

"And the Doctor – the Prince entrusts him with such private matters, and issues of the Regent's personal safety because he too adheres to the same *faith?*"

"Yes, Carême. So you see, the Prince was risking much to bring you into his inner, family circle. He and Fitzy are married; have been for nearly 30 years now, but all of this is a State Secret. George's political enemies would kill to get a hold of this information – it could bring down the whole monocracy."

"That means Charlotte is a—"

"Yes. She is, but no one must ever know."

Carême refrained from smiling. This was indeed intelligence not to be dispatched without careful deliberation.

"I feel I must reinforce my earlier message for you to watch your step in the Pavilion. Many are incensed that a foreigner like you should have such daily contact with the Prince. There are rumours among the staff that someone is out to get you."

Carême brushed it off with a chortle. "My dear Lady, success will always breed contempt. Being well-hated is a sign I'm doing my work correctly!"

"Well, I'm serious. I don't want anything to happen to you."

A new concept entered the chef's head. "If you would like to help—"

"Yes, anything."

"Perhaps you can do a little research on a pair of the kitchen undercooks."

"Discreetly?"

"Always."

"I mean, involve our friend Doctor Kitchiner in this?"

Carême smiled in his suave, Gallic way, letting it speak a decided "No" when it would be rude for his words to do so. "I leave it entirely up to your wisdom, *Madame.*"

What Carême had diplomatically failed to state was why he had his suspicions on the couple working for him in the first place.

Time was pressing for the chef, so he politely stood and held his hand for Lady Morgan to follow suit. As the friends returned through the Gardens, Morgan bade farewell at the street leading to Castle Square, obviously with intent on her mind. She dashed across the road, leaving Carême with the wily novelist's assurance of "Leave it to me."

The chef continued on to the Pavilion's east lawn. A nagging professional decision he still had to make haunted him as he entered one of the veranda doors into the southern withdrawing room.

John Lightfoot and his Table Deckers were busy, focused on dressing the dining table now running down the centre of the space. The chef nodded his approval at him, and the professionals continued with their tasks. As Carême strolled through the room, he placed his hands behind his back and became lost in concentration; so much so, the chamber's pretty decor of blue *chinoiserie* and imported Chinese silk lanterns hanging regularly around the room's perimeter barely broached the artist's consciousness.

So too was the noise of bustle and heated voices coming from the open doors to the Banqueting Room, and so, when he entered this massive space, he was stopped in his tracks by a spectacular sight.

For where he'd only to this point seen a plain plaster dome, now all the stuccowork and paint decorations were in place. Enormous, painted palm leaves fanned out on a blue-sky background from the centre of the ceiling in almost breathtaking realism. Suspended below this was a nearly life-sized flying dragon carved out of wood and polychromed with scales and open bat wings. Clutched in its talons was a ring, and hanging from this ring was the rising object that robbed Carême of his wits.

A crystal chandelier, at least three stories in height, was being hoisted into position. Many of its lead-glass bangles chimed in euphonious harmony as the lighting device inched its way into position. Below the ceiling dragon's clutches, crystal chains descended to the top of the fitting, and from here projected a sunburst. Several lengths of spiky triangles – done in brilliant mirrored glass, with the longest on top – glinted the flames coming from the main body of the pendant, for some twenty feet below, the central band of the fixture supported the busts of six silver dragons. Their necks and wings, which were each the size of a man, bent their open mouths skyward. Satin glass lotus pods erupted from their lips. Here jets of light were shaded by the glass, each flame coming from a tank of compressed coal gas hidden within the body of the chandelier.

The workmen kept shouting injunctions to one another: "Not so much your side"; "Keep it nice and easy over there"; "Slow and steady on your end." They referred to it as a 'Gasolier,' and suddenly Carême's attention shifted to the other four gas fixtures. Simpler versions of the main fitting, each was suspended from a craned phoenix head erupting from the centre of the dome's pendentives.

These had the same mirrored sunbursts, the same crystal ropes, but the main body was entirely lotus leaves in satin glass.

Carême saw two workmen testing the one closest to him, for these, presumably like the central Gasolier, were counterbalanced so a footman with a pole could hook onto the bottom of the device and pull it down. Now the workmen tested the lights hidden inside, and the lotus leaves lit up beautifully. The men raised the smaller chandelier into position to see how it looked. It looked spectacular. Ten-foot torchieres were also being tested. These were porcelain columns in two sections – black below and blue above – with gilded Chinese dragons curling around the top lotus-leaf blossom. These lamps stood around the perimeter of the space, lighting every corner of the room.

The central Gasolier made one final shimmying set of crystal clinks as it slid into its full-height position, and in Carême's head, he knew he was witnessing something historic. For surely nowhere in Europe was another lighting fixture to match this one's grandeur and size. He doubted there'd be a larger crystal chandelier anywhere in the world for a hundred years.

As he began to walk through the commotion of the space to the Decking Room's door, Carême glanced at the magnificent gilt sideboard where his sugar work *pièce de résistance* would go for tomorrow's dinner. He wondered how anything he'd produce could compete with the flights of full-on fancy comprising every inch of this dining room.

He was still thinking about this as he entered a Decking Room devoid of footmen, but stocked with cleaned and polished silver to set out for today's main meal, when all at once, a different sound caught his attention; a very human one.

He slowed his gait as he approached the door into the Central Service Corridor. Here resided a door with steps down to the Pavilion's cold storage rooms, and it was open.

The wily chef glanced about to make sure he was unobserved, then peeked down the stairs. The Kitchen Comptroller and teenager Thomas Daniels were having a heated discussion on the first landing.

Carême placed himself out of sight of them, against the wall bordering the door frame, but well within earshot of the two. The back of his head rested on the wall, and his heart rate went up with the thrill of possibly being caught spying like this.

The chef's ears rang.

The Comptroller was lecturing the lad. "Carême is selfish. He cares for no one but himself." There was a pause before he continued. "Don't scoff. You know it too. Look at the way he's taking money out of the pockets of undercooks like you."

Carême heard Thomas' distinctive laugh. And the chef knew any derision shown within sight of the Comptroller's face was sure to goad the man.

By way of rebuke, Thomas said, "I for one don't blame François or Carême for getting the straight dosh for what they make with their own hands. Shure seems democratic that way."

"It's not egalitarian! It's egotistical . . . . " The Comptroller sputtered to a halt. Perhaps Thomas' expression told the accountant his words were lost in the youth's ideals.

"Besides"—Thomas drove the nail home—"I like the man."

Donald Bland made such an unguarded, gut-wrenched sound of pain at this point that confirmation suddenly congealed into Carême's head who the Comptroller's mystery lover was.

"Listen," Thomas continued in more measured tones, "think of it from my position, please, Donald. Carême's presence in the Great Kitchen is a *great* opportunity. Others line up to pay for the chance to work with him, to be his student, and they pay dearly. Yet, here I am, earning a salary *and* getting taught by him for free!"

"But, still—"

"Besides their cost, these lessons are worth a great deal to young professionals like me. You have to understand—"

"All I have to understand"—the Comptroller's clip slowed to a men-ace—"is a Froggie cook like that greaseball will not last long around here. I'll see to it myself, even if I have to . . . . "

Carême slipped away, wanting to hear no more.

A few minutes later, his mind returned to more pressing subjects, the chef entered the Great Kitchen. All was action and well-oiled coordination as various teams worked towards the completion of the day's dinner.

He glanced up at the clock. The regulator's large and easy to read face told him it was 10 minutes to Noon.

As if sensing his desire, *sous-chef* Bauda and *maître d'hôtel* Distré appeared by the chef's side. A few moments later, a thorough status report had been delivered by Carême's two aides, and he was satisfied matters were well in hand.

Parting from them, Carême went to his office, slipped off his jacket, slipped on his apron and sat down. Leaning against the desk was his drawing board. He pulled it up, scowled at the flight of Chinese fancy he had been considering for tomorrow's dinner, and then glanced up. Thomas had reappeared at his station with a crate of the fresh vegetables he'd needed from the cold cellars.

Carême inhaled deeply, stood and abandoned his drawings on the desk. Instead, he placed his chef's cap dignifiedly on his head and checked himself in the mirror.

A short time later, he'd gathered a few things on a tray and went to Thomas. He stood in front of the boy, holding up an implement he'd retrieved from the tray. It had a handle, a cone-shaped bell of continuous wire and a flat bottom.

"Do you know what this is, Thomas?"

The lad wondered if it was a trick question. "She's a whisk."

"Correction: *She's* a sauce whisk. Always use one when making a quick *roux*. Let me show you."

To Thomas' amazement, the greatest chef in Europe took his tray and stepped to the nearest hot burner on the range. He put on it a small saucepan.

"Sauce velouté; observe."

With a deft hand, Carême scooped a pat of butter which went into the pan. "The proportion for a basic quick *roux* is equal parts butter and flour. Stir."

Carême handed over the sauce whisk, and the undercook moved the butter around the bottom of the pan to melt it completely.

The chef dumped in the flour. "Whisk slowly, and you will see the starch and fat amalgamate."

Thomas did. The liquid of the butter was taken up by the flour to produce a pale nut-coloured substance slightly thicker than whipping cream.

"Do you yet see cooking bubbles?"

Just as the chef asked this, the *roux* appeared to burst everywhere in the pan into a molten mass of foam. "Yes, Chef."

"At this stage, cook by whisking continuously for two minutes. No more; no less. The taste of the raw flour is being converted to warmer, more caramel notes. This is important, but do not let it burn."

Thomas stirred and continued to watch the *roux* slowly, which, degree by degree, became more and more golden. He counted the seconds.

At exactly the two-minute mark, Carême handed the boy a small syrup pitcher. "In here," he said, "is a half-pint of veal stock. Whisking all the time, pour it over the *roux."*

When Thomas did, the first few drops of liquid made the flour and butter mixture sizzle, but adding the rest slowly produced a flawlessly smooth sauce. It was delicately scented, and glossy on top.

"This," Carême said patly, "is why it's called a 'Velvet' sauce. It is done, Thomas. Take it off the heat and taste."

Thomas retrieved the tasting spoon from his apron. He coated the back of it with some of the piping hot sauce. It tasted like none of its individual ingredients but a brand-new thing. Smooth, flavourful, inviting – it would enhance almost anything.

"Now, Thomas, season it to your taste and I will try it."

On Carême's tray were open cellars of salt and three or four kinds of pepper. First went in a small pinch of sea salt. A stir and taste by the boy, and that was all right. As he reached for the cracked black pepper – instinctively eschewing the cayenne – he stopped. Something about the velouté's smoothness made him instead reach for a small portion of white pepper.

Carême had been talking the whole time—"Proportions - two spoonfuls of butter and flour for a pint of hot stock . . . "—but he stopped with a smile.

He took the youth's hand with the tasting spoon, dipped it in the sauce and brought it up to his mouth. Holding the boy's eyes, he tasted it. It was acceptable; there was nothing needing adjustment. Just as he was about to tell the lad so, his gaze slipped off the boy. François stood several paces behind him, one hand on hip, one hand leaning on a prep table, both eyes on Carême. While behind him, François' none-too-pleased scowl was mirrored by one from the Kitchen Comptroller.

Carême patted the young man's back. "Very well done, young Master Daniels."

The youth blushed with the pride of achievement, while glares from the boy's rear flared with jealousy.

Hours later, the chef's staff sat to their evening meal in the Household Kitchen. They'd pulled off a flawless dinner for George and his guests and could now settle for a bit. The day was not over though, for soon super would need to be prepared and served, and the day's last clean-up performed.

Using this time-break for his own purposes, Carême sought out his sure-to-be brooding François, and thought he knew where to look.

He mounted the circular staircase of the Pavilion's water tower with sometimes laboured breaths. Certainly the most commanding structure in Brighton, the dimness of the steps and the overall height made the chef somewhat dizzy. Nearing the top, Carême's eyes adjusted to the light again, for the landing led out to a top level open to the twilight breeze and colour coming from the west.

And François *was* there, sitting on the handrail, dangling his legs over the hundred feet of air twix him and pavement. His head rotated, realizing the chef had come. In another instant, he'd twisted his body too and was standing next to his partner while Carême admired the view.

The chef joked, "Leave it to you to find the highest place in town. I don't think I would have ventured up here on my own."

François, knowing they were safely by themselves, hugged him very affectionately.

Carême returned the embrace, and François kissed the man's cheek, saying, "I like the peace and quiet up here."

And it was true, for the younger man had grown to maturity in France during a time when privacy itself was outlawed.

The pair leaned on the handrail side by side and watched the sun slowly sink.

François said without emphasis, "The Princess suspects she's pregnant. She's been suffering spells of sickness in the mornings."

"Oh." Carême's mind began running through recipes. "I'll plan a list of dishes for her accordingly."

He was so engaged in sorting out his *riz à l'impératrice* from his *potage santé* that he scarcely caught the sudden dim cast come to François' eyes as he had said this. By the time he'd collected his thoughts, it was gone.

"Did you pause today to see the progress of the Banqueting Room?" the maitre-d' asked.

"I did." Carême caught his own enthusiasm. He tamped it down. "I was there when they raised the great lighting fixture. It was really"—the chef cast about for exactly the right underplayed expression—*"le grand poisseux."* Uttering a euphemism meaning *the big sticky,* the tacky connotations had more than slightly betrayed Carême's true sentiments in the process.

François chuckled. "Isn't Marie-Antoinette supposed to have said that at her first sight of Versailles?"

Carême joined in the laughter. "My plagiarism has been sussed out. But actually, I believe, she merely commented 'There are a lot of people around here.' And I suppose she was right – whether about Versailles or Brighton."

After a few moments of silence, François was lost again in his own thoughts.

Carême enquired, "And speaking of the concept of many people around here, how are working conditions with the Chief Footman?"

The maitre-d' scoffed. "Gris Thorndyke? As well as can be expected, one might suppose, considering he's convinced I took his position."

"With the Banqueting Room opening now, he may find more obvious means to show you up in front of the Prince."

"Let him try. I keep my eye on him, just as I keep my eye on all of them." François took his mentor's hand. "It's just you and me in this cruel world."

"Yes, and tomorrow will be long and complicated. And I have a radical idea – at long last – for our sugar work sculptures tomorrow. I will show you my sketches later this evening."

François smiled, warmly. "I'm raring to go. Your first official dinner in the Banqueting Room will be a triumph, trust me."

"I do, François. I do."

That made the young man's heart sing. Inexplicably, François said while stroking the chef's hand, "The way you look after your wife, and your young daughter . . . it just. It fills me with comfort."

"I know, François." Carême drew the young man's head to his own. They touched foreheads and locked eye to eye. "It's because you and I, *Villon,* are both orphans of a sort."

Chapter 6: *ab ovo, ad mala* & Hope for the Future

"Ah, Carême!" the good Doctor exclaimed, clasping hands. "The temperatures may be trending colder, but look at the skies!"

It was a full twenty-four-hours since the master chef had watched the sun go down with his partner, and here he was – exhausted after a twelve-hour day of work – on Kitchiner's roof-top perch.

The western horizon burned itself in gold and crimson, but a discordant colour smothered much of it as well.

"You see the sharp orange and brown smudges in the clouds?" It seemed the Doctor's ability to read Carême's mind was uncanny.

"Yes. They don't look 'healthy'."

"They're not. That is the culprit for a year with corrupted light and heat; the suspended soot and ash from the Tambora explosion." The man removed his blue spectacles for a thorough wipe with his handkerchief. "A poet might say the mountain threw itself into the air, and we're all subject to that rocky monarch's mighty fall."

Carême shook his head. "I hope future generations will never look at polluted air and think this orange-brown pall is 'pretty.' It's sign of a serious, worldwide disease."

"Hear; hear, my friend. I see you are something of a poet too."

Carême laughed. He began to truly like Kitchiner. "I am, with all sincere hope, the master poet of the saucepan."

"Dear Chef, if I had a wine glass, I'd offer up a cheer this very moment to second the motion. You are a master, indeed."

"And you, Doctor – you are a master lens-maker, a physician, a botanist, a food enthusiast, and . . . perhaps, a master secret agent?"

The Doctor shifted just a little. By now the glasses were back in place and looking at Carême from halfway along the ridge of his nose. "I believe the first time we met, I said I assist His Highness with . . . personal matters, and that is indeed the case."

"Nothing is more personal than an individual's security, *n'est-ce pas?*"

The Doctor chuckled. "Right again, dear Carême, and by now you see some of the complexities the Regent must navigate. I *assist* when and where I can."

"Well, you are a kind and loyal friend to His Highness, just as you also told me at our first meeting. You do well to advance hope for a better future."

"At some moments, Carême, it seems a heavy burden."

"What does, Doctor?"

"The knowledge that what we do today, even if it's a decision we take lightly at present, can have profound consequences for the times to come."

"I know what you mean." Carême tried not to think of François. "The world we are making every second of the day will contribute to the success or undermine the conditions later generations will find it in. One personal triumph, or one intimate tragedy can, like Tambora, affect the possible outcomes for all."

The Doctor nodded slowly. "To be aware, Chef – to be conscious of our power – is a gift and burden to the thinking person. I agree."

"As I say, you do well to advance hope for a better future."

"Sometimes I wonder if my son feels the same way about me." The Doctor's mood had clouded over.

Carême, for his part, was surprised. "I didn't know you were married."

"I'm not," Kitchiner replied much too freely. He reeled it back. "By which, to say, I am – technically – but not to my son's mother. She, the boy's parent, has her private lodgings at the rear of my London house, and the lady and I are on equitable terms. It was good for Willi to grow up with his *ma-ma* so close to hand."

"Willi?"

"William Brown Kitchiner, my adopted heir."

"And may I assume, by your careful wording, that your 'wife' resides elsewhere?"

"Oh, yes. Entirely on her own. My wife and I have no contact, other than her cashing of my quarterly bank draughts."

"D'accord. I see, and how old is your Willi?"

"My boy, he's thirteen now, and he grows so fast. It gives me pause. I mean, did I too change so rapidly before my father's eyes? How was it my *pa-pa* recognized me?"

What Kitchiner was revealing to the Frenchman, struck Carême very close to the bone. He debated internally whether to share with the Doctor his own, remarkably similar, domestic arrangements back in Paris, but the shrewder part of him, the Talleyrand-trained part of him, said to hold the information in reserve a little longer.

But the heart of Carême – that had been deeply touched.

The chef said, "I too, Doctor, if I had a glass of a cognac to toast you, would raise it to your good qualities, and bless the future happiness of your son."

Now Kitchiner looked emotional, but refrained from saying anything. Instead, the two men heard the unmistakable jangle of bridles and carriage wheels turning into the driveway below. The vehicle pulled up to the Club's door five floors down.

The Doctor stood. "I believe, dear Chef, that is our signal. Shall we join the others?"

"Certainly." Carême stood as well.

The men descended the ladder into the penthouse studio of the good Doctor, and Kitchiner closed the roof hatch.

Inside, the room was warm with good smells and a crackling fire in the cooking hearth.

Meanwhile, a mile off and something like a world away from the Club, François Distré and Thomas Daniels had most of the muscles of their upper torsos tensed. One on each side, they gingerly slid Carême's first sugar work *pièce montée* into one of the Pavilion's glass-fronted cabinets.

"Watch the clock tower," François chided hastily.

"I'm all right. You watch the palm tree."

And François saw the boy was correct. The exotic date-laden plant was top heavy and had some of its delicate green foliage close to the cupboard's edge. François adjusted accordingly.

Soon, about a quarter of the edible monument's base rested securely on the shelf, and the two could begin a slow and calculated pushing, sliding the display straight back into the cabinet. Once there, the undercook and maitre-d' stood back to admire Carême's work side by side.

"You know," said the boy almost reverently, "the way the logs are constructed . . . and their colouring . . . they shure look real."

"Yes. The sculptor's chisel for the first, the artist's palette for the second. Carême leaves nothing wanting in his Art."

"Now I can see that." Thomas grinned, showering François with it by turning his head.

When François glanced over, the Frenchman realized how close they were; close enough to kiss. This caused François' expression to deaden into a scowl, for the undercook was undeniably handsome, especially once mirth decided to light up the welkin of his azure eyes.

He closed the cabinet door, then leaned his backside on the counter's ledge. With folded arms and kicked out legs, François eyed the winsome teen. "How long have you been cooking, professionally?"

Thomas stiffened his spine, allowing his smirk to fade away. "Since I was thirteen, or five years now."

"You still have much to learn."

The lad flushed with enthusiasm. "Oh, I know! Each day I watch and learn; each day I shurly try to improve."

There was something so open, so unguarded and free of any cunning in the boy's attitude that even François couldn't keep up a hostile front. "You're hungry to improve yourself. That's a good trait for a *garçon* of your age . . . . It was the same with me."

"Carême's methods are so modern, it's a privilege to learn technique from him. Tell me, do any of the big kitchens in France still use the all-night *roux?"*

François laughed. "No! They all use Carême's fool-proof manner of making it, instantly, when needed."

"Yes. He taught me, but still the sauce cooks here prepare *roux* to cook for twelve hours, then grab a spoonful or two to mix into stocks. But, in this case, the old way is *not* better."

"Tell me why." François was cagy, knowing but wanting to see if young Master Daniels could articulate it.

"It's simple. The old *roux* is hard to control. She's sometimes too dark; sometimes not thick enough; sometimes downright bitter – and the sauce could be ruined before it's even started. Carême's roux gets rid of everything that could go wrong. It is in a word, Genius."

François was impressed.

Suddenly, they became distracted. A noise, like hushed voices wrapped in travelling cloaks, invited both to gaze towards the open door.

In the hallway leading from the service entrance, Prince Leopold's Private Secretary passed, heading for one of the behind-scenes staircases. He was turned and oblivious to his audience in the Pastry Larder because he spoke quietly – but insistently – to a pair of gaudy working girls. The three of them drifted out of sight and started to go upstairs, to the Royal Couple's bedchambers.

The passing tableau had been all too obvious, especially in light of the fact the entire Pavilion knew Princess Charlotte was out for the evening.

François motioned for the young man to come over; he wanted to ask in a low tone: "Does Leopold always . . . *amuse* himself . . . in such fashion?"

A mischievous sparkle appeared in the teen's gaze. "Well, to be perfectly honest, no. Sometimes there are two boys; others, a boy and a girl. The Prince Consort is, I've been told, shurly diverse in his tastes."

François tut-tutted. "I doubt the heir-apparent would be very forgiving of her dear Leopold, the lowlife *Bosche,* if she knew."

"Bosche?"

"Kraut; German; pickle-eater."

Thomas laughed. "Ah, *them!"*

A new closeness had arisen between the two; shared laughter will do that.

The undercook returned to the old topic. "So you were the same age when you started training?"

"A little older. Both Carême and I began at fifteen."

"At Bailly's pastry shop for Carême."

Astounded, François asked, "How would you know that?"

"Oh, I've read *Le pâtissier royal parisien.* Carême says Monsewer Bailly gave him his start."

"Yes, that's right. Apprenticed at fifteen, to one of Paris' best confectioners, he began teaching himself right away."

"And you, how did you come to be working with the master?"

"I was just another eager face; one of the cooks at the Élysée Palace." François' tone grew rounder with recall. "Carême, by that time a free-lance caterer, would come there regularly to make desserts, *entremets* and *pièces montées.* He . . . we . . . just noticed one another, if that makes sense."

The younger man nodded gravely. He knew exactly the type of connection François was referring to. "Personally, I feel lucky. I was no one special. Just a lad from the streets, shure, but I went around to the back door of every posh house I could find."

"Why?"

"I'd clean my face as best I could, stand there wringing my cap in my hands, and ask if they needed a boy to help out in the kitchens."

"And?"

"And eventually, one took me in; a fancy establishment over on the Esplanade. After a few years there, they told me there was an opening at the Pavilion, and shure enough, here I am, the luckiest street kid in Brighton. I feel honoured as well."

François merely nodded.

"And," Thomas added with unexpected sincerity, "as lucky as I am to have a position in the Royal Household, I admire the position you have in Carême's heart. You're lucky too."

No part of François could disagree.

There was an awkward "Ahem" from the doorway. The Kitchen Comptroller fidgeted like he was loath to interrupt, although peeved to be required at all to state his wishes. "Thomas, we should"—his head jerked vaguely down the corridor, to the steps of the servants' quarters—"be . . . going."

"Yes." The boy inhaled deeply. "The Comptroller has some figures to go over with me."

François tried not to smile, knowing the only figure on the moneyman's mind was the lad's.

"I'll see you in the morning, *monsieur* Distré." Thomas walked to the exit; the bean-counter having disappeared into the hallway.

"Good night, Thomas Daniels." François cheekily adding "Sweet dreams," although he knew the boy was not going to be allowed to sleep for several hours.

Alone now, the Frenchman stood upright and moved to a position to peer into the display cabinet.

He reflected on what he'd learned from this curious little scene. He'd gained confirmation of the power-mismatched relations between boy and functionary. And he'd learned, despite the maitre-d's jealousy, he liked Thomas and found him beddable himself. The young man appealed too in that he was similar to François: they were both ambitious boys from the streets, trying to stay away from trouble. So he could not really resent the kid; Carême's attraction to the boy on the other hand . . . . Maybe that he could resent.

Several minutes after the figure had alighted from the carriage in front of the Club, the scene in Kitchiner's penthouse was a cozy one.

At the end of the large kitchen table closest to the ranges, Mrs. Lister stood with a handsome young man in his mid-twenties. Aproned, and although an apparent novice at his light-duty task, he chopped parsley and laughed freely with the caterer.

Also chatting thick as thieves, Mrs. Fitzherbert and Princess Charlotte worked well together at the other end of the table. They were laying out seven place settings for their informal supper, one at the end and three on each side flanking it.

The men had clambered down from their exterior perch, with Doctor Kitchiner's lank frame leading the way. Once off the telescope platforms, he and Carême were just in time to greet the new arrival at the doors from the greenhouse.

"Good evening, Your Highness." Kitchiner helped Prince George remove his indigo cape.

"Doctor, always a pleasure. And Carême, I'm glad you could slip away too." He had said this like an inside joke, and the chef smiled in response.

Hearing his voice, the Regent's wife and daughter came forward to greet him. They happily converged with cheek-kissing before the library steps. Kitchiner, ever a conscientious host, had arranged for a table to be waiting here with glasses and a bottle of white wine chilling on ice.

While the Prince and ladies chatted – and George set about his responsibility of opening up the wine – Kitchiner went into his curtained napping area to hang the regent's cape with the other coats.

Carême followed and found the peculiar iron stove set up in this space was lit and pumping out a delightful amount of heat. The chef took a closer look, for there was something unique about the range section. It was round, and although only a small kettle steamed merrily on it now, there were four burners.

Kitchiner stepped near. "Ah, ha! I see you've spied my Rotary Galley Stove."

"Rotary?" enquired Carême.

"Oh, yes!" The Doctor removed a handkerchief from his pocket and folded it over. Then he latched onto a crank Carême had failed to notice earlier. Kitchiner put his shoulder into it, and the round top began to move. A quarter of the way round, the kettle went off the boil. "Two burners are for cooking and two for warming. There are baking ovens around the side." Kitchiner cranked the kettle back the other way, returning it onto the heat.

"How exceptional. How did you come to invent this?"

"Among my close acquaintances is Sir Joseph Banks. He accompanied Captain Cook on his first voyage, and Sir Joseph often regales dinner parties with tales from his adventures. However, his description of the inadequacies of British galleys, particularly their cooking arrangements, got me to thinking how I could improve life at sea. This is my solution: compact; lower consumer of fuel – and thus, efficient; convenient; and versatile. Many ships are now using them, much to my pleasure."

"How extortionary, especially as I do not see stoves in England at all! Only smelly, cold-air producing fireplaces."

"Ah, yes; here you hit upon a conundrum – the English lip-service to advancement and total shunning of anything practical but 'Foreign' in our collective consciousness."

"I'm afraid, Doctor, I fail to follow—"

"*Pardon, Chef.* I meant the very concept of a fuel-efficient heating and cooking device strikes us as too damnably 'European' in nature, even though two Americans, Franklin and Rumford, have brought the technology to perfection. But"—Kitchiner laughed— "a Yank connection only makes the very word 'stove' taboo here. We'll call it cooker; hob; hasenpfeffer; bob's-your-uncle – anything to avoid the correct term already appropriated by *them.*"

"Cooking stoves are beginning to replace charcoal ranges in France."

"And well they should. Because they vent directly to the outside, they are healthier to the cooks' constitution."

"Yes, that is true."

Kitchiner began leading his guest and himself to re-join the others, concluding the conversation with a falsely chipper, "But not here, in either kitchen or parlour! We'd rather tell ourselves how 'English' it is to sit in the cold and damp, having all the heat from our Newcastle coals sucked through barn-door-sized voids in our walls. The alternative would be to install Franklin Stoves or Rumford Grates, and that very notion is forbiddingly alien."

The good Doctor also conveniently omitted to inform his French friend, at least for the moment, how British coal-gluttony favoured him personally, as his family business – the one still quarterly stuffing the fortune his father amassed with fresh funds – was one of fuel brokerage.

The men joined the party around the little table. For, in the interim, George had opened and filled glasses – this time from a Portuguese *vinho verde.* He handed one glass each to the Chef and Doctor.

"A toast," the Regent said, "to our most amiable host, William Kitchiner!"

A communal "Cheers!" got followed by unrestrained drinking, except by the Frenchman who only sipped.

As the Prince re-filled glasses, he commented, "Not much of a drinker, eh, Carême?"

"Oh, *Pa-pa* – you mention that every time."

The ladies laughed.

By way of changing the subject, the Doctor interjected with a brightening voice, "Well, I think we will enjoy our little Autumn supper tonight. Perhaps you'll even find it worthy of Horace's supreme artlessness; that poet's summary of a Complete Roman Meal as *ab ovo usque ad mala* – From the Eggs to the Apples!"

Everyone drank to that, wondering what it exactly entailed for the evening.

Mrs. Lister called them over to the kitchen table. "It's ready."

George grabbed the bottle, telling the woman, "And you, Good Lady Caterer, will eat with us. No excuses this time!"

She executed a blushing protest, but undid her apron at the same time.

Kitchiner strode up to the young man, saying, "Naturally, you too." He then suggestively turned the fellow around and untied the apron himself. Kitchiner took him by the wrist, bringing him to the table, announcing, "For those of you yet to have the pleasure of meeting him, may I present one whom I'm proud to consider my acolyte, Philip Hardwick."

Carême nodded at the Doctor's *protégé*.

People began to settle, and the seating arrangement was informal: Kitchiner sat on one long side with the Prince to his right, and Hardwick on the other. Across from them sat Mrs. Fitzherbert, Carême, and Princess Charlotte. This left the seat at the table's end open for Elizabeth Lister. From here she could pop up when the food preparations demanded her attention.

As George filled Hardwick's glass, the first course arrived.

Mrs. Lister proudly placed a platter of devilled eggs on the table.

Carême examined the unusual arrangement, seeing hard-cooked egg whites split lengthwise and re-filled with a spicy looking yolk stuffing. It appeared quite pink from cayenne pepper to the chef's eyes, even below the parsley Mr. Hardwick had just chopped for the topping.

The ladies helped themselves first, passing the plate to Carême. He took one and handed the tray to Philip with a smile.

As for the flavour, the chef was pleasantly surprised. He tasted sweet herbs – like summer savoury and marjoram – the yolks bound with butter, and perceived the heat and a dash of lemon zest to tie all together and brighten the taste.

Kitchiner had been watching. "Although these eggs are fresh, naturally, the procedure of 'Devilling' is useful for left-overs."

"Devilled ham!" Prince George interjected.

"Yes, Your Highness," said Carême. "We have a similar method in French cooking called *rillette*. It is mainly done with fish, but ham or game – or anything – can be treated in this fashion."

Lost in her own thoughts, Mrs. Fitzherbert asked, "Is it true, my darling – you are with child?"

Charlotte Augusta shot a glance at her father.

"Yes, dear. I told Fitzy," the Prince admitted.

"Well, then – yes, it's true. Leopold and I are very happy."

"Congratulations" went round the table.

"The very best of happy circumstances," added Carême. "If you'll permit me, I'll create a special menu to aid in eliminating your morning sickness."

"Why, thank you, Chef, that would be most appreciated." Then the Princess turned enthusiastic. "And I wanted to tell you how much I admired your sugar work centrepiece today at dinner."

"My *pièce montée?*"

"Yes. It was delightful, and so capital in its originality – a rustic log cabin church to entirely contrast with the 'Oriental' flare of the Banqueting Room." Then she asked her father, "Don't you agree?"

The man was non-committal; silent.

Carême felt crestfallen. After all, it was only his Royal patron and employer's opinion that was supposed to matter to an artist, right?

Charlotte – mildly miffed – directed her attention to Fitzy. "Well, I wish you could have seen it. It was frightfully marvellous."

In a moment, it was clear Charlotte regretted saying this.

Carême studied the suddenly pained expression of Maria Anne Fitzherbert's face and comprehended something profound. Sad notes like an arpeggio lingered in the air, because the Prince's beloved wife was blocked by societal prejudices from ever setting foot in her husband's home.

It started to rain outside. Large drops pelted the roof over their heads and the panes of glass to their sides.

He realized Royals were like caged animals when it came to their public lives, and how much moments like these – this private supper – meant to them. This perhaps applied to Kitchiner and his shy-but-handsome London friend as well.

The Doctor caught Carême eyeing his young man. "I don't think I mentioned it, but Master Hardwick is a promising young architect in Town. At only twenty-four, he's already secured some important commissions."

"How interesting." George stood and moved off to the Welsh dresser to open another bottle of wine – a burgundy this time.

"And," Kitchiner announced, "Hardwick, Lister and myself all reside in the same neighbourhood."

"Where?" enquired Charlotte.

"At the north-west edge – Fitzrovia."

"Oh, very *chic,*" cooed the Prince's wife.

"We like it," replied Kitchiner. "Our backs may be up against farm field and forest, but it's worth it not to have too many long-nosed neighbours monitoring our comings and goings."

"Isn't it round the corner," asked Mrs. Fitzherbert with a warm smile, "from Russell Square?"

"Yes, indeed," replied Kitchiner. "In fact, that is where Master Hardwick resides. I'm west of there on Warren Street, closer to the Royal Hunting Preserve of Marylebone. Its southern edge at least, as it's massive. Mrs. Lister is west of me by a few blocks."

"London," Philip chimed, "is growing in all directions, unchecked like a weed."

George uncorked his selection and returned leisurely to the table to pour.

"Yes," Mrs. Lister agreed. "Growing like a ramble of a bramble of unorganized weeds."

"What's required," said Hardwick with conviction, "is a Master Plan of major boulevards, public squares, and parks with open land. If the 'bones' of the city are healthy, then the neighbourhoods can infill later to everyone's benefit."

The Prince, listening in without comment, was suddenly struck by the soundness of the idea. A central London Plan; the huge potential income to be made if the old Hunting Preserve were developed into its own residential and commercial area – and all on rent-bearing Royal land. Yes, he'd have to think how best to implement such a large-scale redesign of London's north-west quadrant.

Considered in another way, it was his chance to make his permanent mark and leave London far better than the way he'd found it.

Seeing all the egg halves gone, Doctor Kitchiner jumped to his feet. "What say you, Carême? Shall you and I fry the sole and give Mrs. Lister a chance to catch up on gossip?"

"Oh, pshaw!" Mrs. Lister sputtered, but made no effort to move from her seat.

"*Oui,*" said Carême, rising. "Let us cook, Doctor."

The two men went to a pitcher and bowl to wash up. With sleeves pulled high, Kitchiner asked, "Enjoying your time away from the Pavilion?"

"Always, Doctor. As ever, you host delightful gatherings."

They dried hands and drifted to the range.

"I'm glad, Carême. I'm getting serious too about my book. Lister and I are holding our Committee of Taste nights once a week. The 'approved' dishes and their procedures are piling up."

Laid on the prep table were the things they needed. Wordlessly, Doctor Kitchiner saw to the coal, reviving their vigour with a few well-placed puffs of air. Once rekindled, he set an oblong griddle above the grate to heat up.

Carême took three sheets of parchment paper. Checking them against the size of the matching number of sole fillets, the chef folded them in half. Then, with breath-taking ease, he used a waiting chef's knife to cut a half-heart shape. The excess paper fell away, and Carême opened up three apparent valentines of substantial size. "Butter these for me, good Doctor."

While Kitchiner set about his task, and Carême seasoned the fish on both sides with salt and pepper, the Doctor said, "With the Autumn harvest in, meagre as it is, it's nice to relax and cook *avec la famille* in this manner."

"I'm glad," said Carême. "You do my heart good, and, if I may be allowed, perhaps you will find *chez-famille* the more familiar form, Doctor."

The man smiled. "Good to know."

As they were buttered, Carême took the paper and laid half of the heart flat on the table. He placed the seasoned sole down the centre of this section, and moistened the edges with a brush dipped in egg-wash. Then he folded the other half over the top to join the cut edges together, which he crimped with his fingers from bottom to top.

Carême had finished encasing the second *sole en papillote.*

Kitchiner grew animated. "Oh, oh – Chef! I almost forgot the dressing. I'll finish wrapping and get these on the griddle with lots of oil. In the meantime, you go to my Sauce Kitchen and find the nearly full bottle on the shelf called 'Wow-Wow!' We'll have that with the fish."

Carême, drying his hand on a towel, did as instructed. When he got to the Doctor's concoction testing grounds, he scanned the line of prepared and carefully labelled bottles. Sure enough, one had bold red letters spelling 'WOW-WOW.' Carême glanced over his shoulder. The other guests, and the Doctor too, were oblivious to the chef's activities, so he un-corked the bottle and sniffed. A faintly herbaceous note first greeted his nose. Basil, if he had to guess. Stronger, meatier elements were second, like beef stock and anchovy paste. And lastly, tangier notes from shallots and white wine vinegar.

Re-corking it, he thought it reminded him of some of the steak-sauce recipes surviving from Roman times in *Apicius*.

Several minutes later, all were back at the table with three steaming-hot sole packages on a platter.

Kitchiner did the honours, opening the paper parcels with a pair of forks as he served every guest a healthy portion of fish.

Carême, looking down on his own plate, enjoyed the prospects. The fish was done to a tee, and the buttered wax beans with chervil made an inspired pairing for it.

The un-corked 'Wow-Wow' made the rounds, and the Frenchman dutifully glugged a portion near his fish. To his surprise, he could see chunky elements were also present.

Glancing at Kitchiner, the Doctor read his mind. "Chopped pickled walnuts."

Everybody dug in, and Kitchiner watched discreetly for Carême's facial expression. As it soured upon first taste of his bottled preparation, the Doctor wondered if he should have served lemon wedges instead.

For the chef's part, the 'Wow-Wow's flavour was not wholly unpleasant, but his senses reeled at the inordinate amount of salt present. He thought if 'ready-made' condiments of the future were going to be this injurious to health, they should never come to market. They needed the salty preservatives to be 'shelf stable.'

While they ate, Kitchiner directed the focus to Mrs. Lister. "As caterer to all the Capital's best and brightest, you must, *madame* Lister, regale us with one of your experiences."

The woman's lips sputtered. "Here, and now?"

"Do, Mrs. Lister," encouraged the Prince's wife.

"Well, there was one"—Elizabeth Lister dabbed with her napkin—"the present company may find amusing. It seems a Lord So-and-So, a top Whitehall bigwig, had a problem. A new lover with a six-thousand Pound a year income, and an 'old' wife of twenty-nine at home. He needed divorce testimony—"

"How jolly rotten," exclaimed the Princess.

"—So he hired me to arrange for a dinner to which he invited his Lordly Peers, his wife's paramour, and from which he excused himself, last-minute, for reasons of 'urgent business'."

"It's getting good," Kitchiner said, rubbing his hands together.

"So he told my staff and I to keep eyes and ears open for untoward behaviour, but had decided to take no chances and paid off the wife's lover with both cash and threats of ruin to make scandalous overtures on the Lady in front of all, which he did. Sadly, in this society, it's not the one acting the cad who comes in for criminal rebuke in the courts, but the woman who's the object and victim of his obscene advances. Anyway, Milord So-and-So got his wish – the entirety of his wife's fortune in the divorce, and a pretty young thing whose fortune he's next devising to abscond with."

The effect on the table was bifurcated: the men – excluding Carême – gushed with laughter for the 'charming' anecdote they thought it was, and the women shifted uncomfortably on their seats. Theirs was an unease unable to seek relief.

It suddenly dawned on poor Elizabeth how much her company was spent in the presence of men. She had no desire to upset the ladies.

"Well," the caterer added in a more sober vein, "I only agreed to participate for the *other* intelligence I could glean . . . . " She stopped, using her napkin to deflect the fact she'd said too much.

"There are others tales to tell . . . " Kitchiner's chin was rubbed. "Ah, perhaps that adventure you had with the cash-poor young man—"

"The Heiress-Hunter?"

"Yes. That story's delightful."

Mrs. Lister chuckled. "The Doctor is referring to a case I had a few years back. There was a young blade who bet all of his dwindling family fortune on a single dinner. He did indeed invite his intended heiress, but he hedged his odds by summoning two other wealthy widows as well. I had to accommodate three tables in three differing salons, while the flushed young rake progressed from course to course – room to room – three times over."

The Regent, giddy with anticipation and Burgundy, asked, "And did he snare his quarry?"

"Not once, but twice!" Mrs. Lister laughed. "By the time the cask of dessert wine was burst into, he had a pair of proposals from which to pick and choose."

Everyone smiled on hearing the outcome.

Doctor Kitchiner said, "Three times over, I know the food served was the best. Mrs. Lister is a student of all the glories of Britain's cookery past."

"Well, if so," the caterer demurred, "it's because I have borrowed much from your store of knowledge."

The Doctor was gratified. "I do try to live up to my name."

"And what does it mean, old boy?" enquired the Prince.

"Simple, Your Highness. In the days of William the Conqueror, the official Royal taster and personal cook to the crowned head was a noble relative titled as Magnus Coquus, which, re-rendered in good old Anglo-Saxon, became *Master Kitchiner.*"

"Very informative," Carême said.

"Yes, but as I've mentioned before, if I could have my druthers, young English cooks would receive as complete a background education in *English* cookery as young French chefs trained in your historical cuisine."

"How so?" asked Mrs. Fitzherbert.

Hail began hitting the roof and glass.

"For example, Richard Cury, Master Kitchiner to King Richard II in the 1300s, and Robert May, cook to Charles II's men in the 1600s, both left invaluable cookbooks behind. Cury's contains the world's oldest surviving instructions to make ravioli; and May's, the first brawn – that staple of British breakfasts now. And these two momentous figures in our National cuisine are unknown to the young student-cooks of these lands. How entirely different it is with our neighbours across the Channel. There, a healthy appreciation of the past is what young French chefs have that ours don't. One does not need to invent the wheel afresh with every guffawing generation."

The Regent chuckled darkly. "Sometimes I wish my Foreign Ministers *would* re-invent the diplomatic wheel. If so, we may not have to cycle in and out of constant crises, the only solution for which they propose is another state of endless war."

The Prince may have laughed at them, but the prospects of 'the next war' being only around the corner upset the remainder of the guests. It was particularly disturbing to Charlotte, as she'd eventually have the ponderous burdens of Empire crowned on her head.

Mrs. Lister suddenly exclaimed, glancing at the wall clock, "Oh, I nearly forgot!"

She bounded to her feet and called for Philip's assistance. The young man removed the wooden cover from the top beehive oven, and Lister used a peel to pull out a gallon-sized iron mould.

All gathered around to see how the contents would 'turn out' as the caterer lifted the shallow, careful-fitting lid. Good smells greeted them, and the woman placed a flat plate over the top and inverted dessert and plate together. She set the serving dish on the table and slowly lifted the mould. A golden-brown Apple Charlotte awaited.

Everyone's seat was re-taken; everyone's glass was re-filled; and everyone tried to tune out the violence of the storm raging outside.

The dessert – with a sauceboat of *crème anglaise* by its side – was before them. But before he did the honours of cutting into it, Kitchiner lifted his glass for a toast.

The Doctor gestured to Charlotte and her unborn baby. "From these dark days, we send our hope out for the brightest possible future. Here's to Her Royal Highness, Princess Charlotte Augusta of Wales – a very long life to thee!"

"Hear; hear" passed cordially around the table as everyone but she drank to her health.

Carême wore the weight of the day's heavy obligation on his shoulders. These slumped now, late at night, as he sat at his desk by the window, writing a coded report to Talleyrand.

The lit lamp seemed to be his only companion, and he found himself pausing, simply staring into the sputtering flame.

He considered how an hour ago, one of the Club's discreet black carriages had dropped Carême off at the 'back door' of the Pavilion, just to the side of the south-end gate.

He considered how dark the rest of the chamber was outside the pool of lamplight. He was tired, for in retrospect, the day had been a parade of one long hour of him being on display followed by another. Here, at this time of night, he could gather his thoughts and be alone with his own company; but he could not enjoy it.

Instead, he was being forced to scrutinize everything he might potentially relay to the Grand Chamberlain.

He set his pen down, rubbing his eyes.

How much of George's private life – of the Regent's and Kitchiner's trust of him – should he betray.

The chef leapt to his feet, having decided to destroy this 'evidence.' He took the lower corner of the missive, lifted it off the desk and held it to the flame. Once it caught, the chef carefully walked the burning parchment over to his fireplace.

Bending down and resting on his haunches, he tossed the letter in, eyes now aglow with the relieving sight of its destruction. Assuring himself it would be totally consumed, comfort came to Carême as he knew he'd have to start anew.

While down here, he grabbed a stick of waiting kindling from a tin holder attached to the fireplace surround and caught it alight in the flames.

He stood and lit the candles on the mantle, suddenly not wanting his environment to be as dark as before.

Carême's timing was significant, for just at that moment, tapping sounded gently upon their interconnecting door, and François let himself in. He closed the door with the utmost care and walked over to the chef.

The men kissed briefly, François holding the other's eyes as he said, "At least it's stopped raining."

"Yes"—Carême's tone was still absorbed in thoughts of being guarded— "for the moment, it has."

"This time last year was worse. Damp and the earliest frost ever - half the Autumn harvest lost." The maitre-d' became lost in forced memory-recall. "And worst - our hero had been captured again." A bit of his angry nationalism slipped out. "And now times are so uncertain because of it. Things *regress* instead of moving onward like they should."

Internally, Carême again lamented his partner was such a child of the Terror. The young man tended, as did his whole generation, to see things as black and white. "At best, François, Napoléon was a flawed leader. He was not 'all good,' just as Louis XVI had not been 'all bad.' I blame the Revolution, for where the greatest potential is released, so too is the chance for the greatest chaos."

François remained moody and silent, glancing towards the window.

Carême tried to lift François' burdens - give him something to look forward to - brighten his spirits. "Cheer up, for soon we'll start our preparations for Christmas, and we won't have any time to brood on the past."

François attempted to be less dour for his mate, but the mention of Christmas was fraught with its own unanticipated reactions. These complex sentiments too were coloured by the dark times in which the young man had matured. "I've never felt close to *la fête de Noël.* You have to remember, for part of my upbringing, it was still outlawed in France. Anyone caught – or ratted out by neighbours – celebrating it were arrested and tortured to name co-conspirators for their 'crime'."

"I'm sorry, François. You are right to remind me of this."

"Anyway, my point is, that now as an adult with pressing responsibilities, I'm not sure how I feel about honouring it. As holidays go, these days, Christmas seems to be only for those who can afford it."

Carême was caught between an impulse to tut-tut the notion, and a more carefully considered repetition of 'I'm sorry.' Instead, he said softly, "One gets out of Christmas what one puts into it."

The chef's words were sufficiently open to interpretation for François to let the topic drop. "And how was your evening; your supper with the strange doctor at his club?"

François had tried not to sound confrontational, but Carême sighed anyway.

"It was, you know, tiring. Exhausting mentally – English concerns; English food; English thoughts; English manners and conversation." The thirty-two-year-old lifted his arms and drew François into an embrace. "I feel the loneliest when removed from, and deprived of, the genie's spark of our native language."

François held the man's eyes. "You have me to talk to."

"Yes, *Villon*. This is what I mean. It's such a relief to be back in your arms, both physically and via the warmth of our shared tongue."

François smiled at Carême's – admittedly – coarse joke.

The two men kissed, exploring the connection just alluded to.

As his partner was still smiling once they'd separated, the chef ill-advisedly tried to continue the joking. He caressed the hair near François' ear, teasing, "And how was *your* evening of skirt-chasing. Bag yourself any?"

François stiffened and backed out of Carême's embrace.

The man said nothing, but the column of blushing overtaking François' neck enflamed the chef's passions. He strode up manfully and started kissing the reddening area, causing François to let his eyes half-close towards the ceiling and moan in desire. With the young man's neck craning back like that, Carême turned his boy's head and continued on the other side.

As his partner's lips shifted to pet his throat and upper chest, François' hands moved helplessly to stroke Carême's arms. He mumbled through the fog of pleasure, "You know my dalliances with women are just that – dalliances." He took Carême by the cheeks to hold his man's gaze. "It's you I love, you who keeps me safe in a hostile world"—the young man was near tears—"you who give me hope for the future—"

François could say no more, for Carême had stopped up his words with a passionate kiss.

They groaned in one another's mouths and intensified their lovemaking.

"And I protect you as well," François forced through his ever-increasing breaths.

Carême, apparently not hearing, walked the boy backward, lifting off François' nightshirt and caressing the freshly exposed flesh underneath.

He lay him face down on the bed.

Far from helpless, François extended his hands from where he was set and undid Carême's trouser buttons. The chef lifted off his own shirt.

In another moment, the chef had kicked off his lower garments and smiled to feel François' fingers drawing him back in close. They gripped and released –

teased and cajoled – Carême's upper thighs and backside, pulling him ever nearer to the young man's lips.

He took him in his mouth, and now it was Carême's turn to moan in pleasure and look to the sky. François was expert at loving him in this way, and the chef's stiffness only grew more resolute; more insistent.

Glancing down, he placed his fingers within François' hair and guided the boy to take him ever deeper. As he did, the chef's only reaction was to pulsate with spasms of extra hardness down his partner's throat. The lover was earning the sweet reward deposited there each time his calling went above and beyond.

"Oh, *Villon* . . . . Oh—"

The boy substituted his fingers for his tongue, stroking Carême's member with maddening gentleness as he changed positions.

Seeing his partner on his back – his moistened lips mumbling "Please" – increased Carême's enjoyment as he knelt on the bed and lifted François' legs.

Gathering spit from his mouth, Carême applied it to François' waiting portal, which was already trembling with intermittent waves of excitement, and gently worked it in.

François moaned, gripping his lover's lower arms; his eyes letting Carême know it was all right.

Another dab of moisture applied to the end of Carême's member, and the chef expertly positioned it by feel against François' passage. He applied a little pressure, quite literally putting his back into it, and waited for François' response.

The boy tightened his hold on his partner's lower arms, but his threshold helplessly relaxed to his belovèd's assault and let him in.

Carême didn't relent once admitted and sank all the way, thrilling all the more to watch François' eyes grow wide; his jaw slacken to an open-mouthed muffle of exhilaration.

He loved François. Loved him immensely.

As the younger man's hands slid down and took up positions behind Carême's thighs again, Carême pulled partially out and established a rhythm. At the same time, he took hold of François' erection and joined the pair of motions as one.

This lovemaking was not destined to last long, as both men entered it with heightened emotions – and as Carême drew closer and closer to release, François took over the management of his own need.

This freed up Carême to use both hands, and he leaned over, casting the boy's legs over his shoulders, going deeper and longer.

"*Villon . . . Villon—*"

"I'm . . . I'm . . . too."

In rapturous agony, François shot ropes of liquid snow upon his belly, upon his abdomen, upon his upper chest and throat.

"Oh, *Villon!*"

The chef did not withdraw, as neither man wanted that, and he orgasmed deep where he belonged, collapsing on his lover and feeling his boy's fingertips glide atop the layer of perspiration covering his back.

Several minutes later, and after their clean-up, their post-climax glow and conversation upon the top of the bed led to François' inevitable sleepiness. As his partner drifted asleep in his arms, Carême finally let the import of François' final statement before their lovemaking settle in.

Once the younger man was heavy with total sleep, Carême kissed his forehead and gently maneuvered out of bed.

The chef had to get back to his intelligence report, but did so guiltily and wondering if his work would ever be done.

The man sat, pulled close a piece of paper, even bothering to pick up a pen. However, all he did was stare out the window, up to the illuminated clock on top of the Pavilion's water tower.

PART III

Christmas 1816

Pavillon Chinois sur un Rocher

Chapter 7: Monday, 23rd December, or *Paix pour notre temps*

"December's a democrat;
O'er coronet and peasant head
An equal doling of bleakness
She insists on all men be spread."

Doctor Kitchiner's merry twinkle defied Carême to disagree, and his begloved hands clapped to let the chef know the physician regarded the atmosphere as festive.

The Frenchman's only response was to pull his coat a little tighter. This would have to do as acknowledgement of his friend's clever phrasing, for overhead, the weather was drear with cloudiness – and yet otherwise free from rain and wind. Notwithstanding the outside conditions, everything under the roof of the Market House appeared jolly and fair; it and its surrounding buildings served as the hub of Christmas preparations in Brighton.

As people bustled about them, and while the pair strolled down the central aisle, Kitchiner continued with his original thought.

"Bleak outside; merry and bright within. This seems so much the summary of Christmas spirit to me."

"I agree with you, Doctor."

"As it's only two days before the Holiday, I'm delighted you could take your midmorning break with me."

The pungent scent of fresh-cut, resinous wood attracted both men's attention. A smiling vendor, who was selling evergreen boughs and garlands, held up her wreaths for inspection; a tall stack of them stood by the side of her aproned skirt.

"François is at the Pavilion, working with Herr Bauda to see today's dinner preparations are moving along smoothly. In addition, we finished our *pièce montée* earlier this morning, so its completion is a weight lifted off of my mind."

"Then I'm glad you don't think my suggestion of coming to the local public emporium too 'pedestrian.' Or, do you?"

"Ah, mais non! Not at all," insisted the chef. "It is always refreshing to get away for a bit, and markets are my favourite place to visit in other towns, away from Paris, that is." Carême smiled.

"And when in Paris?"

"Ah! When in Paris, there is only Les Halles. But then again, one could not wish for more. It is the finest shopping arcade in the world of wholesale."

They approached another country person – this time an apple-cheeked young man – come to town to sell holiday greenery. But this time he stood amongst an assortment of young trees. The tallest was no more than five-foot, while most of the conifers ranged from two to three feet in height.

"And what," asked Carême, "do people do with these?"

"Why . . . don't you hang trees in France?"

"Not in Paris, *Monsieur.* And, hang?"

"Yes! From the ceiling, in a corner of the front room, or wherever the family spend the most time – the tree is decorated and hoisted up on a hook to hang freely."

"C'est extraordinaire!"

"Some even devise small candles to sit on the branches and be lit on Christmas Day. But sadly, our English Yule tree customs are becoming less and less popular. Soon there may be no more Christmas Trees in England. It's waning out of fashion."

Almost by the alchemy of happenstance, the next stall they passed was of a bonneted white-haired lady selling candles of every size and length. For indeed, more people splurged on the luxury of nocturnal light for the Twelve Days of Christmas than for the remainder of the long trail of winter days after them.

Set up next to the wax lady was a barrow full of cottage-crafted toys – simple wooden drums, dolls and noisemakers. Each was cheerfully painted and guaranteed to bring smiles to recipient children's faces Christmas morn.

"Charmants," said Carême brightly.

"It *is* festive this year, isn't it, Chef? Talk of Charlotte's pregnancy is National News, and it's the first Christmas since the Wars started that people face a new year without utter trepidation for the future."

Carême replied with 'peace in our times' in French, a little sardonically.

"It's a prayer we all have." The Doctor was serious. "It feels like, if we can just make it through this winter without treachery, everything will be all right."

"If?"

"I know. This *will* be a lean winter, possibly brutal. What with the endless precipitation, crops have failed, and other resources are low. However, because of the hard times, the Regent is being extra generous this Yuletide to the destitute."

"Mon dieu, I know! In addition to preparing large dinners for the Prince and his visiting family on the 25th, our kitchens have been ordered to roast five hundred pounds extra beef to be handed out. But . . . it is a worthy cause."

"Yes, and not only Brighton, but the same amounts are to be given from Carlton House, Buckingham House, Holyrood Palace, and Windsor Castle too. All the Royal fires will be burning to feed the poor." The Doctor chuckled. "Soon, *la salle de rosbif* will be trading at Pennies the pound."

Disregarding the Doctor's laugh at this point, Carême stopped to run his hand through a seller's bin. The cook let the ripened grains of rye pass between his fingers, thinking, to be honest, they were not the best examples he'd ever seen. Their deficiencies he chalked up to the miserable weather, and thus – being inferior – they were consequently overpriced.

Perhaps thoughts of money led Carême to ask, "Seeing, Doctor Kitchiner, that you are a renaissance man of many interests and blessed with abundant time to pursue them, may I enquire how you came to possess your fortune."

"Coal," Kitchiner replied bluntly. "Tonnes of it."

"Oh, yes?"

The Doctor removed his glasses to be more circumspect with the chef. "My father established a fuel speculation business – one geared to holding back reserves of the sooty stuff until the London Exchange paid enough for it. His middleman-operation is still running, but I have no day-to-day duty with the firm."

Only receiving the fat bank deposits that allows for your life of dilettante leisure, the chef thought—

"But it can be a dangerous occupation," the Doctor added darkly.

"How so?"

The spectacles went back on to shade Kitchiner eyes, which regarded Carême with a blue-cast sincerity. "Naturally, being an adherent of the Church in Rome is a criminal offence in Great Britain, but that only adds to the blackmailers and rumour-mill operators, by those both in and out of official power. Sometimes the Governing Few decide it's best to sic a bigoted mob on those they want to take down a peg. When I was a child, in 1780 to be precise, there was a Catholic massacre in London the authorities allowed to continue for weeks. The first night turned out to be the most frightening string of dark hours in my life, for there was a torch-bearing horde of ruffians outside our house to hang my mother and father in the street. Hundreds of others, unlike my parents, were killed in exactly this way."

"*Mon, dieu.* I never heard of—"

"Gordon's so-called Riot, as it is known, is not taught in our schools, has not been written about – except in Foreign papers – and is an unofficial 'never happened' in polite society."

"How could such things occur? And so recently."

"My dear Carême, England has had its own Terrors for centuries, only nowadays, they're incited by Whitehall's agents – like Lord Gordon – for the mayhem that suits them best. In my family's case, the Government wanted a cut in the coal dealings, got it, and we were allowed to keep our own heads in the exchange."

In addition to the horrors of the religious riots, another minor-key chord had the chef's mind turning to darker thoughts. Though the massacre was in the past, Kitchiner continued to profit off of human misery, as surely the energy speculation business is designed to do. It was blood-coal, wrung from the infected lungs of Northern miners, making the Doctor richer than ever in this year with no natural warmth. People in the Capital were actually having to choose between food or freezing to death with no fuel. It all coalesced in Carême's third eye as a fleck of airborne soot landing on the Pavilion's pristine, still-wet stucco rooves – a literal acidic black spot.

Kitchiner patted the chef's shoulder. "Shall we renew our amble? I did not intent to—"

"Yes. Let's see what else the Christmas Market has to offer."

After walking on moodily for several minutes, eventually a higher, more holiday energy lightened their step.

As the two continued on their way, they encountered a fantastic fragrance all of a sudden. One fruit vendor was craftily studding Seville oranges with clove pods. The dimpled skin received these in all-over decorative patterns like stripes and dragoons. Next to her, a boy pinned pre-cut ribbons to their tops, forming hangers for the citrus, and several completed ones hung across a rod for ready purchase. They smelled wonderfully like Christmas to Carême, and the stoic chef even let slip a smile of warmth for the ribbon lad.

A teen girl in the next stall was making decorative – and edible – festoons from dried apple slices and plump rosehips. The red skin of the fruit complemented the red-orange rind of the seed pod perfectly. They would bring cheer hanging from any home-fire mantelpiece.

These were near baskets of walnuts in the shell, and imported barrels of Spanish raisins and Turkish sultanas – the sweet golden raisins loved by British pudding makers.

"Like the roast beef, Dukes are selling three-a-Shilling in Brighton for the Christmas Season."

"Pardon?"

"I mean, it's a strikingly family affair at the Pavilion. In fact, my informants tell me the house is so chock-a-block with Royals, the unfinished attic is laid out like military barracks to accommodate all their servants."

The pair of browsers next came to a confectioner displaying pretty little parchment baskets. Two thirds of these were filled with sugarplums, and the rest with either candied violet or rose petals. They all glittered with the finest toppings of sugar granules.

"The attic?" Carême was unaware of the domestic situation at home.

"Yes, There are even two levels of cots in the onion dome to accommodate all the visiting lady's maids and gentleman's val-its."

They were passing into the section of the market reserved for potent potables. Particularly, the delectable smell of cordials, like farm-pressed examples of summer-cherry and apricot, brought the scent of warmer months with them as they only now came to full mellow strength at December's end.

Carême puzzled for a moment, and then corrected Kitchiner's pronunciation. "You mean *valet,* no?"

"Well, yes." The good Doctor grinned caustically. "But I *mean* VAL-itt as well. We English delight in being wrong collectively, after we've decided a particular eccentricity suits us better than a mere accuracy."

"I do not - *pardon* - believe I follow."

"This pleasure in being incorrect relates to Foreign matters primarily. Lord knows how butchered Church-of-England Latin is compared to the original. Centuries-old *Je-su* became new-age Jesus just so we could stand out on purpose."

"On purpose?!"

"Yes. We mangle with intent, *mon Carême*. We do it to reinforce how English we are at the core."

While Carême took a moment to consider it, the pair passed farmers selling fermented cider and perry, and others with true ale, which was made without any hops and only 100% barley. It wafted forth a sweet, unmistakably malty aroma.

These dealers were next to those offering bottles of 'cheap and cheerful' red wine from Spain, and more syrupy Rhenish ones from Germany.

Carême countered the Doctor on the lack of logical consistency. "But dear Kitchiner, if you say *val-it,* then why do you call the front hallway a *foy-ay* and not a *foi-er?*"

The Doctor chuckled like he was good-naturedly warning his friend to be careful. "My dear Chef, *foi-er* is American doggerel, and we'd never intentionally permit ourselves to sound like them!"

Both men laughed and slowly continued on their way. From some undisclosed location, the scent of baking gingerbread suddenly greeted the Frenchman's nose. But now, almost by contrast, they entered the fishmongers' quarters in the market. Fresh-caught colours of every hue represented the fish, but Carême was surprised to peer into one barrow and find the very-alive eyes of a large sea turtle blinking back.

"Has the Regent's mother arrived yet?" asked the Doctor.

"We are told to expect the Queen for supper tonight."

A distracted thought lit up Kitchiner's face. "Do you know how many children Queen Charlotte has had?"

"No, I don't believe I do."

"Fifteen! And of her surviving boys, only George has produced a successor, and then quite reluctantly, as you know. The Duke of Kent: no wife; no heirs. Same with York, Cambridge and Sussex. What an unproductive crew they are. You'll see for yourself. William, the second eldest, *is* married but he and Adelaide have no children of their own, although the Duchess lets William surround himself with his *natural* children."

"Natural?"

"The misbegotten. How do you say it in French . . . *les bâtards?*"

"*Oh, oui – les enfants naturele.* Now I understand, and this policy is very lenient of the Duchess."

"I believe she's an intelligent woman and has come to accept she's the one in the marriage incapable of issue, and so allows William the company of his children. That is mere speculation on my part, however."

"*Naturellement.*"

"In any event, you'll soon see the whole gaggle of Royal relatives sitting around the Regent's table for Christmas dinner."

"All except the King . . . . "

"All except the man who is never permitted to leave Windsor Castle, for any reason, no. He'll have his own Christmas, and may not know that day is any different from all the rest he lives through."

The two men were nearing the end of the Market House where a wide opening let in more light from the outside. But before they could leave, Doctor Kitchiner's eye was drawn to a large display of piscine comestibles.

He strode up to a stall, honing in on a collection of cod sounds – the cut comprising the head, collar and swim bladder of the delectable fish. He poked around until he found the fattest, then his index finger hooked it by the gills and hoisted it up into view.

"What do you reckon, *cher* Chef? This seems to be a nice one."

Carême inspected it visually, and assessed it was fresh-caught by the ruby hue of its gills and the clarity of its eyes. *"Oui. C'est bon."*

"How much, my good man?" Kitchiner hoisted it higher for the monger to see.

"Three Shillings, guv'nor."

Kitchiner appeared dismayed, repeating, "Three Shillings?! No; no; no. I will give you ten Pence."

"For that! I'd stake my life on you not finding that cod head's better in Brighton! Sure, not in all of Kent neither I'll wager. Two Shillings, six Pence."

"Two Shillings, six Pence? No. I'll give you a Shilling, six Pence."

"A hard-drove bargain for you, sir. But a Shilling, six Pence it is." The fish dealer held out a sheet of newspaper – actually, the front page of a local gazette, as it was large enough – and Kitchiner dropped his catch of the day onto it. In another moment, the monger had the cod sound neatly bundled in its newsprint wrapper, money was exchanged, and Kitchiner and Carême began to move on.

The Doctor rang out merrily to his marketing companion, "I'll have Mrs. Lister fry that up for our supper! Philip is back in town."

"Master Hardwick, your young architect?"

Kitchiner was flattered Carême remembered. "The very same!" Then he continued in a more sober strain. "That reminds me; I extend an invitation for you to join us on Boxing Day. It will be the usual small, informal affair, with the *usual* assortment of *characters."*

"When is this Boxing Day?"

"The day after Christmas; the 26th."

"Ah, oui. Then I will be delighted to attend."

They exited the market, and Carême saw an amazing sight across a little open plaza. Behind more holiday vendors in the Square, a poulterer had its little three-story building entirely covered with fresh fowl. Turkeys, geese, capons, pullets and chickens hung by their unplucked necks – their fat white bellies and breasts defeathered and on full display. They hung from street-level up to the eaves, and then around the corner, all the way up to the third-story gable.

Kitchiner sensed Carême's surprise. "It's quite a display, isn't it?"

The chef nodded.

"But it's nothing unusual. Every poultry shop in England hangs up their holiday birds like this."

"On the outside?!"

"Yes. And why not? The December air serves as a natural frigidarium, and by Christmas Day, every one of these birds will have been sold and carted home for cooking."

They began to walk through the plaza's collection of vendors, towards the way out nearest the Pavilion.

The Doctor glanced up at the dreary sky and pulled his lapels a little closer. "There's talk of 'Troubles' from around Europe. Uprisings in Russia, for example. We will see how the Czar handles the situation."

"And Ireland? What of London's Empire there?"

Kitchiner stopped walking, adjusting his glasses for a less better view of the chef. "When the oxymoronic notion of a 'United Kingdom' was imposed a hundred years ago, it meant the English centre of government would never let Scotland, Wales or Ireland be free – ever again. So the English army will always do what's necessary in Eire, and it's up to us Loyal Subjects to never ask what 'necessary' involves."

Carême had no words other than *brutal,* and that was the one he dare not voice.

The two continued strolling, drawing close to the end of the little public market square. Just at the end of the plaza, the men saw a final pair of country swains selling bundles of holly, ivy and mistletoe. The lads stood by a pile of enormous oak logs.

Kitchiner asked, "Do you know what that wood is for? It's a special tradition."

Carême shrugged, quite uncharacteristically for him.

"The Yule Log is another dying tradition in England. Once, on large estates, the trunk of a mighty oak tree would be selected, felled to dry for months beforehand, then dragged into the Great Hall and set on a fire lit Christmas morning. It was then meant to burn continuously for twelve days. So you see, it had to be an enormous piece of wood. Now, in the cities, we make do with a piece of timber that can burn all of Christmas Day."

"The Yule Log – *une bûche de Nöel* – I will remember that."

As the men turned to admire the market square they'd just freed themselves from, they spied the unmistakable gait of Leopold. On his arm, rosy and full of half-concealed smiles, Charlotte Augusta of Wales strode with wide-eyed curiosity for how the other 99.999% lived. Hatless, this time she had her hair gathered into a tight crown atop her head, and this in turn was ridiculously encircled by a choker of oversized daisies; those of the silk variety. For this alone, she stood out like a sore thumb.

And so, as the Royals made their way through the open-air bazaar, an older fishwife recognized Charlotte with a clasp of her hand to her heart. "Bless ye, Princess – may God keep Thee," she said, drawing the attention of others nearby.

Soon a well-meaning crowd cordoned in around them, with Her Highness clearly perturbed their incognito had been thus dashed.

However, Leopold became magnificent. He kept the pair moving forward at a relaxed pace, despite those in front turning to face the couple.

The murmurs of the crowd grew to a consistent chant, unifyingly crying out: "God Save England's only hope!"

"Perhaps we should lend assistance—"

Kitchiner stayed the chef's arm as Carême raised it to point to the couple. "Steady on, old soul. I have my men trailing them for protection whenever they leave the Pavilion. Leopold and Charlotte are in no danger."

And then Carême, despite knowing how despised her father was, saw young girls run up to the Princess. Each held out a posy, and Charlotte took them with a kind word for the children. She seemed genuinely touched.

After this, Leopold re-extended the crook of his arm for his wife to take, and they began easing themselves out of the market. The pair took the street closest to them – by the side of the be-fowled poulterer's shop – heading out to Castle Square. Naturally, the growing crowd trailed after them.

Kitchiner and Carême followed suit, using the passageway they were on to enter the Square as well.

They maintained distance, but kept their eye on the Royal Couple casually making their way back towards the Pavilion's South Gate.

The Doctor bent confidential tones in Carême's ear. "Charlotte is having a difficult pregnancy. The Regent wants her removed from excitement, but she's only twenty *and* an excitable girl. Her high spirits and optimistic view on the world are part of why she is so beloved by the people. The Wars are over! They don't want *staid* anymore."

In a few minutes more, the Doctor and chef parted ways at the Pavilion gate, with Kitchiner heading off to the Club, and Carême gaining admittance to the house via the servants' front door.

As Carême finished hanging up his winter-damp coat in the vestibule to dry out, movement in the hallway caught his attention. For just at that moment, François backed out of the Cold Kitchen in a slightly stooped posture. His hands were gripping the edge of the base supporting Carême's freshly completed *pièce montée* – the grandest, most detailed, central confection for the Banqueting Room.

Inch by inch, the whole of the sugar work sculpture emerged from behind the doorframe. A *chinois* extravaganza, the long 'building plot' of its board contained there tall pagodas, bamboo bridges – spanning rock-candy gorges – and spun sugar waterfalls. Architecturally speaking, all was red and black, with details like coiling dragons and bells hanging from the tip of every roof-point, which were themselves tricked out in edible gold leaf. The full piece finally made it entirely into the hallway, revealing a steady-handed footman manning the other end of the board.

And this *pièce de résistance* was merely one of three made especially for the Pavilion's 1816 Christmas celebrations. For two more – designed for the Banqueting Room's flanking sideboards – were nearly as elaborate, but 'only' featured a single pagoda atop a waterfall-spouting rocky outcrop. Never again would Carême allow himself to be impugned for making pieces too highbrow for his princely English employer to appreciate.

François and the recruited footman continued on down the corridor – the French *maître d'hôtel* walking backward.

Carême followed, giving the men plenty of leeway, but as the *pièce montée* cleared the halfway point of the Decking Room, Carême ducked through the other, closer door to the Banqueting Room.

What he saw shocked him, and events unfolded much too quickly to do anything but react. For crouched down within the room, hidden behind the portal François was just about to come through, was Gris Thorndyke, the disgruntled Chief Footman. His tightly coiled body told the chef he was moments away from leaping up and tripping François, no doubt causing Carême's right-hand man to dash the Pavilion's principal holiday treat to the floor.

The chef raised his hand, preparing to yell out, when John Lightfoot –who had been arranging place-settings at that end of the table – leapt over and tackled Thorndyke from the side. The two men tumbled harmlessly to the carpet at the precise moment François entered the Banqueting Room.

Carême sprang into action, directing the maitre-d' to the central sideboard before his hothead partner could get distracted as to why two grown men were wrestling on the floor by the door he'd just used.

By the time he and the footman slid the *pièce montée* into its safe-harbour position, François had correctly deciphered Gris' sinister intentions. He stalked up to his enemy, demanding, "And what plan did you have in mind, *hein!* To destroy Master Carême's masterwork, *hein!* To disgrace me—"

"Ah, keep your Froggie trap shut," the Chief Footman shouted.

François shouted back a stream of vernacular French, cursing the twenty-eight-year-old man as if he were a pickpocketing youth caught in a Paris back-alley.

Thorndyke didn't need an interpreter to feel the insults hurtling his way, and his face grew redder and redder with rage. His fists clenched at the ends of his piston-rigged arms.

Just at that moment, more footmen arrived from the Decking Room. They were followed by the Kitchen Comptroller and Thomas Daniels.

The moneyman flew into action, pushing the others aside to stand before his fellow Englishman, back turned to Distré.

Into the silence that followed, Thorndyke raised a wickedly self-controlled leer. He gently pushed the Comptroller aside. Into the face of the man he hated, he spat, "I was tying my shoe. Prove otherwise."

François' Gallic pride tore through his body like a flash of lightning. "How dare—"

"Now; now"—the Comptroller tempted fate by putting his hand flat on Distré's chest— "the man has given you a perfectly reasonable explanation. It's time we—"

"*Quel baratin!*"

Again, no one needed help translating François's charge of *Bullshit!*, for at this point the look of homicidal fury returned to Gris Thorndyke's face.

This, naturally, goaded François to further action, but Carême took over, murmuring a plaintive *"Villon,"* and causing the maitre-d' to glance around.

His men, his servers – the footmen – seemed to be on François' side . . . but were they really?

Thomas Daniels, the undercook with hand-drying towel still in his clutches, looked to be sympathetic to the Frenchman's cause, but in the end, François realized it was as it had always been – Carême and he alone, against the world.

François straightened up, backing away from the Comptroller's hand. Then he said, "Apology accepted."

Still, all in all, the glint in Thorndyke's glare remained as determined for a nasty comeuppance as ever.

Carême's midmorning break saw him running an errand to a Brighton jeweller. He'd placed his order weeks ago, and so was relieved the gift had been completed just in time.

The chef's course home took him through the Pavilion grounds. Having used the West Gate, the domed grandeur of the Prince's stables was to his left, and pleasantly laid paths and borders spread their leisurely way towards the marine villa.

However, far from an idyllic springtime saunter, Carême's pace was brisk, for the leaden skies had opened up half an hour ago with snow. It fell gently and began clinging to the marble stucco rooves of the Salon's onion dome as an incongruous fuzz. The white fluff also collected picturesquely on the tent roof of the Banqueting Room and its recently completed set of colonettes. Beyond this, behind and to its side, the golden weathervane of the moody Water Tower pointed its dragon tail towards France, and the black smoke of the Great Kitchen's just-lit roasting fires rose up to mingle with the ill-boding cloud cover.

Carême quietly ruminated on how those fires would not be extinguished for days – perhaps a fortnight – for the poor of Brighton were going to be coming to the Kitchen Court seeking meat and liquid merriment. The chef simply hoped it was the poor receiving the Regent's beneficence, and not a chance for someone like Donald Bland to funnel Royal vittles to brokers of 'trend' and pocket the money for himself.

The man reached the relative comfort of the Pavilion's *porte-cochère,* or the covered entranceway for carriages before the home's front door. Here he kicked the light accumulation of snow off of shoes, and brushed the same down from his shoulders and arms.

At his approach, a handsome but unsmiling youth in a livery uniform opened one of the glass doors for the chef. "Monsewer" was his only greeting.

Carême nodded at him and moved into the Octagon Entry so the young man could block out the wind at Carême's back by closing the door again.

The chef loved this room. The architect had designed it thinking of days like this, for the angled back wall – to the left of the double doors leading into the house – had been arranged to host a fireplace. Now a warm and smokeless coal grate easily kept the cold at bay, inviting every visitor to loosen their winter attire and feel at home.

The paint scheme was also inviting, for an array of pale greys tricked out the raised panelled flanking the enormous, opposite-set windows, and carried up this grisailled subtlety to the plaster tent ceiling. At each of the eight meeting places of the 'fabric,' charming little bells in burnished silverleaf only hinted at the riot of colourful *chinoiserie* beyond.

Suddenly, Carême's eye was caught by holiday cheer. A topiary of oranges, surmounted by a pineapple, stood on the reception desk in this room. It was placed next to the open visitors' book where departing guests could thank the Regent for his hospitality.

He walked into the Reception Hall, immediately appreciating the architect's forethought once more, for in this nearly windowless space – as large and rectangular as it was – Mr. Nash had arranged a stunning wall-to-wall clerestory where each of the arched panes of glass were polychromed with a long-tailed phoenix.

The walls of this room stepped up the decoration of the Octagon, as they were a pale blue-green with a tone-on-tone overpainting of Chinese dragons and coiling serpent motifs in a lighter tone. But now the large, central rondels were covered with glossy wreaths of magnolia and holly berries above the pianoforte against one long wall, and the mantlepiece of the other.

Striding through the room to the open door on the right, Carême's thoughts ascertained what was 'wrong' with the decorations, for, concerning colour, they were lovely, but without scent, these particular evergreens plants offered no real Christmas spirit.

Through this portal, into a vestibule leading to the guest chambers and their shared parlour known as the Red Drawing Room, another discreet door to the chef's left was of the swinging variety – the staff access to the Pavilion's end-to-end Service Corridor. Nash had even thought to submerge the portion of this corridor intersecting the Reception Hall. He'd stepped it underground so staff never need delay their valuable tasks simply waiting for guests to clear the Hall.

What Carême failed to notice, being lost in his own thoughts, was how a friend had been sitting quietly in the Red Drawing Room.

"Oh, Lady Morgan—"

She'd come up behind him and snagged his arm. "Just the person I was wanting to see."

She led the chef through the 'green baize' door into the service passageway.

Maintaining her arm tightly through his as they walked, she added low and conspiratorially, "My enquiries into James and Audrey Keenan have finally been answered."

"Oh, yes. And what information have you found?"

"The parish priest in Ireland confirmed their origin story; their age and names; and their parentage too. Lord DeWitt's secretary in Ireland also corroborated the couple's employment in their household kitchens, as well as Lord Aire's butler in Yorkshire testifying to their satisfactory engagement with the Duke of Cambridge at his country estate when he was head of staff there. From this position, already in Royal employ, they came to work at the Pavilion two years ago with positive references."

As Carême was digesting this information, he must have scowled, for Sydney Morgan was swift to add, "They seem on the up and up, as we would say back home, but truth to tell – one can never know."

"*Oui, Madame.* One never fully knows."

"Also, I needed to see you today because we've been given a delicate mission." The hush-hush tone was back in Lady Morgan's voice.

"Of what nature?"

"It's from Prince Leopold. He's worried about Charlotte's constitution. She suffers dreadfully from the morning sickness and hardly eats anything at all. The father-to-be knows Charlotte needs her strength, and wants us to meet with her."

"When?"

"Just about now. She'll be rising and calling for her morning tea."

"*Comment ça.*"

The pair entered the hurly-burly of the Great Kitchen.

Extracting his arm with a kiss on her wrist, the chef bowed and said politely, "*Madame, s'il vous plaît.* If you will wait for me while I give instructions, I shall return with something for the Princess."

The chef went about his tasks.

Ergo, cunningly left to her own devices, Lady Morgan suddenly found herself 'alone' and nearly invisible amongst the swirl of action. Drifting to one of the two great preparation tables, she pretended to be taken by a delicate chive florette. It was a ruse and employed the mundane action of drawing it up to her nose as a means of spying on Charlotte's lady's maid.

Brigitte was standing at the end of this table, the Princess' breakfast tray near the hand she used to lean on the wood in mid-flirt with François.

The maitre-d' suddenly coloured and stood more erect; so did Brigitte. Carême had arrived with another chef-hat-wearing gentleman – one whom Lady Morgan immediately assumed was Herr Bauda, the Sous-chef. They ignored Brigitte, who slipped out of the conference by mumbling something concerning "Sweet rolls" and "Pastry Kitchen"; the men continued discussing battle plans for the day's dinner.

Oddly then, a young woman in chef whites retrieved Charlotte's tray and set it much closer to Lady Morgan's position. The novelist casually strolled her way to it while the undercook turned her back and returned her attention to something on the range. A man lingered there waiting for her, and Morgan instantly knew *this* was the Irish couple – James and Audrey Keenan.

Using deft motions, Morgan inspected the contents of the tray. It was what one would expect for a young lady's wake-up service, except, inexplicably, there were two tea pots – one in highly polished silver; the other in humble, everyday crockery. The lids were off, and Morgan wanted to peer inside each—

"Begging pardon, mum," Audrey said, returning unannounced with a boiling kettle, which she held via the facility of a folded towel under the bail handle. She filled each pot, giving the novelist a tantalizing whiff. One was heady, earthy Ceylon tea – that she knew – but, as for the other . . . .

"Ah, Lady Morgan." Brigitte was back. She held a porcelain plate of sugar twist buns. "This is a surprise."

"Nevertheless"—she smiled—"you had better run along to your mistress now. Carême and I will be up shortly to sit with her."

"Ah, oui?" The experienced companion maid's tone was controlled, first admonishing anyone telling her what to do who was not Charlotte, and secondly, it managed to simultaneously convey the displeased 'irregularity' of the Royal heir-apparent having people "sit with her" just out of bed.

Lady Morgan – in the meantime – assessed the little snicker of approval coming off of Audrey Keenan. At least the undercook liked the French maid being dressed down, and by an Irish Lady at that.

"Yes. So see to it there are enough cups, *oui?"*

Brigitte played her ace, unnecessarily curtsying. *"Oui, Madame."*

James, oblivious to the entire display of female intrigue, had slipped matching shawls around the tea pots. It was a relatively long trip to the other end of the house and up one flight of stairs. No Pavilion drafts would be cooling the hot beverages along the way.

The maid hefted the tray and departed.

Sydney Morgan engaged the couple, her smile fixed as she indulged in that casual, Irish way of word-dressing designed to get at what one wanted to know without seeming interested in it at all. "Back in County Dublin, where I'm from, a shawl is for the shoulders, not the tea pot!"

She laughed; the other two exchanged awkward grins.

"Say, I noticed," continued Lady Morgan, "there were two pots on the Princess' tray."

"Yes, ma'am," replied James. "The Princess' usual drink of choice is herb tea."

"Oh." Sydney Morgan pushed her luck. "May I taste some?"

"Begging pardon, mum"—Audrey chose to become offended—"but I've been in charge of making Charlotte's teas for years at the Pavilion now. I know how she likes it."

"Yes, but—"

James interrupted. "We would serve you a cup, ma'am, but there's none ready-made, and we don't have the authority to make a whole pot just for one, curious sip."

"Well, then, just tell me what it is so I can try some of it back home – on my own." She smiled in full deceptive innocence.

Audrey paled a moment. Her husband responded, gesturing to a sealed porcelain jar on the table. "Chamomile. The Regent himself ordered it given to her; to calm her nerves, you understand."

Morgan laughed it off. "Of course! Why, of course." But still she whipped the lid off the jar and took a deep whiff. It was the same herbaceous fragrance she'd scented coming off the crockery tea pot.

"Been drinking it, ma'am," added James, "since she was a lass. Very fond of it she is too."

Lady Morgan re-lidded the canister. "I see." She copped a happy expression. "Very good. By all means, do carry on."

She walked away, knowing exactly what she must do.

Later, away from the great Central Corridor with its ceiling of skylights, up the leisurely paced North Staircase to the Chamber Gallery – and in the suite of rooms identical to the Regent's – Chef Carême and Lady Morgan sat in morning *levée* with the Princess.

They were gathered around the sofa table in the antechamber: Charlotte slouching on the couch itself with her back to the window; the visitors perched on armless chairs drawn up to the table for the occasion. Brigitte stood with folded hands by the Princess' side.

Morgan and Carême had a cup full of tea before them, while Charlotte ignored her buttered sweet-roll.

Brigitte served the Princess her third helping of herbal tea, and again, while Charlotte lackadaisically stirred in far too much sugar, Lady Morgan found herself acknowledging the scent of chamomile flowers, but couldn't shake off the hint of something more medicinal being in the tea's vapours as well.

Carême had brought his portfolio of sugar work architectural drawings and held them up across the table – away from Charlotte's greasy fingers – while he expounded upon them. As he did so to the bored Princess, Sydney Morgan noted the cold, dagger-pointed glares the maid shot at Carême. Perhaps the French-woman was merely miffed at the chef's failure to detect Charlotte's disinterest, or, Lady Morgan considered, it was possible someone felt jealous of a certain chef's connections to a certain maitre-d'.

"And this one, Princess"—Carême was concluding his miniature lecture—"I title *l'ermitage Russe;* a Russian Retreat."

Charlotte sparked to attentiveness. "Oh, yes! This is the superior example you made for the Banqueting Room inaugural."

The chef was flattered she'd remember. *"Oui, ma Princesse.* Your first official dinner here."

"But tell me"—she plopped dish-rattling elbows on the table—"why a palm tree for a Russian church? And why chicken-wire windows, made of sugar, of course, for such an *ermitage?"*

Carême coloured a bit. He tried to be as plain-spoken about it as he could. "It is a new school of Art called *le pittoresque.* Elements from one place or time are shown juxtaposed against others."

Charlotte wasn't following.

Lady Morgan lent assistance. "As I understand it, Mr. John Nash, your father's architect, is a leading figure in the 'Picturesque School' over here. For example, have you noticed the small, Gothic rose windows he has placed on the

Pavilion's onion domes? They don't belong there by any stretch of logic or application, and yet they produce a very harmonious effect for the eye."

"Oh . . . . " Both Princess and lady's maid got it. "It's a damn curious thing to do when—"

Sydney Morgan cut her off, knowing the other was about to insult Carême. "But, artists will be artists." Her sidelong glance at the chef, with eyes snapping back to the Princess' own, drove the message home.

Charlotte collapsed on the sofa cushion, sighing an apology. "I'm sorry, Chef Carême. Here you are, so gallantly trying to lift my spirits, and I . . . . Well, and I simply feel in too much pain to even remember my manners. Do forgive."

"*Naturellement,* for there is nothing to forgive. But, are you in much discomfort, Princess?"

"Yes"—she straightened up and drained her now-tepid tea—"I am."

Brigitte de Saint-Exupéry re-filled the cup once it was back on its saucer.

The Princess inattentively stirred in her usual three spoonfuls of sugar. "The old bother! It really is such a horridly unfair thing . . . . " She nibbled on some buttery flakes. "Morning sickness is, that is."

"From what I've observed," Lady Morgan said, trying to offer comfort, "moving past the three-month mark, young mothers-to-be don't suffer from it anymore."

Above a gay, princessly laugh, Charlotte replied, "Well, I do!"

"Doctor Kitchiner and I saw Your Highnesses in the market yesterday." Carême suspected correctly: even the mere suggestion of the Prince Consort's existence would raise her spirits.

Charlotte replied with glee, "With all the people; you saw! But my Leopold, he ambled us home, right through the South Gate, just to walk us straight through the North Gate again, *sans entourage!* We had a lovely, beachside stroll after that in perfect quiet. It was divine, although the overcast weather was not. When will this beastly winter of the summer of 1816 end?" As she had aimed the tail end of her rhetorical question in Brigitte's direction, the lady's maid raised her shoulders, and then - with pursed lips - shook her head.

Returning her attention to her guests, the Princess continued, "Sometimes I have my doubts." She was back in the doldrums again, glancing around. "Sometimes, I don't like this place – too many eyes about me. I much prefer Claremont House. It may be small, but it's all Leopold and I need to be happy. And it does my spirit no good to be in Brighton so often in pain."

Carême and Lady Morgan exchanged meaningful looks. Before the chef could ask what kind of pains, the Princess went on in a pettish way.

"How dreary I find dinner at the Pavilion right now. No reflection on your skills, *Monsieur,* but these trying and testing days leave me with no appetite to sit and look amused for hours while the men drone on so about famine in Russia, revolts in Dublin, starvation in India – again – and on and on and on. It's horrendously dull and bores me to tears; and they've only *just* stopped talking about the Congress of Vienna."

Carême thought this was much too cavalier an attitude coming from the head destined to wear The Crown of the English Empire – but naturally, he said nothing.

The Princess grew thirsty, and after having swallowed half of her cold tea, suddenly showed considerable interest in her pastry. She took a heaping teaspoon of sugar and liberally doused the buttered flakes of her roll with it.

Tearing off shreds and chewing crunchingly, her elbows landed on the table once more. "My Consort is always correct in his judgement . . . thinking, I mean. He is so bright and attentive to details, I rely on Leopold's ears to gather the intelligence I need but am blind to during my current condition. Ergo, this is why I prefer to sup alone with him at night, here in our chambers, so we can privately chat about the day's activities."

Carême reconsidered his slighting of the young woman's sagacity, and felt a bit ashamed. This led to the chef announcing brightly, "To cheer you up, I will personally prepare a treat for you and the Prince Consort tonight."

"What is it?" A sprinkle of sugar fell from the young woman's mouth.

The lady's maid was also quite engaged with learning the answer.

"A *baba.*"

Crestfallen, Brigitte apparently considered this far too humdrum.

Despite the maid's folding of arms with a dubious expression, Charlotte sat a little straighter and smiled. "Oh, how jolly well mysterious, considering I don't know what that is!"

At that moment, the little gathering indulged in free and easy laughter.

Hours later, the main course of the Royal Couple's late-evening meal having gone up thirty minutes before, the Great Kitchen was shuttering itself at nine – as usual – while Carême, François and Thomas placed the finishing touches on Charlotte's and Leopold's dessert.

The original *baba au rhum* had come into being during the reign of Louis XV's pretty Polish wife – the one who not so famously uttered the line that cut off Marie-Antoinette's head: "What, the peasants have no bread?! Then let them eat brioche, ha-ha . . . . "

She might have instead suggested they eat her favoured *baba,* baked in fluted moulds said to resemble the flaring skirts of contented old women, for as Carême knew the true Polish tradition, this slowly risen yeast cake was prepared with rye flour, and such staples were cheaper and more readily available to a France in crisis in the 1760s. But sadly, history cannot rewrite itself except in wistful or deceitful ways – never the practical.

And the rum? Ah, the chef whose inspiration to take the somewhat plain-Jane *baba* of the tea table – which was, no doubt, a stale one by the time he got his hands on it – and spoon a luxurious dark rum syrup over the top, has been lost to culinary folklore.

Suffice to say, it was now an item a hungry Parisian proletariat could splurge for as an everyday treat from Carême's pastry shop; the *baba au rhum* was famous throughout France – especially the master chef's version.

And glistening on one of the Pavilion's silver platters was just such an example. Admiring it, Carême felt sure it would please the young couple sequestered at supper on the opposite side of the house. Whipped cream filled up the centre where the plain tube section of the baking pan had been, and on the exterior of the cake's rum-burnished, mahogany crenulations, precise dollops of more Chantilly creme were being hand-piped by François under Carême's watchful eye.

"No; no," François chided Thomas. For the 'chucklehead' was following in Distré's wake with perfectly cut diamonds of candied angelica. "That's crooked! Straighten it."

Thomas quickly saw which decorated highlight was amiss and righted it to a proper up and down.

Just as this team of two completed the final garnish, they looked up. It struck François that the kitchen was suddenly depopulated from when he first began his task a few minutes ago. In fact, now only James and Audrey Keenan were working. Near to them, to François' embarrassment, Brigitte de Saint-Exupéry stood observing the man at his task; Carême slyly observing her at hers.

The *chef de cuisine* gently lidded the dish with a large silver cloche, and Gris Thorndyke lifted it to walk the dessert upstairs. As Chief Footman, it was his appointed prerogative and pleasure to receive compliments due the Great Kitchen's staff. He was trailed out by Charlotte's lady's maid with her pot of herbal tea for the Princess on a tray.

As Thomas collected the used utensils and bowls, returning them to the sink, Carême and François settled into shared observations.

"*Villon,* I am concerned the Princess consumes too much sugar. It's far better to try and curb its use for her here, in the kitchen. *Babas* have not so much sweetness."

François surveyed the Keenans tidying up too. Audrey was sealing the canister containing the Princess' special tea. His own thoughts towards Charlotte were not as flattering as Carême's. He chuckled, telling the chef, "Certainly as a Princess, she'll decide to have exactly as much sugar as she likes."

Carême was not sure how to take the suddenly caustic remark, nor indeed, what mood inspired it.

François explained in a lower tone. "You are too nice to them, at least to that stuffed-shirt *Bosche,* Leopold."

"Chef Carême, sir . . . " Thomas interrupted them, instantly drying up what little good humour François was showing. "I've checked with the spit-jacks and the first shift of roasters. They will be up by 4 in the morning to stoke the fires and begin roasting the beef for the poor."

"Good," replied the distracted chef.

"Also, begging your leave, but I had a glance over your menu for Christmas dinner tomorrow. The number of entrees is staggering . . . . " The teen boy's voice trailed off in personal uncertainty.

This caught Carême's attention. He was nothing if not a mentor *par excellence.* "Thomas, my boy, do not be intimidated; but do get a full night of sleep."

He placed a warm hand of encouragement on the lad's shoulder. "Tomorrow's activities will be like going into battle. Like any soldier, the best you can do is be prepared, and calmly fall back upon your training to get you through challenges. As you *are* prepared, I know you will play your part well."

To this supreme compliment, Thomas Daniels smiled.

However, unmistakably to François' eyes, the boy also blushed to receive this kind of personal attention and praise. The man quickly blotted out unbidden memories of feeling the same nearly a decade earlier with simmering jealousy; he became angry at both the boy and the maitre-d's fickle lover.

Oblivious to any of this, Thomas said in a holiday-making tone, "And the Staff's Christmas will promptly start at noon on the 26th." The young man split glances between the Frenchmen. "I wanted both of you to know you are warmly invited."

Carême rather curtly replied, "I won't be here. I have other plans for Boxing Day, but thank you."

This stunned François. It was the first he'd heard of it.

"Pardon." Carême left them, heading to his office, his hand reaching around to take off his apron for the day.

There followed an uncomfortable moment for the gloating kid and dejected man. But François Distré pulled himself together and bid Thomas a cool but unhostile "Good night." He then went to confront Carême.

When he got to the chef's glass-boxed sanctorum, the chef was taking off his knife scabbard and locking it away for the evening. Unseen by François, Carême had to shove a certain package aside in his desk drawer to do it.

François closed the door behind him.

"My God"—François was impassioned but under control—"you flirt with him in front of me? And worse yet, puff up the ego of that block-headed boy."

Carême stayed calm, turning the key in the lock of his drawer. "He has potential, and everyone has more to learn in their craft. In fact, I'd suspect he's only slightly less educated on culinary matters than when I discovered you in Laguipierre's kitchen."

François dropped all pretence, mumbling "It hurts," hoping it would soften his partner's heart. It didn't.

Walking towards the wall where the chef's coat hung on a hook, he stopped behind François' right shoulder. "It hurts me that you are sleeping with Charlotte's lady's maid."

François thought for an impulsive moment to deflect; to try and laugh it off. Instead, he gave up and honed his tone with a slight vindictiveness. "I have to entertain myself somehow, considering you're always with your new 'friends'."

Carême, slipping on his suit jacket, replied rather flatly, "Just because I'm not in the kitchen, it doesn't mean I'm not working."

After a drumbeat of deafening silence, François slammed the kitchen towel from his apron down in frustration on the desk. "You never consider me or my situation, do you?!"

Carême, stunned and perplexed, watched as François tore open the office door and stormed off.

François went back to the middle of the Great Kitchen, not really knowing what he was doing. In another moment he had stopped, and stood leaning on the still-warm steaming table, emotionally mute.

Lost in misery, he barely noticed the lights dim as the kitchen officially closed for the night.

A hand landed on his shoulder from behind. Cheering, masculine words erupted with an Irish lilt. "It's about time you made good on that promise to let us take you out."

Audrey strolled up smiling towards her husband, fixing her bonnet. Both were in their street clothes, and the kitchen was otherwise deserted, save for the three of them.

François stood upright. *"Oui!* Why not."

Chapter 8, Part Two:
"Here and Now"

In a non-descript section of Brighton, fronting an also-ran street, stood a public house of untold importance to the life of one of the town's populations. Evanescent as the numbers of patrons might have been, the Irish-owned pub functioned throughout the year as an information hub, a social venue, and a place to get some traditional fare and drinks. But on nights like this – this holy Christmas Eve – many sought out their own community under the sign of "The Barrel" because the Law barred them from gathering later under the sign of the cross. There were no Catholic Midnight Masses in Britain, at least not ones officially regarded as anything but criminal if not licensed by Whitehall, and those were few and – by design – far between.

Nevertheless, what one found on ordinary days was present this night in gleeful abundance, including the aromas of roasting meats and vegetables, along with potent bottles of Whiskies on the back-bar shelf and nearly explosive barrels of beer in the cool cellar below. What would any visit to an Irish pub be without an expertly pulled pint of stout? A glass filled so perspicaciously, it's topped off with a head of foam as savoury-sweet as a dollop of whipped cream. "It's all in the wrist"— the wrist working the tap handle—"and I'm the best," any barman worth his salt will tell you.

As François Distré approached "The Barrel" from the outside, bundled against the snow on the ground and the damp coldness rolling in from the sea, he saw it was the only building on the block with a lit candle in its front window. "Is this the place?"

"It is indeed!" replied Audrey Keenan, two paces out in front with her husband.

James strode up manfully, opening the door inward to let spouse and guest enter before he did. When François caught the man's eyes to nod 'thank you,' the maitre-d' noticed a vibrant wreath of holly behind Keenan's head; the one hung on the outside of the pub's door.

While the three shed their outer layer of cold-weather attire to hang on hooks in the vestibule, François was amazed by the life and vitality emerging from the taproom just beyond. He never would have guessed it from the staid, mostly dark exterior of the establishment.

"Where will we sit?" Audrey was already scanning for a spot.

"There!" James pointed to a table near the back.

They made their way through the crowded bar area, and the Frenchman grew surprised to see children round about.

"Harry!" James called to the barman above the ruckus "Three pints," and pointed to their final destination.

The barman grinned and held up his free hand to acknowledge the order.

Once they'd settled at their table, François renewed his inspection. Near them, on a table pushed against the back wall, stood a manger scene with simple but brightly painted figures. Oddly though – and the maitre-d' had to look twice to make sure he saw what he saw – an empty, up-turned crate stood on the floor in front of the *crèche.*

Another glance around him took in a bit of greenery on the far-end of the bar closest to them. It was a wreath of evergreens laid flat and appointed on the inside with several stubby candlesticks – four lit tapers of purple and pink, and an unlighted fifth candle of white standing in the centre. Oddly, here too stood a discordant element in the form of broad-mouthed snuffers lying at the back of the burning candles. Their placement was all-too obviously planned for in advance.

A barmaid turned up with three overflowing pewter tankards. She set them down with a hurried, "Here you go."

"Three for dinner too, love," said Audrey.

"Set course?"

"Yes."

"Coming right up." The maid went her way.

James picked up his glass, inviting the others to do likewise. "So, I'll say – here's to—"

"—New friends!" His wife finished his thought.

"Cheers!"

François waited for a moment as the couple drank deeply with obvious enjoyment. He more cautiously brought the beverage up to his nose. He sipped some foam, pleased with the creamy texture. Then he drank and was less satisfied with the taste.

James asked, "Do they have much beer in France? I don't even know."

François wiped the froth from his lip. "No, not much. In Alsace, yes; in Paris, not so much. Although Lambic beer from Flanders is starting to be seen."

"What's that like," enquired Audrey.

"Fruity, because to normal ale they add fruit juice to give a second fermentation."

"So it's stronger too," observed James.

"Yes, that is true. Which is why Parisians are needing it these days." He chuckled.

The couple exchanged non-committal looks.

François asked, "What is it you have ordered to eat?"

"Oh, you'll soon see." It was Audrey's turn to chuckle.

James replied enthusiastically, "It's none of that pouncy stuff intended for the Regent's table. It's real food tonight! Genuine Irish fare."

That was it; François took the comment as fair warning to stay away from the subject. He'd have to grin and bear whatever was placed before him.

Suddenly, one of the little girls in the room ran up to the crib. She climbed on top of the upturned wooden box to get the best view.

"Ah!" François said. "So the crate is there for this reason. I wondered."

Audrey handled this one – after glancing at her husband first. "That and, another more, practical reason."

François was all ears.

"You see," explained Audrey, "these so-called 'papal displays' are out-lawed. If, and just if, the fine dishonest men of the Brighton Constabulary decide to try and slip one of their spies in here tonight—"

"—So they can later send the mob to bust down the door, looking for Christmas *crimes—*" supplied James.

"—The crate can pop up and hide the manger; the stranger gets shown the door; the decorations get swept up and hid in the cellar, so we stay safe."

François saw the light. "Oh. Same with the Advent Wreath: candles ready to be snuffed, and candlesticks which can be quickly moved away from the green-ery."

"Precisely," Audrey confirmed. "We've been made fugitives in this so-called open society where we dare not be open about anything!" Her laugh, attempt-ting to enforce an air of levity, fell flat. In fact, the hollow sound of it wound up rein-forcing how serious her 'humour' had been.

François sighed, moving closer to his beer. "I wish the world were a lot more free."

"I'll drink to that!" James raised his tankard with a grin, inviting the French-man to do the same. The little party of three drank deeply, and François even began to appreciate the malty flavour.

Their waitress arrived with an opening cold course to be shared amongst the table occupants. As soon as she set it down, François could see neatly trimmed slices of clove-studded ham dominating the platter, around which were piles of pickled cucumbers, radish pods, and pearl onions no bigger than fat cherries. Off to one edge of the dish was a healthy dollop of mustard to be taken with the meat as desired.

"Let me play 'Mam'," Audrey said, already using her knife and fork to lift a choice hunk of ham; it was bound for the Frenchman's plate, so he held it up to receive it. "The pickles and condiment," she added, "you can take as you see fit."

Audrey served James next, and François took small helpings of each of the preserved vegetables. The mustard looked formidable, so he lightly coated the tine-end of his clean fork to taste it first. It wasn't too over-powering, so he took some more and spread it over his slice of ham.

Everyone was served now, so James said, "Let's eat. How do you say . . . Bone?"

"*Bon appétit.*"

"Bone appa-tea," the couple repeated.

They ate in silence for a while, and the life and noise of the pub around them reasserted themselves.

The little girl at the crib had long since drifted off. Now a pair of roisterous boys were playing a make-shift game of tag, running helter-skelter beneath tables and ducking out of one another's touch with uproarious laughter.

One of the boys' mothers came up and took both by an upper arm. "Stop actin' the maggot, you two! Behave yourselves." She guided them back to the booths their parents were occupying.

François gestured with his knife. "I'm surprised to see young ones around. Is this always the case?"

"No; no," James said. "It's just for tonight – or, more correctly - for nights like this one."

"How so?"

Audrey took over explaining. "You see, normally, back home, we'd socialize in each other's front rooms, and then meet up as a community for Mass at Midnight. But, here, no. So on special nights of the year, including the Saturday before Easter, this pub functions as a more wholesome meeting house for the regulars to bring their children."

"Yes," James added, "but they're strictly to be on 'best behaviour' only."

They tucked in again, and in no time, their plates were bare.

"How was it?" Audrey enquired cautiously.

François sputtered his lips. "Good. The ham was moist, though still a bit salty. The pickles? *D'accord;* but I truly like the radish pods. This is a vegetable I will be taking back to France with me." After a pause, he added, "Eventually." He drank some of his beer.

The couple displayed obvious joy in having fed the maitre-d' something 'good'.

"Speaking of France," James slyly inveigled, "what was it like growing up there – when and where you did."

François felt he was being pumped for information, so stayed generic in his reply. "Awful, and wonderful."

"The Terror, you mean?" asked Audrey.

"The *Terror.* I was just a little boy, but everyone I knew growing up had been touched by it. Like a madness in the blood, first flowing through Robespierre and his Committee, then from his henchmen to their victims; and then worst of all – the madness jumped to the victims' survivors as paranoia, as lust for vendetta . . . for blood; blood; blood."

François had sobered himself, so it was a relief when a mug boy showed up just then with fresh pints for them to take. The Frenchman didn't mind the taste now, and quick swallowed a third of his tankard in one go.

James had eyed him oddly. He finally asked, "And 'wonderful' – what was wonderful?"

François grinned like a little kid. He wiped the foam off of his lips before saying, "Napoléon. Not only for France – defeating, crushing the Austrians right away, but the hope he represented – a United Europe. A democratic community of equals he was willing to fight to achieve. *That. Him.* He was the French Revolution redone a second time; a right way."

The Irish couple paused.

Audrey asked, "Then, what happened? He was guilty of atrocities, in Syria and elsewhere."

"Oui; oui; oui! My boyhood icon was gold leaf and not gold. He shattered the heart of my nation a second time. But what does it matter? We children of the Terror weren't allowed to have childhoods, and not allowed to live as free, grown men. So maybe one like me, of my age and homeland, goes back in our memories to the few, brief springs of optimism."

James reached out and warmly jostled François by the upper arm. "We're really not so different, you know."

"How so?"

"You may not be up on your Irish history – and trust me, there's a shit-show – but when Audrey and me was coming up, our folks, everyone we knew, was still traumatized by the Irish 'Rebellion' of 1789."

"Touched," Audrey added, "just like you say. People walked around with hollow eyes, dug out it seems by the horrors they witnessed – and hearts too heavy to bear."

"They were sad?" François asked.

"No," James replied. "They were angry. Angry and full of a sense of sub-jugation. I mean, what was the British lion doing on the throat of the Irish people in the first place!"

"And the aftermath was something awful." Audrey grew upset.

James explained her thoughts. "Not only were the actual lads involved in the fighting round up and shot, but so were all the intellectuals. All of them; a whole generation. You see, they'd set their names to a document – like the Yanks did to their Declaration of Independence – only, just as Ben. Franklin boasted, the pat-riots of freedom would either 'hang together, or assuredly be hanged separately,' and the signers from Trinity College in Dublin were indeed strung up in the University's courtyard by . . . those . . . . " Now James was upset.

"So"—Audrey picked up the ball—"your Terror, and our Freedom Strug-gle of '89 – it just means we grew up pretty much the same way."

Their waitress arrived and scooped up the empty entree platter. Right behind her was the barman. He had an oval dish piled high with pieces of roast goose, around which were brown-butter mushrooms.

The waitress came back with a covered vegetable tureen. She unlidded it, and familiar smells wafted out to François. He righted himself a bit in his seat to see inside. "What is it, please?"

The barman supplied the answer as he set down the gravy boat of creamy bread sauce. "Them is potato rounds cooked low and slow in the renderings from the goose."

"Pomme au fondant!" François was clearly pleased. "Wonderful."

"He's French," James explained to the barman, who was parting with a queer look for the other man at the table.

This time, François didn't play 'Mam,' but he did play *maître d'hôtel,* stan-ding and making quick work of carving the goose and dishing it up. Almost absent-mindedly, he asked, "And kids? Don't you have any?"

Being busy, hungry and a bit buzzed, François missed the on-rushing veil of sadness wash over Audrey. He did catch James' hand reaching out to rest atop his wife's. "Soon after we were married, Audrey was . . . with child. But, come a few months later, we lost the baby."

"*Oh, mon dieu.* I'm sorry to hear that."

"It's all right." Audrey had bucked up. "What matters is the here and now. A Christmas Eve in a foreign land: we share that in common too. We've been removed from our mother cultures by circumstances, but we have one another to lean on."

François, still standing, was taken by surprise. Despite his ingrained caution regarding 'outsiders,' he felt a warmth build towards the couple. He set down his cutlery, picked up his stout. "I'll drink to that. That, and to a happier future."

"A more equitable future," James amended.

The three touched rims and drank. Feeling just a tiny bit warmer inside than before, François half wondered if it were the beer and not sentiments heating him up.

Audrey rose too and spooned out a couple of potato rounds onto each plate.

As they sat down to dig in, someone near the window at the front of the pub began playing a concertina. The tones were slow and sombre, and yet imbued with a diffuse spirituality.

"Some of the little ones will sing now," said James.

"Sing and busk," corrected his wife.

"*Busk?*"

"Yes," continued Audrey. "Back home, child carollers will go door to door in the villages and cities and collect a few coins for their Christmas cheer the next day."

"But here," said James, "they carol from table to table, collecting *more* than a few pennies in the process!"

Now a group of fine-looking children stood patient as angels before a booth and started putting lyrics to the haunting melody coming from the squeeze-box.

> "*Good people all, this Christmas time,*
> *Consider well and bear in mind . . . *"

Enjoying his roast goose, but more specially, his potatoes, François asked, "What song is this?"

"The Wexford Carol," replied Audrey.

"It's beautiful."

The undercooks nodded agreement as they continued to eat.

> "*Near Bethlehem did shepherds keep*
> *Their flocks of lambs and feeding sheep . . . *"

"There are no *English* carols this old. This song dates from the 1400s and it's been sung every Christmastime in Ireland from its day to ours."

François let James' words sink in. It was so different in France, where *le Noël* was an issue more than a holiday, buffeted by political and conservative winds to the point that any true sentiments surrounding the ceremonies were lost to almost everyone.

While he was musing these 'grand,' public-wide considerations, a quiet scene at the bar caught his attention. A young couple – working class, by their tidy-but-worn attire – stood oblivious to the hurly-burly going on around them. Close together, in fact, face to face, the young man extracted a small bundle from his coat pocket. The brown paper- and twine-wrapped gift was gently placed in the young woman's hand. She kissed him briefly and then unwrapped – but François could not see whatever the gift was.

> *"Good people all, this Christmas time,*
> *Consider well and bear in mind . . . "*

It made him sad. Sad that Christmas was ever politicized in France in the first place. For it was at essence no more than this: people sharing intimate moments with the ones they loved.

François drained the rest of his beer, looking away.

James suddenly laughed; he'd been observing the Frenchman. "And where's the boss-man tonight?"

"Honestly," said François, "I don't know or care."

Audrey laughed too, her tone joking, "Maybe Carême's with his new convert!"

"Who?" François puzzled.

"Thomas Daniels!" James blurted.

"Yes, he's taken particular shine to a certain ashen-haired youth. If I were you, I'd better watch out . . . . "

Although Audrey continued in the spirit of levity, it all became too much for François. He set his silverware down. He stared at his plate. "I fear I will be set aside; replaced. Replaced just as I 'replaced' Carême's old protégé. He makes me feel alone, but I care for him no matter how often he leaves me to go hobnob with Kitchiner and the English gentry."

The couple were taken aback.

François regarded them with brimming eyes. "You can't understand how much he's done for me . . . things closer than any brother would do—" François tried to gather his thoughts. "How great a love must a person have to *do* that for another?"

James and Audrey may not have understood the drink-laden and mawkish words, but they drank down the intelligence greedily.

"Perhaps," suggested Audrey, "you are too much under his sway. Maybe he dominates you without you realizing—"

"You do not understand *l'égalitarisme*. No two men are more equal than Carême and I, and I owe him everything."

The carollers drew closer to their table; they were finishing up with the Wexford Carol.

James reached out to take François' hand. He said very slowly, "You, *mon ami*, have tippled a bit too much stout." Then he laughed, patting the hand before pulling back. "We should indulge in another old Irish Christmas tradition."

"What's that," François said, gathering himself to wipe his eyes.

"A jump in the sea! Nothing better than a cold-water plunge to drive off the doldrums!"

François chuckled despite himself. A dip in the sea didn't sound half bad. He wasn't used to being emotional with strangers. When he glanced up, the five children of the singing group stood at their table with the concertina player a few paces off by the bar. This man struck up a fresh tune.

The new melody unfolded at a slow walking measure. It had an underlying beat like a soldier's drum.

All the room grew hushed as a five-year-old boy started off in solo.

> *"The Minstrel-boy to war is gone,*
> *In the ranks of death you'll find him;*
> *His father's sword he has girded on,*
> *And his wild harp slung behind him—"*

The other children sang the chorus.

> *"'Land of song!' – said the warrior-bard,*
> *'Though all the world betray thee,*
> *One sword, at least, thy rights shall guard,*
> *One faithful harp shall praise thee!'*
>
> *The Minstrel fell! – but the foeman's chain*
> *Could not bring his proud soul under;*
> *The harp he loved ne'er spoke again,*
> *For he tore its chords asunder."*

François' emotions swelled as the little boy continued on to the climax of his solo verse.

> *"And said, 'No chains shall sully thee,*
> *Thou soul of love and bravery!*
> *Thy songs were made for the Brave and Free,*
> *And shall never sound in slavery!'"*

After several moments of moved silence, applause began from the front of the taproom. It made its way back, and soon, the little party of three Pavilion workers were on their feet. Audrey wiped her tears, and the men fished out a generous supply of coins, which they made sure to press into each child's hand.

By the time the ruckus died down, and they'd re-taken their seats, the little ensemble had moved to another corner of the establishment to continue their serenading. This coincided with the moment the table was cleared of the main-course dishes and a plate of three single-portion-sized pies was set down. In addition, the empty stout tankards were taken away and replaced with a trio of whiskey tumblers.

To François' inquisitive glance at the pastry, James replied, "Mince tarts. It wouldn't be Christmas without having at least one a year. Help yourself!"

François took one, but Audrey proposed a toast. She raised her glass, waiting for the other two to do likewise – and said, "Again, let us drink to a brighter future to come - and to a liberated Ireland!"

"Amen," muttered James, with a steely glint in his eyes.

After they downed the amber drought in one go, François felt the burn and sliding warmth move from throat to belly.

> *"... With the poor, the mean, the lowly,*
> *Lived on Earth our Saviour Holy ... "*

Just then, Audrey turned serious. "And, François, remember the words of Jeremiah. 'For it shall come to pass,' saith the Lord of Hosts, 'that *his* yoke about your neck will break; that *his* rope about your arms will burst; that *by* him you shall no longer be enslaved to foreign powers.' Take control, like James and I have."

"Get freedom at any price. All means justify the ends." The dark cast was back upon James Keenan's eyes, but François didn't have time to think about it.

> *"... And our eyes at last shall see him,*
> *Through his own redeeming love ... "*

The regulator clock on the wall above the bar began to strike twelve. All in the room fell silent, except the now *a cappella* children.

> *"We shall see him but in heaven,*
> *Set at God's right hand on high,*
> *When like stars his children will be crowned*
> *All in white and gathered close around."*

The midnight hour was struck with the chorale's crescendo. Slowly, voices all about the room began wishing a low and earnest *"Nollaig shona dhuit"* to their loved ones.

James and Audrey did too, briefly kissing before turning to François. In unison, they said:

"And a Happy Christmas to you."

Chapter 9: Wednesday, 25th December, or Tales Out of School

Christmas Morning broke damp and drear over Brighton. At the first peek of cloudy light upon the eastern prospect, coal fires across the city sent up polluted smudges. These got widened into inky trails by the westerly breeze, choking the already Lenten air with the sharp smell of sulphur.

None of that mattered to the residents of the Pavilion. Thick curtains before clamped windows ensured the 'natural' was kept at bay. And the roasting flames coming from the meat on spits for the poor formed a special little smogbank lingering around the onion domes, tent rooves and dragon weathervane of the Water Tower ensured the Pavilion took on an especially unhealthful aspect.

But inside – under those Venetian stuccoed follies – the staff had no time to think of their health, or indeed to make themselves merry; those would have to wait until tomorrow. For now, their focus was to serve, and to serve the Regent's Royal Guests to the best of their abilities, if on this one day and none of the rest. For like Trimalchio's sign hard upon his dining room door, the Prince would keep 364 Christmases at his board, and on the one day a year he should by established rites entertain his staff, he'd go out to eat.

Christmas Morning also found Carême occupied by his usual *levée.*

As he departed George's suite, he found Lady Morgan in the North Chamber Gallery. She pretended to read a book in one of the faux bamboo chairs she'd drawn up to the fire.

"Ah! Dear Carême."

"Madame Morgan, enchantée." He gifted her a slight bow; that is, once she'd risen, closed her book, and approached.

"May I have the honour of walking you back to your kitchen?"

He extended his arm. "My pleasure, My Lady."

They began descending the grand staircase. The natural light behind the elaborately painted Chinese figures seemed to dim this morning.

They reached the landing. "I trust your confabulation with the Regent went well."

"Yes, we went through the plans for the day's dinner at 3 o'clock, and the supper buffet for the ball later tonight."

"Oh, yes, the ball." Sydney Morgan sounded weary already. "What time will it commence, again?"

"Half-past ten."

"Well, I will do my *duty,* which, as I am a woman, requires me to put on a brave face, and an equally courageous frock!"

"Courageous?"

"Yes, loose in all the right places; tight in all the wrong."

The friends shared another heart-felt laugh.

"The Prince also enquired after my special menu for the Princess."

"I do so worry about Charlotte's constitution, and what's proving to be a very touchy pregnancy."

They turned and started descending to the principal floor. The chef, for his part, was in no hurry, having reason to anticipate with dread a potential meeting with François at the end of this walk.

Carême gestured to all of the sumptuous décor. "I sometimes wonder if Brighton and the Pavilion are simply too much stimulus for the girl. The girl the Princess still is at twenty years of age."

"Yes, Carême, you could be entirely correct. The Pavilion is a haven of excess, as is every home the Regent pulls around him like a blanket of comfort against the 'imposing world,' but still, concerning Charlotte's health, I . . . . "

"But still, what, *Madame?*"

Lady Morgan smiled and shook her head. "Perhaps I'm too cagy, and it serves a body no good to tell tales out of school—"

"However?"

"However – let's just say I have my suspicions, suspicions you yourself have raised, and I've enlisted the help of the good Doctor."

Carême did not press her for details, knowing they would emerge if, and only if, her misgivings proved true. Instead, he rendered a polite laugh. "Ah! In that case, Lady Morgan, you have placed your mission in capable hands."

They stepped through the stair hall into the Central Corridor. As the illumination through the skylight was none too great, the charming metal torchieres were lit. These rose floor to ceiling, standing away from the walls with their elaborate design of crossed weapons behind shields and a large serpent wrapped around the top; the snake craned its neck forward to support a lantern in its mouth. The authentic Chinese lights were silk octagons painted with flowers on their panels, and had long red tassels. These wall fixtures matched a central, European-made example hanging - as high as a man is tall – from the middle of the skylight.

Carême had never seen this space fully illuminated, and it charmed him.

Lady Sydney Morgan gripped the chef's arm a little tighter. "There are such resplendent hopes for Charlotte, and I suppose for Leopold too. He is so dashing and charming—"

"But what of the *régent?*"

"Please do not mistake me. I do not disparage the Prince Regent, but George inherited his father's men, and as the King is not . . . departed from us . . . there is nothing the Prince can do to move the country along."

Carême found Lady Morgan's comments relevant to his own experiences. "We French believed we had such a One to move our nation along."

The Irish novelist joked, "And now you're lucky to have a country at all!"

A column of heat rose through Carême, and he hoped the woman did not notice.

Sydney Morgan slowed her gait and drew the pair up to the great model of George's completed marine villa. Their eyes scanned the veritable cityscape roof of colonettes.

"I apologize," she cooed softly, "but on the other hand, your nation has had uninterrupted leadership."

His puzzled expression played about her mercurial features.

"Talleyrand!" she exclaimed. "Prime Minister under Bonaparte, the Provisional Government, and now, under the restored Louis Bourbon. *That's* leadership."

"I believe, *Madame,* we in France have another word for it, but it won't bear repeating before a lady."

Now both laughed.

The chef continued, "And we've yet to find the right element that will exterminate him."

"Or combination of elements. But tell me, is it true Talleyrand had such a contentious relationship with his counterpart, Cambacérès? It almost strikes me as a love-hate working arrangement."

"Arch-Chancellor Cambacérès was a uniquely gifted survivor. In that, the two men were alike."

"Was; were. You prove my point. Cambacérès, the greatest legal mind of our age, the author of The Napoleonic Law Code, is no longer in government. The man's presumably on a farm somewhere out in the countryside, while meanwhile, Talleyrand in Paris only continues to consolidate *his* power."

Carême nodded. "I dare not refute the obvious."

"But what I wanted to ask, is this"—Lady Morgan's tone bent low—"is it true Talleyrand disparaged Cambacérès for – shall we say – the other's *Grecian* inclination?"

She grinned, having no desire to run down a person born under the self-same star as Carême.

"I can assure you, Prince Talleyrand has no qualms working with anyone, even society's lowest of the low – like Archbishops."

The two shared a genuinely warm bout of laughter.

On the move again, Lady Morgan led the way through the door to the servant's central passageway. They continued on at a leisurely pace towards the kitchens.

"You said," Carême stated, somewhat hesitantly, "Leopold is admired in England, but what manner of character do you think the real man, the one under the uniform, possesses?"

"Difficult to say. Shrewd, for sure. He too is a wily survivor, riding the winds of change instead of allowing himself to be buffeted by them."

"He was the Czar's right-hand man."

"True. From what I know, when Napoleon's troops invaded his German Principality, he travelled to Paris and threw himself at Bonaparte's feet. The Little

General was so charmed to be given the role of a forgiving Alexander the Great, he made Leopold a member of his inner circle."

"Yes," observed the Frenchman, "but it did not last long."

"No. Leopold embezzled a fortune, fled to the Czar and took up arms to free his homeland."

"Very sagacious; very far-sighted, it turns out. And now, *he* is here, married to the most powerful second-in-line to a throne in Europe."

"Your point being, my dear Carême?"

"My point is to wonder how much he truly loves Charlotte. I have grown quite fond of her."

They arrived at the portal of the Great Kitchen.

"I think the question you raise will only be answered in time, Chef. But perhaps it is a moot point."

"Ah, oui? Why so?"

"Because there is no doubt whatsoever that the Princess loves him."

"Yes. That is true. He makes her happy, and that takes priority over all else, for now."

The friends entered the busy beehive kitchen and stopped. Good Christmas smells enveloped them.

"It's like a battleground in here!" she said. Adding, "Is it true Talleyrand is fond of quoting the Great Macedonian King: 'I'm better afeared of a hundred-sheep army led by a lion than a hundred-lion army led by a sheep'?"

"Yes, Lady Morgan, but kindly remember, Talleyrand is also fond of saying: 'God gave mankind small-talk so that we may safely disguise our true intentions'."

They chuckled and disengaged arms.

Carême asked, "Will you be at Kitchiner's tomorrow?"

She shook her head, becoming mysterious as she added, "He did not invite me."

"No; no; no; *Madame.* It must be an oversight on the Doctor's part."

She blushed, befuddling him a bit.

In another moment, her gaze alighted on the large regulator clock. "It's nearly ten. I must be off to meet my husband at the stables. We're planning on riding down the coast and working up an appetite for your magisterial dinner today! I told him I simply must try some of everything you put on the table. I know people in the coming years will want to know what it was like."

Her smile kindled the chef's heart.

They parted with Lady Morgan kissing Carême's cheeks.

"Que votre Noël joyeux et lumineux, mon ami."

"Et votre aussi, ma chère madame Morgan."

Once she'd passed through the door, Carême stiffened. He sensed a pair of eyes on him, and he didn't have to look to know to whom they belonged.

The *chef de cuisine* made his way to his office, leaving the door ajar.

François quietly slipped in. He closed the door behind him in reverse fashion, leaning against it slowly. As he began to speak, Carême was occupied by taking off his street jacket and putting on his chef's whites.

"Chef Carême, there are no incidents to report in your absence. The Undercooks of Roasting are ahead of schedule, and you'll be able to dress the cold quail soon. All the base sauces are made and being kept warm in the *bains-marie* for you to season and create the compound sauces at your leisure."

François took a couple of paces into the room.

"*Oui?* That's good." Carême started strapping his scabbard of knives atop his apron.

"Furthermore, the staff in the Cold Kitchen are ready to turn out the *entremets* for you to decorate examples they should replicate."

"Good." Carême was fully dressed. "Anything else to report?"

"Well, one. Thorndyke has been temporarily demoted to rank-and-file server for his antics in the dining room when we moved the *pièce montée*. Word came down 20 minutes ago, and needless to say, the former Chief Footman is angry."

Flatly, Carême replied, "I see."

"I know this slice of just deserts is your doing, even though you have rankled the Kitchen Comptroller to no end by sidestepping him."

In the same monotone as before, the chef replied, "His Highness wants to be informed, and makes the decisions; not I."

Carême made to leave, walking towards the door.

François stepped in front, touching the other man by the arm. "I realized something last night. I know part of my current state is due to pure homesickness. The Irish couple woke me up to this."

"You were with them, last night?"

"Yes. They took me to an Irish pub for supper, and many people there were already celebrating Christmas."

In his head, Carême was relieved to know François spent the night with them and not in the arms of Charlotte's lady's maid. He softened his stance, withdrawing his arm from his partner's grip. "As for homesickness, I can understand. I miss so much of Paris. But, we must bear it for the higher, artistic purpose of why we are here; we must be the homeland for each other, François."

"Yes. I know that now. Know it after seeing so many families away from home leaning on one another. In a way, it's the first real Christmas I've ever experienced. It's made me see what's important."

"I'm sorry you never had any joyful *Noëls* when a child, and then, afterward – like me – you were too busy making other peoples' Christmases merry to feel much joy for yourself."

"Yes, Chef. I wanted to tell this to you . . . last night, but you locked your door. I tried it when I got back at one."

"*Oui.* I needed my strength for today's campaign."

"But still, it was hard to go to sleep thinking I'd upset you. And . . . it was even harder to get to sleep while not next to you."

Carême, thoroughly melted, tried to lighten the mood. "It's your own damn fault. You and your Lyon stubbornness."

François chuckled. "I can see that you know it's true."

For a moment, Carême quavered audibly, like he was debating something. In the end he went behind his desk. "I had thought I would give you this later tonight, but . . . . " He unlocked the drawer and extracted the wrapped bundle he'd stashed there earlier. "I have this for you."

"But—"

"No buts. Here." He gently pressed the gift in François' hands. "Go on. Open it."

François merely stared at the package.

Carême continued softly, "I know you never had a proper Christmas before, so I wanted to do something personal for you – for us. Won't you open it?"

François tried to control his emotions, remembering the glass-bowl nature of Carême's office. He tugged on the string and unwrapped the paper, soon finding himself holding a heavy cardboard box. Although small, the top contained an embossed oval with black letters: *Smith Bros., Brighton.*

Prying off the lid, the man saw a silver locket on a long sturdy chain.

"Open it up," Carême said.

When François did, he found the plain door snapped on a hinge. Opposite the lid, under a bevelled crystal, nestled a lock of Carême's hair. The strands were secured by a tiny blue ribbon.

"Only you need know, *Villon,* whose hair is in that locket."

Without Carême comprehending it – or suspecting why – François' heart broke a little further. "I don't know what to say. Perhaps only, thank you, and I don't deserve it."

"Of course you do. You said yourself you saw last night how Christmas is about having those near you consider family. And you are certainly that to me."

François mumbled, more for himself than anyone else, *"Mais, ou sont les neiges d'antan?"*

Carême asked softly, "What was that, *mon cher?"*

"I was quoting my namesake: 'But where disappear the snows of yesteryear?'"

The chef grew unexpectedly emotional. He lived for François' rare moments of vulnerability like these.

"I truly love it, Antonin. I'll treasure it always."

François let the empty box fall on the desk. Clutching the locket manfully, he strode up to Carême, took him by his upper arms and kissed both his cheeks like a true Frenchman. *"Bon Noël, mon amour."*

"Et toi aussi, Villon."

Then François stepped back, making sure his eyes were dry, kissed the locket once while holding Carême's gaze, and slipped the chain around his neck.

As he lifted his collar to let the silver rest against his bare chest, he said, "Your army awaits, *Général."*

The words caused Carême to unconsciously grip his knife holster.

The pair opened the door to the sights and sounds of a battlefield kitchen.

Four and a half hours after the start of the celebratory meal, an exhausted Carême glanced at the clock: it was a quarter to nine, and the banquet was almost over.

There was still a frenzy in the Great Kitchen, but it mostly related to cleaning and putting away. However, at least the roasting fires had been dampened, which for days had fed a noxious kickback of fumes into the whole of the servants' quarters. Now, the cool of the night from the open clerestory windows could stroke Carême's cheek. In the chef, the weakening effect of the carbon monoxide in his system felt like a pang of hunger. It niggled at the back of his mind as well.

François, wearing his best 'Republican Suit' and face flushed a rosy hue, came to the chef straight from the dining room with an update.

"Chef, all the plates are cleared, and the guests are having Port while exchanging small pleasantries. They'll break up into parties of men and women soon and head to the Drawing Rooms."

"But," Carême asked earnestly, "how was the dinner received?"

François stood fully upright. "All were amazed and delighted. This was surely a meal—"

They were interrupted.

"What is it, Henry?" François asked one of his suddenly ashen footmen who'd walked up to them.

"You are wanted."

Carême and François exchanged a silent glance, as if to say, 'Who, me?'

Henry cleared his throat and started again, this time, unable to contain his excitement. "Monsewer Carême, the Prince is asking for you to join him in the Banqueting Room!"

"Oh."

Still, not one of the three moved a muscle.

Suddenly, Carême began fumbling with the strap of his knife holster. "François, help me."

The *maître d'hôtel* did, and in another moment, the man was also free of his apron. He started straightening his jacket and neck scarf. "Do I . . . ?"

"Yes," a beaming François replied, "you look splendid."

"Merci. You will come and be by my side, François."

If the young man had something to smile about before, now – with validation from his mentor and beloved – François Distré glowed from within. Chef and *maître d'hôtel* began their glorious march of triumph. Those in the kitchen stopped what they were doing to watch. It was the same with table deckers and footmen in the Decking Room.

Almost in a daze, the pair entered the banqueting hall. The Regent was seated at the far end of the table. This walk afforded Carême a chance to drink in the sights and sounds of the room. The lights were blazing; the décor, charming; and never before had the chef been in a space so simultaneously grand and intimate. The glint of gold did not have to compete with the sparkle of the Royal family members chatting and admiring small gifts. At the table's narrow end closest to the fireplace and doors to the Decking Room, Queen Charlotte was ensconced with two of her senior Duke sons on either side. Carême noticed William and Adelaide on one side with another woman and several ruddy children – all of them a Royal *his,* but none of them of Royal *hers.*

François, for his part, admired their fully *chinois* sugar work *pièces montées* on the three huge sideboards. The table itself was set with flowers and fruit on silver-gilt stands, *à l'anglaise,* between sparkling candelabras. He saw the happy faces, wondering how real any of their interactions were. He noticed too the signs of gift-exchange, but focused on the carton boxes, like the one he had received, from which jewellery had been extracted.

The two Frenchmen drew up to the Prince Regent's left. It was Charlotte, seated at the right-hand of her father, who met Carême's eyes first. George was talking with Leopold seated to Charlotte's side.

The Princess appeared bored in her fancy gown, tortured-up hair, from which rose three enormous ostrich feathers à la Prince of Wales. More so, she was pale to the point of looking colourless. As she clutched her tea cup – for she had no wine glass, only her nursery tea pot before her – her sorrowful expression seemed to plead with the chef 'Rescue me.'

The chef almost wanted to ask if she felt all right; however, Leopold then noticed Carême and drew the Prince Regent's attention to the man.

"Ah, Carême!" His Highness exclaimed, *"très magnifique!"*

By the Prince's slight slurring of words, Carême could tell George had overindulged already on his favourite maraschino liqueur.

"By the by, Old Sport, I don't suppose you've met a fellow architect of yours – one who works in limestone and stucco instead of sugar-paste and icing."

The Regent gestured to a middle-aged, balding man seated to the Prince's immediate left. To Carême's eyes, the 'fellow architect' was frumpy in his attire and anything but distinguished looking. "No, *mon Prince,* I don't believe I've had the honour."

"Mr. John Nash," the Regent continued, "I'd like *you* to meet my cook, *monsieur* Antonin Carême."

The chef bowed his head. "It's a pleasure to meet you."

"The pleasure is mutual, Mr. Carême. Your eye for colour, design and detail is unsurpassed."

As Carême was of the same opinion, he glanced briefly at François and nodded.

In the maitre-d's thoughts, now that he'd finally seen the Pavilion's architect, he examined Nash's pug-nose, realizing a beautiful mind lived behind a not-so beautiful exterior. In a Classical sense, Carême was young and composed, while Nash was wild and Socratic in his maturity.

George chuckled. "My two *wunderkinds* of design – architect and pastry cook – and both are the greatest of Regency Britain." He took a sip of spirits, leaving everybody hanging, before he continued. "As a matter of fact, I think Nash has further abilities yet untapped. We may be calling upon your urban design skills in the near future."

The sitting man bowed his bald pate. "I'm always at your service, Your Highness."

Without further ado, the Prince groaned as he hoisted himself, and his full belly, to an upright position. He tapped his glass with a dessert fork. "Please, dear Mother; dear worthy Royal peers of my family; join me in cheering the remarkable architect of this feast!"

Chairs slid, food-weary bodies rose – some, like the Queen, with the assistance of attendant footmen.

François himself went to assist Princess Charlotte, but as soon as he got behind her chair, a brusque Leopold was there waving him off.

François stepped back with a hostile bow.

The Regent continued, holding his glass mid-stomach. *"Our* valuable chef has worked for the likes of Cambacérès, Talleyrand, the Czar of Russia – and indeed, the vanquished emperor, Bonaparte – but under My family banner, he has come to full blossom. Such is evidenced by his . . . . "

The voice of the Regent faded in Carême's hearing, and despite a brief glance at François to confirm he was none too pleased by George's comments, the chef's attention was focused on Charlotte. If possible, she was even paler than when he'd first seen her. She gripped onto her Consort's arm instead of standing fully on her own. The cook wondered if she'd eaten anything tonight other than sugar lumps and chunks of candy.

George's words came back into range.

He raised his glass higher, saying, " . . . And so this day will be one to remember, the first true Christmas after a generation of wars, and the *first* with reborn hope for the future." His loving gaze fell on Charlotte and her belly.

She put on a brave face. It was a dutiful one for all those around the table turned to her.

The Regent's toast crescendoed: "Here's to Princess Charlotte Augusta of Wales, and to Antonin Carême - a prince among men, and a Chef amongst Princes!"

A chorus of "Hear; Hear" went around the assembled, and glasses were brought to lips.

As they drank – Leopold's hands off of her – the tea cup tumbled out of Charlotte's grip. It shattered noisily on her silverware and broke a vase of flowers.

In the next instant, the girl collapsed unconscious, her chin smashing ignominiously on the edge of the table.

Women screamed; men drew in air. There was panic coaeval with the impulse to suppress it.

Elements of chaos instantly arose. Female relatives voiced opinions almost as shrieks: "Lay her flat!"; "Sit her up!"; "Get the child water!" Men mumbled optimistic retorts: "She's all right."; "Silly, excitable girl."; "No need to make a fuss."

All of this contributed to a riot of indecision, one which continued as George and Leopold looked on the crumpled figure.

Then, when others began to move from the table to crowd her in, Leopold quieted them with the simple lifting of his finger. With that single, silent motion, he took command as a true, dominant leader should ever do – by example.

He told his father-in-law "Clear a path" before bending and scooping up Charlotte in his arms like a lifeless ragdoll. Leopold carried his wife from the room with a nearly preternatural calm.

The Regent touched Carême's shoulder. "Call for Kitchiner."

Hours later, the initial hand-wringing uproar of the entire Pavilion, both upstairs and down, had settled into a staid nervousness concerning the Princess. Being an age of Faith, many hands were folded in supplicant fervour that the cup would pass from "England's Only Hope" and Charlotte would feel better by sunup. Naturally, news of the heir-apparat's status as *under the weather* was to stay under the roof of the Royal Brighton household at all costs. The night time onset of what-ever was ailing her helped keep it under wraps for the time being.

Alone in his room, Carême barely noticed the clock's advance. Now at 2 in the morning, he still sat at his desk, still recording the day's culinary triumphs and setbacks in his cooking journal, the notes that one day he'd use to write his culinary *magnus opus*. Perhaps unknowingly he did it as a form of his own secular prayer – waiting anxiously for news of the Princess but not impotently focusing on it in his thoughts.

In the sputtering light from the candle lamp, he wrote:

Cette journée a marqué une avancée dans la nouvelle esthétique de la grande cuisine classique, je crois. Car, pour la première fois, j'ai osé servir un plat composé entièrement garni d'autres préparations de poissons. Fini les tranches de jambon, les coqs

I believe today marked an advancement in the new aesthetic of *la grande cuisine classique*. For, for the first time, I dared to serve a composed fish dish entirely garnished with other fish prepar-ations. Gone were the slices of ham, the poached cocks-combs, the quail legs – all the silly luxuries of the ancient methods – replaced by practical and taste-appropriate accompaniments.

Today's dish was some excellent-tasting local pike, the flesh ten-der, white and flavourful, so I poached some dumplings of sole, and some dumplings of crawfish, and decorated the rim of the tray in a pretty white-and-pink alternation.

In honour of the occasion, I believe I shall call the dish *brochet à la Régence* – or, Pike à la Regency. The recipe begins with one entire, five-pound fish, as fresh as possible. Clean—

Carême's thoughts were interrupted.

He listened closely for a repeat of the sound he'd just heard. There it was again – a light rapping on his door. He stood, realizing how dark the room had become. The chef grabbed a candle and walked it to the interconnecting door to François' room. Just as he placed his hand on the knob, the knocking appeared for a third time – on the door from the corridor.

"I say there, Carême"—Kitchiner's voice sounded from the other side—"have you gone to bed?"

"No; no – I'm awake." He let the Doctor in, who was carrying his medical bag.

As Carême went and lit more lights, growing astounded at how late it had become, Kitchiner dropped his kit and collapsed in the chef's armchair, his lank frame almost sixty degrees in exhaustion against it.

Carême closed the door.

The Doctor's spectacles glinted in the fresh lamplight as he relayed, "I've just been with the Queen. Poor woman; a thoroughly decent sort, she's had to live with upset for years. Her husband's madness, sons' – in the plural – moral recalcitrance, and now this."

"And how is the Princess?"

"She's fine! A lot of to-do over a fainting spell. And that's what I told the Queen; and that's what I told Prince George. She's fine. Merely tired from all the festivities and"—the Doctor winked—"the fine food."

A whinge of comprehension contorted Carême's face for a moment. "And what is the Princess', eh . . . level of awareness?"

'Her conscious level?"

"*Oui.*"

"Embarrassed! She wishes to get out of bed, but I advised Leopold to keep her there at least until breakfast tomorrow."

"Sound advice, no doubt, but I . . . ah, wonder if . . . she's—"

"Wonder what, dear Chef?"

Carême replied awkwardly. "Oh, please forgive me; it was a mere stray of a thought. Never mind."

Carême's worst suspicions were just at that moment confirmed. The door from the hallway burst open, and François and Brigitte rushed in, panicked and panting.

The lady's maid gasped for air. "Come quick, Doctor. She's . . . she's—"

"*Échoua,*" François said.

Kitchiner got to his feet. He removed his glasses to see less better. "She's what?"

"The baby, sir," said Brigitte. "A boy, stillborn, just now."

Kitchiner fumbled for his medical bag and rushed away with Princess Charlotte's companion maid.

The two Frenchmen were alone.

"What happened, François?"

"Everything seemed fine. I was with Brigitte in her chambers, when suddenly, there was screaming from Charlotte's room next door. We rushed in, found blood, and Leopold already there, holding his crying wife. Oh, Carême—"

All at once, François' naturally engaged human emotions of pity got shut out by a hard smile of the kind Carême had often seen during the reign of Terror.

"I'm sorry for the Princess," François continued, "but it's just deserts for Leopold; that abuser of France's rights."

Carême paused his thoughts to shake his head. Politics, at a time like this? Although it slightly sickened his stomach to think about it, nevertheless, a message would have to go out to Talleyrand right away.

"*Villon,* it's horrible news, but if you will excuse me." He gestured vaguely to his desk, lying, "I want to finish my recipe for *brochet à la Régence* while it's still fresh in my head."

François appeared stunned. Then he started to cry. "All right. 'It's horrible news,' but don't worry – I won't be bothering you later tonight either. In fact, I'll go lend a shoulder for Brigitte to cry on; to comfort her. It's what normal humans do – lend comfort where and when they can!"

He stormed out, leaving the door wide open.

As Carême went to close and latch it, he thought how sorry he was to inadvertently make François feel unwanted again, but the chef acknowledged to himself he had larger obligations to fulfil.

Chapter 10: Thursday, 26th December, or Boxing Day at the Doctor's

In a reprisal of its performance from the morning before, the sun rose like a coal smothered in the folds of a grey blanket. Boxing Day arrived cold, and the Royal Pavilion – usually so warm and gay – seemed but a gem lodged in the heart of an iceberg.

The crews of the Great Kitchen were busying themselves with the post-breakfast clean-up. It was supposed to be the household's Christmas, with a grand dinner in the Staff Dining Hall at noon. This was the occasion many had been waiting for, for the presents exchanged included a slip of paper to each of the kitchen workers from the Comptroller stating how much their end-of-year bonus would be.

However, news of the Nation's dead baby prince cast a smothering pall over The Peoples' holiday. It was one to match the dreariness of 1816 in general.

At one end of the room, outside his office door, *chef de cuisine* Carême stood in conference with *sous-chef* Bauda and *maître d'hôtel* Distré.

"Per the Regent," Carême said, "His Highness and the Queen will take luncheon together in his chambers. A reduced dinner will be laid at 4 o'clock, Herr Bauda, in the Yellow Drawing Room. You know which items from yesterday are going for the staff's dinner, and which can supply the *relevées* for the Family's meal."

"What about," asked the Sous-chef, "the zugar work monuments in the Banqueting Room? I suggest they be moved to the Ztaff Dining Hall so they can enjoy them there, and the Family – well, they von't have to zee them again."

"A sad necessity," confirmed Carême, "but a good idea. Please have them moved, François."

"Yes, Chef."

As Carême carried on with instructions, the tensions between François and himself were nearly palpable. Although making for an awkward working relationship at the moment, neither dared touch upon what had happened between them early that morning.

"In addition, François, I would like you to prepare a *baba au rhum* for the recuperating Princess. You know how, so I entrust it entirely to you."

A flush of pride coursed through the maitre-d'. It was a badge of honour to be given responsibilities over a dish carrying the master's name on it. *"Oui, Chef!"*

"And when you do, pull Thomas into it so he can learn."

François was crestfallen. "Understood. I'll pull in the *boy.*"

Before Carême had time to react to this, James and Audrey Keenan laughed at a private joke between them. The wife was at the range with an iron kettle, and her husband stood chopping vegetables at the preparation table opposite her. Their jolly – nearly ebullient – mood stuck out like a sore thumb in the down-cast kitchen.

Without any warning, the three men turned the other direction to see an odd sight: Lady Morgan and Doctor Kitchiner entering from the courtyard entrance, both still bundled in their outer winterwear. Right behind them came two dour-looking men in cut-away uniforms – not military; more like a constabulary police force.

The Irish couple very obviously noticed the visitors' presence, but tried to carry on for the moment unconcerned.

Suddenly, they bolted.

Audrey had the longer way to go, while James had a more or less straight line to the Great Kitchen's other door.

He took off, but as soon as he cleared the preparation table, Thomas Daniels kick-slid a crate of cabbages right across the man's path. As Keenan was glancing over his shoulder to gauge his wife's progress, he fell head-long over the crate, spilling it. James twisted his torso to land on the hard stone floor with his back. That knocked the wind out of him, but not enough to prevent him from drawing his chef's knife.

Without missing a beat, Thomas kicked it out of his hands, landing a hard blow on the back of James' knuckles.

Just in time to apprehend him, two more of Kitchiner's men arrived through the door from the Service Corridor.

Meanwhile, with her escape route blocked by the cart and her fallen husband, Audrey quickly mounted and clambered over the preparation table's narrow side, but Lady Morgan arrived there at the same time. She was the one to halt Audrey's escape by grabbing her upper arm. Rage coloured the noblewoman's face. She slapped the cook, hard.

The two constables who had followed her, restrained Audrey from behind and immobilized her. Joined by James pinned between the other policemen, they were led back to where Kitchiner stood waiting.

Lady Morgan joined them, first grabbing the canister of the Princess' special tea. She uncovered it, holding a pinch of it before the Irish couple's faces.

"Chamomile? To soothe the Princess; to keep her quiet and calm."

James and Audrey exchanged a brief, confirming look of guilt.

Doctor Kitchiner took over. "Lady Morgan followed her suspicions and had a sample secreted away for my laboratory to analyze. Not chamomile—"

Lady Morgan threw it in the woman's face. "Yarrow. A known and powerful abortive. You poisoned the Princess' child!"

Audrey's face washed over with a sneer of accomplishment. Almost possessed by a rebellious fever, she recited:

> *"The blood which here was streamed,*
> *With justice to heaven cries!"*

Sydney Morgan was stunned. These were part of the famous poem on Irish Independence by Robert Emmet, chronicler of the 1789 Revolution. Audrey's voice rose in volume.

> *"I claim it on the oppressor's head*
> *Who joys in human woe,*
> *Who drinks the tears by misery shed*
> *And mocks them as they flow."*

One of the constables tried to hush her, but Audrey only became more frantic to get it out.

> *"I claim it o'er his ruinèd isle,*
> *Her wretched children's grave!*
> *Where withered Freedom drops her head*
> *And man but exists a slave."*

Woman to woman, poetical mother to poetical mother, Morgan was desolately sad.

"But part of that poem also says, 'By marked mercy may freedom rise, by cruelty unstained.' For not *all* things are fair in love and war. Not all."

Kitchiner cleared his throat and ushered the constables and prisoners out of the room.

Irony always seems to dog the tracks of honest men; more so, the sincerer they are in their endeavours, the closer to his heels come the biting scorn of others.

So too appears to be the fate of Nations and their people. For British history had been altered irrevocably with Charlotte's stillborn boy, but *the nation* went on about its business unaffected because it did not know. How many course corrections in the night transform what our daylight reality will be in the years to come without our reckoning them. How to tell time, then – properly – if one can never truly make out the hands moving against the Clock's face?

Thus Britain, and the world along with it, had been changed in ways untold because of Charlotte's miscarriage, but on Boxing Day 1816, none of those ways were yet imagined.

At precisely three in the afternoon, Carême rolled up to the Club. As he mounted the final steps, Kitchiner swung wide his portals.

The chef entered amidst the man's smile and twin aromas from the pine-bough wreath on the Good Doctor's door and the smells of simple, substantial food from within the house.

"Ah, *mon très cher, Carême!* Let me take your coat."

While the Doctor closed the door, Carême sloughed his outer winter cape, which Kitchiner took and handed to the waiting door porter.

"Won't you follow me?" Kitchiner proceeded down the corridor. The Club was particularly quiet today. All the office doors stood open and the chambers beyond them appeared dark and unpeopled.

Not trusting how alone they actually were, Carême asked in a confidential tone, "How fares the Princess?"

They had arrived at the lift. Kitchiner let Carême go first, then came a-board and spoke into the mouthpiece. "First floor, please."

As the elevating platform began to rise, the Doctor removed his glasses and told his companion, "It is all so sad, but life must go on." He turned professionally jovial. "I'm pleased to report Charlotte . . . is young and strong."

They arrived at their floor, just one flight up from the street, and the main level of the establishment.

Kitchiner again led the way off the vertical conveyance and into the main corridor, heading back towards the front of the building. The Doctor continued with his original thought.

"Despite the Princess' difficult time with pregnancies, there shall undoubtedly be many healthy, normal children born to the Royal Couple."

To Carême's mind, these wily assurances were fundamental projections of a deeply held hope. But, so most declamatory statements must ever be.

Light poured through the open double door at the end of the passage. Kitchiner explained: "This is the Front Room of the Club. A gathering spot for members to trade in . . . well, intelligence from around the world."

The chamber spanned the entire width of the property along the Esplanade, and was thus as long as Kitchiner's penthouse upstairs. Five tall windows brought an excellent view of the sea beneath their arches. Within this room, leather sofas and arm-chairs clustered about various tables. Some of these were stacked with Newspapers and Periodicals; Carême's stray glance caught one pile topped with *24 heures,* a Swiss daily from Lucerne. He'd seen many a copy in Paris, but none in England.

He could imagine the well-appointed room populated with men smoking cigars, holding papers and chatting with each other about events occurring far and wide. But today, the place was deserted.

"Perhaps," Kitchiner said as he strolled, "we could convince you to roll up your sleeves and prepare something today. Something simple; untaxing, naturally."

Carême hemmed. "Well, I don't know . . . . "

"My holiday larder is full. Perhaps take a look once you get upstairs and see if inspiration strikes."

"I doubt, Doctor, inspiration will be lacking, but may I ask why you want me to cook at this gathering?"

"Simple." He hauled up before the fireplace at the end of the room. The coals were lit and pumped generous heat into the unoccupied space. "In times of grievous woe, there is an honesty in hand-to-hand food prepared for one's friends that all the tributes of *gourmandise* cannot match."

Carême bowed, slightly. "Then I will acquiesce and look at what manner of provisions you have, *and* I'll coordinate anything I make with Mrs. Lister's dinner plans."

"Excellent." The Good Doctor radiated warmth.

Suddenly, the hollow grandeur of this space struck Carême as a metaphor for 'the spectacle' of an empty high-class life. Appearances may rule, and luxuries are often pointless simply for lack of another person close enough with which to enjoy them. The Doctor's invitation to cook was an attempt to let pretence drop in favour of the personal connection they'd experienced preparing the sole several months ago. Carême would embrace the opportunity.

The Doctor gestured with his right hand. "Shall we?" He led the way into a second chamber whose double doors stood open at this end of the parlour.

A grand library was laid out for dessert service. The central round table, under a tiered crystal chandelier, was spread with a damask cloth. Upon this were arranged various sweets, buffet style. The item closest to the chef was a four-pound round of Stilton blue cheese. It sat on a silver platter with a linen napkin wrapping the comestible's lower third.

In proper symmetry to this – on the opposite side of the table – sat a cake the same proportions as the Stilton, only this confection was a marzipan-encased 'Christmas Cake.' It made Carême smile to think such holiday fruitcakes were an unbroken tradition dating from ancient Roman times to the very present day.

Kitchiner explained, "After our meal, we'll adjourn here to stretch our legs, and"—he motioned to a sideboard with decanters of Port and Sherry—"offer a toast to the Yuletide season."

"Delightful." Carême continued his way around the table. There were many plates of *sablé* and other sugared biscuits for the ladies to sample. When he got halfway between the blue cheese and the Christmas Cake, he encountered a third cardinal-point of the layout – a glistening *blanc-manger,* that classic moulded jelly of almond milk. Frosted grapes, in colours ranging from pale green to deep purple, surrounded the base of the *entremet* and glistened in crystalline sparkles.

Kitchiner, arms behind his back, came up to the chef. "Do you approve?"

"Oh, yes, Doctor. A wonderful choice – a dish unaltered since Taillevent's times in the 1300s until today."

Kitchiner was pleased. "I knew you and I are kindred spirits when it comes to 'understanding' the value of culinary tradition."

"Yes," the chef agreed. "It means enjoying the past creations as living gifts; not mouldering curiosities for the library shelves."

"Most assuredly so," confirmed the Doctor.

Carême's eyes were drawn to the fourth compass-point of the arrangement; an empty spot on the table.

"Ah, that!" exclaimed Kitchiner. "That is for the guest of honour – the Pudding – the King of every Englishman's Christmas."

"*Enchanté.* I look forward to seeing it later."

"That you shall! But, I suppose we should be wending our way up to the other guests."

Carême reached out and stayed him, hand on arm. "Before we do, and I hope you don't mind me asking, but how is it the Keenans, as radicals, could have slipped past your security checks?"

"Simple, Carême, old boy – they weren't *radical* when they were cleared for Royal work."

"*Comment?*"

"The answer lies in the fact that terrorists – like heroes – are born by on-the-spot circumstances. Any one of us could answer the call of it if the stress *and* opportunities were ripe enough."

A blushing sensation rose through the core of Carême. He understood this all too well, and said so. "Yes, Doctor, I witnessed for myself such things during the Reign of Terror. Neighbour against neighbour; brother against brother; children against parents – it was horrific."

"Indeed. That's why we hope a French-style revolution will never come to Britain's shores."

Echoing the Doctor's words from before, Carême replied, "It's all so sad, yet, life must go on. But what of the fate of James and Audrey? What will happen to them."

The Doctor laid it out very matter-of-factly. "First, they'll undergo ten days of systematic torture – mental and bodily – to reveal names of co-conspirators—"

"What if they acted alone?"

"They still have compatriots of like sentiments, and they'll cough up their names. In addition, we've shuttered their local den of criminality – a pub called *The Barrel.* The family who owned it, and several of the regular *habitués,* have been apprehended and will likewise spit up names, naturally. National Security is at stake."

"And after the Keenans' torture?"

Kitchiner shrugged. "That is up to His Highness to decide. After all, it's a Family matter to him."

The Doctor paused, defensively. It was all-too easily read upon the cook's face that Carême was judging Whitehall's techniques harshly.

He continued in a sharper vein, removing his glasses first. "I should warn you, Carême, so you know, that whenever the British mind is confronted with facts concerning English brutality at home and abroad, it quickly makes peace with itself and thinks, all in all - despite all evidence to the contrary – 'British Empire' is and was a good thing. A civilizing force on Earth whose ends absolve any savage means to form and maintain Her."

"But . . . . "

"It may sound complex, but the simple fact is, it's automatic. At even the first syllable of criticism against 'the English,' we – with our insular natures – shut it out as so much Foreign balderdash. We know how good we are, despite what the greater world holds up as a mirror to our actual ugliness."

"Gentlemen, am I interrupting?"

A female voice made them move to the front room. Lady Morgan strode towards them from the corridor doors.

The Doctor called out, "The woman of the hour! We might not have known yarrow was the culprit without Lady Morgan!"

She came up to the smiling men, the chill of the outside still upon her cheeks when Carême kissed her.

"Welcome," the Doctor said. "I'll excuse myself now and go upstairs. You two follow at your leisure."

With that, Kitchiner was gone.

"How is it you are here?" Carême asked. "You said the Doctor had not invited you."

"Oh, it was not, my dear *ami,* Kitchiner. The Regent had not wanted me, but he changed his mind." Her smile was radiant at this point.

"Well, I'm very glad he did!"

Several minutes later, after an elevated platform ride and a stroll through the Doctor's combination greenhouse and biology lab, the old friends Lady Morgan and Carême approached the open doors to the Doctor's penthouse retreat. Even before they could make their way in, the source of the good smells radiating throughout the building revealed their origins.

They entered unnoticed, for the bustle of activity and well-disposed voices seemed confined to the cooking-end of the room. Carême did perceive Kitchiner's galley stove was lit and pumping a pleasant amount of warmth to this end of the space. He shrewdly closed the doors behind them to make sure the heat stayed in place.

"*Après vous, Madame,*" the chef said with a gesture.

Lady Morgan and he made their way to join the others. Both were surprised to see the Doctor's rafters draped with garlands of evergreens. They swagged in great loops, decorated here and there with sprays of holly and mistletoe. The scent they offered the space was lavish.

A giant wreath of the same stuff hung on the wall of the cooking hearth, and Carême observed something similar in the left-hand corner of the room up ahead, but could not make it out. It flickered with pinpoints of lights.

"Ah, they've joined us!" Kitchiner called out.

Prince George and Mrs. Fitzherbert were seated at one end of the spacious kitchen table; the lady was pouring what Carême assumed was the Regent's favourite cherry liqueur into a sherry glass. He appeared to be drinking more than was his usual, at least judging from the high colour on his cheeks. But with the all-too recent death of his grandchild, who could have blamed him?

"Lady Morgan," Mrs. Fitzherbert said graciously, "though a day late, may I wish you a Happy Christmas."

The mood was anything but joyous, and if compared to past gatherings hosted by the Doctor, the day's atmosphere was cast in sombre hues.

"You are too kind, and may I wish the same for you, Madame. I'm delighted to be here."

"As am I," added Carême. "A *bon Noël* to you, and to Mrs. Lister."

As if via a stage cue, the London caterer arrived from the working end of the table rather excited. "Good," she said in a pat manner. "You're just in time to do the honours; everyone else has already had their turn."

She took the two late-arrivers to a large basin sitting in the centre of the workspace. "Take your stirs for luck," Lister said, producing a large wooden spoon.

Lady Morgan evidently knew what was brewing, for she clapped her hands quickly and hopped like a schoolgirl. "What fun!"

The Doctor had to explain. "It's an old custom, Carême. Everyone in the family has to make a wish and stir the Plum Pudding before it's cooked."

Lady Morgan took the stirrer, closed her eyes and stuck it in the thick mass of raisin-studded dough. She moved it around, and mouthed something below the level of hearing.

Once done, she handed back the spoon. "Thanks ever so much. I haven't done that in years!"

"Your turn." Mrs. Lister coaxed Carême to her side of the table.

Being new to the custom, the chef was a little reluctant.

"Like this," Elizabeth said. "Take the spoon, close your eyes and make a wish for the one thing you most desire in the coming new year."

Carême did take the spoon, but as he hesitated, Mrs. Fitzherbert recited gently from memory:

> *"Stir up, we beseech thee,*
> *The wills of thy faithful people.*
> *Bring forth the fruit of good works,*
> *That they may be plenteously rewarded."*

As he stuck the spoon into the uncooked pastry batter, he wished for greater harmony to exist between himself and François.

No one watching the chef from the outside could have guessed, except perhaps, Sydney Morgan.

Carême opened eyes to applause, and Elizabeth Lister handily lifted the bowl to dump the contents onto a floured cloth laid flat on the table. She picked up two corners, tying them twice, and then guided Carême to hold the spoon still in his hand under the knot while she tied up the other two ends.

"There," she announced. "Now I'll set it into the pot of water I have simmering on Kitchiner's 'Sauce Stove,' and by the time we're done with dinner, it'll be ready to eat."

As Lady Morgan settled in a chair next to the Regent's wife – preliminary to exchanging some breathless court gossip – Kitchiner caught Carême's attention and led him towards the long side of the room fronting the street.

Now the chef could understand what was hanging in this corner of the penthouse: an evergreen tree, which was suspended by its top from the ceiling. From the tip of many of its sturdier branches, glass spheres the size of large apricots flickered with tiny flames inside.

"The lights are an invention from across the pond, although over there they don't put them on trees like this," Kitchiner said.

"How do they work?"

"Simple really. Fill half full with water – to keep the glass cool so it does not break from the heat – add some oil, which will rise to the top, and set in a floating wick. *Presto!*"

"The effect is so . . . charming."

"Why, thank you." The Doctor was truly flattered. "But I doubt me the novelty of lighting Christmas Trees will ever catch on."

"That's a pity."

The pair moved back along the range to get a better view.

"It is," agreed Kitchiner, "but as I pointed out in the market, the tradition of having a Christmas Tree is dying in England. Another ten years, and I'll wager you'll see none hanging from London ceilings."

Carême's hand brushed a tray. Glancing down, the Doctor grew enthusiastic; his eyes twinkled. "Ah, you've uncovered my tartlets filled with rice pudding and dried cherries. Later on I will sprinkle them with brown sugar and run a red-hot salamander over them."

Carême had a hard time concealing his revulsion. "Why?"

"*Burnt Cream,* old boy! It's an ancient schoolboy tradition at Eton. Boys left behind at Christmas were fed Burnt Cream on the Holiday."

The chef mulled it over. *Crème brûlée.* . . . It sounded schoolboy indeed. "I doubt, Doctor, the novelty of eating it will ever catch on, as you say."

"Then that's a pity as well!"

"Besides the *entremets,* what else is planned?"

"Ah, yes, the full *menu.* For the soup course we'll have a ham and parsnip potage, and Mrs. Lister's brown bread with a devilled terrine of pease and aubergine to spread on it. A *rillette,* I believe you'd call it."

"No meat?"

"No, only vegetables."

"Then I'd call it a *pain de légumes.*"

"I stand corrected." The Doctor smiled.

"And the rest of the meal?"

"The entree will be grilled steaks with potato puree. And the main course will be a grand turkey pie. Followed by dessert downstairs, as you know."

Carême turned over possibilities. *"Purée* of potatoes, you say?"

"Yes. What have you in mind?"

"Potato croquettes."

"Wonderful!"

After that, Carême took off his jacket, rolled up his sleeves and washed his hands. He and Mrs. Lister camped out at the far end of the table with her basin of mashed potatoes.

As he loosened them up with a spoon, Carême became chatty. "Your anecdotes from your adventures catering, to London's best and brightest, are similar to ones I've had."

Elizabeth Lister kicked hands on hips in surprise. "Do tell, dear Chef!" After a warm laugh, she added, "But I suppose the dealings of caterers the world over provide privileged access to all manner of goings on. Things outsiders normally wouldn't know about."

"Goings on," Carême repeated with his own good-humoured chuckle. "That is a fine way to put it!"

"As an independent, for-hire chef, you must have been in great demand."

"*Ah, oui.* From *bourgeoisie* to *grande-dame* – I've seen the homes and secrets of many."

"*Bou-jee*"—it was time for Mrs. Lister's own repetition—"that's a perfect new adjective; I'll have to remember that one! As for London's 'best houses,' the good Doctor puts in a good word for me with those he thinks . . . . Well, with those whose acquaintanceships might benefit both Kitchiner and myself."

And the Regent, Carême thought to himself. The chef glanced over what he had to work with, and turned all-business. "I'll need a dish," he told Mrs. Lister, "where I can beat two eggs and another one filled with breadcrumbs."

"Oh, yes, Chef, right away."

As the matronly woman trundled off to hunt up the ingredients for the crisp, golden shell of the croquettes, Carême allowed his mind to once again consider how their careers overlapped as caterer-spies. He had a *soupçon* of how her intelligence-gathering operations meshed hand-in-glove with the Doctor's security mechanisms.

Carême suffered an inexplicable moment of looking at the plump middle-aged woman and seeing himself. Such a fleeting realization made him glance at Kitchiner, because that insight signalled the eccentric Doctor was Lister's Talleyrand – no one casually looking towards Kitchiner would suspect the power he and his cook wielded over world affairs.

The chef's moment of introspection was broken. Elizabeth Lister returned not only with the two requisite items he'd called for, but the needed ingredients to complete the dish.

He broke in a pair of eggs, and poured on a good slug of cream. He mixed all well together and reached into Lister's open spice box for salt and white pepper, which he was relieved to see.

In another moment, Carême gasped. Just barely in time had he arrested the woman's hand from adding a huge pinch of Allspice.

Aghast, the Frenchman thought, in spying, yes. But in food, they did not resemble one another at all!

After this near-miss, the pair of cooks harmoniously formed the croquettes into cylinders with their hands. Next, Mrs. Lister double breaded them – first in flour, then in eggs and breadcrumbs – and laid the assembled morsels on a platter.

Once they were all formed, Lister smiled. "I'll call a boy up from the Club kitchen. They're all set up to take and fry them down there."

"Ah," Carême instructed, "tell them, no more than three minutes on each side – turn only once!"

"I will."

After a clean-up, Carême rolled down his sleeves, put on his jacket and re-joined the group at the table. The Regent was in mid-sentence.

". . . And that's why," George concluded.

Mrs. Fitzherbert kindly filled Carême in. "His Highness was just now say-ing—"

"*We* was saying"—the Prince cut her off—"Fitzy, dear, how much I appreciate Kitchiner's evergreen decorations. It's made me recognize how the *smell* of Christmas is missing from the Pavilion's exotic decorations. Virginia magnolia leaves do not smell; nor do the pineapples. Festive, yes. Christmas, no."

"True." Mrs. Fitzherbert, undaunted by the Prince's growing inebriation, added, "He was saying there's no match between fragrant greens versus the villa's pop and colour."

George slurred slightly. "Quite right."

"And he used to have *such* Christmases as a lad with his brothers and sis-ters growing up at Buckingham House."

"Indeed," agreed the Prince, "splendid, family Christmases at the place we called the Royal Nursery. What fun we had in London!"

As the Regent soon slipped into a moment of maudlin introspection, Lady Morgan smiled and asked Mrs. Lister, "Speaking of London, how goes this year's Social Season?"

The caterer chortled. "Oh! With the weather being so dreary, people are throwing more balls than ever. Anything to celebrate the end of the Wars, *and* stay indoors."

"It sounds exhausting for you," said Mrs. Fitzherbert in commiseration.

"Oh, it is." Elizabeth placed her hands on the table and inspected them. "Quite frankly, I'm tired. So I'm glad to get away to Brighton for a few days and cook with dear friends." She smiled at Kitchiner.

"I heard," the Doctor confided in low, conspiratorial tones, "they're build-ing an ice house in your neighbourhood."

"Oh, it's true!" Lister failed to hide her enthusiasm. "A huge excavation – the size of an opera house – all underground and going to be bricked over with a dome to keep the ice cool all summer long. It will be such a convenience to send a boy down there anytime I need to make ice cream, or chill a pudding."

"Such structures always fascinate me," said Sydney Morgan. "So much effort for a utility storeroom that would make a Roman emperor blush at the extrav-agance."

"Well, I fancy the one they're building on the edge of London now will be even larger than the one buried beneath the Pavilion's grounds."

The Regent looked suitably dinged, but before he could reply – or Lister apologize – Kitchiner interjected with his own news.

"Carême, old boy, did I tell you?"

"Tell me what?"

"I'm doing it! I'm writing my book on food, diet and cookery."

"C'est merveilleux!" Carême diplomatically pretended as if the Doctor hadn't already said as much a mere hour ago. "And what title will you give it?"

"That I am still debating, but with Lister's help, the London Committee of Taste is busier than ever. I want to vet every recipe and make sure it works. I strive to balance flavour with nutrition—"

"Spoken like a true M.D.," the Regent cut in. The Prince laughed, so the others could too.

"I look forward," said Carême, "to having one of the first copies."

"That you shall, my friend. That you shall."

"And what," George asked Carême, "have you prepared for us today with your own hands?"

"Crème croquettes des pommes de terre, Highness. Such hot dishes, along with meat-based kromeskies, were ones preferred by Napoléon."

"Is that right?" said George, perked up to learn something new about a personal 'hero' of his.

"Yes, Your Highness. Deep-fried morsels such as these were favourites of the *Empereur,* although he was embarrassed to be seen eating them."

During the saying of this, the respective host and hostess of the party rose from the table. Kitchiner assured everyone had a glass of white wine, while Lister fetched the warming soup terrine, bread and *pain de légumes.*

As the caterer dished up a bowl of the ham and parsnip potage for each guest, Kitchiner announced, "Tonight's supper will be *service à l'anglaise* – that is, course by course."

Fitzy ventured to ask Carême, "What is it he means, Chef?"

"No doubt, *Madame,* the Doctor is teasing me about how I only ever serving dinner *à la française,* that is; in two respective table courses where all the dishes are laid out at once."

"Yes, indeed," Kitchiner added. "Two 'Tables' – first, soups and entrees; followed by a second setting of roasts, vegetables and desserts."

Carême smiled. "You make it sound as simple as it's intended to be."

Everyone began eating.

"Simple?" asked the Doctor. "But elaborate enough that such a meal can last three hours or more."

Mrs. Fitzherbert gasped.

Carême reassured her. "With a half-hour break, *naturellement,* to reset the table."

"Why is it"—the Prince wagged his spoon in Carême's direction—"you al-ways start with soup? You never vary, and yet I believe there's a new way now in France – something called an *hors d'oeuvre.* "

"Well, Highness, the answer is related to why I only do *service à la française.* I serve soup because it is the great equalizer. All mouths will have the same flavour at the same time. It's communal and democratic, like the *service* itself, which forces neighbour to serve neighbour as equals." As he dabbed some vegetable spread on a piece of bread, Carême grew wistful. "Soon after the Revolution, we would have neighbourhood meals in France once a week. Whole streetfuls of Citizens would build a central table down the middle of the road, and food from every kitchen would be shared in warmth and conversation. There was so much hope back then . . . . We had actual equality."

Carême stopped speaking then, realizing he'd probably put too much of himself on display.

"Anyway," he wrapped up briefly, "that is why I prefer *service à la française.*"

"Mrs. Lister," Lady Morgan interjected at this point, "the soup is delicious!"

"I agree!" added Mrs. Fitzherbert.

The men thought so too, shining with reaffirming smiles and nods. Carême took his first bite of the *pain* and found it very pleasant – if a tad overly seasoned.

"In addition, your Highness"—Carême had thought of something else—"it may interest you to know of another food trend in France. It's having coffee at the end of a meal."

"Instead of Port?!" exclaimed the Prince.

"Yes, indeed. The fashion was begun, again, by Bonaparte. He ordered it served to countermand the sleepy effect that may come from long, State Dinners."

"Very interesting, Carême. But your former emperor won't need fret over State Dinners ever again."

The effects of George's long day of drinking were catching up to him; it was not for nothing the man's *chef de cuisine* had swung the conversation around to sobering caffeine.

"The new peace treaty with France," continued the Regent, "saw to that. He'll never have power again. Not even over a laughably small island like last time. No, not again."

"George, please." Mrs. Fitzherbert laid a hand on his arm.

"Oh, Fitzy – this talk offends no one. Right, Carême? I mean, it's just the new world order; the proper re-establishment of monarchy over men. Louis XVIII ruling France – and Russia, Prussia and Britain ruling over him. Otherwise, what else did we fight for?"

"Well, I for one," chimed in Lady Morgan, "am glad the Wars are over. It took too long to bring peace to the Continent."

"Did it?" George scoffed.

"What do you mean?" Doctor Kitchiner had suddenly gone off his soup.

"I mean," replied George sharply, "British blood spilled on European soil entitles us to more power; more control there."

The table seemed stumped.

The Regent proceeded as before. "And war *is* the best way to consolidate it. Already we're supplying guerrillas in the southern part of the Netherlands to carve off a piece of Dutch territory to hand to Louis XVIII in France."

"Why?" asked Morgan.

"Simple. *We* hope to lure Prussia into honouring their alliance with Holland and escalate the conflict into a war between the French and Germans. That way, with them both weakened and distracted, *our* empire can keep expanding colonies around the globe for the British flag, unchecked."

Again, the table's occupants were stunned and silent but sober seeing the evil genius of the plot possibly working.

George drained his wine – and then his maraschino liqueur right after it – before saying, "What French Belgium needs is a King – one appointed by, and utterly beholden to, us."

A maniacal grin arose at this juncture, and everyone else returned to their soup, suddenly conscious of staring at the Regent.

Carême shivered to think what the consequences of such national interference could lead to in a hundred years—

The Doctor broke the reverie. "And, Your Highness, just before we sat down to sup, I got confirmation via signal towers that the Royal Couple have safely arrived home at Claremont House in Surrey."

"Oh, excellent news, Kitchiner. Excellent." The mentioning of his daughter went a long way to sobering up the Prince. He explained to the rest of the guests, "Charlotte and Leopold set off today right after noon-time tea. I felt resting at home, away from all the excitement at the Pavilion, was best for her, the excitable child. Oh, Carême, by the way, the Princess departed by saying, 'My compliments to the chef for the baba. Truly delicious!'"

"*Merci.* I shall pass along the praise to François, who made it for her today, following my strict guidance – naturally."

The bubble of contentment was deflated by Kitchiner announcing, "And just so you know, Chef, the entirety of the Pavilion staff and functionaries have been debriefed. They've all been sworn to regard Charlotte's 'misfortune' as a matter of strictest family confidentiality. A cover-story is being generated that the Princess and Leopold left Brighton on the 24th of December, and her grandmother, the Queen, on the 23rd."

"The Nation's *enemies,*" the Regent said, "will never know either, dear chap. Never!"

After the silence which followed this pronouncement, Lady Morgan sighed dreamily. "But Prince Leopold is strong; so strapping. Charlotte draws a great deal of strength from his calm decisiveness."

"That character," hazarded Mrs. Fitzherbert, suddenly doubting herself, "is what first swayed you – right, darling – towards a . . . a marriage."

George grinned a little, totally disarmed. He took his wife's hand, explaining to the rest, "What Fitzy is referring to is my initial refusal. I mean, Leopold came to England as part of the Czar's high command, an unknown here, and somehow Charlotte and he spent time . . . . That is to say, naturally, when they first came to me, I said, no. I said to Charlotte she'll marry a prince of my choosing, but . . . . But thanks to Fitzy's warm advice, I got to know Leopold myself, and realized he's a decent fellow. And I got to see how in love he and Charlotte really were - are." The man teared up. "So how could I say no, when my own father had said no to us . . . ?"

As several napkins around the table rose to eyes, a pair of lads arrived from the Club's kitchen below.

One grinning boy held a platter of still-sizzling steaks, and the other, Carême's golden-brown croquettes.

"Ah! Our entrees," Kitchiner said, rising to his feet. "Set them on the table. I'll get the wine!"

A few minutes later, the kitchen boys gone back downstairs, each person served the food of the second course, and with a filled red wine glass raised in hand, Doctor Kitchiner offered a toast. It ran in verse form:

"Lift one to the future, by rights,
For no matter how dark the day,
We must thereupon set our sights
And cherish our Hopes, come what may."

PART IV

Winter 1816~1817

Pavillon Rustique

Intelligence Communique No. 43

Jj3m ofe5vn8xskr qc9jrp am8hw,

*Wr9j fp9wj hn5d hr2md on1nrjf 1 hn8som8jhcmp n jh mb2k
km ih3 un9ew9rc. Pq4cuex 1 fl4jednfcg nu8 2 od7d jn
lm4hb4md ns8 sc9xjr jn2l8f, yb9s qf5k sd1hbx 3 ihd8hdbwp 4
gcz7ihlimv wk8s rd3khee dc 3 inmd4t on5 mf8henks 4 fr9skeb5*

Cher Instituteur Marron Glacé,

*Nous avons reçu votre rapport de renseignement n° 52 avec un
vif intérêt. Heureux d'apprendre que l'état du Pavillon est plutôt
sombre, nous vous dirons de continuer à travailler sans relâche
et d'ouvrir vos oreilles à toute information utile. Il semble que*

Dear *Instituteur Marron Glacé,*

We received your Intelligence Report No. 52 with keen interest.
Pleased with news of the suitably gloomy state of the Pavilion,
we'll tell you to continue keeping your hands clean, but your
work relentless. We'll add how advisable it remains for you to
keep your ears open for any and all usable information. It seems
you have recruited a valuable asset, so continue to keep her close.

We are also pleased to be kept abreast of the upcoming ball in
celebration of the Princess' birthday on January 7th. After its
conclusion, we'll await report with icy anticipation. This gathering
shall, no doubt, afford unique opportunities to overhear tongues
wag freely under the elixir of champagne's liberalizing effect.
More news concerning the Prince Consort is also warmly welcome.

As for your colleague's changeable nature, I'd advise you not to
worry. He may yet prove a valuable asset to your ultimate assign-

ment's success. I'm glad to know you both have nearly un-watched access to all parts of the Regent's marine villa.

At the moment, my time – although not my talents – are taken up with Louis' ridiculous, newly proposed treaty with the Vatican. I shall continue to work behind the scenes to ensure it never comes into effect. The separation of Church and State must survive in France, and will. Fortunately, the king's favourite lackey, the Comte de Blacas – and a possible Royal bedwarmer – has been put in charge. As I dupe the Count everyday as a matter of course, the outlook for the Church's reconquering of France appears suitably dim.

I hope you'll appreciate this piece of sunny Republican good news in your lonely exile amongst cold English monarchy, but remember the importance of your long-term mission. *If,* by which I mean, you *must,* pull off your assignment, a firm piece of your patriotic honour will be assured. Your name will enter the History books small children in France shall read forever. If not . . . well, just assume, for you, there is *not* an *if not.*

Incidentally, my trusted 'friends' - the ones who keep an eye on them for me – relay Marie and Agathé are quite comfortable in their settled life right now. But alas! As you yourself, a child of these dark times, know only too intimately, a terrible upset could dispose of anyone's comfort, liberty – and dare I say, life – at any moment. Such caprice of Fortune has an all-too keen blade to sever ruthlessly.

Well, I see I have digressed, and so for now, will bid you a good-bye and an even better *bon courage!*

Please accept, *Monsieur,* my best regards,

Doyen de l'école de la Concorde

Chapter 11: Charlotte's Ball & *perché crudo destino*

While much of the world hunkered down, sheltering from the drag of failed crops and dwindling food supplies, the first month of 1817 found the Pavilion in a warm flurry of activity. The pitiless effects of the summerless year before were barely visible in the Regent's marine villa, and certainly never mentioned to the Regent's face. Instead, the long-neglected interior of the Music Room rang out with hammer blows beneath its still-wet, silver leaf, fish-scale ceiling. While the priority had rested on completing the Banqueting Room to give a proper venue to Carême's food, the ball room had lain ignored. But now that the French chef's food was served daily under the great Gasolier of its dedicated space, another mandate rained down from the Prince's suite above: "Finish the Music Room in time to celebrate Charlotte's birthday." And today, the 7th of January, all hands of the Pavilion's workmen were assembled to see the chamber complete before their appointed 8 o'clock 'stop work' order. The doors then were to swing wide two hours later, and the Pavilion's ball room inaugurated with dancing to commemorate the 2nd in line's natal day, despite the icy, winter-clad weather just outside its walls.

In the Cold Kitchen, Carême and François had been working at a calmly concerted pace for hours. Carême had devised eight showstopping pastry pieces for the day's dinner and ball refreshment table. Four of them were sugar work building models, two rustic hermitages, and two weed-encroached 'ruins'. Everything for which the master planned was symmetrical by kind, but never mere duplication. Thus, he devised a Chinese retreat to counterpose a Moorish gazebo, and a Carthaginian ruin to complement a ruined Gothic church in a German forest. These were assembled and waited his deft hand at colouring and final decoration.

Besides these architectural fancies, two of the eight *pièces montées* were large cakes – a turbaned *brioche au fromage,* and a star-pointed *biscuit à l'orange.* These were baked and cooling to one side.

They would have to wait, for now the French chef and his trusted *maître d'hôtel* focused on the last pair of treats. Carême had set the Confectionary boys to cut out fluted rounds – bite-sized pieces – from trays of quickly cooling nougat. The half-inch-thick slabs of almond and hazelnut candy had to be stamped out while still hot, and there would be six more trays coming!

The rounds would be racked and allowed to cool completely before Carême showed the boys the piped icing decoration he wanted on each. They had steady hands, so he trusted them with this. Eventually, all the morsels would shingle a four-foot-high pasty cone standing by to receive them.

Meanwhile, Carême and François worked harmoniously on the nougatine tower's counterpart. François piped pistachio *crème* into mouth-sized cream puffs. Then he dabbed a tiny amount on the back to serve as glue.

Carême took each, one by one, and symmetrically placed them on an identical pastry cone as the nougat treats. He arranged them *à la religieuse* – or like a 16th century nun's cap – first in vertical stripes from base to tip, plotted out in even columns at the 12, 3, 6 and 9 o'clock positions. Once these 'guidelines' were complete, he'd go back and infill the background with slightly smaller pistachio cream puffs. As a final garnish. Hot spun caramel sugar would be allowed to run down the 'nun's cap' and glaze the *croque-en-bouche* to glossy perfection.

The sculpted finial, which would rise above it all, was the waiting bust of Charlotte modelled by Carême's own hands in white chocolate.

A complementary bust of Leopold stood by to cap off the nougatine tower.

These two would form the glories of the ball's refreshment table served at midnight under the great sky-painted dome of the Salon. Like the Banqueting Room, this circular space featured its own flying dragon supporting the crystal chandelier, although this one was all in trompe l'oeil.

While François was handing him the next cream puff, he jostled his head at Carême. "You really captured his insufferable sneer."

"Whose?"

François gestured to the white chocolate sculpture. "You faithfully reproduced his smug, German sense of superiority."

Carême chuckled, affixing the guide-line *pâte à choux* with care. "Well, I was aiming for 'true to life,' so I'll take your comment as a compliment."

François chuckled in turn. "Yes, do."

Carême was pleased the Frenchmen's relationship was on the mend again.

Donald Bland suddenly tore open the closed door from the hallway. The eyes of the working cooks all lifted to him, upper torsos still stooped in their tasks.

The Kitchen Comptroller stalked up to the *chef de cuisine,* and behind him appeared an office boy. The lad cradled one of the Estate's green-bound ledger books upright in his arms. A careful observer would have noticed the boy's finger being employed as a bookmark.

Once these two had arrived in front of Carême, Bland cracked open the volume and made the young man stand there holding it like a Bible for a parson. It seemed Bland was about to read a passage of damnation over the head of a lacklustre fearer of God.

Carême interceded. "We are busy, which I'm sure you can see. Now is not the time—"

"Monsewer Chef, I have been trying to reckon the books for last quarter. I'm afraid you need to know your demands for produce are more than the thousand acres of working land at Kensington Palace, Hampton Court, *and* Kew Gardens can grow."

"Perhaps this is better discussed later, when—"

Bland's finger slid along the red text of his ledger. "You wanted – just in October alone – you *demanded* 1,200 stalks of asparagus. That's a dozen bunches of 100 each!"

"So?"

All the chefly eyes in the room were trained on the Comptroller's rising fury.

"So?! They're out of season. We had to make a considerable outlay in attempting to procure them on the open market."

Carême refrained from asking 'So?' again, though it seemed the obvious retort.

"And what's worse"—the kitchen moneyman turned the page—"in the same month you had the Pavilion spend 258 Pounds, 12 Shillings, 8 Pence and 3 Farthings on beef. Beef alone! Not to mention making me pay for 1,600 pounds of lamb, 1,700 pounds of veal, 262 fresh hams – 118 aged ones as well – plus 600 chickens, 88 quail, 31 capons, 12 geese and 61 lobsters, which had to be imported – horror of horrors – from America!"

Carême waited to see if Bland was through. Once assured the out-of-breath functionary was, the world's greatest chef calmly replied, "I believe it was Mozart who countered a claim he used too many notes by saying, 'I use just as many as required; neither more nor less.' My art, in a like manner, Mr. Comptroller, requires what it requires."

The scorched red in the lackey's face reminded François of a certain Italian volcano about to blow.

"I ask you"—Bland stated staccato—"to be more reasonable—"

"And *I* ask you," the chef replied, "to remember I work to achieve the Prince Regent's wishes, not yours."

Bland raised his arms in frustration, knocking the book from the boy's hands. It went spilling in a mighty clatter upon the floor, and provided the pastry cooks something to titter over.

The Comptroller boxed the poor lad's ears. "Pick that up!"

Once he had, Bland shooed him towards the door and followed. As the moneyman got to the frame, he turned spitefully on the chef. "You've gone too far this time, Carême. Too far!"

In the moment or two of silence following their departure, all eyes were on Carême, but the Confectionary cooks' gallant General appeared unflappable.

François made hand gestures for the others to get back to the nougat, which they did, while he made his way to close the door from the hallway's noise and dirt.

Just as he got there, Doctor Kitchiner came breezing in. "François! Nice to see you." His usual high spirits were well in place.

François closed the door behind him as the Doctor made his way to Carême, apparently with the intent of shooting the breeze. "And there's the man of the hour! What are we up to today?"

"The usual, Doctor," said Carême, "preparing our *pièces montées* for today's festivities." He motioned for François to resume filling and handing him cream puffs.

"Ah, yes! Your *pièces de résistance!* Or, pieces of resistance - which, come to think of it, loses much in the translation."

All of the cooks in the room resumed their meditative work.

The good Doctor wandered over to the eye-level cooling shelf hosting the portrait busts. His attention was drawn to the base of Charlotte's, for there, in the most flowing, legible hand, Carême had piped the Princess' name in dark chocolate.

He drifted back to the *croque-en-bouche* assembly station and asked in a tone of wonder, "Carême, old boy, why have you written Charlotte's name, when the likeness is so obvious?

"Because," answered Carême matter-of-factly, "imagine the thrill of walking up and seeing *your* name on something so special. Now magnify that feeling and place it in the heart of a girl turned twenty-one today. She deserves it."

The Doctor's odd reaction to this emotional vignette took Carême by surprise, but he only made a quick mental note of it and returned his focus to the pistachio cream architecture under construction.

"I was wondering," Kitchiner said after a long while, "if I might ask you . . . about—"

His book, Carême thought.

"—My book. As you know, I wish to approach it from the standpoint of nutrition."

Then don't boil your vegetables for an hour, Carême further thought.

"And from the standpoint of organization—"

"Dear Doctor," Carême replied in an even tone. "Why don't you – if you wish to be here – roll up your sleeves, wash your hands and help us."

The undercooks snickered in their tasks. However, Carême knowing him best, knew what the Doctor's next actions would be.

"Righto!" Kitchiner was already shedding his jacket and hanging it on a hook by the door.

As he folded up his shirt cuffs and began washing his hands, Carême told François, *"Villon,* show the Doctor how to do what you are doing so you're able to instruct *les garçons* how to decorate each nougatine piece."

"Yes, Chef."

And so it came about that Doctor Kitchiner was shown how to pipe just the right amount of pistachio *crème* into each cream puff and provide a little tack on the back before handing it to Carême for placement.

In the meanwhile, Kitchiner got his wish and asked for the chef's opinion on the Doctor's book; and Carême got his wish in that the nougat tower was kept moving towards completion.

After about 20 minutes of this harmonious effort, the door opened once more from the hallway. This time the visitor remained unnoticed until the Regent's Private Secretary was standing by Carême's side.

"Chef Carême, you are summoned to the Royal Chambers."

"What? Now! Can't you see I have my hands full?" A bit of frustration was let show in his voice.

"It's the Prince Regent's orders. You are to come at once."

Several minutes later, with Carême's hands washed and hair combed, the cleaned-up chef in his street clothes followed Cornelius Hook through the *chinois* splendour of the Central Corridor.

He had kept the *pièces montées* production going, and was glad Kitchiner had shown up; Carême switched the roles between the Chef and François so the maitre-d' could continue 'gluing' the cream puffs as Kitchiner filled them.

But now, as they mounted the steps to the North Chamber Gallery, this long walk from the kitchens put the chef in mind of the Secretary's tour on Carême's first day; he did not like the man then, and had even less motivation to conjure a fondness for him these many months later. Carême felt sure the funct-ionary had talked the chef down in George's company whenever possible. Carême expected no good would arise from today's "summons." The courtiers were flexing their muscles, and Carême remembered a private moment with Kitchiner in which the Doctor had laid out Hook's particular arrangement among the Regent's circle. Namely, how the Secretary used the appearance of having the Prince's ear to bully his way with people, *and* undertable cash to move others' agenda items to the Regent's at-tention. In reality, Kitchiner had the man on a short leash due to some choice scuttlebutt he held over the functionary's head, thus putting the Prince's mind at ease that Cornelius was actually trustworthy.

The good Doctor, for his part, fed the Secretary false intelligence on the Prince's 'new ladies,' to throw the rest of the court off the scent that he and Fitz-herbert were still together.

Such circumlocution was always the way with aristocratic matters, and Carême felt lucky to be mostly an outsider to their machinations. For the greater part of his days, he was allowed to cook in peace and gather intelligence for others at his leisure. But every now and then, his on-the-sly existence was upset by being dragged into others' flash pans of courtly posturing.

However, as they entered the gathering area within the Regent's suite, Carême knew he'd been trained by the slickest courtier of all, and was well armed not to let Talleyrand down.

The pair reached George's bedchamber, where – to Carême's total *lack* of surprise – Donald Bland stood waiting by the Prince's desk. George sat behind it, his hands already up from his elbows on the wood, fingertips touching to indicate he was ready to 'be the judge' of the forthcoming dispute.

"Ah, Carême, do join us," the Regent said. Once they had, the Prince gestured to Bland. "Now, Mr. Comptroller, will you kindly repeat what you told Ourselves and my Private Secretary before the chef arrived?"

Put on the spot, Donald Bland demurred; but he soon recovered and assumed a hard expression. "Your Highness, the Frenchman is well aware of the financial particulars I outlined earlier for your scrutiny, and which details will not bear repeating. The point remains what to *do* about this problem. The Household accounts have been put under substantial strain since . . . since . . . that man's arrival."

"And you, Hook?" The Prince turned to his secretary. "Will it bear repeating what considerable observations you made upon 'that man' before he joined us?"

The Private Secretary underwent a violent, instantaneous attack of blushing.

"No," surmised the Regent, "I thought not. The truth is, your money-grubbing 'revelation' is an offensive one to Us. And your supercilious snooping into gossip concerning one of my most important retainers is an affront to Us personally." He stood and made a warm gesture towards Carême. "That is why I wanted you to be here, Chef. To know"—he made a sneer a Bland—"that I do not trifle myself over the price of pumpkin on the 'open market,' or"—now he frowned sternly towards Hook—"care if tongues wag that you are too close to a certain teenage undercook." The Regent's tone rose hostilely at his lackeys. "I care that particular parties are attempting to undermine your valuable time, especially as *monsieur* Carême has tonight's festivities to prepare!" His eyes narrowed at his toadies; his voice lowered too. "The pair of you do think birthday preparations for my daughter, who is second in line to the Throne of both England and Empire are important, yes?"

Meek as boys dressed down by a schoolmaster, the appointees replied in off-kilter, off-timed, "Yes, Your Highness."

"Good. Then you men should listen very closely to what I'm about to say."

He reached out to shake the chef's hand. "Carême – know that whatever your artistry requires in the Pavilion's kitchens, you shall have it. Furthermore, you shall have it knowing it comes liberally blessed by your humble Prince's blessings and appreciation."

The two functionaries were stunned.

Carême, for his part, was so touched, he bowed deeply, which was something he rarely did, owing to his upbringing as a free and independent Citizen of France.

"Now"—George made his way back to his seat—"Bland; Hook, you are dis-missed. I wish to confer with my *chef de cuisine* concerning a few critical details for tonight."

Looking at one another, daring the other to express the roil of indignation buried beneath their surfaces, the Comptroller and Secretary turned for the door. They were silently berating each other: 'It's all your fault!'

"And, oh"—the Regent stopped them on their way out—"I'd find some *productive* pursuits for your time, men."

The pair cast murderous glares at Carême.

"That is all. Now, be gone, out of Our sight."

Quiet as angry rats going down with the ship, the functionaries reluctantly quit the Regent's suite.

"I feel as if I know you, albeit, only vicariously, through Carême's . . . um . . . remarks concerning you."

Doctor Kitchiner's awkward attempt at breaking the ice with François was less than meteoric.

The two of them continued with their work per Carême's instructions. The guidelines of the *croque-en-bouche* were finished, and Kitchiner filled and handed smaller cream puffs for the Frenchman to infill the background.

"Remarks?" François echoed the Doctor's word-choice back to the man.

"Well, that is not the correct . . . term. Shall we say, his"—equally inappropriate options cycled through Kitchiner's brain: discussions; comments; banter; revelations—"his *thoughts* about you."

"They are warm ones, I hope."

"Yes, very. He's mentioned how he relies on you as the only one in the Pavilion who gets him – as we say in English. Or, understands him."

François sputtered his lips in a deflective way. "Ah, well – we are French! We 'get' one another."

How much did Kitchiner dare replay the perceived depths of feeling he sensed from Carême for François? Glancing about the room, with the Confectionary undercooks hard at work but relaxed of ear, he decided, nothing. Besides, no exposing of confidences with persons unknown was Kitchiner's – any intelligence-gathering operative's – most basic doctrine.

François rotated the plate holding the *croque-en-bouche* to begin infilling the final quadrant. In his heart was a tumult of emotions. He'd never spent a moment 'alone' with this somebody he was inclined to regard as a rival. So cold suspicion vied with a species of hot jealousy; jealousy that at the drop of a word from this funny little man, François' lover was ever-ready to abandon him for "an evening at the Doctor's". But over the maitre-d's conflict of heart, his mind inter-ceded and took control. The better exploitation of his time alone with him was in calculating an attempt to figure out this mysterious M.D.'s overall place in the Regent's world.

"Carême tells me he enjoys the *soirées* you invite him to; says you are a remarkably fine host."

"Does he?!" Kitchiner smiled. "I'm so glad to hear he feels that way."

"He does. He says your hospitality is warm, and as I have heard the ex-pression over here, 'second to none'." François could tell by his adversary's body language that Kitchiner was flattered.

"Well," the Doctor gushed, handing him a pistachio cream puff, "good company, good conversation, good food make the event, I always say."

François grinned. "And Carême agrees!"

Although the eccentric Doctor continued to smile, François nevertheless detected the man's demeanour shift to the inquisitorial. "By the by, old boy, I feel obliged to mention something unpleasant."

"Oh, yes?" François' hands came to a halt.

"I'm afraid so, yes." Kitchiner eyed him directly. "It seems, in connection to cleaning up the Keenans' mess, you understand, certain parties at the now-close Irish den of inequity known as *The Barrel* have mentioned a Frenchman being there . . . a servant of the Pavilion, they seem to think."

The maitre-d' had to knit his brows, but not in consternation; he genuinely had to think about it.

"Oh," he exclaimed, recalling all at once, "Christmas Eve supper – yes, I was there the one occasion, as the Keenans' guest."

The Doctor's ensuing silence was a bit puzzling.

"Was there any . . . are there any suggestions I was—" François was cut off.

"No; no, old soul." Kitchiner's grin re-lit his features. "Let's merely regard it as a detail that lingered about, floating; one that has now been put resolutely to bed."

Unconsciously, François resumed his tasks.

"So, you ate Irish fare at the pub. How did you find it?"

The Frenchman indulged in a brief sputter of lips. "Oh, it was substantial, I believe you'd say, but generally of a good quality."

"I see." The Doctor's tone lowered a concerted hitch or two. "So, what does the Chef . . . say about . . . . "

"About what, *Monsieur?*"

"Well – about *my* . . . food?"

Ah! At this point, François stood erect. He knew he'd have to avoid an-swering directly. Decorum prohibited out and out honesty at this juncture. That being the case, the Frenchman was not averse to foisting the same type of in-sincerity the Doctor had just dumped on the maitre-d's shoulders.

"Tell me," François asked in stark honesty, "why did you evidence such a 'complex' reaction to Carême putting Charlotte's name on her bust?"

Had the Doctor's hands been free, he would have occupied them in his force-of-habit ritual of taking off and cleaning his glasses. As he did not have access to this moment to think, he merely glanced around the room and, in coast-is-clear confidential tones, confessed, "Because the Princess will never see it. Leopold has decided, last minute, they shall not make the journey from Claremont House to Brighton today. Not over the icy roads."

"I see. And why is that something you could not tell Carême?"

The Doctor was taken aback; he appeared to feel the answer was obvious. "Because, the Chef will take it to heart. There is no need to dampen his artistic fire with the knowledge that the guest of honour won't be here tonight. It's better to let him proceed as he is, and execute his vision to its full glory."

And just like that, François tacked the last cream puff in place; with it, their joint assignment was complete.

François glanced at the ever-ticking clock on the wall, and told the Doctor, "I must run now and check on how the Table Deckers are doing for the banquet placement. Would you mind taking the pastry bags to the sink and washing them out . . . ?"

The Doctor smiled. "No. It would be my pleasure!"

A few minutes later, the *maître d'hôtel*, un-aproned and re-jacketed for his proper role, strode down the Service Corridor thinking of the Doctor's parting words to him. "Thank you for this chance to work with you. I'm always seeking to learn new things."

François mulled this pronouncement in the context of Kitchiner's reluctance to tell Carême the Princess would not be in attendance at her own ball. Was the Doctor being overly sensitive to the chef's feelings, or simply secretive. If indeed the latter proved the true motive, then so too must his words about enjoying François' company be mere platitudes.

Instead of unravelling any of the 'enigmas' surrounding the Doctor, François only sensed more layers being added.

Suddenly his inward focus snapped. As he neared the door to the steps leading down to the cold cellar, he perceived it was open and heard voices emerging from somewhere behind it.

François quickly assessed the coast was clear and placed his body at a ninety degree angle to the frame. Slowly, he peered beyond it: Donald Bland was copping an aggressive stance over Thomas Daniels on the first landing.

By their impassioned tones, it was clear the Kitchen Comptroller and his cornered boy were having more than a common lovers' tiff.

François settled back out of sight to listen.

"Don't deny it," Bland said. "I know you've been unfaithful."

By the teen-boy's plaintive reply, François could tell he was hurt.

"And I *told* you, that is not true—"

"This place is full of foreigners," the moneyman complained. "No good can come of sustained contact with these continental types!"

Thomas chuckled in derision.

"Funny!" Bland demanded. "You think it's funny, do you?"

"The way you sound—"

"As far as I'm concerned, we should drive a mighty ponderous wedge through the bottom of the English Channel and be free from 'Europe.' The future of this country lies in the hands of our armies colonizing lands overseas anyway, not in the clutches of garlic-tainted Froggies or vinegar-swilling Krauts!"

Thomas laughed outright. "And not with Russian piroshki-eaters either, despite the fact we're going to be entertaining one in the spring, owing to the fact we *never* would have won over Napoleon without German, Russian and Portuguese help. Never."

François dared to take another sustained peep; their voices were growing ever hotter. The boy had moved from the corner, but Bland still blocked his access to a way out.

The older man's ire kicked into a more rabid state. "Sometimes I wonder about you, Thomas Daniels. Wonder about your loyalties."

"What is that supposed to mean?"

"I know it means you've been unfaithful!" He latched onto the teen's upper arm, hard. "Guilty of . . . of un-English behaviour with those two—"

The young man wrenched his arm free. His tone once again showed he was hurt. "I haven't been a boy on the make for a better position – but who knows now – because it's over shure between you and me. Over!"

François turned to leave, but could hear Thomas' footsteps coming up followed by Bland's voice rising to a bloody threat.

"I'll see to it Carême is ruined for this. I'll make that man pay dearly if it's the last thing I do!"

Meanwhile, outside the insular walls of the Pavilion, more than just the bone-chilling temperatures and howling winds were frigid. Winter-like too were the possible zephyrs of British Imperial change. The salient points to the powers-that-be were that Prince George was not worth his keep, which was considerably more than his weight in gold. In debt, he kept right on spending – on himself and his considerable pleasures – while in exchange for Parliament floating a personal balance-due three times larger than the entire Empire's National Debt, what did the Lordly few receive as returns on the tax-payers' Farthings? Nothing, except a leadership vacuum, headed by a corseted strawman taking no evident interest in what the Lords held as critical agenda. In fact, many were the discreet Duke, Earl, Marquess, Viscount and Baron of the Peerage who questioned if George's disgraceful excesses actually provided opportunity for regime change. Then again, change to what?

The Country was not in a holiday mood January 1817, but some few comprehended tonight Charlotte would turn "legal." She became eligible, as an emancipated adult, to convert her formerly groundless epitaph of "England's only hope" into a bright sign of change. A new, twenty-one-year-old Regent over the Nation with her grandfather as King-in-name-only. The powers-that-be knew few in the Home Counties, or Foreign Colonies, for that matter, would mourn Beau Brummell's 'fat friend' being exiled to his own version of Napoleon's African isle of Santa Helena.

However, inside the insular world of the Pavilion, all minds were focused on the fantasy escapism of George's 'Brighton.' Lady's maids were scattered throughout the house, anywhere behind the scenes they could find a window, to mend and toughen their employers' ballgowns for tonight. Likewise, valets stitched hems or polished the gold-plate of inherited military titles – not earned honours – for the be-paunched extras who'd accompany the ladies on the dancefloor.

But for Carême, as he lighted through the North Chamber Gallery – having just been dismissed from the Regent's suite with a list of new requirements for the ball – his thoughts focused on repercussions. There would be a price to pay for the Prince's dressing down of his functionaries in the presence of the chef, but he found it hard to grasp all the manifold ways in which their revenge could play out.

He heaved a heavy, stifled sigh, taking the first step downstairs. Wherever Carême went, new enemies arose. Though it was pikestaff-evident in his mind, and simple, that he only ever sought out a venue where he'd be able to execute his artistic vision, others popped up to get in his way. Jealousy, the man thought, was at the heart of all unprofessional feelings. He had yet to devise a way to defuse the petty rancour serving as doorman to every opportunity opening before him.

Suddenly, as he turned on the landing to head to the main floor, his contemplations were interrupted by sound. It was in fact the type of sound first perceived by one's ankles and lower legs as bass-toned rumblings through the architecture. It seemed to be emanating from directly below him.

He continued down to the bottom of the steps, and now the deep vibrations transitioned into notes. Carême followed them through the open pair of mirrored doors under the landing. The pipe organ erupted into contrapuntal melody.

The chef's breath was taken away. He'd never before been in the Music Room, and consequently had no series of impressions of the space under construction to fall back upon. He saw it in nearly all of its intended glory.

The centre of the wall opposite from where he stood was taken up by five bays of pipes from a mahogany-cased instrument built into the wall. At a console beneath them, the organist-installer was running tests and trills to ensure each of the metal reeds were sounding, and there were hundreds of them. Occasionally these test-runs would burst into snippets of Bach gigs and Mozart minuets to test the keyboard's response time.

This auditory background was also punctuated with the voices of work-men. One crew of drapers were by the windows, wrestling with acres of pale blue and cerise velvet. The heavy gold fringed swags of this fabric rode an incredible pelmet of long-tailed dragons and writhing serpents. The unspoiled freshness of their silver leaf scales made them look like solid metal.

Silver leaf scales also covered the shallow dome ceiling, which was sup-ported from below with eight octagonally-placed pendentive windows. These, some thirty feet above the floor, were stained glass and shaped like ovals coming to points on both ends. Every place one of the eight sides of the ceiling structure met, gigantic arms in the shape of pineapple-tipped leaves, stuck away from the wall and sup-ported dish-shaped chandeliers of exotic, painted glass panels. These eight lighting fixtures were now aglow with their concealed coal gas flames, and were miniature versions of the central chandelier. This behemoth hung from the middle of the central dome on chains and a crystal-beaded Chinese pagoda.

But as splendid as these appointments were, it was the overall mood of the space that struck him. Measuring a perfect sixty-foot square, the Music Room was an equal match to its Banqueting Room sister on the south end of the house. But this new chamber was also the ideal counterfoil to the villa's dining room. That's because, while that hall was designed for late afternoon use, and featured pale blue walls to host murals on cream backgrounds, the Music Room was a space designed for the night. For here red and gold Chinese landscapes were framed by *trompe-l'oeil* dragons and snakes on dark green backgrounds. The fantasy world escapism of this chamber was stunning – Nash's masterpiece example of the European fascination with 'Oriental' luxury. It was enough to make both Kublai Khan and Samuel Coleridge jealous of Prince George's pilfered wealth and sheer dedication to voluptuousness.

As he walked to the Great Kitchen, new creativity was already gripping the *chef de cuisine's* keen mind.

Sugar work inspiration notwithstanding, Carême's admixture of awe and adrenalin upon seeing the Music Room was repeated many times over in the minds of the Regent's official guests as they began arriving for the ball at 10 o'clock.

George, for his part, was suitably impressed with his own grandeur and ensconced himself on the built-in velvet divan to let his guests one by one to come up to him and gush – as much as one's English ways would allow one to gush, of course.

Standing by his side was the event's representative Hostess, one Miss Minney – Mary Georgina Emma – Seymour, daughter to Mrs. Fitzherbert. Pretty, youthful and quiet, the eighteen-year-old was everything the Regent was not.

However, undaunted, and with personal reasons of his own in the selection of Hostess, the ruling Prince of British domains sat beneath his finally completed 'Pleasure Dome,' transmuted into the Emperor of delight; his own, naturally.

After this reception ritual was complete, the band assembled, and together with the organist for the evening, played fanfares to announce commencement of the dance. The first was led by the most senior Royal in attendance other than the Regent. His brother the Duke of Clarence took Lady Cholmondeley to the centre of the floor. Once launched, and the array of mandatory applause died down, the far more youthful and exquisite couple of Prince Esterhazy – the highest ranking foreign dignitary present – and Miss Seymour joined them. This pair received their own ovation of handclaps, which were arguably tendered to a greater extent, and the dancing thrown open to those in general attendance.

From this point onwards, people relaxed. The orchestra initiated the playing of Quadrilles, Cotillions and the merry 'country dances' the Regency's best-and-brightest expected.

Among the crowd of forty or so were Lord and Lady Morgan. They'd arrived fashionably late and danced several numbers, with the novelist thoroughly enjoying being in her husband's arms. However, soon after, one of the gentry ne'er-do-wells requisitioned a spacious round table in the Red Drawing Room and started a cigar-smoking card game. Like moth to flame, soon Lady Morgan's escort, and his bulging wallet, were drawn away from her.

She peered at the faces in the Music Room and decided that she did not recognize any of the dancing ladies as particular friends.

Paused in this manner, Lady Morgan caught the occasional glance of Miss Seymour being whirled past her by the next handsome beau on her dance schedule, and the novelist began to muse upon the girl.

Well-known as Mrs. Fitzherbert's adopted daughter and ward, Sydney Morgan understood how the young woman's presence here – in an official capacity, forcing everyone to pay her the dignity these self-same people believed the girl unworthy to receive – was causing many heads to be agog.

'Too bad,' she thought, stifling a chuckle, 'this condition won't prevent their tongues from being awag!'

Tired by this observing, she withdrew into the North Drawing Room, knowing she'd would become nauseous continuing to stare into the convoluting circles of dancing partners.

Crowded as it was in here as well, she felt relief spotting a friendly acquaintance, and proceeded to Lady Rugsby with the intention of chatting.

"Ah, my dear! It's wonderful to see you," said the older woman, latching onto the novelist's gloved hand. Rugsby drew Sydney Morgan in for a contact-free kiss on the cheek. "I positively haven't seen you for an age!"

"Oh, yes, indeed. It was at the ball the Lord Mayor threw in honour of Lord Nelson's victory that I saw you last."

"Was it!" Rugsby exclaimed falsely. "Well, I suppose it was, dear. As I say, it's simply been *an age.*"

Lady Morgan laughed; a delicate, appropriate laugh.

The music from the ball wafted pleasantly around them as they both used one another for cover to spy who else was milling about the 'Yellow Drawing Room'. Gossip would surely follow the trails their eyes had blazed.

In the Music Room, the next number began, ushering in an air of lighter key and quicker tempo.

"Ah," sighed Lady Rugsby. "A Spanish Dance. Much more to my taste – don't look now, my dear, but there is that beastly, ghastly, so-called American Princess, Elizabeth Patterson."

"Who—"

"You can look now, quickly. Lord only knows who brought her down from London for this event."

What Lady Morgan saw was an attractive, well-mannered woman in her early thirties. The brunette, with Roman finger-curls draping her forehead, formed the centre of a small group of men across the narrow end of the drawing room from the ladies' position. "Is that—"

"Yes – the abandoned *madame* Bonaparte, Maryland-born and bred wife of Napoleon's youngest brother."

"Oh, yes. The 'American Princess,' as you say. Her story is such a sadly moving one."

"She doesn't look sad to me!" Lady Rugsby exclaimed, *sans* humour.

Morgan chuckled. "Well, she doesn't wear black constantly and act like her life is over, so on that account, she has my admiration."

Having not heard it, Rugsby ignored Lady Morgan's comment and latched onto an earlier remark. "And speaking of Princesses, it does seem a lot of bother to mark Charlotte's birthday when Her Highness deigns not to attend her own ball."

"I imagine it's the wisest choice. Her father hardly need make an excuse for a party when he's in Brighton, so it's possible Charlotte was not consulted about this celebration. Anyway, it's better for the Nation if she's warm and safe at home."

"Well," Rugsby hmphed. "I wish others had stayed at home as well."

Outpaced by the English Lady's inimical inclinations, the novelist asked simply, "Who do you mean?"

"Really, you do sometimes *surprise,* Lady Morgan. The 'who' in question are a pair of undesirables now in our midst: our hostess and the would-be in-law of an *empereur.*"

"Oh, those two." Morgan supressed a grin.

Rugsby continued, this time fanning herself casually, "Indeed. These, and their types, are no better than climbers, reaching for heights beyond their social grounding, clinging to the merest of *incidentals* as excuse to act equals amongst their betters."

Against her opponent's frosty frame of mind, one to beat the howling January winds outside, Sydney Morgan glowed warmth, suspecting the English noblewoman spoke to others with inclusion of the writer as the third *undesirable* at the ball.

"Well, admirable friend, some do cling to their natural charm and talents to raise themselves up in the world. I, for one, see nothing worthy of heated comments concerning the fact."

Knowing she'd been trumped at her own game, Lady Rugsby shone admiration upon Morgan. "Your mind *is* so penetrative, my dear. You conceive of problems as no problems at all, as only the best of novel writers can."

After a shared chuckle over the barbed compliment, the pair stood in companionable silence for several minutes, and then spent several minutes more chatting with a young and vapid associate of Rugsby's who had glommed onto them. Fortunately, a young man appeared through the mirrored door of the Music Room and snatched her away "for the next dance." Unfortunately, for Sydney Morgan, the girl's removal left her alone once again with Rugsby.

When the next dance did begin, Lady Rugsby immediately made a sour face. "The *Duchess of Devonshire's Reel.* One must not approve of this particular set of gyrations."

Morgan found herself bemused by Rugsby's vehemence. "And why mustn't *one* approve?"

"Because it is unseemly. This dance requires men to . . . gesticulate with one another."

A quick survey through her mind of the dance steps revealed to Lady Morgan the moment when the gentlemen of the couples mirrored movements with one another while the lady partners linked hands and raised them to execute a circle.

Lady Rugsby lowered her voice while raising her own ire. "It's the sort of *dance* Lord Byron would do with his voluptuary, Doctor Polidori."

Morgan stifled a giggle. If only Rugsby knew the half of it; knew that amongst circles 'in the know,' the latest sybaritic interest was paid to how Shelley and Byron - England's two greatest poetic "bad lads" - had returned from summering in Switzerland closer than ever. This new intimacy was causing raisin tongues to wag along Community grape vines.

The arrival of a second young socialite – one hoping to ingratiate herself in Lady Rugsby's good graces – provided the Irish novelist with an escape route. After saying 'how do' to the new arrival, she excused herself to go look for Lord Morgan.

Walking farther through the Yellow Drawing Room, Sydney Morgan felt only the tiniest twinge of guilt for her white lie. Her true intentions were not to pull her husband from his card game, but to go see the rest of the Pavilion in her merry-making finery.

She strolled into the Salon, not realizing what she would encounter. For nearly the entirety of the three window bays to her left were taken up by Carême's refreshment tables. These formed a semicircle with the central part given over to giant *sorbetières* – porcelain tureens with ice in their bases to keep fruit sorbets frostily refreshing. After a dance or two or three, nothing was as soothing as the ubiquitous 'Pineapple Ice' awaiting a person's enjoyment.

But Lady Morgan's eyes were more than taken with the array of pastry laid out on silver trays. These treats were anchored at either end by edible towers, the one closest to her topped with a bust of Princess Charlotte.

"Excuse me . . . . "

Lady Morgan turned, startled. She was just about to reach for a cream puff and suddenly felt 'caught,' as if a little girl.

"Somebody told me you're the writer, Lady Sydney Morgan. Is that right?"

It was the American Princess, shy and rosy-cheeked in beauty close up.

"Why, yes, I am."

"I hope you don't feel it's too forward of me, but I am Elizabeth Patterson-Bonaparte, and a great admirer of your work."

"I'm flattered." And Lady Morgan truly was, part of which was helped by Patterson's considerable magnetism. It was instantly easy to see why this woman was the current toast of London, *and* how she'd been able to attract a French prince to her. "Shall we . . . ?"

Morgan gestured to a pair of open seats on one of the built-in sofas, curving away in yellow silk upholstery on either side of the fireplace.

After they settled themselves, Lady Morgan said, "I didn't know my books were being so closely read in America."

"They certainly are. Especially *The Wild Irish Girl,* but I have to confess to holding another of your books in higher regard."

"Oh, yes? Which one?"

"Saint Clair."

Lady Morgan sputtered. "Oh, I wish you wouldn't."

"Not hold it in high regard . . . . My goodness, why?"

"Because, dear, *The Heiress of Desmond* – or, *Saint Clair* – was my first attempt at full-length fiction. I sometimes feel embarrassed by the quality of that novel!"

The Irish woman's tone of laughing self-deprecation was lost on the sincere American.

"Now it's my turn to advise that I wish you wouldn't. It may have come out in 1803, but its themes are just as stirring now as ever. The elevation of Nature as the supreme metaphor for human suffering, *à la* Goethe or Rousseau; the tragic heroine's choice of an ill-considered marriage, while all the time, the star-crossed passion of great love haunts her. Well, as you can see, I gush – but I do so love the book."

Lady Morgan was suddenly deeply touched. Here was a real-life "Saint Clair," a heroine who loved and was abandoned. Patterson's was yet another 19th century love-match wrecked on the wheel of political manoeuvring, all because Napoleon could not accept his baby brother marrying a commoner. But in Karmic grandeur, Napoleon too felt pressured to toss over the woman he loved and marry someone – anyone suitable – who could bear him a son and heir. And in the end, the baby 'King of Rome' is forgotten; his father, a war prisoner.

As if sensing what Lady Morgan was thinking, or then again, perhaps due to rote repetition to a person she talked to wanting to know her personal mindset, Patterson said, "If you ask me, I'll tell you I believe Jérôme will someday be coming back to me and our son Bo. He can and will, now that the Wars are over."

Sydney Morgan doubted she'd ever heard a more tragic string of words. "Yes, Elizabeth, I hope so too."

Then a faraway cast came to Patterson's eyes. As melody faded from the receding world of the Music Room, the American Princess began to recite an intimate quotation from Guarini.

> *"Perchè, crudo destino,*
> *ne disunisci tu, s'Amor ne strigne?*
> *e tu, perchè ne strigni,*
> *se ne parte il destin, perfido Amore?"*

The novelist clasped hands gently with Elizabeth's. Moved, she knew the quotation by heart in the translation of William Ayre, and softly replied:

> *"Why, cruel Fate, dost thou*
> *the Hearts divide which Love has joined?*
> *Or why, fickle Love dost thou,*
> *when Destiny would split, unite?"*

Half an hour later, at a pre-determined time set by the Prince, Carême appeared at the back of the Music Room dressed in his finest. François was by his side, and the pair paused motionlessly near the door. Carême waited for his young hothead to speak first.

He did. "Don't be angry with me, Carême. I am sorry, as I always am, about my . . . dalliances. But you know I only ever want to do better, and patch things up to be stronger than before."

Carême half-smiled, teasing *le garçon*. "You will demonstrate how sincere you are to me later, *oui? Dans la chambre.*"

A quick glance took in François' helpless grin. The chef fully enjoyed the flush of colour coming over his stiffening young man.

The music stopped abruptly. Footmen circulated through the crowd with trays of champagne. All eyes turned to the Regent.

"Today, dear friends, is my belovèd daughter's birthday – her twenty-first birthday, to be exact – and although she and her Prince Consort cannot be with us on this occasion, she'll be pleased to allow you to be the first to know of some important Statesmanship. To wit, in the spring, Brighton will be blessed with an official State Visit from Nicholas, Grand Duke of all the Russias, and brother to the Czar. We have much to do to get ready for the stay of His Highness. So, join me in drinking a thrice-blessed toast to Charlotte, Nicholas and our glorious Victory over France!"

"Cheers!"

Now, as Carême began mentally listing all the 'things to do' worthy of a State banquet, he glanced to François and wondered what the enigmatic cast on his lover's face could possibly mean.

Chapter 12: Dalliance at Rottingdean & Crossroads

Several weeks after Charlotte's birthday ball, with the Princess safely tucked away at Claremont House for several weeks more until she'd need to travel for State affairs, Carême was feeling weak.

The famous *chef de cuisine* was, as usual, driven in his unforgiving pursuit of self-disciplined perfection. He competed with no one but himself at this stage in his career, but he always chased that better, more naturalistic flavour or appearance to his work, and it required much from him.

The reasons for this he confided to Kitchiner's care. Carême relayed how the spells of his 'chef's lung' were cropping up to slow him down more frequently, and to a greater degree, than previously. When asked what and how severe these effects were, the chef described a period where he could feel a weakness in his muscles accompanied by lightheaded pains and rapid, shallow breathing.

Kitchiner diagnosed it as chronic air-intake compromise – "diminish-hed oxygen in the circulatory system" – and indicated rest and fresh air.

Providentially, the climate had decided to cooperate, presenting a spate of mild weather. What struck inattentive denizens of the City of Brighton as 'unaccountable' was uncontroversial to those closer to the land. The old folks of the countryside knew the unseasonable weather was nothing inexplicable and had a term for it. Yes, for Primaveral Summer was upon southern England, and, which like its better-known cousin, Saint Martin's Summer in autumn, presented to people a pleasant stretch of warm and dry days, in contrast to the main season this period interrupted so welcomely.

Thus, the good Doctor's prescription of a "day off" was timely. For one, the hard-working cook had had nothing resembling one since December 26th, Boxing Day. And two, the clear skies and southern sea breezes opened a window of opportunity not long to remain unclosed.

The Doctor simply told Carême to spend his holiday outside; to draw in deep draughts of renewing air; and refresh his system. The chef had agreed only when Kitchiner announced whom the Doctor had asked to go with him, *and* remind the Frenchman that, according to the calendar, days to rest and recreate were vanishing quickly as the Grand Duke Nicholas' visit loomed ever closer.

Such a State Occasion at the Pavilion would require Carême to give his all; and he would too, which is what troubled the chef's friends in England so much.

These thoughts and others filtered through Carême's head as he made his way across the Pavilion's property to the Regent's horse stables.

Ever a designer submerged in a world of design, Carême strolled on the gently curving paths of crushed stone, noticing the natural grouping of trees and shrubbery – almost as if mounded islands amidst the sea of grass – varying by height and shape. Around the base of these 'islands,' flowerbeds stood in for fields and meadows *en miniature*. This picturesque approach was so different from the formal, regimental combination of low boxwood bordering rectangular beds of flowers he'd expect a palace the size of the Pavilion to have in France. He liked the effect the English gardeners had achieved.

He turned the corner of one such island and was greeted by the full glory of the Royal Stables. This structure found situation on the far north-west end of the estate, and frankly, dwarfed the marine villa itself. A central dome – some eighty feet in circumference – rose six and a half stories to a colonette-style cupola. Composed of iron ribs alternately dressed in stone and glass, the ethereal structure reminded Carême instantly of a Paris monument built just around the time he was born. *La Halle au blé* was constructed as the world's first modern grain exchange – auction house and storage facility – to feed a hungry capital city. Its dome was of the same proportions as the Prince's private horse barn, and featured the same broad ribs of skylights to illuminate the interior.

As Carême continued crunching gravel underfoot towards the Moorish grand entrance, he thought how ironic it was that the Paris structure was built to house nutrition for the people, while the Regent's extravagance was only ever intended to provide for his personal property, things more valuable to the Royal than human life – sixty horses, several of whom were money-making champions on the racetracks.

His reverie was broken by a figure waving at him, for parked on the wide crushed stone expanse before the stable entrance was an open-top carriage. The yellow lower half featured the Prince of Wales feathers painted on the door. A team of perfectly curried horses were hitched and standing by in glossy black perfection. A groom stood in front holding the bridles. Lady Morgan waited next to the team, so he smiled and hastened his step.

As he strode up to her, Carême also noticed a red-liveried driver in black top hat, and a boy in street clothes, buzzing about the carriage.

The two old friends kissed cheeks.

"Look, Chef! The Prince lent us a carriage. We'll get to Rottingdean in the best of style."

"Ah, oui. And will Lord Morgan be joining us?"

"He shall meet us there later this afternoon, but he'll ride out on his own."

Just then, the chef noticed the driver and boy lifting flat baskets onto the board along the rear of the conveyance; otherwise known as the "boot."

"Do you see, Carême? Kitchiner provisioned us with half a dozen groaning picnic baskets."

She stepped aside, giving the chef his first unencumbered view of the two at work at the rear of the carriage. The 'boy' was Thomas Daniels, difficult for Carême to recognize right away for not wearing his chefly whites.

Carême turned smiling eyes back to his hostess for the day.

"Doctor Kitchiner also," she said slyly, "thought we'd need a steward to shepherd all the food."

"Oh, the Doctor did, did he?"

"Indeed. He may or may not have also indicated – via prescription, you understand – that the Chucklehead may form part of your *personal* refreshment."

"Lady Morgan!"

"Now, now, dear Chef. No need for protests, for I can assure you, as the well-worn novelist that I am, I'm skilled in the art of being both the most trustworthy and inattentive of chaperones."

After a momentary pause of digestion, the chef understood the thrust of the reassurance.

Just then, the men had finished their task. Thomas ran over, whipped off his cap and said to Sydney Morgan, "Baskets all stored, mum."

He dared to grin at Carême for the briefest of moments, his mercurial blue eyes not risking a lingering sparkle there. He too had barely seen his brooding, Byronesque boss out of his work clothes either.

"Very well done, lad," Lady Morgan replied. To Carême she extended her arm for the chef to crook. "Shall we?"

"*Oui.*"

The young man gallantly jogged and opened the carriage door for them, offering a hand while the lady stepped up.

As the pair of old friends settled in and positioned the charcoal-burning foot warmer and thick lap blanket over legs, Thomas closed the door and dashed up to sit next to the liveried driver. As he repositioned his cap, he looked back for one more glimpse of his handsome mentor with a happy beam.

And so with a gentle slap of the reins, the horses picked up their feet and crunched the gravel on the path winding around the corner of the massive enclosed tennis courts forming that end of the stable building. Soon, they turned onto a broad road lined on both sides with a double planting of stately poplar trees. This grand-yet-natural *allée,* in the best of true Mogul landscape design, pointed like a die to the Pavilion's North Gate. The grandest adit and exit to the palace grounds, this "front door" was a tall stone Indian-style arch capped with a copper-clad onion dome.

The gate attendants saluted the approaching carriage and stood by open iron *portails* as the merry little party sailed on through. As they did, Carême looked up to see the intricate plaster work ceiling of the gate house.

Turning right on the public thoroughfare, the carriage soon made another right onto the wide, grassy parkway of the Steine. Rounding one of the Pavilion ground's island of trees, the vehicle was rolling smoothly along in front of the building's fenceless east front. Here a few well-heeled gentry strolled their morning constitutionals. Nash's tent rooves for the Music and Banquet Rooms, and their rising towers of complementary colonettes, anchored the two extreme ends, while the cladding for the great onion dome over the Salon was rising halfway between them. The Salon's exterior loggia of delicate stone tracery was also under construction and would eventually be part of a continuous walkway around this side of the marine villa.

Carême closed his eyes. Although currently a work in progress, the completed form of the Pavilion based on the architect's great model in the Central Corridor filled Carême's sight as they travelled past the structure.

After a matter of several minutes, the carriage turned left and began rolling out of town on the King's Road. Soon there was nothing but open sea to one side, and open countryside on the other. The fresh air felt invigorating, and Carême breathed it in deeply.

Lady Morgan was pleased to see this. She adjusted the coach blanket a little higher, and Carême glanced at her.

"So, what is on the agenda today, *Madame?*"

"Rottingdean is just the next settlement up the coast from Brighton, but a world away. Quiet, self-contained, I thought we'd stop when we get there and walk the beach. Then I know a peaceful, grassy place where we can spread out and relax."

"Sounds marvellous."

They enjoyed the views. Mostly sunny, a few grey clouds occasionally cast shady patches on the blue sea rolling onto shore rocks. The open fields periodically resolved themselves into low stone walls, fencing farm houses set well back from the road. Some people were out when they came up to these farmsteads, like women doing laundry and men slopping hogs.

Tranquil coastline, with a broad ribbon of stony beaches, glided past. The highway began to rise in elevation and take a gentle bend inland. The beaches disappeared, becoming limestone bluffs with no margin between them and the surf.

The landscape transformed into a broad-shouldered meadow, gently rising a few hundred feet in the air to blot out the western horizon-line with a jade mantle of grass. On the crest of this hill stood the most picturesque and perfect of windmills. Five or six stories in height, it was the type where the top "barn" of the building – sitting upon a fixed, octagonal tower of sloping sides – could be rotated in and out of the wind. Now its four blades turned in lassitude with the mild offshore breeze.

"That's Beacon Hill."

The chef nodded affably at the Sydney-Morgan-supplied information, but in another moment found himself wondering what this single, weather-worn sentinel was doing up there. It seemed a lonely island unto itself.

The road rose in elevation again and grew narrower. Houses came up to it that now featured low fieldstone walls topped by white picket fencing. Their coach was rolling into a town of two-story masonry buildings with leaded glass windows and high thatched rooves. Windows boxes hung in place, and no doubt, in season added gay colours to the earth-toned village scene.

The artist in Carême wished he'd brought his sketchbook.

After a couple of blocks, the houses stepped back and an impressive set of accommodations fronted the road with its back to the open sea. "King of Prussia" read the Inn's sign as their carriage glided past.

Beyond it, all manmade shelters disappeared from the scene. To the left, more grassland rose in smooth undulations to the north-west, while a spectacularly clear view of the English Channel greeted them to the right. The road was now hugging the seaward rim of cliffs sixty feet above the shoreline.

The carriage slowed, drawing up to a narrow pathway off to the right.

"Here's where we get off." Lady Morgan smiled to her companion as the coach came to a stop.

Thomas gallantly hopped down and again opened the door, offering his hand for Lady Morgan to use as she descended. Once she was down, he left it extended, and this time Carême took it. He didn't need help, but the relaxing ride has softened him a bit; he therefore squeezed the young man's fingers with affectionate gratitude.

"This way,' Sydney Morgan called.

Carême reluctantly let go of the boy's hand and followed. The narrow path wound its way along the cliff-face down to a half-mile strip of sandy beach. When the chef glanced back, Thomas had re-taken his seat, and the driver pulled the carriage away.

He caught up with Lady Morgan. "Where are they going?"

"They are heading to the place we will have our picnic. Rottingdean is tiny, and we'll have a pleasant walk joining them later."

"*D'accord.*"

Down the trail they went. The sounds and smell of the surf carried by the mild sea breeze lightened both their hearts. For a moment, this place seemed a world away from all their earthly cares.

In another minute or two, they were walking the seashore, and Carême could now see the sheer vertical of the cliff-face made of the same white chalk for which Dover is so rightly famous.

Lady Morgan interlaced her arm with her friend's. "I do hope the scenery meets with your approval."

"It does, *Madame.* Only a short drive from Brighton – *et voilà!* We are alone, as if the only two people in the world."

"Yes. Sometimes it is best to feel this way. To embrace the ephemeral as the here and now that matters. Let our niggling and nagging concerns leave us for a while."

"*Oui.* I have had little opportunity to experience it, sadly, but there was one place where I've felt this peace."

"Oh, yes – where?"

"In the woods and countryside around Château Valençay."

"That is Talleyrand's private—"

"Napoléon's gift to Talleyrand. But not for private use – it was given for work."

"Yes, I've heard it functions as a sort of diplomatic guesthouse."

"*Oui.* Consequently, I was very busy there, modernizing the 16th century kitchens to give State Dinners three times a week"—a lick of salt air greeted the chef's nose, and he inhaled deeply—"but on my midmorning breaks, François and I could stroll out of the formal gardens and see some of the beautiful Loire Valley. Some days we'd go out for much longer – pack picnics, find shaded glens to be by ourselves, to reconnect. We'd always bring *Le grand testament* by François Villon with us. My François is so good at reciting the tragedy-tinged words of the old poet, he knows several of the Ballades by heart now." Carême paused, slightly overcome by the memories of their past closeness, wishing perhaps heroically – if somewhat naïvely – that their personal good times would return.

Lady Morgan's words came back into range. "Sounds ideal," she said.

Carême smiled. "Yes; nearly as wonderful as being here, with you."

Sydney Morgan's spirit lit up. She so relished the moments when she thought Carême was happy.

They continued to walk the beach with thoughts turned to enjoyment of the moment. Up ahead, the white cliff angled sharply towards the sea. This was the place the sand ended, so the strolling pair turned and made their way back.

Half an hour later, they walked along the residential streets of the village, and Carême could see the fancy patterns some cottages had in their thatched rooves, either scalloped borders along the line of the eaves, or egg and dart motifs at top along the ridge. He also noticed the carefully maintained evergreens, most shaped to resemble megalithic standing-stones, planted in the margins between houses and their low-slung stone walls.

Soon they turned the final corner, and the village church appeared off to the left. Another masonry monument, its most striking feature was a truncated tower rising above the crossing of the nave. Its pyramidal roof looked accidental; as if its red clay tiles were meant to serve a year or two while money was collected to continue raising the tower. But, as that was evidently a century or two ago, the temporary cap still in place looked exhausted from a too-long life of service.

Lady Morgan led Carême around the front of the church, and to his surprise, the long flank of the building facing the south-west had a sunny lake studded with swimming ducks. It also had a clear view of the rolling open countryside outside of town. This side of the building was infinitely preferable to the other, which housed the parish graveyard.

Parked to the side of the water by a wide margin of lawn stood the carriage and men.

As soon as he saw them, Thomas Daniels dashed to the boot. A moment later, he came running towards the chef and novelist and whipped out a blanket for them to sit on in the grass.

As they were lowering themselves onto it, Sydney Morgan reached and took the boy by the wrist. "Why don't you join us too."

To the lower-lip-bit glance he shot him, Carême nodded, letting Thomas know it would be all right. To show he acquiesced, Thomas removed his cap and scrunched it in his hands.

The newly formed trio sat in easy comfort: one looking at the lake and waterfowl; one glancing at the church; one gazing up the grassy slopes to the breeze-turned windmill about a mile away. Then the three would trade off points of interest to admire.

"The sea is much quieter here, eh, Carême?" Lady Morgan observed.

"*Oui, Madame,* but if one listens very closely, the low-toned rumbles are always there."

"So they are; so they are," she replied. "Young Master Daniels, have you been down below the cliffs, on the beach, before?"

"No, mum."

"Oh, you simply must go." She suddenly turned sly. "Perhaps in summer you can bring *monsieur* Carême again, this time with his sketchbook."

"Yes, mum."

"I hear," clipped Sydney Morgan in a far-too casual manner to be casual, "The King of Prussia has some lovely, private accommodations as well."

Carême suppressed his smile as he watched the teen boy colour all ways to Sunday.

Lady Morgan continued as if she'd seen not a thing. "Chef Carême and I were having a very interesting conversation. Weren't we, dear friend?"

"On the beach? Yes, I suppose we were."

"About what," Thomas asked.

The chef replied, "*Ouf* – about setting troubles aside, *sans souci.* About relaxing into the moment and enjoying it." Now the chef blushed on his own, sensing what the novelist's point had been all along.

"Oh, yes." The boy smiled. "Lettin' your hair down, as we'd say around here."

Lady Morgan laughed, thrilled to have been discovered. "So true! Although the fashion for men these days is to eschew the ponytail, I suppose – like all fashions – long hair will be back soon enough."

After that charming if vapid bit of *bons mots,* the trio once more relaxed into their respective living for the moment, only this time, all eyes settled on the blue sky and rolling clouds above the windmill.

A few minutes later, Carême observed, "Odd, its being up there all by itself. In Holland, for example, windmills to pump water are lined up in a row."

"That one's to grind flour, Chef," the lad said.

"I think"—Lady Morgan suddenly sounded adamant—"a trip up there is warranted for a closer inspection, don't you, Chef? The views are spectacular."

Carême took a breath of fresh air and shrugged. He wasn't opposed to a little hike across such pleasant meadows.

As the novelist had just stood, man and boy were obliged to follow suit.

Carême extended his arm. "*D'accord.* Shall we, *Madame?*"

Lady Morgan acted surprised. "Oh, I'm staying put. After all, I've seen the *views* already. But Thomas will accompany you, and in the meantime, the carriage driver and I shall unpack and lay out the picnic for your return."

"Are you sure, *Madame?* You will get lonely—"

"Heavens, no, I won't! You see, I've packed a book to read. So, let's say, you two go for your walk – as it's about noon now – and at 2 o'clock, the driver will pick you up from the windmill and bring you back so we can eat." While Carême referred to his watch, she added, "Lord Morgan will be here by then as well, so it's settled!"

Carême lacked proper reason to protest, but in the meantime, Thomas Daniels smiled, setting his cap back on his head, and said, "Shall we?"

The walk up the gentle hill was easy. The slope was verdant, as sea air seems to tweak the vigour of all grassy patches growing close to the water.

Thomas, with hands in pockets and eyes cast upwards, suddenly recited something in tempo with the sound of the men's feet stepping and dragging through the grass.

"Blue skies shall overarch us at the end
When innocent sleep will aid our choosing,
And every love's a melted lover's sigh
Reborn fresh under some new warm-weather sky."

After a few unharried paces, the chef remarked, "That is lovely, Thomas. Who have you quoted so well in the context of our current situation?"

"Ah, a farmer lad. A humble poet of our age I think future times will shure regard as our best: John Clare."

"Well, it is certainly measured and perfect in its beauty."

The young man grinned helplessly. "I couldn't agree with you more."

As they slowly drew near it, the windmill assumed less and less the character of a feature on the landscape and more of an impressive destination. Once the silent pair crested its hilltop, they found a wooden bench for visitors a fair distance off. They went up to it and did what it invited hikers to do: sit and admire the vista with the sight of the turning windmill and endlessly rolling sea in the background.

Once several minutes of private contemplations had passed, the boy removed his cap, shoved it in his jacket pocket and sat on the edge of his seat. Leaning forward, and with elbows on his knees, he regarded Carême with curiosity.

"It's a pleasant day, *n'est-ce pas?*" said the chef.

"She is indeed." The undercook's eyes cast glances behind Carême. "Although it seems some darker clouds are rolling in from the west."

"*Ah, oui?* Well, still, it is warmer than I anticipated—"

"I liked what Lady Morgan and yourself were saying back there; back there by the church."

Carême fidgeted.

"About living for the present," Thomas explained. "Though I like to consider it from another angle as well."

"Which is?"

"Regrets. Fundamentally, don't have any. They're impossible to live with."

Carême grinned, feeling like challenging the teen's philosophical turn. "And what manner of regrets are you speaking of?"

The boy sat back, confidently placing hands behind his head. "Missed opportunities. You see, it seems like life intersects our paths every now and again with crossroads." The boy's voice shone with sincerity. "What do we do when we encounter one? Put on blinders, ignore what opportunities the new direction could offer – and, possibly regret it later. Or, explore the new path, even if only for a little while, so later, a person has no regrets and feels they've made the right choice all along."

Carême wiped the contentment off the young man's face. "Is there something you want to tell me?"

Thomas' hands slowly descended into his lap. "Well, for one, I appreciate all you've taught me so far, and I look forward to what more will come my way in the Great Kitchen. The end-of-year bonuses you paid out were also more than generous. You shure made a lot of people very happy."

"Well, as for the rest of the kitchen, it's wise for a chef to make his people happy. But for you specifically, as I have already mentioned, stay focused on your career, and you will go far."

"Thank you, Chef. And I suppose there is a second . . . thing . . . I might want to tell you."

Carême was silent, knowing the boy would venture information on his own. The chef noticed the darker clouds were suddenly right over them.

"Well, on a personal note – we're split. No longer together."

"We means you and the Kitchen Comptroller?" Carême asked.

"Yes, that's right. She's officially ended."

It started to drizzle. First, randomly timed drops no bigger than pinheads fell.

"*D'accord,* Thomas, but you should also know that François and I are not 'split,' officially or otherwise."

The skies opened up, pelting the pair with large, fast-falling raindrops.

The youth suddenly stood, grabbing Carême's hand. "Come on. We'll make a run for it!"

The ground getting soft where they trode, the two bolted for the windmill's door.

It was unlocked, and Thomas ushered the chef inside. The sound of the rain squall was reduced to muffled pinging on the exterior clapboards, for inside was a different world.

The steady sound of wooden machinery at work was accompanied by the smell of timber meshing with timber and the axle grease used to keep all running smoothly.

Thomas shouted: "Haa-looo?"

There was no reply.

They were alone, and Thomas closed the door to the outside world.

Exploring for a few moments, they peered up the length of the great revolving wooden shaft. It went all the way to the mill's loft, where light filtered in through the opening. Ladders rose here and there, tier by tier, up the building's height.

After this, a new sense of boldness illuminated the younger man's face, which Carême noticed as a fetching glow.

The chef found a sturdy pillar to brace his back against, waiting for the teen boy's tempest to break upon him as well.

It did, although it was a gentle, tender assault on the handsome chef's resistance.

Keeping himself a good way back, Thomas glanced to the dusty heights of the space, reciting:

"But for my joy, I stamp my lonely footfall
Upon the wild's shadiest gravel path."

He slowly lowered his eyes, locking them on Carême. He continued:

"With no ear to listen, nor eye to see,
Or mind to judge what wrong from right might be,
My sole companion, a soul free from wrath,
With hate for none, and abiding love for all."

The chef smiled. "More of your John Clare?"

Thomas, full of shy glances and uncomfortable gesticulations, came to stand before his mentor. "No – Byron this time; the poet who resembles you so dearly, Chef."

Despite himself, Carême was moved and reached out to take the young man's hand. The boy, under the master's touch, calmed down right away.

Thomas asked in a pained way, "Why is it François hates me as much as he does?"

Carême was slow with his answer, but he was honest. "Because he thinks we are sleeping together."

"A dalliance? That's shure rich."

"Why?"

"Because"—Thomas re-thought his reply midstream—"well, because we're not." The young man took a step forward.

"No, we're not. But, in fact, you and I already have a relationship, don't we?"

Thomas was taken aback. "We do?"

"Oui. Only in the last few days have I realized it's you – you are my official 'minder' for Doctor Kitchiner. You have been the Doctor's man in the Great Kitchen the whole time."

Young Master Daniels didn't act particularly surprised by this confrontation. In fact, he closed the gap between them a little more, saying, "I help out where and when I can; for the Doctor's sake, but also for yours."

"And it was you who obtained a sample of the yarrow-laced tea for Kitchiner's laboratory to analyse."

"Well, yes. That had to be a discreet, in-house job."

The chef's estimations of the boy's potential had just been confirmed. He couldn't help but look at the young man with newfound respect for having fooled spying veteran Carême these many long months. But, on the other hand, the chef had no doubts what Thomas Daniels did now was motivated for personal reasons.

Thomas laid the palm of his hand flat over Carême's chest. The accelerated heartbeat he felt there was all the validation his actions required. "But getting back to François, he thinks we are, but we're not sleeping together – yet."

"Yet?"

The boy let his hand wander south, drawing his face closer to Carême's. "Not yet, that is, but since François already thinks ill of me for it"—he licked his flushing lips—"I might as well deserve his bad temper." Thomas put his hands on Carême's waist, leaning his lower half full against the chef. "Ness Pa?"

Carême uncharacteristically shrugged, feeling the boy's blue eyes hard upon him, as well as how hard the young man was against his inner thigh. The chef teased: *"Oui, n'est-ce pas?"*

Thomas kissed him; once, briefly. "Besides, what he doesn't know of this dalliance won't hurt him."

He leaned back for another kiss, and this time stayed.

Carême found the young man to be an expert, experienced kisser, and in return, grew resolutely hard himself. The combination of the boy's tongue moving across his lips, and Thomas' hand pressing against the chef's member, made Carême's need insistent for release.

In a natural moment of breaking apart for air, Carême said in artless sincerity, "I never imagined you English could play so passionate the lover." His comment made the boy laugh, Thomas' smile warming Carême's heart profoundly.

The young man replied, "There are many other *passions* this English lad knows." He undid the flaps of Carême's trousers, easing the man out to the fresh air, and caressed him – all with his tender gaze searching every corner of Carême's visage. He then dropped to his knees to pleasure his master.

Some ten minutes of bliss later, as a slow but relentless climax built to the fore, Carême closed his eyes and let his head loll back. The sound of the Beacon mill's blades turning, the wooden axle and mechanism creaking, the luscious – almost edible – scent of the lubrication, all contributed to a spinning sensation of body and mind.

Carême's hands reached down, latched onto the boy's rabbit-soft flaxen hair and held his mouth still.

He climaxed as suddenly as the showers had come upon them, oddly seeing the gilded dragon atop the Pavilion's water tower getting pelted by driving rain as he filled the waiting young man's mouth.

After panting, grunting and nearly melting in pleasure, Carême barely perceived Thomas Daniels rising to a standing position again. Carême felt the boy's weight as the young man leaned his head against his pounding heart. But in another moment, the chef gradually drew the English lad's lips up to his own. This repast was finished with a sensual *entremet* of their own making.

PART V

Spring 1817

Pavillon Polonais

Chapter 13: A Ruse &
Ladies at Tea

"Ah! my most welcome, thrice-honoured guests."

Kitchiner had again invited the Club's doorman to step aside. Redundantly, he stood by the open portal while his employer radiated good cheer on Chef Carême and Lady Morgan.

"As always," the Doctor continued, "wonderful to have you here at one of my little get-togethers."

In the vestibule, the doorman had something to do at last, as he could assist with the removal of the guests' springtime outerwear. He moved off to store them, and Kitchiner, ebullient as ever, led his little party down the hall, chatting brightly. "We'll be eating later, but I thought you'd both like some time to relax beforehand."

"Thank you, Doctor," replied Sydney Morgan. "You are always so considerate."

"Well, I do what I can to assist." Kitchiner glanced over his shoulder. "And, Dear Chef Carême, you will have such a taxing time day after tomorrow, handling the State Dinner for the Grand Duke Nicholas."

"Yes," agreed Lady Morgan, "and it's already been six weeks since our day out at Rottingdean."

Carême flushed a bit to have his interlude in the dusty light of the windmill spoken about, albeit indirectly. The heat of the accelerated blood settled down below his waist, and all of a sudden, made him adjust his walking carriage to try and conceal the fact.

They arrived at the elevating platform, and the Doctor graciously let his guests board first.

"Third floor, please," he said into the speaking tube.

As the conveyance jolted to a smooth-but-slow ascent, Kitchiner beamed on Carême. "Speaking of the banquet, I cannot express how proud I am to know you've decided to include our National Dish on the menu."

"And it's your recipe, Doctor," said Lady Morgan. "I know it will be a sensation at the start of the meal in two days' time."

"Yes," agreed Carême. "I have placed François in charge of preparing this himself, and he's been experimenting and practicing it all week to assure – both himself and I – that every detail will turn out a flawless triumph!"

The lift came to a shuddering stop; they had arrived at their floor.

Once again, Kitchiner showed the way along the corridor back towards the front of the Club. "And incidentally, I've just learnt about a corresponding season: how the migratory *Streptopelia turtur* spend their nesting season – all lovey dovey – on English shores from May the First until the start of October." He grinned a bit suggestively. "Isn't that interesting?"

Neither Carême nor Lady Morgan knew exactly how to reply. The Lady had to resort to a banal *"Very* interesting."

He stopped the pair before the closed door of one of the private rooms inhabiting this level. "Lady Morgan, if you please, the Chef and I have some foodly matters to discuss. We will join you in the bye and bye." Kitchiner opened the door, leaning in a bit to maintain his grip on the handle and ushering Lady Morgan in with his free hand.

"But—" is all the novelist was able to get out before the Doctor shut the portal again – but now with her inside the room.

On the move once more, Kitchiner led Carême to the quieter, rear portion of the floor.

The chef queried, "And what matters of food are so private that—"

"None, old boy. I'm afraid it's a ruse." He placed his fingers on a door lever. "And I'm afraid I told Lady Morgan a fib, because *I* will not be with you."

After gently guiding the still-puzzled Carême inside, with the Doctor's face disappearing behind the closing door, the chef turned.

A figure stood up from the neat and tidy bed in the chamber. It was Thomas Daniels.

Without removing his eyes from the excitedly grinning young man, Carême reached behind himself and locked the door.

"What is going on?" the chef asked, smiling as well.

Thomas was wearing youthful stockings and knee-britches; on top, he still wore a warm-weather linen jacket.

"A surprise from the good Doctor," Thomas said, bashful all of a sudden. "I'm here as a pre-banquet course: an *assiette volante* – or one of your 'morsels on the fly,' as you call *hors-d'oeuvres—"*

The boy could say no more, for Carême strode up, took the teen's head manfully between his hands and kissed him.

This kiss led to another, deeper one. And was followed by fingers removing the young man's jacket.

Thomas reciprocated, shucking the chef's coat off his shoulders but keeping his hands moving across the Frenchman's flanks to his waistband. A little farther down, and to the front, and the young man felt the excitement he was raising in his mentor.

They stepped out of shoes and went tumbling on the bed. Shirts got pulled off, followed by trouser buttons becoming undone. The kissing grew ever deeper; bare skin came into contact with bare skin.

As for Sydney Morgan, she had turned around to find quite a surprise of her own. For in the pleasant little sitting room made up for luncheon sat Mrs. Fitzherbert.

"Ah, Lady Morgan! Won't you come join? They've laid out a lovely tea for us."

"Why, yes." Lady Morgan crossed the room. "It's an unexpected pleasure." Part of her comment was directed at a three-shelved satin wood stand of sandwiches, pastry and cake.

Before she sat down, she made sure to say, "You're looking well. I haven't seen you in quite a while."

"Yes; Boxing Day, I suppose. Tea?"

"Yes, please. And we are so beholden to the Doctor's hospitality."

Mrs. Fitzherbert poured Lady Morgan a cup of green tea, and gestured to the sugar bowl and cream jug. "Do help yourself."

"Thank you. I have to say, the baked goods look tempting as well."

The Prince's secret wife plucked off the dish of cut cake slices, which she placed on the table between them. "Indeed. Mrs. Lister is always so considerate in everything she does."

Out of sheer upbringing, both ladies stared at the selection a silent moment. Indecision paid its mute lip-service, the novelist said sheepishly, "Perhaps we should . . . . "

"Yes." Mrs. Fitzherbert giggled very sprightly. "Why don't we?"

Each selected a slice and placed it on their respective plates. Once again, through cozy proximity, the Irish noblewoman noted the large and charming bracelet her tea companion wore. The top of which was oval and encircled with size-matched pearls.

Lady Morgan took a nibble. "Will we be having dinner upstairs?"

"I believe we shall. For the time being, Mrs. Lister arranged for tea down here to keep me 'out of the way.' Although, she's much too polite to say such a thing aloud."

Sydney Morgan sampled her tea. "And is there any particular reason why today would be different? She's usually contented as a clam to have us sat around the kitchen table while she bustles about."

"Ah. Well, there you see – today *is* different. Doctor Kitchiner arranged for one of the young Pavilion undercooks to be her apprentice for the day."

"A young man?"

"Why, yes."

"A certain Thomas Daniels, to be precise . . . ?"

Mrs. Fitzherbert raised a lopsided grin. "That is the young man. You know the lad?"

Lady Morgan deflected by having more of her cake. "You could say that, yes." The crumbs helped disguise her own grin. "I wonder what spurred," mused the novelist, "this sudden apprentice day . . . . "

Mrs. Fitzherbert replied dutifully, "Because, as the Doctor explained, he's seen quite a marked devotion to his craft from the young man over the last several months, and wouldn't mind furthering the boy's career."

While Lady Morgan sipped her tea again, it gave her mind a moment to consider the devotion Thomas had for Carême was more a matter of the heart than apprenticeship, but in the end, it equalled about the same display of competence. Surely there wasn't much the London caterer could teach young Master Daniels that Carême didn't have *firm* in hand. In fact, Lady Morgan suddenly suspected the master chef had the young man *still* under his educational control at that very moment.

Now the novelist could settle back and enjoy her tea. Being conspiratorial was fun. "Incidentally, do you know if Kitchiner's young architect friend also came down from London for today's festivities?"

"Mr. Hardwick – Philip?"

"Yes, that's the young man."

"I'm not aware if he could get away," said Mrs. Fitzherbert. "But, it's early still."

"Well, I do hope he's able to attend."

Now it was Mrs. Fitzherbert's turn to feel conspiratorial. "I know what you mean. The good Doctor's face does light up so whenever Philip enters the room."

"Yes, it is true."

"And speaking of architects, I had a chance meeting with someone I know: William Porden."

"The designer of the Regent's stables?"

"The very one. But Lady Morgan, the man and I have more of an immediate relationship than that . . . he designed my house!"

"Your home in Brighton?"

"Yes, on Castle Square, just a stone's throw from the Pavilion."

"How very interesting."

"Porden made plans for the Pavilion too, but George rejected his idea for a Chinese exterior. I think he was quite right to approve Nash's Indian-inspired redesign. And quite ironically, Nash was inspired by Porden's Mogul style for the stables. Sometimes it can be quite a paradoxical old world."

"I quite agree, Mrs. Fitzherbert."

"Please do call me Maria Anne – or, 'Fitzy' like the Prince."

Lady Morgan shed a warm smile. "Then you should call me Sydney if you like, Fitzy."

The women laughed and moved on to the plate of buttered sandwiches.

"But I do like working with John Nash," said the Regent's wife. "He's such a straight-forward soul, but polite, and a genius. And he wears his genius as lightly as some men wear a riding coat, yet the ideas come from a profound, apparently bottomless source."

Morgan attempted not to sound too interested. "And, have you been working with Mr. Nash?"

"Well – I'm sure I can tell *you,*" said Fitzy like she'd been caught with her hand in the biscuit barrel. "You see, George is planning new private quarters for himself, on the ground floor by the Music Room. And the Prince has devised – with Nash's help – a secret staircase from his bedroom up to the floor above."

"Oh, my goodness. Secret passages; how intriguing. But why?"

Mrs. Fitzherbert proceeded to blush like a girl of seventeen. "Because, above his bedroom, I will have my own private quarters for occasional, shall we say, dark-hour use."

Sydney was stunned. "But how will you ever get into the palace in the first place?"

"Ah, see, here the good Doctor's good egises come into play, for he's directed Nash to provide an underground service tunnel running from the new block development on the south-east border of the property, all the way under the east lawn, and around to the north cellar of the Pavilion – the location of the Regent's new suite."

"How extraordinary." A sudden pang in her heart had Lady Morgan realizing how difficult it was for Mrs. Fitzherbert to live in Castle Square – a stone's throw away – and yet, despite the closeness, never be able to stroll across the plaza and see him in his home. What a painful situation for man and wife to endure.

The Irish woman's eyes must have been lingering on her companion's bracelet.

Tenderly, Mrs. Fitzherbert asked, "Would you like to see inside?"

"Oh. I didn't know it opened up. A locket?"

"A miniature painting." She popped a small clasp on one long side. The lid hinged open.

Lady Morgan was expecting by the term 'miniature' to see a portrait, but instead found herself regarding only a person's eye and eyebrow.

"It's a gift from George," the bracelet's owner explained. "He said whenever I'm feeling lonely, lost or isolated in the world, to look him in the eye and know I am loved." She regarded it now, moving it closer to her sad smile. "Window to the soul, as they say."

Mrs. Fitzherbert gathered herself, slipping off the bracelet and giving it to Lady Morgan so she could inspect it at her leisure. She continued in a brighter tone, "It quite humbles me really – all the fuss and expense of a tunnel and secret stairs and two suites – but on the other hand, few are the tokens of love that could possibly signal a greater devotion." She took a sip of her tea with relative calm.

Internally, the lady-novelist heart of Sydney Morgan could not have agreed more sympathetically than it did. She was touched by the tragic nature of it all, for both George and Maria Anne were so faithful and yet forced by the nameless, heartless "State" to live in secret, always fearful of a knock on the door.

It also caused Lady Morgan to realize the depth of importance Doctor Kitchiner's involvement played. He facilitated their happiness in a literal, tangible way.

Although only removed from the polite ladies at tea by a few dozen feet, Thomas and Antonin Carême might have been on the other side of the world.

They lay atop the sheets of a dishevelled bed in the cozy security of one another's arms. Eventually their post-lovemaking languor gave way to a revitalized connectedness.

Carême sat up, using the headboard to support his back, and invited the young man to re-settle his head against the man's chest, which Thomas did eagerly.

Thomas chuckled without warning and lifted his light eyes to his mentor. "The good Doctor may not look much like Cupid, but he can play one shure when called upon."

Carême smiled. "No matter how good he is, if I had the choice, I'd rather see *you* in pair of wings and diapers."

Thomas, youth that he was, twisted involuntarily as he convulsed in laughter, hugging his lover even tighter. To Carême's ears, the silvery tones were like high scudders blowing threatening clouds away.

Once the boy settled down again, Carême's smile only grew larger. "Maybe I shouldn't tell it, but Lady Morgan has a special name for you and all your cohorts in the Pavilion's kitchens."

"What is it . . . ?"

"She says you are all 'chuckleheads'."

Thomas' blank expression raised into a grin. "And you, I'm sure you defended my honour, right?"

Carême shrugged, caught red-handed. "I may have agreed that in French we have an equivalent term."

"Which is?"

"*Tête de linotte.*"

Thomas mouthed the unfamiliar sounds. "*Tete* – that's head, correct?"

"*Oui.*"

"And – *Lee - Nooo*—"

"Linotte – that is, *lee-Note.*"

"*Tête de linotte.*" Thomas was proud of his mastery of the new phrase, but then scowled. "What's a linotte?"

"It's a particular, chattering, laughing bird. Perhaps in English it is similar."

"A linnet, I guess. She's noisy. So, a 'Linnet Head' in your French is a chucklehead in my English."

Carême bent forward to kiss the boy's flushing ruby lips; he could not resist. "You look so endearing speaking French in your English way. But if you come to Paris, you must learn to speak it in their accent."

"Oh"—a light went off behind the young man's eyes—"like the French capital's version of Cockney English. How would they say it in their dialect?"

"I'd say *tête de lee-note,* like I taught you, but in Paris, they'd say *tête de lee-nut,* and really bite off the *Nut* at the end."

Thomas tried it a few times: "*tête de lee-nut; tête de lee-nut; tête de lee-nut.*"

"*Oui.*" Carême was impressed. "You pick up the sounds quickly. You would learn French rapidly if you lived there."

"In Paris . . . ?" Thomas was suggestive, not needing to state the obvious 'with you' part of the question.

Carême grew uncomfortable, only responding to the above-water portion of the query. "In Paris, or Dijon, or Orleans – anywhere."

Perhaps this small break in their connection caused Thomas to pull himself upright.

He sat against the headboard next to Carême and sobered his tone. "The next few days, they'll be hell in the kitchens. State banquets require everyone to function to their highest level."

"That they do. However, each one in the Pavilion knows what they need to do and who to report to. We are well positioned to win the battle."

"Battle positions – that's what it's like. Equivalent to our guest's strategy in the Wars. Nicholas was good pursuing Napoleon every mile back to Paris from Moscow."

"Don't let François hear you say Grand Duke Nicholas was good at anything."

"Why?"

"Well, it's no secret *monsieur* Distré hates him. He loathes him as a cock-strutting boor who . . . . Well, the *maître d'hôtel* has a pronounced dislike for brass and braid."

Thomas was struck. "Yes. All military 'glory' is vainglory if weighed against the human misery it took to achieve."

"Vainglory . . . " Carême mumbled.

"What's that?"

"I said, vainglory," repeated the chef. "I keep my politics to myself, but to think Russian and England will be the two Empires to shape the course of the world over the next hundred years – quite frankly, it makes me shiver for the fate of *la libertè.*"

"Well, forgive me, but 'the next hundred years' is too large a timescale for me to think about." The young man attempted a chuckle. "I still have the next few days to get through. And then there are thoughts of what happens, as we say, after the ball."

"What do you mean? Your position at the Pavilion is secure."

"Yes, true, but I won't be there all my life. Is that all my future might hold?" He suddenly picked up Carême's hand and interlaced their fingers.

"Perhaps," Carême suggested, "going to London and working with Mrs. Lister would be good for you. You can take what you've learned and improve her business, and I know you'll continue to grow. I myself learned the most from *monsieur* Bailly during my catering days in Paris."

The boy was quiet, merely playing with the man's fingers. His 'future,' but what kind could the chef and lad possibly have of one together . . . ? Right now, it was not possible.

"But after this week," Carême said, "things will go back to normal."

Thomas held his eyes. "After today, you mean, things will go back to your normal."

Thomas referred, of course, to François, and Carême could not deny it. Instead, he raised his arm and placed it across the young man's back and shoulders. He slowly drew Thomas close to him again.

Carême spoke very softly, "The Doctor was talking about turtle doves. They fly all the way from North Africa to find safe nesting spots on English soil. With you in my arms, Thomas, the Doctor has provided a cozy nesting place for us on his personal shores."

The boy closed his eyes. Their lips met, and in quick succession, first touch turned into impassioned embrace. Mouths opened, essences flowed as tongues mingled with breaths grew choppy and fevered.

In one deft motion, Carême took ahold of the willing young man's waist and laid him flat on the bed.

Like a cunning feline hunter, the man pulled Thomas down towards him so the lad's backside pressed against the chef's thighs. Then, hand behind each knee, he lifted the boy's legs in the air, letting the tip of his erection come into contact with the boy's portal.

Thomas moaned, using spit from his mouth to moisten the insistent head of his mentor. Inside, he was relaxed though, delighting in the internal feel of the chef's earlier anointing.

Carême entered him, holding the boy's eyes as Thomas' expression went from a sad one to another teetering on pain and ecstasy.

The young man lifted his hands to behind his lover's head, saying, poignant with emotion, "I've longed for this; too many eyes at the Pavil—"

Carême sunk in, delighting too at how silky smooth the boy's passage felt with his initial loving still making Thomas all his.

As he pulled back, settling into a primal rhythm melding the lovemaking souls of the men together, Carême had a wicked thought. He unwillingly saw François and Brigitte in their trysting – flesh enflamed and rubbing together – under the exposed framework of the onion dome; on rooftops, beneath the shadows of the colonettes; over the handrails at the top of the Water Tower.

They never had trouble finding out of the way places in the Pavilion, away from prying eyes.

That very minute, unbeknownst to Carême – but perhaps intuitively felt – the French maid was ensconced in her duties at the Prince Regent's seaside home, the very place the chef had abandoned François in favour of Ser Cupid's hospitality and an unexpected *liaison* with Thomas Daniels.

Yet, with typical Gallic efficiency, Brigitte worked through determined mental steps to "prepare things," as ordered. For not more than twenty minutes previous, the Royal coach from Claremont House had deposited the maid and her mistress on the back steps of the marine villa.

From this hush-hush point of discretion, the Princess informed her servant she had a pre-arranged appointment to attend to, and called upon the Butler to hail her a cab.

All of this was done without Brigitte having the least chance to enquire after details. Therefore, the neglected companion maid bustled about her tasks with hot speed, relishing the moment the noisome chores would be at an end and she could fly to François' side. She imagined how she'd inform the handsome man of *Brigitte's* return.

Meanwhile, being of sound mind – and a body well rested from the cloying pleasures of Brighton – a figure made her way unescorted through the empty spaces of the Club; she headed instinctively towards the private air of Kitchiner's penthouse.

Mrs. Lister was already there, half-facing a hot burner of the very Good Doctor's sauce stove. Knackered from preparation work for the day's Club dinner, and taxed by a pair of promised helping-hands never showing up, she became lost in considerations.

Now, taking the moment of stillness to heat water for her own tea, she stared at the warmed teapot and meditatively chewed over the rounds of Scotch shortbread spread on a plate.

'House of intrigue,' she mused, imagining the goings-on behind each of Kitchiner's closed doors and shuttered windows. The Doctor's Brighton base of operations was a world unto itself. And the woman suddenly realized it was not exactly fair to say her assistant for the day never showed up. But on the undercook's arrival from the Pavilion, Kitchiner had whisked him away – before the lad even had a chance to peg his cap, or switch his street clothes for chefly whites.

Then there had been the rigmarole of orchestrating "a private" tea-service for Mrs. Fitzherbert and Lady Morgan.

The kettle began its rumble towards a steady simmer, masking fainter sounds coming from behind the caterer. As she took it up and filled her teapot, Lister wondered what the Prince's wife and Irish novelist could possibly find to talk about. She laughed.

"House of intrigue, indeed!"

But while she thought these things, she'd failed to recognize Charlotte's calling to her as the Princess strode through the penthouse.

Consequently, Elizabeth turned and was surprised to find the Royal standing on the other side of the communal table, peeling off her long white travelling gloves.

"Sorry to have given you a start, Dear Lister, but you didn't seem to hear me singing out as I approached."

The Princess was also clad in a dark riding cowl, still dusty from errant road dirt that had somehow made its way into the coach.

The caterer flustered a hand. "My, I am a silly goose. Why, lost to my own ruminations that way, I wouldn't even hear an army sneaking up. Pardon." She began a stiff curtsey.

"Oh, no! No need for that. Remember the Doctor's rules: under this roof, we are merely a collection of old friends, gathered to our own equal society."

Charlotte disrobed her riding mantle and plopped it on a chair before plunking herself down upon it.

Lister explained, as she trundled over to fetch another cup and saucer from the Welsh dresser, "I was just about to sit to tea. Your timing could not have been more perfect."

Elizabeth placed items on the table within easy reach of her Royal guest: sugar bowl, creamer, teapot, and the dish of shortbread.

The London caterer poured the Princess a cup of the steaming infusion. "We were expecting your company a little later on."

"Yes, I *escaped.* As soon as the hideously long coach ride from Claremont House ended, I left my maid, and here I am!" She stirred in lumps of sugar, several at a time.

"Prince Leopold—"

"Is travelling separately, with his Private Secretary. They are getting a delayed start from Mayfair, where affairs detained him last night. They're not expected till suppertime."

"I see. And Brigitte knows nothing, concerning the Club?"

"Heavens, no! That's a *family matter,* as well you know." Charlotte sipped her tea, eyes noticeably inspecting the biscuits. "Speaking of supper, the Prince Consort and I are eagerly looking forward to renewing our eating customs in Brighton. Carême ever and always arranges the most delectable – and appropriate, or so he tells me – post-supper puddings!"

Elizabeth added a little cream to her own cup. Moving her spoon about, she relayed, "Well, you'll be able to thank Carême in person soon enough. He's already in the Club somewhere."

"Oh, yes? Where?"

"I shouldn't tell tales out of school"—Lister grinned—"for I do not know for sure, but presumably the Good Doctor has him holed up in some private study, poring over Kitchiner's manuscript for his cookery *exposé.*"

"Oh, dear!" Charlotte laughed, very ladylike. "Such intelligence makes me glad to have a few, quiet moments just to think, sip tea, and"—her eyes alighted on the buttery treats—"engage in less weighty discourses."

Did Elizabeth Lister, London caterer and spy *extraordinaire,* dare risk speaking frankly? She did. Picking up the serving dish and offering the Princess a piece of shortbread, she said, "Honestly, me as well. The Doctor's drive for culinary perfection can sometimes be wearing."

Charlotte lifted her selected biscuit. "I can imagine, especially on you, as he relies upon your years of expert service to coax his cerebral considerations towards matters more practical."

"Maybe so, but in that regard, Chef Carême outranks me decidedly." She topped off the Princess' cup. "So I'll leave them to it."

"Quite correct." Charlotte Augusta of Wales finally took a bite. As she chewed, with Lister following suit with her own morsel, the Princess sank through degrees to a more reflective state of mind. Eventually, she lowered her hand, saying, "Dear Mrs. Lister, I would like to offer sincere apology – for what I said."

The face muscles of the caterer went slack. She did not know what the Princess meant.

Sensing clarification was needed, Charlotte added, "That one time we were having dinner here and . . . well, I *intimated* that women who worked in business were somehow – dare I repeat it – deceptive. For that, I am sorry."

Lister insisted, "It's not necessary—"

The Princess interrupted with a frown. "It is. It's something that's been on my mind. Ofttimes, in reflection, the extent of my sheltered isolation from life comes to me. I hope you do forgive me, because I am sorry for being a beastly boor that day."

Elizabeth was touched by the young woman's sincerity. "Forgiven," the caterer intoned as a fetching blush stole across her face. "To be transparent about the matter, Princess, I didn't necessarily start out seeking to be a 'woman of business.' At one time, I harboured quite different ambitions."

"Oh, yes?"

She nodded. "You see, I had a beau, and once contemplated marriage and motherhood with him."

"What happened?"

"What happened . . . ? He proved himself to be anything but . . . constant."

"Oh." Charlotte angled her lower arms against the tabletop, drawing herself closer to the more mature woman. The Princess' pitch also dropped as she said, "Some men never seem to learn the world is *not* their oyster; never learn they cannot rely on status to shield their infidelities from societal view."

Did it strike the Royal, just at that moment, how her words might have unconsciously been directed towards Leopold as well? An observer – say in the form of one Mrs. Lister – could not be sure. But keen observation did regard Charlotte stiffen at that precise moment, set her shortbread down, and fall back into her chair. The slightest bit of colour rouged her young cheeks.

Elizabeth acted like she hadn't seen a thing, returning to the topic of fellows at large. "Oh, you are so right. Some men can never seem content with happiness, always stirring the pot, knowingly or not, to bring threats of danger to their domestic arrangements. It makes one wonder what is on their minds."

Charlotte let loose with a remarkably un-princessly chortle. It continued to hang hoarsely in the air as she said, "My Dear Mrs. Lister – I think we both know what that one *thing* is!"

Communal laughter followed. Both women pulled up and tucked into their collation with gusto.

"Oh, Princess! I feel truly blessed to know you like this. As beloved as you are, if people could see your inner sparkle and wit – why, they'd only treasure you all the more."

Far from taking the comment in stride, Charlotte's countenance grew sad. "I am *beloved* while my father – Dear Pa-Pa – is . . . not."

"Princess; pardon. I didn't mean—"

"No, I know you didn't intend the comparison, but I often feel the unhappiness it must bring to him. However"—a newly honed edge crept upon her resonance—"they do not know him. He would be beloved too if ordinary subjects knew of the hard-choice reforms he's working on behind the scenes. Reforms that will make people freer of both the Peerage and the spying abuses of Whitehall."

Lister responded viscerally. She commented with a tear in her eye, "The people have those hopes for you, Princess. Few Royals have been invested with a nation's aspirations as you are."

Though intending to have no such results, the London caterer's words set Charlotte to considering how loved the Princess' offspring would also be, certainly when they were infants.

The young woman longed to be a parent, but the notion also held dread for her. She had no direct experience of mothering in her childhood, growing up lonely, separated from the girl's Danish Princess ma-ma for "political reasons." Her Grand Pa-Pa schemed to ram an illegal Act through Parliament to pretend Prince George was not already married. After Charlotte's birth, George drove her mother back to Denmark. What person would want their illicit 'wife' around them once her role as child-bearer had been fulfilled?

But Charlotte had suffered. And this suffering explained the young woman's "tolerance" of her father's arrangements with Mrs. Fitzherbert.

Yes, knowing her own bastard status was not entirely un-useful to the Head of State in training.

It was through such training she'd gained great confidence in herself.

And yet . . . she had so far failed to produce an heir. Politically speaking, she knew the incompletion of her *rôle* left her vulnerable.

She reached out to the woman across the table for understanding.

"I suppose you want to know," Charlotte began tentatively, "how things fare with me since . . . since I lost the baby."

Touched deeply, near the heart of Elizabeth's own womanhood, Mrs. Lister nodded gently.

"Well, I'll confess to being worried: it was not the first."

Into Lister's pall of silence, Charlotte inserted a sputtering glibness. "Come now; it isn't all bad news. And according to my Palace-appointed physician at Claremont House, I remain 'Fit and Able' to throw a whole stable-full of princely brats – just like Dear Grand Ma-Ma did."

The caterer instinctively drew her apron hem to her mouth, attempting to shield her smile. But in the end, the action proved fruitless, as the laughing sparkle in the woman's eyes prompted Charlotte to giggle at the Princess' own 'wickedness.'

Then, linking hands once more, both let loose with unguarded, sisterly laughter.

When she had sufficient breath, Charlotte hastened to add, "Of course, horrid old Doctor Hogarth didn't put it in *exactly* those words, but his meaning was nevertheless *exactly* the same!"

Rocked back on their chairs, Elizabeth blurted: "God bless you, Princess. You have a truly fine disposition."

Meanwhile, with the London caterer hardly noticing it, Charlotte had refilled the woman's teacup. After this, Charlotte suddenly reached for one of her gloves. Her eyes had filled with tears.

"Oh, Princess," Elizabeth uttered in muted tones, "bear up. Be brave."

"I am, Dear Lister; I am to both. And yet, until I have a child, I'll somehow feel less of a person."

"You are still young! You have the rest of your life ahead of you. Doctor Hogarth will undoubtedly prove right about you and your *litter* of princely pups."

"I also worry about Leopold losing interest in me—"

"I wouldn't!"

"And I worry about the State, for the sooner I bear an heir, the quicker my amoral uncles recede into the background as irrelevant. There they can continue their lives of quiet dissipation in quiet non-contemplation. That of course, Dear Lister, *is* best for England, as well as the U.K. and rest of our Empire abroad."

Elizabeth replied with a heartfelt, though soft, "Amen."

And of course, Elizabeth Lister, caterer spy, was correct, although she lacked in the proper understanding of just how determined Charlotte Augusta of Wales was. For, trusting in herself to a high degree, she'd move heaven and earth to prevent one of her unworthy uncles from ascending to the seat of Saint Edward's throne.

A deep-seated part of Charlotte understood she *was* England's only hope. And she felt it about herself as devoutly as any one of the grubby-faced subjects genuflecting before her on one of Leopold's public ambles.

Chapter 14: A Morning in the Life of a Banquet

– 7 A.M. –

As Carême strode out of his office to begin the workday, he was aware the Great Kitchen had already been a bursting hive of activity for a couple of hours. And not merely the Great Kitchen, but every nook and cranny of the Pavilion's suite of concoction spaces had been organized to play their part in pulling off the Regent's State Dinner for the Russian heir-apparent, Grand Duke Nicholas.

The chef locked hands behind his back while he inched past the preparation tables. They were laid out for his inspection with all the fresh produce and herbs the cooks would be relying upon today. One leaf out of place, one black mark, and the master of this domain would pluck the offending vegetable matter out of service.

However, having worked with Chef Carême for the better part of a year now, the leafy greens and plump root bulbs selected for use were all of the best, unblemished quality. Because of this, Carême let a little smile of satisfaction show; he knew from his own days as underchef this was reward enough for a job well done.

His staff, waiting patiently on the other side of the table, responded by relaxing a bit. Over their shoulders, he spied stocks, roux, fonds and aspics – all in closed pots on the ranges – waiting for use.

While he inspected the staggering array of poultry, game, fowl, rabbit, pork, veal and beef arranged for his inspection on the other preparation surface, Carême noted the activity opposite this second table. The roasting fires were being lit. Spit-jack boys stoked the coals, and the first whiff of stifling carbon monoxide clogged the kitchen airways.

There was a loud thud, rattling stacks of silver cloches on the great oval warming table in the middle of the room.

Carême turned to chastise whoever it was disturbing his morning peace and saw Donald Bland, the Kitchen Comptroller, with a scowl on his face.

The chef, keeping his hands behind him, walked over to the man.

"There," said Bland sharply. He'd banged a string-and-brown-paper parcel on the table and now flashed his carbon steel penknife under Carême's nose.

"Here are your *cartes de menus* back from the printer." He angrily cut the string on the bundle. "I hope you know it will take an Act of Parliament to pay for this meal: *Forty entrees?!*" The Comptroller ripped the paper off. "In a year when thousands have starved to—"

The chef stayed the functionary with the mere lifting of his finger. "I thank you, *and* will let you know if you're needed or wanted in His Highness' kitchens today. Now, go."

Bland, slowly, methodically, sheathed his blade, his eyes glossing over with contempt. "Fine, but get ready for your master's tables to be meagre for months after this. What? – two soups, four entrees – you'll be bored to tears making apple sauce to go with the tough old goose his creditors will give him to roast." He turned to walk away. "Artist! Ha."

To characterize Donald Bland's leave-taking as curt would be an understatement, but Carême did not care. The chef's task was to create a meal fit for the annals of history, and by God – or the memory of the French Republic – he would do it.

He picked up a gold-edged menu card from the stack, admiring the engraved emblems of Empire at the top, both British and Russian. But as his eyes scanned the neat, dense lines of text below, he scoffed at Bland internally. *Forty entrées!* As if that were our biggest concern, when there are also forty *entremets,* eight soups, eight fish and sixteen roasts. Not to mention more than a dozen trays of *hor-d'oeuvres,* and a hundred-fifty individual servings of hot dessert – soufflés of apple and vanilla, plus molten chocolate fondant cakes. The latter was yet another of Carême's inventions.

The chef placed the card back, suddenly confronted with what an overwhelming day it would be.

– *8 A.M.* –

As the new hour struck, half a dozen covered trays from the Great Kitchen's steam table were picked up by the waiting army of footmen. These young men would troop into the Salon with the Family's breakfast service. As soon as the servers departed, a second round of fifteen footmen picked up identical trays for the guest's breakfast service in the Red Drawing Room.

Cornelius Hook was also there, glancing at his pocket watch and tapping a surly foot. The Regent's Private Secretary personally waited to take up the Prince's breakfast tray. But he was not alone. Besides the black-suited valet to the Grand

Duke, Brigitte de Saint-Exupéry scanned the line and instantly recognized her charger to take up to Charlotte and Leopold. The Royal Couple had been at Brighton for a week now, and the pair had grown so fond of Carême's version of *baba au rhum*, miniature versions even appeared on the princely breakfast tray. She inspected to insure that nothing was amiss, and hurried off with the tray to the other side of the villa.

Removed from the bustle and steam of the Great Kitchen, Carême and François, and the entire battery of pastry and confectionary chefs, camped out in the Cold Kitchen.

Eight sugar work *pièces montées* needed to be completed: two scenic; two rustic; two pavilions; and two Classical-style trophies.

The bases for the scenic sculptures had been finished the night before, and now that they had set rock-hard, were being decorated. A pair of boys applied goldleaf on a rocky cliff-face and burnished it with agate irons to flawless perfection. Surmounted on top would be a sculpted double-headed Russian eagle made of 'feathery' prunes.

Another set of young men applied green tints to the other scenic base – a grassy island isolated by ribbony blue waters.

Carême and François worked side by side.

Using marzipan modelling tools, the master had already converted an uninspiring four pounds of sweetened pork lard into a work of art – a lion asleep, his shaggy-maned head resting in the crook of his right arm. Later, its whiteness would disappear as a fine brown powder got blown into each of its sculpted crevices for a realistic effect. Eventually, the lion would be placed upon its island, nearly covering it entirely.

"I don't know," François said, shaking his head and partially laughing.

"Do not know what?" Carême glanced at François' task. The *maître d'hôtel* busied himself making the shields: Romanov for the eagle's breast and Plantagenet to lie against the recumbent lion's flank.

"I don't know why we work this hard," explained François, his tone more mirth than menace. "After all, this banquet is to celebrate France's humiliating defeat at barbarian hands."

Carême returned to his task, relieved to know only rhetoric was at stake.

"Because," François concluded with a grin, "now the pigs are swilling their way through the pearls of French Cuisine. But you and I, we know they are unworthy."

Now it was Carême's turn to smile. *"Oui, Villon.* Why do you think we are doing the Russian eagle in prunes and the British lion in lard?"

After a pause, both Frenchmen laughed openly – it was their little comeuppance on 'their betters.'

– *9*A.M. –

The Great Kitchen was awash in flesh. It all had to receive preparation for cooking: large, lean joints larded with laces of fatback for internal basting on the spit; poultry, trussed and seasoned for the braising pans; wiry game, like rabbit and venison, barded with pure-white drapes of caul to add moisture while they were grilled. It was here Thomas Daniels showed his assertive self, for Carême had put him in charge of prepping the roasts, and seeing the *grosses pièces* all the way to completion.

"What's a gross piece again?" a fellow undercook asked Thomas.

"She's the centrepieces of the First Table. No flowers! Food is on display – they'll be placed down the centre, evenly spaced."

The other young man peered over the impressive lay-out of meat and poultry on the prep table. "Which to do first?"

"Start with the centrepiece roasts – the turkey, then the round of beef, the quarter of veal, and those three pheasants. They have to be prepped and given to the Roasters first."

"Oh, yes," his companion remembered. "They have to cool completely so Carême can decorate them."

"That's right, with sauce and thin-cut chives, *et cetera*. The other eight roasts for the main course can be barded now, trussed up in string, and then taken to the cooler downstairs. We won't need them finished cooking for hours; not until about 15 minutes before we set the Second Table."

"Don't they need much time to cool?"

"No. They'll go to the table hot! And with minimal surface decoration, but with tasteful accompaniments on the planters, like tartlets of salsify root; whole, simmered black truffles, and pan-fried potato balls. *Lyonnaise,* she's called."

The other young man nodded, already trussing the turkey.

Thomas paused a moment, surveying the table of fresh. A small surge of panic edged his tone, saying, "Hurry! After the roasts, we've got to start on the forty *entrées!"*

Meanwhile, in the Table Decking Room, François glanced over the nearly sixty-foot-long sideboard completely covered with freshly polished platters. Near the doors to the Banqueting Room, carts stood by, stacked high with the Pavilion's china dinner service. Today, all 120 place settings would be used to set, and then *re-set* the fifty-foot table for Carême's two courses.

Close to these carts sat houseboys and sweep-up lads from the kitchens. They were on the floor, set to their task by the maitre-d', with rags in hands going over every piece of flatware to ensure it sparkled.

Suddenly Gris Thorndyke was there yelling at François. The usurped Chief Footman had his own ideas on priorities. "Distré – what the hell! These boys should be wiping down the glassware for the table, not the soup spoons."

François walked over to be very close to the jealous Englishman. "Anyone who is not an amateur knows, *monsieur* Lightfoot, the Head Table Decker, needs the flatware first to compose the basic table settings." François deftly snatched a rag and threw it in Gris' face. "If *you* want to be helpful, then you can start wiping the glasses."

"Mr. Lightfoot . . . !" Thorndyke was already storming into the Banqueting Room to play tattletale.

François returned to his task at the sideboard. He glanced over the platters, knowing he'd have to come back and assign each one a number relating to a menu item. But for now, he inspected the sixteen stands Carême had selected yesterday for choice *entrées* and *entremets* that needed higher positions on the table. Gratified they were all immaculately polished, he set them aside for later use.

François had also singled out two round and two square trays for the *pièces montées* not architectural in nature. These he grabbed and headed back to the Cold Kitchen.

When he arrived, after closing the door quietly behind him, he set the round trays close to where the completed trophies were drying. The *marine* example was a Classical column with the prows of Roman ships sticking out symmetrically in three levels. It represented Britain's power at sea. Next to it was another Classical trophy, but this time, round shields formed a core against which Roman armour was attached. Like a barbed porcupine, spears stuck out from behind the armour and represented Russia's land army sweeping across the European continent. François considered it a bitter memorial for raping and pillaging from the Prussian frontier all the way to the steps of the Louvre. What *Glory*.

To clear his head, he went to observe an artist at work.

Carême was seated on a high stool, busy with his sugar work pavilion – a miniature version of Nash's onion dome and arcade for the Salon. It was breathtakingly beautiful, for months ago, Carême had drawn the Pavilion's architects' intricate trefoil design of the stone tracery for the arcade onto a block of wood. One of the Royal Household carpenters had carefully incised and cut the pattern into the wood, and Carême had used the mould to make sugar-paste grates for his model. These rested on the table before him – all sixteen of them – while Carême finished the drum to receive the dome. He applied shingles all around the roof just below the onion dome, and which resembled fish scales to François' eyes. The magnificent dome itself was complete and accurate right down to clear panels of candy glass in the dome's windows. François knew Carême had also bettered Nash with a small lamp ready to go inside the dome and illuminate the windows from the inside.

The matching piece to this gazebo was not as complete, but as "the Russian Pavilion," it featured baroque columns supporting an undulating dome of the type one might see in Saint Petersburg, designed by Bartolomeo Rastrelli, the great architect who built much of the Czar's city.

Eventually this sugar work dome would be burnished in blue gold leaf, and a second lamp stood by to illuminate its edible windows from within.

The door rattled open without warning. "Begging pardon, sir." One of the red-cheeked spit jacks was standing there.

"What is it?" François asked.

"Begging pardon, sir – Chef Carême – but you are summoned to the Great Kitchen."

Carême turned, eyeing the lad narrowly. "Summoned, by whom?"

"Prince George, sir."

Carême stood. "François, take over for me. Continue applying the shingles as I've started."

"Yes, Chef."

During what seemed an interminable walk back to the main kitchen, Carême feared the Regent's presence signalled a change to the 4 o'clock serving of dinner. It would be disastrous, but not uncommon for the caprice-prone Prince.

The second reason was almost worse – George on one of his house tours for 'very important people.'

As soon as the *chef de cuisine* cleared the corridor doorway, he saw it was the second reason. The Regent's group of seven blocked the natural flow of work, standing as they were at the far end of a preparation table.

He took a deep breath and strode over to them. "Your Highness."

"Ah, Carême, I've brought you some visitors. They are dying to see how things 'work' at the Pavilion."

The Prince's Private Secretary sneered over the Regent's shoulder like a lurking shadow.

Carême bowed, slightly. *"Enchanté."*

"May I present," the Prince continued, "the Marquess of Londonderry"—he motioned to a mousy man—"and Lady Frances, the Marchioness. Also, their son Charles Stewart."

The Regent didn't have to gesture to him, for the strongly good-looking, blue-eyed Adonis was standing – left hand leaning on the table – like a party bored-partly amused Apollo Belvedere. The mere mention of his name conjured his *résumé d'action* for Carême, for the notorious blade had first 'distinguished' himself at the Congress of Vienna by fist-fighting cab drivers for fares, and then by pinching first-rate ladies' backsides in the Opera's foyer.

The Prince patted the boy's shoulder, breaking the young man from his stupor for a bit. "Stewart's our Ambassador to the Austro-Hungarians, but his diplomatic star may be rising even farther very soon."

The final two persons of the Prince's party were demur, middle-aged women, one of whom cleared her throat.

"And, yes"—the Regent got around to them—"may I present Miss Caroline Law and Miss Jane Octavia – friends of Ma-ma, Queen Charlotte."

Miss Law could stand on no more ceremony and gushed, "What a thrill to meet you, Monsewer Carême. I so look forward to this afternoon's dinner!"

"Me as well," enthused Miss Octavia.

"It's my pleasure to present it to you, *Madames.*"

Carême suddenly noticed – to his discomfort – the Regent had one of his menu cards in his hands. All of the Prince's guests did too.

The Prince held it up. "Very impressive, Carême. Of course, *We* personally went over all the precise details with you previously, but to see it in black and white—"

"And gold," Miss Law interjected.

"—Is gratifying." The Prince quickly scanned for an item about which he could seem knowledgeable. "Especially looking forward to the . . . the . . . . " He stumbled over the French. "Fill-its doo leparow n lorge-netts."

No one, including Carême, knew how to respond.

However, functionaries are never at a loss for words, even when silence is to their benefit. "That's the rabbit, Your Highness."

The Royal turned to the shadow behind him. "I know. But, as you are such a culinary expert, perhaps you'd care to read a few more items to us – with explanations."

He passed the *carte* back, and after an audible swallow, the Secretary began.

"Let's see – there's the . . . the *côtelettes de mouton glacés,* with *purée de navets* – that's . . . um . . . um—"

The young rake provided the answer. "Glazed mutton chops with smashed turnips."

The bravado was such, Carême could not help smiling; it also helped that Charles Steward was completely correct.

"Yes," muttered the weakened functionary. "But there's also the *salade de homards aux laitues*—"

"The American lobster salad on curly-leaf lettuce," the Ambassador supplied immediately. "But tell me, Carême"—he focused his beautifully cold eyes on the chef—"why all this fuss with sitting down to a table already loaded down with vittles? I mean, over here we eat as God intended – in courses, served to us by servants, come to spoon-feed us one by one."

Carême derided like a true diplomat – with dead-pan face and overly sincere tone. *"Ah, oui. Le Yorkshire pouding, n'est-ce pas?"*

Ambassador Steward smiled in spite of himself. What the chef could not have known is to what extent the British aristocrat took a shine to Carême from that moment on.

"I guess what my son is asking"—Lady Frances tried playing peacemaker—"is what is the rationale behind the way you serve; how does it work the way you do it?"

"Yes," agreed Miss Law. "To the untrained eye, it just looks like a sea of food."

"Well," Carême said, calmly resisting the urge to look at the clock on the wall. "It is simple: it follows the Classical model given to us by the ancient Greeks and Romans. The First Table is the appetizer course – soup, fish, *entrées.* Then there is a break to stretch legs while the Second Table is set with the main course of roasts, vegetables and sweet dishes. It's all about sharing the experience with others, exploring the flavours, and"—his glance shot to Steward—"serving one another as equals."

Carême was relieved to see François had arrived.

"Chef Carême, you are required in the Cold Kitchen."

The chef bowed slightly to the VIPs. "Nice to have met you all, but, Highness, duty calls."

"Yes, Carême," replied the Regent. "Be off with you and work your foody, comestible witchery!"

– *10* A.M. –

Thomas worked at the range in the Great Kitchen. He had two pots on the go for dressing the centrepiece roasts of the First Table: readying the *sauce allemande* – pure white – and the *sauce chaud-froid* – with its amber glow of aspic. The *chaud-froid* needed to cool to a syrupy thickness and allow the natural gelatine of the chicken stock to set before being able to spoon it over the cooked and room-temperature quarter of veal.

He had to take what range space he could, for Sous-chef Bauda was busy on another battlefront; the eight soups were beginning to come together.

Thomas took the *allemande* sauce off the heat, putting on its lid with an already-designated paper label of identification.

The second pot he also lidded, but picked it up to walk to the Cold Kitchen to rest.

Meanwhile, in the Household Kitchen next door, the preparation of the staff lunch – their "dinner" – was well underway, but so too were the scaling, gutting and be-boning of the eight fish *relevées*. Some were already gently sim-mering in specially-shaped fish kettles. The delicate smell of citrus, champagne vinegar and lemon juice – to keep the prepared fish white – deliciously pervaded this usually meat and potatoes cooking space.

In addition, croustades were crisping in the ovens to kick off Carême's *assiettes volantes* – "flying plates" – or, his version of hot finger-food to come after the fish dishes were removed from the dining table. Far from an afterthought, the five different kinds, spread over fifteen platters, required meticulous planning and execution.

Returned to the Great Kitchen, Thomas gave his attention to the centrepiece roasts' decorations. He cut a carrot into even slices, and then shaped each round into a triangle. He had to be precise, as each three-sided 'tile' would be matched to a neighbour in a border design.

Unbeknownst to the concentrating young man, François was approaching from the Silver Vault in a sour mood. The velvet-lined tray he held contained long, decorative skewers in sets of differing shaped finials. The maitre-d' was being forced to hand over to Thomas four dozen incredibly valuable *attelets* made by *Maison Odiot,* the silver- and goldsmiths to the French Crown since it the house's founding in 1690. François groused internally that the teen boy had been put in charge of the highly prestigious garniture of the eight *grosses pièces.* Carême planned to prepare one skewer for each roast for Thomas to replicate, and François could envision how the chef would allow the young man the honour of sticking each completed *attelet* into the roast right before the *maître d'hôtel* took them out to place for the First Table.

François set the tray down with a rattle. He told Thomas, "Be careful with these. Even one is worth more than your entire life."

Young Master Daniels attempted a chuckle, but soon saw François was far from joking.

"You have to be aware," continued the maitre-d', "the skewers are of First Grade silver, which is a far purer than your 'sterling,' and easier to bend."

"Thank you for the useful information." Thomas' smile fell flat.

François made to go, but instead leaned over the table and lowered his voice. "I know, because Carême *used* to let me have the privilege of preparing his *attelets.*"

The Frenchman left, and Thomas glanced down on the glinting implements on the tray, feeling intimidated.

And just as he lifted his chin, Donald Bland was there.

"What a waste of money." The Comptroller sneered. "Who will eat the things Carême sticks on these? No one, that's who!"

Thomas slowly shook his head. "I'm afraid you do not understand."

"Understand what, boy?"

"Art. Carême's art, my art, she's a feast for *all* the senses, including sight."

Bland's appearance became ominous, revealing the bottom whites of his eyes. "Well, your *artist* may not make it to see another waste-of-money dinner like this one."

Thomas' resolve grew flinty. "You should stop saying such things, Donald, or very important people could hear them very soon."

The threat only made Bland more punch-drunk with notions of revenge. "Mark my words, boy – I'll get him—"

The undercook curtly cut him off, stress cracking the normally even-keel boy's voice. "Kitchen Comptroller, sir, I'm *shure* busy here, even if you are not!"

– *11 A.M.* –

Great progress had been made on Carême's eight *pièces montées*. The chef worked alone in the Cold Kitchen, attaching miniature fruit to a spectacular tree he'd crafted from molten sugar candy, when a beaming man entered from the hallway.

"Ah," Doctor Kitchiner announced, "there's the man of the hour!" He chuckled. "Or, of the day, I should say."

Carême set down his tools, carefully rising from his stool to not upset his work. He greeted his friend with a smile. "What brings you to the Pavilion, good Doctor?"

"You." He laid a flat palm over the chef's heart. "How has your breathing been? Any light-headedness or muscle weakness?"

"I'm feeling fine today, Doctor. It helps I have been so much in the Confectionary this day. Even for a short while it helps to be away from the coal fumes."

"I am glad to hear you are feeling strong today. Today of all days—" The Doctor was suddenly distracted by what Carême had been working on. He approached the chef's table in awe. A sugar model of a two-story house stood on the grassy banks of a river. It was a country cottage with hipped roof and modest stonework details around the windows and at the corners of the rectangular structure. "Is it a real place?"

"Yes," the chef replied. "It modelled on Peter the Great's rustic summer house on the Neva, in Saint Petersburg."

The Doctor then noticed the *pièce montée's* most astounding feature, for a towering tree anchored one end of the abode and rose above the ridgeline. "My goodness. I'm amazed at the, pardon the expression, 'artistic conceit' of causing a fruit-laden date palm to thrive along the shores of a mostly frozen waterway."

Carême smiled with a well-studied shrug. *"Vive l'art!"* He gestured to the second 'rustic.' "Did you see the English companion to this Russian cottage? You recognize . . . ?"

The Doctor glanced to the second worktable and was astounded afresh. "My goodness! It's a perfect model of the Rottingdean windmill, complete – or, perhaps I should say, *more* than complete – with a giant coconut palm!"

The chef felt gratified. *"Oui."*

It was at this point Kitchiner looked around and caught the other *pièces montées* complete and mounted on silver salvers: the two Classical trophies; the two patriotic animals; the two palatial pavilions. Now, at last, the concept of Carême's art struck him viscerally. What an accomplishment.

All at once, the Doctor remembered his own noteworthy achievement. Now he was as giddy as a schoolgirl.

"Say, old boy, I nearly forgot. I have good news to tell you. Great news, really."

"What is it, Doctor?"

"I've found a publisher for my book!"

"Congratulations. That is indeed wonderful information."

"And I've decided to call it *Apicius Redivivus, or The Cook's Oracle* in honour of all our long, intimate discussions about food, my dear friend."

"An inspired title, to be sure. When does the book appear?"

"The printers say they'll have it ready by the start of summer."

"*Bon.* I will buy the first copy, dear Doctor."

The Doctor's warm smile said how much he appreciated Carême's kind encouragement, but the two did not have much time to enjoy the sentiment of the moment.

François rushed in, clipping his speech as he said, "That *Bosche* is now giving tours like he owns—" Distré saw Kitchiner, stopped and bowed slightly. "*Pardon.* I thought the chef was alone."

Kitchiner asked Carême, "*That* Bosche? Who is—"

"Well, it's a joking nickname François has for a certain German Prince."

"Ye Gads!" The Doctor glanced around playfully. "Has he sneaked his way back-of-house?"

"*Oui, Monsieur.* Leopold is in the Great Kitchen and now cornering Sous -chef Bauda. The Prince Consort is giving a tour to Grand Duke Nicholas, and Charlotte is looking bored and agitated—"

The Doctor interjected: "Ah, yes. Those fellows are old comrades; brothers in arms."

"Oh, dear," Carême said, shaking his head. "I feel bad for the Princess, knowing how taxing these long days of State business are on her restless mind."

"The worst part," François confirmed, "is that now Leopold is summoning you."

The chef explained to Kitchiner, via a tiny grousing sound, "The Family have all day been giving kitchen tours, and I need time to work!"

Suddenly they heard Leopold's voice.

The sound of it was coming from beyond the open dutch-door to the Water Tower Court.

First exchanging covert eye-movements, the three repositioned themselves there, staying out of sight. A quick glance confirmed Charlotte, Leopold and Nicholas stood at the other end of the sun-drenched court, squinting up the heights of the water tower.

Leopold was saying, " . . . And so the Prince has the finest spring water pumped up to a reservoir tank that the Pavilion might have optimal water pressure."

"Water pressure; water pressure," the Princess mocked in an odd, annoyed tone.

"Yes, darling," Leopold said, apparently tone-deaf. "But, Grand Duke, as I was saying—"

"When do we get to ride the horses!" the Princess exclaimed, apropos of nothing evident.

"After Tea, *Männchen* – I mean, *München* – no, I mean, my darling." Leopold's flight of fancy took a tour through a failed term of endearment.

"Are you *quite* all right, Leopold?" The Grand Duke asked. "I think we should retire out of the sun and rest in the Salon. Yes, Princess?"

"Well"—she genuinely did not know—"what do you think, Leopold?"

"Ja." He gathered himself together. "Some tea in the Salon. That would be best; *aber ja."*

With that, the three Royals exited the courtyard for the Service Corridor and their proper side of the marine villa.

Carême, Kitchiner and François were left silenced, wondering at the peculiar display they'd just witnessed. For Carême's part, he'd noticed François' baleful expression the moment the Russian began to speak. It was as if the maitre-d' could have stalked over to the Grand Duke and spit in his face. However, to the chef's relief, it seemed Kitchiner was too giddily caught up in the 'naughty' act of eavesdropping to note François at all. At least, it appeared that way.

As the men relaxed and stood upright in front of the door, a beaming Thomas Daniels entered the court from the same door the Royals had just vacated. He strode over drying his clean hands on his apron.

The young man came straight up to the dutch-door, leaned his elbows on its shelf. "Gentlemen, the guest of honour has arrived."

Within another minute, the men followed Thomas across the court, through the corridor and the Household Kitchen to the Kitchen Courtyard. There he gestured to a low-sided, but enormous crate.

Kitchiner, Carême and François glanced down through the lidless top and saw a massive sea turtle, a hundred pounds or more in weight. It was alive and glanced back at them.

Kitchiner was the first to speak again. "I feel I must convey once more how proud I am you're using *my* turtle soup recipe for today's banquet."

Carême replied, "It is a privilege to use it, and François is in charge of preparing it today."

The Doctor smiled. "Then I know it will be delicious."

"Chef Carême," Friederich Bauda called from the door to the staff kitchen. "Are du free?"

"I am." Then Carême apologized. "If you gentlemen will excuse me."

After his departure, Kitchiner, François and Thomas continued to look down on the creature.

"Someone will have to kill her," Thomas said.

"Oh, by the way." Kitchiner was suddenly all smiles for François. "I hear Princess Charlotte is comfortably ensconced back in her chambers, and so is Brigitte . . . quite comfortably."

The suggestive tone was all the rebuke the physician needed to reprove François, who shed a nervous squint at young Master Daniels.

In the silent moment that followed, François felt revolted that Carême had shared such 'private information' with the eccentric Englishman. The *maître d'hôtel* of course did not know Kitchiner had connections in the Pavilion who could have told him, and not Carême.

The Doctor clapped his hands. "Well, young men – I know you are busy boys, and so I will take my leave, and leave you to it." He winked at Thomas Daniels, before strolling out of the court towards the street and Castle Square.

François told Thomas in ice-coldness, "Time's ticking. Kill it; butcher it. I need to start the soup *tout suite.*"

"But – but, that's below me. I—"

François lowered his chin as he came up to the young man with the whites of his eyes showing. "Nothing is below your type, boy."

Chapter 15: "Dinner is Served" & Call for Kitchiner!

The Banqueting Room was fully lit.

The natural source provided bright spring sunlight to pour through Nash's ingenious stained glass clerestory windows. Positioned thirty-five feet above the floor level, they cast sparkle and tessellated squares of colour down on the table.

A cathedral to cuisine is what Carême thought as he admired the room's artificial sources of illumination as well. Nearly countless gas flames burned be-hind the frosted panes of this hall's chandeliers, torchieres and great central crystal Gasolier.

Carême slowly paced along, in the silence before the storm, examining every detail. The guests, including the Prince and Grand Duke, were detained on the other side of the closed doors from the Central Corridor and South Drawing Room. No one would get in until the *chef de cuisine* was satisfied with the pre-sentation of his meal.

And what a meal!

The forty entrees of the fully-set First Table were arranged per the chef's vision – in casual precision. There was no over-crowding, and yet everything re-mained in easy reach for the diners to pick up and serve their neighbours. But precision too in the arrangements, for a 'tall' *quenelles de volaille en turban* – dumplings of chicken meat served mounded in a ring – were matched pleasantly with a similar-height stand on the other side of the table of *quenelles de volaille à l'italienne* – stacked artichoke hearts, filled and toasted with tomato sauce and par-mesan. 'Low' dishes, like the deep-fried lamb nuggets served on aubergine slices, or the hash of roast pheasant with poached quail eggs, were likewise equally placed in complementary positions. Everywhere a guest turned, a new delight and pleasing arrangement would be awaiting their attention. This artistry of composition spoke of Carême's Classical mind, even if he himself had to be the one acknowledging it.

Down the centre of the fifty-foot-long table, the eight centrepiece roasts Thomas had prepared glowed spectacularly in the cast light from the gilded can-delabra they rested between. The First Grade silver finials of the decorative skewers shone like jewels.

In contrast, the eight *pièces de résistance* were on the sideboards, set apart as the edible works of art they were for guests to admire before they sat down. They would be moved to the table itself, to replace the *grosses pièces* roasts, when the second course was set.

Admiring it all, the chef felt a fleeting pang; it was unfortunate Lady Morgan could not be to see this, as she was an ardent admirer of his work. Personal thoughts led him back to young Master Daniels, and how the undercook had pulled him into the unoccupied Pastry Kitchen two hours ago to tell him how much François hated the boy. With the Regent's secretary, the Kitchen Comptroller and François, Thomas felt he was being surrounded for assault. Carême soothed him the best he could, first reminding the young man that each of the three he named were really angry with Carême and not Thomas personally; and second, he assured him Thomas' completed centrepiece roasts today would show all the naysayers in the Pavilion the young cook was a force to be reckoned with. After parting – after a brief kiss – Carême had been left alone to contemplate that such tensions as the young man was now navigating always arise in large kitchens. François' actions practically illustrated the frictions felt between the up-and-coming and the up-and-come. Prosaically, the chef regarded the situation between François and Thomas as nothing truly serious. Although, interpersonally – thanks to the cupid in Doctor Kitchiner's nature – the chef found himself in a more emotionally complex situation than he could have anticipated.

He stopped; one wine glass was a fraction of an inch too close to the plate of a place setting, so he gently pushed it back along the table, careful only to lightly touch the foot of the tumbler where his fingerprints would not show. He also adjusted the *carte de menu* on this plate; each place setting had one, along with the dignitary's name who'd sit there.

With that, he passed around the narrow end of the table and began working his way up the other long side. But everything his eyes encountered seemed perfect.

This was Carême's own moment to savour his work. To acknowledge the spectacle of it all. While he cast his gaze over the table and its arrangements, he considered how every monarch in History had only dreamed of hosting a banquet as flawless as this one. But, despite the crowned heads of eons numbering well into the thousands, each one of their foodfare dreams had fallen short, for Carême was the only Carême ever born, even if he had to say so himself.

As a last glance to seal his memory of this moment, he crossed over to the centre sideboard. There rested his sugar work model of John Nash's onion dome and Salon colonnade. He bent down to see his own innovative little lamp light up the sugar-pane windows from the inside. He felt he could have made the Pavilion's architect jealous; and why not. Carême was an architect of fancy worth every jot of praise Mr. Nash regularly received.

The chef stood upright. He nodded at the waiting footmen to let the guests see for themselves. Once done, he humbly made his way back to the kitchens.

His internal clock was ticking. Carême knew he had about fifteen minutes before the guests had finished admiring the table and sideboards, found their seats and settled down.

In the Great Kitchen, he strode around the massive steaming table, seeing the eight tureens were warming to be filled, lidded and set on silver platters to go out hot. Hot was key, as there was something to suit every possible taste – a consommé of capon; a bisque of crayfish; a *potage* of partridge; and five others, including a Russian-style broth with pearl barley cooked in *kvass,* the *russe* version of un-hopped English ale. The fun was in having the guests break the ice at the table and ask their neighbours to pass down their bowl to have it filled with the soup they most fancied to try. In the chef's food world, hot soup was essential.

Carême glanced at the clock. He nodded, and undercooks began taking their soup pots from the range over to their designated tureen.

One of these vessels was special; while the others were democratically alike, this one was larger and featured an oversized painted set of the Prince of Wales feathers. François appeared to the chef's side with his pot of soup. This tureen was to be placed by George's side so he could personally fill the Grand Duke's bowl.

The filled tureens were covered one by one, for once the Prince gave the signal from the dining room that everyone was ready, the soups would go out immediately.

Suddenly Thomas Daniels was next to the chef. He spoke low and urgent into Carême's war. "There's something you have to see."

François noticed the boy pulling Carême away. "Chef . . . ?"

"Keep going, *Villon.* I'll be right back."

Thomas led his master into the Service Corridor, and then through the door of the Household Kitchen. Here, several of the uniformed musicians who would play later tonight at the ball sat having tea while they flirted and chatted with the maids.

Thomas led the way out of this room at the other end, past the pantry and storage rooms, and out to the day-lit Kitchen Courtyard.

More of the musicians were here, standing around in a tight circle, gaping at something in the centre of the court.

The chef and Thomas pushed their way through. Carême saw several dead cats. They were ghastly – stiff, with contorted limbs, grimacing leers, petrified in death with open-eyed faces. They had succumbed through horribly pain-racked convulsions, and then the chef saw 'it' - the reason, for a gnawed turtle shell laid in the middle of them. The same turtle whose meat had gone into François' soup—

The chef panicked, and then bolted, but instead of retreating the crowded way they'd come, Carême ran along the covered passage that dog-legged around the Kitchen Stables, the flank of the Great Kitchen, and led straight to the Decking Room.

Quickly out of breath, and feeling his legs would go out for lack of oxygen, Carême burst through the glass doors just in time to intercept the Prince's soup tureen. It was the last one, and going through the door to the Banqueting Room.

Carême grabbed the arm of the footman, gasping, "Back to the kitchen with that."

The footman obeyed, although with a confused scowl on his face, and Carême followed the server. He told the man, "Take that straight to the sink and pour it down."

"Yes, Chef."

In the Great Kitchen, Carême was first occupied with finding another tureen. He told the appropriate undercook, "Fill that with the barley soup and see it's served immediately to the Prince Regent."

"Yes, Chef."

Carême had yet to think of François, and then suddenly his partner was standing in front of him. The man was trying to speak, but couldn't. Then François' eyes glazed and rolled back in his head. Spittle turned to foaming at the corners of his mouth, and the man's legs gave out under him.

Thomas appeared.

Carême dropped to his knees, reaching out for François, but the maitre-d' began convulsing on the floor, violently.

"Mon dieu," Carême cried aloud. Then he shouted at Thomas: "Call for Kitchiner!"

Chapter 16: Tender Loving Care &
Who Done it?

The night had been an oppressive one. A uniform blanket of discomfort arrived with muggy weather rolling off of the sea, and caused a change in the barometer which could be sensed by one and all as a growing headache in the sinuses.

And the night had been touch and go for François. In the privacy of his room, the Doctor had flushed the young man's stomach several times to assure the residue of the toxin was fully cleaned out.

After that, and after some pain medication and warm compresses for the patient's abdomen, Carême had stayed up all night, calming François' periodic hallucinations of being chased. He whispered his nickname, and François would blink, try to hug him, and settle back to his fitful sleep.

By the time the coal-soot sun rose, it seemed François was out of the deepest part of the woods.

A few hours later, as the Doctor returned to examine him, he was sitting up in bed – deathly pale, but alert and coherent. Kitchiner had forced his patient to drink from a large tankard of tea, knowing the stomach pumping had left François dangerously low on fluids.

Carême closed the interconnecting door behind him. Kitchiner and he wanted to confer in private, in Carême's quarters.

The chef asked, "What have you found out about the . . . culprit?"

"The Kitchen Comptroller sent word up and down the coast to secure 'a British' turtle for the feast, not one imported from the colonies. A Royal bounty of 2 Pounds, 6 Pence was offered for the one who brought him the biggest specimen, plus, of course, a Shilling a pound for the creature."

"Is that a lot for one?"

"Not necessarily, but it's a fortune to any of the hand-to-mouth fishermen around here. An absolute fortune!"

"And so, it was a local turtle?"

"Ah. Well, there's the rub. First, the Comptroller swears the one butchered for the soup was *not* the one he selected. And it turns out the poison turtle is not regional at all. It's not even European."

"*Non?*"

"It's an exotic, Asiatic species – the Hawksbill – known to be extremely toxic and deadly to humans."

Carême paused. He refrained from asking the man standing before him, the Regent's right-hand security man, if he thought this was a plot to assassinate George, and possibly the Russian Grand Duke as well. He channelled his ponderings and asked, "What information have you discovered about the turtle's origins?"

"Well, there's a second rub, for it seems two nights ago, a theft occurred from the Duke of Kent's zoological collections. The only thing taken – one specimen Hawksbill turtle."

Carême thought he perceived undue tension in the way the man had said *Duke of Kent,* but as to why, the chef could not hazard a guess. He replied simply, *"Mon dieu."*

"My operatives think the money prompted some scoundrels, lured by the Regent's prize on the biggest obtainable, to steal the Hawksbill and fob it off as a locally provisioned animal."

Carême had his doubts; this theory still did not account for how the Comptroller could swear it was not the turtle he selected, nor indeed, the one he paid for—

"In the end," Kitchiner continued, "perhaps this was all just an accident – an elaborate one, but an accident nonetheless. Anyway, fortunately François only tasted the poison brew for seasoning in the course of his cooking the soup. Had he had a bowlful, he would be dead."

Carême, sickened by the thought, glanced at the door leading to his partner's room. "And, how is he?"

"Tired and weak. See he drinks the tepid tea I have sent up from the kitchen every hour. He needs the toxicity flushed out of his liver, and fluids are the only way to do it."

The Doctor made to leave, adjusting his glasses before saying, "Now, not to be rude, dear Chef, but you'll have to excuse me. The Regent has arranged for me to see he and Charlotte in private. He feels concerned the Princess' behaviour grows . . . well, becomes . . . more untoward by the day."

Kitchiner paused by the door to the corridor. "I suspect it's mostly evidence of her usually high spirits, but His Highness has forbid the Royal Couple from leaving Brighton for the time being. Travelling could exacerbate the Princess' agitation, he feels."

The Doctor placed his hand on the lever, lowering his tone to a personal one; a warm one. "Don't worry, Carême. François is young and strong. He dodged a bullet, and although he came close to death, he'll pull through and recover quickly."

His voice choked with emotion, Carême replied, "Thank you, Doctor."

Kitchiner touched the brim of his imaginary hat and left the room.

Carême gathered himself – inhaling deeply; patting his cheeks dry – and entered François' chamber. The curtains were drawn, but a light breeze from the warm day outside animated them. The murky light moved in and out with the curtains.

François was awake, sitting up in bed, so Carême sat by the side of his maitre-d'. "You didn't tell me how the dinner was received. What about the ball? Do George and Nicholas know what almost happened?"

"All agreed the dinner was a triumph. The Regent called me in, and especially praised our work on the model Brighton Pavilion. *Our* work. I made sure he knew how vital your hand was in the creation of all the *pièces montées.* And he was grateful."

François – wan and pale – appeared little impressed by this information. "And the ball afterwards?"

"The Music Room was magnificent. The footmen moved the sugar work Rustics to the supper buffet table, and the effect was enchanting." Carême's demeanour changed. It went from matter-of-fact to perplexed. "There was one odd moment; only one offkey happening the whole evening."

"And that was?"

"Well, Princess Charlotte was dancing – in fact, in the middle of a waltz with the Grand Duke – when suddenly she pushed him back, claiming he'd put butterflies down her dress. The dancing stopped, and she soon apologized for her 'beastly' joke."

Carême thought François' appearance took on a strangely gratified cast at hearing this anecdote. It was as if he approved of the action and results. But the chef shrugged it off.

"And George and the Grand Duke, do they know about the turtle?"

"His Highness knows," replied Carême. "But, according to Doctor Kitchiner, the Regent has decided to keep this bit of intelligence from the Russians, feeling what the Grand Duke doesn't know cannot hurt him."

"Pity."

"Is it?"

François did not respond. He moved on instead. "And this Hawksbill turtle, it was taken from a collection?"

"Evidently, yes. But the Doctor and his informants think the whole thing was an accident. That and nothing more."

François looked dubious.

"What, *Villon?* You have other thinking?"

"Yes, of course." François grew animated. "In my gut, I *feel* my enemy – Gris Thorndyke – was in cahoots with Donald Bland to poison me."

"Why? Would they want to put the Regent and Grand Duke, and perhaps European stability, in danger too?"

"But, think about it. They knew I'd be making the soup; that I'd be tasting it as I went along; that I'd get sick and possibly die before it was ever served to the Lordly types."

Carême conceded François did have a point there, however . . . . "If so, what motivation would the Kitchen Comptroller have in going along with the Chief Footman's personal vendetta against you?"

François tapped his temple. "Think about it. Donald Bland hates you; wants you out of the way again. He naturally assumed you would taste the soup too; assumes you would die just as quickly as me."

"Well"—Carême considered it—"perhaps." That was all he could manage to say, yet, he admitted internally something remained 'mysterious' about this entire event, but what it could be he wasn't sure. "So, moving forward, the Chief Footman and Kitchen Comptroller will be put on a short leash. I'll ask the Regent personally. They will be closely monitored."

François relaxed, his muscles deflating from the coiled tension he'd been keeping them under.

The sight calmed Carême. He worried about François's passions, wondered if they'd one day be the end of him.

"And the Doctor says I will be well?"

"Yes. Strong, quick recovery is what he predicts."

"And I have to get well soon so I can go back to making your *baba* for Charlotte."

Carême smiled. "There's no need to worry about that. I'll make it for the Royal Couple in the meantime."

François was oddly crestfallen.

"Of course," Carême hastened to add, "you'll go back to making it for them as soon as you are able."

François attempted a feeble grin, puzzling Carême once more. The chef placed a gentle back-of-the-hand touch on his partner's feverish brow, passing off the unaccountable behaviour as merely the poison talking through him.

Carême stood, kissing François' forehead. "You sleep. I'll go prepare my *eau de poulet rafraîchissante* for you. The chicken stock, along with fresh green herbs, will provide more nutrition and hydration than the Doctor's weak tea alone. That and some of the leftover sole *quenelles—*"

François took his hand. "Thank you."

Carême smiled again. "Sleep, *Villon.*"

Several hours later, Carême burned the midnight oil recording the daily food successes and points to be revisited for improvement. As this was his wont, the thoughts transferred easily from mind to paper. But after a while, his emotions concerning François over-shadowed the practical. He found himself writing:

> *Je dois un rapport au Doyen de l'école de la Concorde. Il me reste à déterminer dans quelle mesure je dois l'informer de la maladie de François et de sa cause mystérieuse. D'autres ont peut-être déjà relayé ici les circonstances concernant le Grand*

> I owe *Doyen de l'école de la Concorde* a report. How much of François' illness, and the puzzling cause of it, I inform him of

remains for me to work out. Others may have already relayed the circumstances here concerning the Grand Duke's visit, so I must be cautious. And, as one must always be, mindful of the *Doyen's* acumen, which oftentimes seems that of a mind reader.

In any event, François' near-brush causes me to wonder if my over-arching reason for being here is worth the personal price. The *Doyen* would reply with narrowing eyes that there is no 'personal' where matters of State are at play. And I'd be hard pressed to dissuade him of his convictions along these lines, but some of us were born to be garter snakes and not strangle-hold pythons like him.

Acknowledging it leaves me chilled to the bone. For what cold comfort is there in recognizing Fate is inextricable; one cannot run from it, be it from Brighton or Paris. Even the powerful are powerless, and hope is the first, last and middle ground for those who wish to survive the caprice of Fortune—

Carême heard a noise.

François had come through their door, and now stood in his nightshirt like a child awoken by a storm next to a parent's bed.

From his chair, the chef asked, "Can't sleep?"

"I've slept enough today; the only thing I did is bathe. I'd rather talk to you, *mon cher.*"

Carême went to him; hugged him, relieved to feel the fever had gone.

Carême undressed, lying down in bed first, and then beckoning François to cuddle down close so he could draw the blanket over the top of them.

The warm, sensual feel of his legs atop his own lightened the chef's mind-set. The young man positioned his ear over Carême's heart, and Carême stroked his hair.

François said, "Maybe it's the muggy closeness of the weather, but it feels like the Pavilion – like there are eyes on me, on us, all the time."

Carême tried to soothe away his partner's paranoia, chalking it up to more fever-talk, but he knew how François felt. They would always be suspect Frenchmen to these people – dodgy frog legs and *velouté* in a land of roast beef and mustard.

"I know, *Villon.* Warm days like these make me long for our time, our spare time, at Talleyrand's country palace." Carême felt François' body tense up, as if the mere mention of the Grand Chamberlain's name put him on edge.

But in another moment, the *maître d'hôtel* relaxed again, hugging Carême close. "Me too. I sometimes find myself longing for the beauty and quiet of the Château Valençay. Longing for our slow, hand-in-hand walks in the woods, feeling truly alone, removed from the 19th century and its crassness and oppression. It was just you and me, alone together, beholden to no one but each other."

"Yes. The books we'd take with us—"

François laughed freely. "And later, take the bring slender volumes in bed to read each other to sleep."

Carême paused. "Yes – I loved to read the sad words of a certain other François to you late at night; read and watch you slowly close your tired eyes to peaceful sleep. It's why I've called you my *Villon* all these years."

"Yes, Antonin, I know"—François was overawed with tender emotions—"I know."

Carême stroked his partner's hair more adamantly. "We'll have that again someday, just as soon as . . . as soon . . . . Well, when the state of the world is calmer."

François replied listlessly, "If we live that long."

Carême misinterpreted the import of the comment and immediately turned his thoughts to the silent killer within himself. Here too he could try to reassure his partner.

"Do you know why I moved you from being my *sous-chef* to my *maître d'hôtel?*"

"So I had grounding not only in the preparation of your food, but also in the ideal ways it should be served."

"Yes, that is correct. But I had other, more personal, motivations. I did it to save you from my fate – the wasting disease that takes every chef too young in life."

François raised his head. "I did not realize – you did not tell me—"

Carême gently guided the young man's head back down. "Yes, *Villon.* I changed the course of your career, because carbon monoxide poisoning may not be as swift as the Hawksbill, but it's just as deadly. In the long run, it's safer for you to be maitre-d', in and out of the fumes all day, and less riddled by them."

"You had faith in me; took me from an also-ran undercook at the Élysée Palace to be a knowledgeable and skilful aspirant to your high culinary Art."

"Yes, I had faith in you. But your success is all your own. I merely identified and then cultivated the latent talent I saw in you."

"And despite what's happened since – the ways in which I've hurt you – you believe me, don't you? You still believe *in* me?"

"Of course, *Villon.*"

François shed the blanket from the upper part of them, took Carême's hand and laced their fingers together. "I love you, Carême. Love you."

Emotion shone from the young man's voice, but before the chef could say anything, François continued.

"I need to thank you for what you have done for me, but how? For your mentoring and love; for your support and forgiveness. I mean, *he* had his hands around my throat . . . . But you; well, who other than you would take in Agathé, the mother of my daughter, so Marie could grow up respectably, and with your good name behind her?"

Carême had stiffened a bit now. He tried to explain, "Notions of respectability for appearance's sake played little in my decision. But love, François, that weighed heavily. I do love you; you know that, right?"

François vowed he wouldn't cry. "Yes, Antonin. You show it – if not say it to me – every day. So I am blessed many times over." Internally, François was breaking down, guilty that his own was so inferior. "Your love is humbling, and I feel unworthy, and relieved to know I won't be a burden for too much longer. But, you will keep looking after Agathé and Marie, no matter what . . . ?"

"Of course." Again, the chef misinterpreted, but his reply steadied his belovèd nonetheless.

Carême's first kisses were tender, gentle ones to wick away the threatening moisture gathering under François' eyes.

François ratcheted it up, placing his hand aside his man's face and kissing Carême's mouth with gleeful hunger. While his lips woke up his lover's desire, François' skilful digits reached below the blanket and made Carême hopelessly hard. He kept at it, making the man moan directly into his mouth at the powerful ability of François' caress.

The younger man broke their kissing, smiling then with a flushed, glossy pout as he slid along the length of Carême's body, uncovering it as he went.

He applied that wet, precocious mouth onto Carême's masthead, thrilling as it became stiffer still at this first, new type of contact. He opened his mouth and slowly slid his lips to the fur-lined base of Carême's shaft.

The chef moaned, gripped onto the sheets, and François was again rewarded with the flaring feel of his man's pleasure within his mouth.

François moaned himself as he brought his tightening lips up again, driving the chef nearly mad.

But the young man did not relent – did not want to. He instinctively knew his personal skills, and the exposed, heightened emotions they both shared, was building in Carême to the point of a powerful explosion.

As he proceeded, François's lips and tongue could feel his partner's predicament, and more so, could taste the sweet nectar which precedes a man's orgasm.

He stopped suddenly, kneeling on either side of Carême's waist. He lifted his nightshirt.

Carême protested, "It's too soon, You are still—"

François shushed him, as if *words* were too much noise for the moment. Then, the young man applied slick moisture to his palm, which he transferred to Carême's standing member. Smoothing it around the tip, he slowly positioned and lowered on it, vowing to himself he would not cry.

He loved Carême more than words would ever be able to express, but what he did not know, is it was ever thus for all lovers. In his way, François was fortunate, for he was the type of lover who discovered the quickest, surest way to communicate love was to let bodies do the talking.

François sank down as far as he could, thrilling to this familiar, deeply intimate sensation of connection, and gratified to feel Carême's hands grip the sides of his thighs with urgency. He experienced even greater satisfaction sensing his man's growing hardness – expansiveness – within him.

He placed his open palms on Carême's chest and gradually worked himself over his belovèd's shaft. François gasped to know Carême could not hold out for long like this, for what in life had ever meant as much to a street kid like François – a child of the French Reign of Terror, which only sought to break intimate connections – to be the instrument to make the one he loves comingle their essences in the most personal means possible?

"Villon .... Villon!"

François sat back, taking Carême all the way.

His lover convulsed with pleasure, bucking the young man up once or twice as he did.

And yet, as content and fulfilled as he felt, he told himself not to cry, fearing this might be their last time together.

PART VI

Summer 1817

Tente à la Française

Jj3m l8hew 3 1 j7kmf 3 1 vnj9jwfd,

1 jwn6hwyp 3 te9c jn 1 lm8jdvw 4 mx6 gt9ckbdp dhxiw 5 wg3 f hifm5hxt kj2nf 7 dhf2j jmc4 1 ou6mdwqz nfo un4 jge nb3ph. 1i gob9jn kg rct lp2krhcvh dl6c 1 dhxiw7 lrnw 1 xlgi3je jhkjhb3 lkj 5vzmvx. 1 h lie 3 uxt lv9jlqxu dn3m kjjjjjdyyhs 1 lkjnhgy3 vgs uhd

Cher Doyen de l'école de la Concorde,

Le banquet d'État en l'honneur du duc criminel russe a été ré-évalué comme un échec dans les quelques semaines qui ont suivi. La rumeur s'est répandue chez les Russes que les Anglais cachaient un complot d'assassinat, et maintenant les relations se

Dear *Doyen de l'école de la Concorde,*

The State banquet in honour of the Russian criminal Duke has been re-evaluated as a failure in the several weeks since it happened. Rumour got to the Russians that the English hid an assassination plot, and now relations have soured.

That is a beneficial development as we approach the midsummer mark in a couple of days. Such buoyant news is needed as the summer of 1817 is every bit as bleak as in '16. Rain, fog, chills hem in this interminable coast where goosebumps are the standard fashion even in the 'best' of English weather.

Hunger stalks the land more than ever. Food shortages have progressed to the dire state of staples running short. Already, mouths from the Colonies are being robbed just to feed the Lords of this nation. The social reform movement known as *Luddite* continues its violence around the country, although the press is forbidden from printing the true story. The newspapers must tow Whitehall's propaganda that the movement was exterminated six months ago, at the end of 1816. Naturally, it wasn't, but now when protests arise concerning sixteen-hour working days at industrial sites, the Red Coats are sent in to slaughter and bury in mass graves, *carte blanche*. Many are the tales of these Dragoons – 'Goons,' as they are known amongst the people – enslaving children whose parents they've mowed down to be receptacles of their daily lusts, and set to degrading, menial tasks not fit for even the raggiest enslaved Christians yoked and castrated by the Ottoman Turks. And yet, 'white slavery' – of the type most especially inflicted on the Irish – is not to be spoken about in this country, for fear the disgrace it would open up like a volley across the closed-off Great British brain.

Most of the Luddites are fighting for basic representation in assemblies. They do this for reasons of fundamental nutrition, for English 'bread' is a travesty of adulteration: chalk and alum to make it look white to the eye; sawdust to swell up in water and bulk out the loaf. All this is malevolent rubbish to those who can barely afford to sicken their children with it. Corruption of this sort is so rampant that all of a town's bakers openly collude to ensure no one shop offers anything better than the others – and the 'Law' lets them. These exploiters pocket their ill-got gains with elitist smiles, saying the courts prevent them from charging more for wholesome loaves, so they in turn sell nothing but starvation bread to a people deprived of any political power in Parliament.

The natural outcome of this inequity is, instability grows, much to the overarching advancement of Liberty for the populace here. Yet, if the trauma of the 'Year without a Summer' produces a Constitution for the English, and freedom – at last – for the Scots, Irish and Welsh, then all the strife and bloodshed will have been worth it; the land will cease to bleed men, women and children to feed the money-grubbing factories and slave-grown cotton mills. What Man produces should be in the hands of free citizens, not their would-be Lordly 'masters.' But naturally on these issues, I preach to the choir, as they say over here, for you've single-handedly done more for the advancement of democracy than anyone alone in Europe today.

That I understand; although your means have sometimes been heavy-handed, your goals began and remain spotless.

As for the blinkered, fairy-tale world here at the Pavilion, I'm pleased to report the war against the entitled English proceeds smoothly right under their noses without them even knowing.

The plot afoot is working, and this might be my last field report as the 'action' may be put into effect any night now.

With this knowledge clearly in your mind, I again plead with you to allow Agathé, Marie and my associate to be released from under the *Doyen's* vengeful eyes. I'm doing what's been asked of me. Uphold your end of the agreement. Obviously, I speak with such candour knowing I probably will not survive the mission, and if that's to be my fate, I wish for this missive to hit your conscience hard. When dead, sacrificed to an International cause – a human monument worthy to have wreaths placed at his feet – do what's right to honour the memory of my commitment to the advancement of Liberty.

In conclusion, I will remind the *Doyen* that I'm close to attaining my goal. And, per your express instructions, my col-league continues to operate oblivious to what I am doing, although I hate to think of the consequences for him if any plot is exposed *and* unsuccessful.

But then again, I can assure you, I am well aware 'failure' is not an option for me or my kind.

Instituteur Marron Glacé

Chapter 17: Just Past Midsummer & Inexplicable Behaviour

"Did you and Lord Morgan have a nice time in Ireland?"

"A family funeral is seldom conducive to a 'nice time.' But we Irish have a saying:

> 'The roads rise up to meet us;
> The winds at our backs compel us,
> With the sun warm upon our faces,
> And the rain softly upon the fields
> Until God sees fit to reunite us.'

"We're prosaic" she went on, "and accept death as part of the life of our lush, green landscape. At home, they are oddly acknowledged as part and parcel of daily life."

"Does not sound odd to me. It sounds natural."

"I knew you'd understand."

Carême and Lady Morgan were out for a midmorning stroll. Their feet crackled the pine chips freshly laid in the Riding House of the Regent's stables. This enclosed space to the west of the horse barn's dome was like a medieval great hall, with a wide, timber-framed roof and towering acres of window glass, peaking in the delicate scallop of a dozen Indian-inspired arches.

Tepid light from the half-hearted day outside now slanted in as a few horses were exercised in the centre of the space. The chef and novelist had plenty of room to amble around the structure's perimeter, as, at the width of the Pavilion's Banqueting Room – but triple its length at 180 feet – they felt cozy and unobserved. A rare treat on the Pavilion's grounds.

"I'm sorry to have missed your State Dinner," Sydney Morgan said. "From the reports I've heard, it was an occasion assured to go down in the annals of Diplomacy."

Carême glowed internally. "The Lady does my heart good talking about 'my' banquet. Most everyone will think of it as the Regent's success, or the Grand Duke's."

She interlaced her arm with her friend's. "My dear Carême, *if* this event is remembered in times to come, it will be recalled as 'your' banquet, no doubt."

After a few silent paces, Carême's ebullience got knocked down more than a few pegs. "However, the Prince's liberality has had unforeseen consequences."

"Oh, really? What?" she asked.

"It sickens me to admit it, but in his way – inadvertently, at least – the Kitchen Comptroller has wreaked his revenge on me."

"How so?"

"Because of the Prince's lavishness with the banquet, he has to 'save' and now pay for it. It means I must economize and eke by on daily menus with a mere *four* entrées and *two* soups. I could accomplish such meals in a trance."

"Oh, dear."

"My Art has even been reduced to serving *l'oie rôtie aux purée de pomme.*"

Lady Morgan chuckled a bit. "Roast goose with applesauce."

"Oui. It is nursery school food, and *I* am asked to cook it. What's next: *'Burnt Custard'?!* No."

Sydney Morgan repressed a smile, simply repeating her commiserating "Oh, dear."

"I feel my talents are being wasted. It might be time to look for better opportunities; bluer skies."

The thought of Carême's departure saddened the novelist. She muttered lackadaisically, "Blue skies. Haven't seen one in months – not since our outing in Rottingdean – and I'm beginning to wonder if things will ever get better."

"I don't know, Lady Morgan; I don't know. I had hoped things between François and I were better after the poisoning, but I don't know. It seems he has taken up again with the Princess' lady's maid."

"Oh. I am sorry to hear that, Carême."

"I had hoped, after François had come so near to death, he'd sort out his priorities, but now I am not so sure."

Morgan replied, "Although the girl is young and pretty – and accomplished – and French, I feel confident whatever François sees in her equals a dalliance. Sometimes in life, we must accept wandering as natural, and treat it with patience and a shoulder-shrug."

The chef considered, and then avoided asking, if these dispassionate shoulder-shrugs were something Lady Morgan could dole out in the light of Lord Morgan's 'dalliances' receiving an airing. What he actually said was, "Perhaps a change of location will be good for our relationship too."

However, Carême's change of mood did not pass Lady Morgan by unnoticed. So, after a few more steps over the resin-redolent wood chips, she felt emboldened to inquire, "Possibly; but if so, what might that mean for your young Master Thomas Daniels? Your *tête de linotte?"*

Despite himself, Carême grew emotional hearing his now-pet-name for the young man. Across his internal vision, Carême recalled how his blue eyes sparkled as the chef taught the kid the 'proper' Paris accent for the term.

In point of fact concerning the question just asked, he didn't know, so Carême tried deflection. "The undercook's skills have come along nicely. It might make for a good fit if he goes to London to be Mrs. Lister's right-hand apprentice. But, the young man is now in a position to be taken on by any chef as a skilled *protégé.*"

"Taken on even as yours?" his friend slipped in, slyly.

Suppressing his complex reaction, replete with thoughts of François, he answered with the truth. "Even mine."

Clearing the air, they walked through the door into the stables. The fine ribs of iron, set with numberless panes of glass tapering up to the dome's oculus, was always breath-taking. A sort of cathedral-hush pervaded William Porden's great equestrian rotunda, and even the horses seemed to tread through the room more softly.

"*Au fait* – I've been meaning to ask how the launch of your book went in London, before you had to go to Ireland."

"My *France,* thanks to your unflaggingly good assistance, is off to tremendous interest."

"'Interest,'" the chef slyly reiterated, "amounts to excellent sales?"

"And good reviews too, thank the heavens."

"Well deserved, *Madame.* Your keen mind has delivered an exemplary *exposé* of the most winning kind."

"Thank you, dear friend, but I have *exposed* myself and wait anxiously for the day my book is attacked in the press by means of denigrating me personally."

The chef, a man of the world, knew what she meant. "But, is it to be so?"

"Women, *mon cher* Carême, are always accused of impropriety if they dare publish anything riskier than an embroidery manual. And such criticism ever starts and ends with imaginings of the woman's love-life. Apparently only whores – according to men sat behind desks at newspaper and magazine offices – write about anything contemporary to the world we currently live in."

"I am sorry, Lady Morgan. I can only hope that in the future the substance of a woman's work will be the only factor considered in assessing what she has published."

"I can only add my wish to yours. Why, at this dreary date, a person who's written a truly original piece of fiction – unlike my travel-log, you understand – will have to publish it under an assumed male moniker to have any chance of it being read for its own sake."

"I wish it were otherwise, *Madame,* but, I'm afraid you're correct."

After several paces in silence, the pair cast their eyes upward, enjoying the play of light and shadow, slowly making their way to the open gate onto the Pavilion's gardens.

"I have heard the Regent has yet to let the Royal Couple go home."

"Yes," replied Carême, "it's true. And Charlotte has 'rebelled' against her father by staying in her quarters for long stretches of time, and insists she and Leopold take meals sequestered upstairs, alone."

"Dinner; alone?"

"And suppers too, which never vary: the meal goes up at 8 o'clock. And then at nine, we send the Princess' favourite *baba au rhum,* made personally by François for them."

Lady Morgan responded with a chuckle. "A girl of habits. That is not such a bad trait for a young woman destined to reign as Queen one day."

By this time they had arrived at the crushed gravel of the foot and horse paths lacing across the estate. Up ahead, to their left, the finished rooves and colonettes of the Pavilion crowded the sky with their white-stuccoed perfection. But the expansion of the marine villa seemed never-ending, for already workmen had excavated the rectangular patch of ground for the Regent's new, garden-level suite of chambers, and brick walls were rising to enclose it.

They stopped. Noise from the bridle path to their far left drew their attention to an unaccountable sight. Princess Charlotte sat side saddle on her steed in a relaxed manner, but Leopold was muddy – as if he'd just fallen – and berating the poor teenage groom holding the reins of both horses.

Charlotte babbled, apparently at her husband. "You make me write too, too many letters—"

"You stupid *Schmutzfink!* Take that, *Schweinehund!*" He began striking the boy's neck with his riding crop.

"Too, too many – I can't seem to get the ink off my beastly fingertips any-more—"

"I ought to beat you to within . . . . " He suddenly seemed to remember Charlotte's presence. "Well, *leibchen* – I mean, bodice – I mean, darling – *lieb-chen,* if I make you do such letter-writing, then I do the same to myself as well, for my fingers – help me up, boy – are as stained as yours."

The groom genuflected so the Prince Consort could step on his thigh, which the man did, simultaneously wrenching his horse's reins from the boy's grip.

"Let us be away." The German rode off.

The groom handed her reins to Charlotte, and she followed her spouse as distracted as before.

"Peculiar," Carême said. "I have never known Leopold to be short-tempered, let alone violent!"

"Yes. The behaviour we've just witnessed is . . . is, well – unaccountable. And in her own way, the Princess is as odd as he."

Carême consulted his watch. "Now, if you excuse me, I must meet the Regent and go over the final details of this day's dinner."

Lady Morgan smiled. "I look forward to eating it, Chef."

"*À bientôt, Madame.*"

"*À tout à l'heure, mon très cher Carême.*"

As she lingered, able to see the Royal Couple's horses retreat off to her left, and the chef's figure moving to a door in the northern part of the Pavilion to her right, she had a sudden flash of insight.

"Could lightning," she asked aloud, "strike twice?"

Sydney Morgan knew what she had to do, and the investigation would call upon Doctor Kitchiner and his Brighton laboratory.

Such a regular sight in the Great Kitchen, Lady Morgan's presence drew little attention – in spite of her not being with Carême.

Her sleuthing *chapeau* was on as she casually removed the lid of a certain cannikin. She raised it up and sniffed the Princess' special tea, smelling only wholesome chamomile now. Just as she was re-lidding it and setting it back in place, a quiet little scene unfolding at the other end of the kitchen caught her attention.

Conferring near the corner of one of the matched Welsh dressers holding the copper crown jewels of the Pavilion's kitchens – the 1,600 piece *batterie de cuisine,* sparkling clean in every size of lidded pot and pan – stood fellow French-men François and Brigitte.

Even from Lady Morgan's slightly removed vantage, their body language spoke loud and clear: she was flirting and he was receptive. Her index finger traced the centre of his chest from neck to sternum before it withdrew and seemed to transfer its static charge to a freshly arrived grin on her face. Her head cocked momentarily to the side in tacit questioning, and François replied with an awkward Adam's apple bobbing up and down.

Sydney Morgan instantly understood such displays, out in the open as they were, must ping Carême's heart.

She considered circumstances a bit deeper. Brigitte was "off duty" while the Royal Couple gallivanted on horseback along the beach, and Carême was usually out of the kitchen at this hour, meaning this was some sort of ideal opportunity for the pair.

With a sly signal, Brigitte left the room – the 'wrong way' – out the door that led to the pantries and Kitchen Stables. In another minute, François, having spied Lady Morgan's spying, appeared irrevocably sad, but turned and trailed after the lady's maid for their predestined rendezvous.

The subtle domestic spectacle had been the confirmation Lady Morgan needed to see that Carême's suspicions were well-founded. It allowed her to perceive the degree to which such sights left her friend feeling desolate.

An unbidden scrap of Byron unfolded across her mind:

> 'What matter the golden rooves of the past? –
> Their sight must falter neath a single tear
> Shed for a loving existence to last
> Beyond the sum total of every year.
> Though the human heart is oft insincere,
> Its past, its future – its glory – endear.'

She then spotted Thomas Daniels going up to a preparation table with a crate of fresh produce from the cold stores. She wound up thinking how the lad unwittingly formed the third side of Carême's triangle of affections.

As the young man began to work, lost to his own thoughts, Sydney Morgan slid into place next to him.

"What is planned for today's dinner table?" she asked with a smile.

"Ah, Lady Morgan – I didn't know – well, the plan for today is to get ready to make cream of barley soup and chicken consommé, to go with my fried sole, and then ham and turkey."

"What for the entrees?"

"A poultry fricassee, grilled mutton chop, pan-roasted capon with asparagus, and a 'blanket' of veal sweetbreads with fine herbs – that's a sort of quick stew. All of this pending His Highness' consent."

The novelist slid in a sly, "Naturally."

"Naturally." Now the boy grinned as well.

Lady Morgan turned serious. "If you don't think I'm overstepping my bounds by saying so, I've noticed quite a change in your work-life character."

"How so, mum?"

"I mean, compared to nearly a year ago when Carême first arrived, I perceive you are now a diligent young man focused with passion on the career ahead of you."

"I'm striving my best to achieve that, mum." The boy's smile transformed into blushing.

"With Carême's help, you can reach your goals."

He glanced away. "I'm not so sure anymore."

"Why?"

Thomas appeared hesitant to speak of personal matters, but assessed from Lady Morgan's warm countenance that it would be all right if he did. "Carême has me aside, which is a hard blow considering I've made enemies of both the Kitchen Comptroller – who pilfers from my rightful earning now, crediting me a mere six Pence from last month's food sales – and François who talks down my cookery skills to all and sundry."

"I'm sorry to hear that."

The boy was sincere, getting down to work. "It was worth it before, but now that . . . now that the chef and François have reconciled – I'm out in the cold for shure."

"Well," the Lady said cunningly, "don't be so positive you're cast away from Carême's heart. In fact, don't be positive of it at all. I'd say, buck up, young man, because things can change rapidly. Trust me; I've seen it many times."

Seeing young Master Daniels beam, she continued to the primary concern pressing on her mind. "Tell me, Thomas, have you heard any grumblings concerning Princess Charlotte or Leopold from members of staff?"

The boy was taken aback. "Why do you ask?"

"The Royals are increasingly – shall we say, eccentric."

"No, mum," Thomas replied artlessly. Then he said with honesty, "There have been no chatterings about them, other than the usual gripes concerning their late-hour wants or inconvenient chores."

"Anything different about what they eat?"

"No, Lady Morgan. Apart from taking their meals on trays, they eat what the rest of the Family do."

"I'm feeling there must be something special about their food; something leading to their untoward conduct of late."

The young man's eyes fell on a half-nipped sugar-cone. "Charlotte likes her sweets, but that's nothing new."

"Well, give me some of the sugar anyway. I'll take it to Doctor Kitchiner and ask him to analyze—"

Lady Morgan halted her own words because the boy's face suddenly held an unaccountable expression.

"This," Thomas said, reaching for a particular jar. "Have the Doctor look into some of this."

Hours later, another gruelling day in the life of the Great Kitchen was coming to an end.

Had Lady Morgan an inkling of how momentous a day this was destined to be, or how pivotal events in motion were, she might have placed in her mind an additional quote to stand by Byron; one by his contemporary Wordsworth.

> *Think how kind Nature's made to weep,*
> *Knowing thus the human soul can*
> *Scheme its atrocities most deep*
> *When he plots 'gainst his fellow man.*

But now as the hands of the regulator clock inched their way forward from five minutes to nine, most in the kitchen were cleaning or restocking various work areas with the washed and dried implements of the next day's meal-making, while only a small group were actively still working.

Carême had a contemplative hand to his chin, inspecting the finishing touches on the night's *baba*.

François stood across the dish from him. It was already on the silver tray upon which it'd go up to Charlotte and Leopold.

While Carême wondered if the lines of piped Chantilly cream and equally spaced candied violet petals were enough – maybe a few angelica slices too . . . ?

The chef caught some veiled-yet-sexual inuendo pass from Brigitte to François. She was right there as well, waiting as always to take the Royal Couple's dessert up to them.

The *chef de cuisine* soured on any notion of further embellishment, wanting things to be over. He stepped back, nodding his assent to François.

The maitre-d' placed the sparkling silver cloche over the top, and Brigitte stepped efficiently forward.

Just as the lady's maid placed her hands on the tray's grips, the peaceful quiet of the kitchen was burst like a bubble.

Doctor Kitchiner and Lady Morgan came bounding through the doors from the Kitchen Court.

"Stop!" Sydney Morgan rushed over. She stepped between the maid and tray, whipping off the cover. "It's here, Doctor, thank the stars!"

"What is this?" Carême asked, confused and personally offended to see his food manhandled. But in another moment, Kitchiner was by his side.

"The Princess and Leopold are suffering from Saint Anthony's Fire. It's in the food – driving them mad."

"Impossible," muttered Carême. "Where's the poison?"

Lady Morgan pointed to the *baba.* "Here - the rye flour. Tests show it's infected with the mould that causes ergot poisoning. The Doctor's laboratory analysis indicates the toxicity levels are off the chart."

Carême's confusion was only added to. *"C'est impossible.* François alone handles the grinding and cooking of the rye for this dish." Stunned and in disbelief, he glanced around the room, feeling his breath shorten. "François . . . ?"

The young man was nowhere to be seen.

Carême told Kitchiner, "He was here a minute ago."

Two of the Doctor's men rushed in at that very moment from the Court.

The Doctor immediately barked at them, "He's escaped! Search the Pavilion, starting with the Servants' Hall."

As people scrambled this way and that, Carême straightened his spine. He very calmly picked up a bin and slid his *baba au rhum* into it.

Then he headed to the Central Service Corridor, not turning to the left as the others did towards François' chambers, but to the right, to the darkened Banqueting Room and the sleepy Pavilion beyond.

Not daring to carry a light, Carême mounted creaky steps. This narrow passage was one François had shown him, for the chef suspected where his partner could be found.

Carême drew his breath carefully, for even the exertion of climbing drained the feeling of strength from his muscles. The tightness of this windowless space also heightened a sense of claustrophobia. Or perhaps it was the dawning of an awful dread that gripped his heart. A helplessness pervaded him.

At the top of the stairs was a small landing and door. He opened it quietly outward and stepped onto the roof of the Pavilion, behind the Salon's now-finished onion dome. Closing the door again, the scent and faint sound of the surf struck his senses. Up above and out to every horizon line, stars filled the sky. A crescent moon was just beginning to rise in the south-east, casting fantastical shadows from the villa's roof on the ground far below. Ironically, it was the most beautiful night he'd witnessed in Brighton.

The chef made his way around the construction site at the base of the dome, still littered with boards, timber and troughs to mix stucco and limewash. He climbed a short ladder leaning against the bulging substructure of the dome, up to the flat ledge encircling the curved walls of the dome itself.

Rounding the platform to the point of where the water was visible, he saw François standing, silently admiring it. The views and sea breeze up here were perfectly unencumbered.

Almost as if perceiving the other man's presence, François said, "Listen. Out there is the seashore, the waves rolling in, and beyond them, our motherland, France. I wish I'd never left her."

"Is it true, what the Doctor claims." Carême came closer.

"Yes."

"Why, François?"

François turned in slack-jawed amazement. "Because that's why I'm here! To kill the entitled brat and frame the *Bosche* for her murder. And tonight it would have been too. One final dose of ergot, and after they were sound asleep, I'd sneak away from the lady's maid. I'd run the Princess through with Leopold's sword, and in the morning, he'd be stark raving mad and unable to explain how the English Empire's heir – and her unborn baby – got killed, except by his own hand!"

"François—"

"The problem with the Irish couple was they weren't radical enough. Why strike out just to kill the innocent offspring when you can kill their actually criminal whelpers! I had my mission – figure out a way to pull down in madness, murder and disgrace the Regent, Leopold and the heir-apparent along with them."

"And you planned this on your own?"

François scoffed. "Antonin, how blind you can be when you want. We work for the same master – Talleyrand."

Carême was confused. "But what possible leverage could the man have over you?"

"You," François said through an ironic laugh. "Blackmail me via you and everything I value. To ruin your career, separate Agathé and Marie from your protection; throw them on the streets as scum to make their own way, and you know what they'd have to resort to."

"But, I don't understand. Talleyrand ruin me?"

"Chef, it'd be as easy as sharpening his fingernails to reveal who you love, create scandal, make sure you're shut out of every palace kitchen in Europe because of it."

"Prince Talleyrand would not do that. We've worked closely on stability for such a long—"

"No?! He wouldn't let harm come to you? Naïve thought, that. A luxury men like you and me – working men – are never allowed to have."

"And the poisoned turtle?" Carême suddenly saw some light, albeit a terrible, dark one. "I thought the scheme somehow had the smell of Talleyrand on it."

"It did. It was his idea, and quite frankly, he didn't care if the success of it brought you down – serving venomous broth to the British leader – you'd be hanged in public, and he wouldn't care; would laugh that he got away with it while you swung."

"My God—"

"But I – me, Carême – I couldn't let you suffer. If the plan had worked and Nicholas and George died in agony in the dining room, I would have confessed and taken the fall. It helps that you were actually innocent; knew nothing; and that gave you sterling deniability. But I would have swung to protect you, Carême."

"Why did you then drink the poison soup yourself?"

"Simple. The plot was exposed. I drank to sicken myself and again divert suspicion away from you. The Doctor concluded the whole affair was nothing but an 'accident,' or a plot by the Regent's brother, so it worked."

Carême suddenly became aware of time. Desperately, he said, "It's not too late. We can get you to Talleyrand's men in Dover. From there, they'll get you to France."

François walked up straight into his man's arms, hugged him; kissed him. "It *is* too late. Right now you are safe – I've seen to that – but if the English catch you helping me, it will mean your head as well as mine."

"Don't talk so desperately. There is always hope."

François was devastatingly sad. "Is there? No, not always, my love. You see, I am a true child of the Terror, and hope is dangled for such as we like a promised treat for a dog, but one always yanked away at the last second by its vicious owner."

"So, Brigitte—"

"I never slept with her through my own volution." Tears appeared. "She never meant anything to me – neither did Agathé, at first at least, but having a child together changes a person."

"Yes, *Villon,* I know. It changed you for the better; made you a better person."

"Made me a mark for Talleyrand to exploit, against you. It's like he told me before we left for England: 'Every one of us scrambles for just a bit of warmth and comfort. It's human nature.' And so too is the drive to keep those we love safe. And I've only ever loved you."

The man became lost in his own sorrow. Carême saw him chance to pull his partner back from the brink.

"François—"

"I had to use Brigitte," he cried out in his torment. "Had to use her to get to Charlotte. It broke my heart to see how painful it was for you to bear"—he struck himself hard in the chest—"and I won't forgive myself"—he hit himself again, dishevelling his hair—"even if you do, but I had to use her."

"*Villon,* it's not too late—"

"Oh, but it is."

Gruff voices sounded from within the stairway.

After a frozen moment of silence between the men, François's face washed over with horror.

He took off, away from the access point, sliding down from the ledge on which stood along the 'fish scale' shingled part of the dome support.

Carême, thinking quickly, rushed down the ladder and to the closed portal. He picked up a short plank of construction timbre, jamming it under the doorknob just as it twisted with the onrush of Kitchiner's men. In another moment, their fists pounded on the other side of the door and voices commanded to "Open up!"

Assured they were locked in, Carême turned tail and followed François' course across the Pavilion's treacherous roof-scape. Parts of the metal flashing were slippery and damp where rainwater had puddled, as he found out while jumping from the dome's ladder.

Carême wasn't fond of heights, so he kept his eyes mainly on the surfaces he had to walk. He tried to regulate his breathing as well, navigating around the blue iron ribs rising like drums for the smaller onion domes over the bedrooms.

As he cleared his path around the second one, Carême glanced up to see François mounting a ladder up to the Banqueting Room's tent roof.

There was no other way around except over it, so Carême followed suit, placing one foot after the other, mounting the workmen's scaffold, trying not to look down. He hauled the ladder up after him, to slow pursuers if they got through the door to the roof.

Up top, the moonlight burst full on the stuccoed-over standing seams of the tent. But as the incline was a curving one, walking on it gave Carême the frightening sensation he was constantly being pitched downslope.

He swallowed the fainting feeling and followed on. But as he rounded the last section of tent roof, his heart sank. Up ahead, and down below a good eight feet, François was holding his arms out for balance as he tight-roped a thick plank across a void. Illumination from the Decking Room skylight, ten more feet below his partner, lit up the maitre-d' as if some eerie circus performer. His destination? The shiny copper roof of the Great Kitchen beyond.

Carême wanted to call out François' name, but he thought better of it in case Kitchiner's men were also roving the Pavilion grounds.

Instead, Carême located the place he could lower himself from the Banqueting Room roof onto the ledge with the board.

He could see François already carefully scrambling on the kitchen roof, so Carême inhaled deeply, stuck *his* arms out for balance, and walked the plank. He focused only on the patch of wood where his feet would go next.

Clearing the void over the Decking Room, Carême suddenly thought maybe he shouldn't have, because the forty-five-degree pitch of the Great Kitchen's roof was perilous. Light from the clerestory windows above his head only seemed to make it worse, for now the copper-clad slope appeared smooth and unaccommodating to any toehold.

But when he saw François round the corner up ahead, he soldiered on.

Once he too cleared the corner of the kitchen, he could see the angle of the Servants' Hall roof was not as severe, and an easy cross-over point existed, which François was using at that very moment.

All of a sudden, the breeze shifted and distant motion caught his eye. The gilded dragon weathervane atop the Water Tower slowly glinted as it turned in the moonlight.

Carême had to stop; his muscles were deprived of oxygen and weak.

François' movement again focused Carême's task. He too got down and onto the more tread-friendly slate of the Servants' Hall. Now, although winded and fatigued, he could make good time and close a bit of the distance between them.

And the Water Tower was François' destination. He climbed through a window of this octagonal structure, and in a couple of minutes, so did Carême.

Inside the tower, the chef paused. The great wooden cage of stairs and landings encircling the interior's perimeter reverberated with François' steps. But then, Carême panicked. His partner's footfalls were not below him – heading to escape at street level – but above him.

Carême leaned his body over the handrail, into the void, and saw François' shadow going up and up. He once again drew in a deep lungful of air, fought back tears, and began to follow.

The last flight was a ladder leading to an open hatch. Carême mounted this, at last arriving at the open enclosure right below the cupola on top and its weathervane. Eight arches looked out in all directions, and François sat quietly on the stone balustrade of one of these facing forward. But his back bent low as he stared at the stone floor, catching his breath; his hands, spread wide, anchored him to the railing.

Carême approached slowly, holding out his hand. Gently, he said, through his gasps, *"Villon,* you don't – it's not too late."

The young man slowly recited his namesake, almost as if in a trance:

> *"Wretchedness tracks us everyone with his trace.*
> *Find it writ on the tomb of our ancestors,*
> *The spirits whom we hope God can yet embrace,*
> *Though we poor lack the rich's crowns and sceptres."*

François lifted his head. A look of utter desolation was upon his face.

"Come no closer," he barked as if suddenly waking; only it was from a dream to a nightmare. Tears blurred his vision, but he gathered his thoughts, slowed his tempo, and added with pleading tones, "You will, won't you? Continue to look after Agathé and Marie for me? And tell my daughter – please, you be the one – tell her her *pa-pa* was a patriot for France."

Carême nodded.

"Thank you, *mon amour."*

François let loose his grip on the edge of the stone balustrade. He fell backward, over the handrail and down the ten stories to earth.

In the awful silence that followed, Carême heard the wind shift outside and the gold weathervane pivot with a terrible screech overhead.

Through the film of his own tears, Carême gingerly made his way to where François had just been. He looked down into the court to see the lifeless corpse of his lover twisted on the paving stones.

Carême's hand brushed something.

He picked it up. It was the locket and chain he'd given to François, right where his *Villon* had left it on the handrail.

Chapter 18: Dinner in the Kitchen & Farewell to Thee

Tragedy ever seems to hound the tracks of dishonest men; more so, the more personal they are in their deceptions, the nearer his heels he brings the torments of Hell for others.

So too appears the fate of individuals against the backdrop of Nations and their radicals. For if any noble soul could be trusted to execute the dire plans of those who would terrorize, not one of us is safe from being made radical. World History had been irrevocably altered by François Distré's actions, and though perhaps unknown to the world at large, had deeply affected the life of the man who loved him. For Carême, how many course-corrections in the night would transform his daytime reality in the years to come without his belovèd. How to tell the chef's time, then – properly – if one can never truly make out the hands moving against the Clock face?

Thus in Britain, and the world along with it, the black skies appeared to recede a bit as summer 1817 crept on apace, but in actuality dark times had just moved out of sight to reappear on the upcoming generation's horizon in ways unimagined.

And yet, none of these cruel broodings mattered on this, a bright day in the history of the Pavilion. Bittersweet are farewells, and bracing are the chances to bid them.

The Regent asked a chamber maid several places to his left, "Charming Miss Beatrice, will you partake of the quail dumpling soup?"

The young lady with the apple cheeks reddened even more. "Yes, thank you, Your Highness." She passed her bowl.

The leader of the British Empire dutifully ladled a portion of the piping-hot consommé and passed it down with a smile. He then asked Miss Beatrice's neighbour if she'd like the same.

A remarkable afternoon in annals of Brighton's Royal household was unfolding. Four weeks after the discovery of François' plot, this sunny mid-July day saw the knock-down and removal of the steam and preparation worktops from the Great Kitchen; then a red carpet had been rolled out atop its flagstones and sections of the Banqueting Room table had been re-assembled down the kitchen's central bay. Clothed in Irish linen and set for thirty-five guests with all the precision John

Lightfoot lavished on the Crowned Heads of Europe, it now played host to Carême's final dinner for the Pavilion. A full menu, consisting of four soups and thirty-two entrees, were set out in Carême's meticulous fashion prior to the diners being allowed in – the Household work force who had attended to George's wants so well for so long.

As the meal commenced, high-spirited footmen and sweep-up boys, plus maids and scullery girls – along with all the members of the kitchen and serving staff – sat to eat with their Prince. George himself anchored the western compass-point of the table, the Housekeeper and Royal Butler took the respective middles of the long sides, and Carême presided from the southern, narrow end.

"Senior" staff bit their envious tongues, and who, including the Kitchen Comptroller, the Chief Footman, the Regent's Private Secretary and others, stalked the outside of the table to remove dirty dishes, re-fill wine glasses and perform other 'menial' tasks for their underlings. Meanwhile, poor Sous-chef Bauda was needed to man the roasting spits in the Household Kitchen for the main course, but he would take his rightful place next to the chef's side after the Second Table was laid.

For now, the good Doctor was seated to his right, and Carême served the same role as the Regent, filling the bowls of those who fancied trying the fava bean *potage* resident in his tureen. As he did so, his gaze fell upon George with deep-seated gratification. As ears also picked up the Regent's queries to his staff, and their delighted replies. It all produced a contented feeling in the chef, for here was true democracy in action, and after all, mankind's fate was destined to resolve that each person's bowl is as worthy as another's for rich filling and true enjoyment. The chef's heart was pleased knowing François would have deeply appreciated this moment as well. Europe's greatest chef had toiled at the Pavilion for a year, and when he tendered his resignation, the Regent suggested this dinner would be a fitting send-off, encouraging the chef and giving Carême hope his time here had changed things for the better.

Carême's thoughts were interrupted by Kitchiner directing some low-toned confidences his way. His blue-tinted spectacles glinted in the light from the clerestory windows as he said, "Old boy, I know I've said this before, but – please don't feel you have to leave Brighton because of . . . well, of . . . *his* treachery. A thorough investigation exonerated you, and what's more, the Prince and I *know* you had no hand in his plots. There'll be no repercussions if you stay on – and none of the staff know what happened at the Pavilion. No one will ever know either, I've seen to that."

The Prince's security man had crafted a cover-story: the maitre-d' slipped and fell one night when he went up the Water Tower to star-gaze. It was a tragic accident; not one in fifty knew otherwise in the Royal Household.

"Thank you, Doctor." Carême's words were measured but sincere. "Your reassurances are politic, but my time with the Prince Regent is at its end. The hour has come for me to move on and look for new horizons." But in his soul, the chef dare not say how desolate he felt to be departing England without his François.

"As you like, dear Carême. I thought I'd try one last time." At this point, everyone at the table had a soup of their choice, and at a signal from the Prince – his picking up of a spoon – all settled down to eat it.

The Regent's Valet approached over Kitchiner's shoulder and re-filled the Doctor's wine glass.

"Oh, I love perfectly fresh broad beans," young Master Daniels, seated to Carême's left, mumbled between spoonfuls of his *potage*.

The remark made the *chef de cuisine* smile; it was the perfect invocation for a meal like this.

"I say," asked Kitchiner, dabbing his chin with his napkin, "what's next for you, Carême?"

"I'm not sure. Paris first, naturally, for at least a few months to reconnect to my grounding—"

"And catch up on the latest trends," interjected Thomas.

"Yes, that too. And then, I will investigate my options."

"What might they be?" insisted the Doctor in a polite manner.

"Well – believe it or not – that young Lord Stewart asked me to cook for him in Vienna. And he offered me very generous terms."

"And the Czar," Thomas slurped a second interjection.

"The Czar too?" asked Kitchiner.

"Yes. Funny enough, the day after the Grand Duke's banquet, not only did Charles Stewart invite me to work for him, but Nicholas conveyed an invitation to Saint Petersburg to be personal chef to his brother, the Emperor."

The Doctor chuckled, having done away with his soup in record time. "You have options! And what grand choices as well." Kitchiner's tone turned sly. "And you won't be alone as you begin your new adventures. As for Paris, this certain someone will love it there; I hear it's the food capital of the world."

Carême smiled, never moving his eyes from Doctor's. "It is, and *they* will love it."

Just at that moment, the Kitchen Comptroller was passing behind the Doctor – replete with a surly scowl on his face and white wine decanter in his gloved hand. No doubt the expense of this "staff meal" rancorously rattled in his head.

"Oh, *garçon,"* Carême addressed the moneyman, "Master Daniels' glass is empty. Go and fill it."

After a pause, and impotent glare, the lackey bean-counter lurched to Thomas' side and filled the glass.

Impertinently, the teen boy replied, "Thanks, Donald. That will be all."

After the functionary huffed himself out of sight, the three laughed and laughed.

Meanwhile, the Regent had begun to repeat his playing host with the fish course. The four soup tureens had been removed and replaced by an equal number of piscine delectables.

Thomas had taken over serving duties for the chef and filled dishes as they came his way.

"You know," said Carême to the Doctor, "I think my Brighton innovation of only serving fish after the soup will be a durable one. It only makes sense to follow the lightness of the soup with the lightness of a fish course, unlike the 'traditional' way of serving *pâtés,* or meat, or any old thing."

"Yes, as I've mentioned before," agreed Kitchiner, "soup; fish; meat, it's a natural progression and I imagine people two hundred years from now will still be eating it that way."

Changing topics, the chef mused, "It's too bad that the Princess Charlotte could not be here to wish us a *bon voyage.*"

"Indeed," answered Kitchiner, "but it is best she and Leopold remain at Claremont House, at least for the time being, where they feel the most comfortable."

Placing a slice of turbot on Carême's plate, Thomas asked the Doctor, "And what became of Charlotte's maid, Brigitte?" He was amongst the very few in-the-know.

The Doctor removed and polished his glasses. "Mamzelle Saint-Exupéry was rigorously investigated. No radical ties could be established to her, so the Princess had her way and Brigitte is still in her employ. Charlotte believes her when the maid says she had no idea what François' intentions were. So, there we are."

What the good Doctor failed to say is that George secretly agreed to Brigitte's retention for only six months. After that, the young French woman was to be bundled away in the middle of the night to a Loyalist Judge who'd condemn her to an insane asylum for the rest of her – short – life. Charlotte was never to be the wiser on the girl's fate. To the Regent's way of thinking, the lady's maid's trespasses could not go unpunished. Justice delayed is still justice served.

Those gathered around to share a meal settled down to enjoy the fish selections. Contented sounds filled the room – for many seated at the table, this was their first chance to see what "all the fuss was about" concerning Carême's food. Many a palate finally got it and understood what the chef meant when we spoke about his Art.

"Oh, by the way," Thomas said between forkfuls, "did the Doctor tell you about his good news, Chef Carême?"

"Good news? What good news?"

"My book, old boy. It's out, at last, and already selling well. The impetus to finally settle down and write my *magnum opus* is due to you, dear friend."

"Well, that is wonderful news. Congratulations!"

"Yes, Doctor," added Thomas warmly, "this occasion, she shure deserves congratulations!"

"And Chef, I have seen to it that three copies be placed in your room, atop your trunk, for you to take with you."

Carême considered it for a moment. "You know, I think I know straight off who one copy will go to."

"Oh, yes. Who?"

"An eccentric acquaintance of mine, an old Royal Bourbon Judge named Brillat-Savarin. I believe he will be most interested in the way you have treated your subject; in its way of physiology, that is."

True as the chef's statements were, he failed to remark that Carême's primary reference to the funny old gentleman was as the 'one' who dared to take naps *during* Carême's banquets. And how more eccentric could anyone be!

At that precise moment, the Regent's Private Secretary was scurrying behind Thomas with the last of the white Bordeaux. "I say"—the Doctor's tone to him had a wicked sparkle—"the chef's glass is low. Be a good chappie and top it off."

Thus, Carême's sincerest adversary in the Pavilion was forced to play servile lackey to the great chef's wine glass, which he did, although with some hostile glares.

After he beat a surly retreat, the three friends laughed again and again.

Finally, Carême's mind resolved around the one shared friend missing from this jovial assembly. "What a pity Lady Morgan could not be here today."

Thomas nodded in agreement. "I very much like her."

"I do as well," agreed the Doctor. "But she's needed in Ireland, where there is 'trouble' again." The man suddenly chuckled, making a shrewd glance in the Regent's direction. "There's trouble again in London, for that matter. But in any event, Lady Morgan has gone home to help be the voice of reason, national figure that she is. Reason is needed too if there's ever to be a smooth acclimation to the new void of power-sharing, with their Parliament being shut down by us as an act of revenge. But still, a smooth transition, if that can ever happen."

Carême showed his Republican stripes. "With your feet on their soil? Where matters of Empire are concerned, good Doctor, it is too late. And your countrymen will soon learn around the globe there must be blood for blood in every act of independence."

Kitchiner replied sincerely, "Well, although we English may hope docility to the yoke becomes ingrained, I suppose I cannot argue against your point. 'Blood for Blood'; I will remember that."

The Regent groaned himself to a standing position. First he addressed the mid-level servers. "Fill up every glass – a bumper is called for."

The men scrambled to top off drinking vessels of spit-jack boy and house maid alike.

The Prince picked up his own full glass and held it chest-height. "I thank you all for attending this dinner with Us – me – in the Great Kitchen. The reason for this decorum-shattering meal is a celebration and a thank-you to all of the Pavilion's staff. The Household Service"—he gestured with his glass to the Butler and Housekeeper mid-table—"have seen that every visitor to this home is treated like royalty. And the Kitchen Staff and Footmen have worked tirelessly to ensure our humble Banqueting Room is the most admired and sorely envied dining room in all of Europe. *Bravo!* I drink to you!"

After the Prince drained his wine, he remained standing, holding out his glass to be re-filled with a snap-to grimace.

Guests' glasses were also topped off as the Regent continued.

"And a second reason for our family gathering today is to wish abounding good fortune to Charlotte and Leopold. Their baby – *Our* grandchild – is due in November. So I raise a glass to them and the bright times yet to come!"

Having downed his second 'bumper,' senior staff thought it must have been all there is. But they were wrong. This time the Prince acted downright testy that should be so poor in reading his mind. The lackeys re-filled glasses once more.

The Regent's cordiality returned as he proceeded with a warm glance directed towards the table-end opposite his. "And I wish to raise my glass to an artist who has graced both my kitchen and board. A man who just today told me this great room would be improved if only palm leaves were added to the column tops"—he gestured to the four round supports holding up the clerestory—"because it would lend the space the feeling of an oasis in some oriental desert. And I agreed, and they are being made. In one way, it will be a tangible display of how this man changed and enlivened this Kitchen forever."

He lifted his glass.

"Carême, although you part from our side, we take comfort in knowing a little piece of England will go with you in the form of your new protégé"—he gestured openly to Thomas, who blushed—"and it gladdens our hearts. So, please rise and join me in toasting the man of the hour."

All but Carême got to their feet.

"To Carême," the Prince Regent said, "Chef of Kings, and King of Chefs."

APPENDICES

for Further Reading

Carême in Brighton Appendices:
for **Further Reading**

Works by Antonin Carême

» *Le Pâtissier pittoresque*
first edition (Paris 1815)

https://archive.org/details/b21533842/page/n7/
mode/2up

» *Le Pâtissier royal parisien*
first edition (Paris 1815)

https://archive.org/details/b29328949_0001

» *Le cuisinier parisien, ou l'art de la cuisine française au XIX*
siècle
  first edition (Paris 1822)

https://archive.org/details/b21525407/
page/n5/mode/2up

» *Le maître-d'hôtel française*
  first edition (Paris 1822)

https://archive.org/details/b21525390
0002/page/n11/mode/2up

» *L'art de la cuisine française au XIX* *siècle: traité élémentaire et*
pratique
  first edition (Paris 1832)

https://archive.org/details/b21526047
0002/page/n7/mode/2up

» *L'art de la cuisine française au XIXe siècle: traité élémentaire et pratique* (a modern edition of Carême's 1832 *magnus opus* with a new essay on his life and work)
Gilles and Laurence Laurendon [Editors] (Paris 1994)

https://app.ckbk.com/book/222888862
1/lart-de-la-cuisine-francaise-au-xixe-
siecle

» *The Royal Parisian Pastrycook and Confectioner* (first translation of *Le Pâtissier royal parisien*)
John Porter (London 1834)

https://books.google.com/books?id=hK7-
ltOfXwEC&pg=PP11&dq=careme&hl=en&new
bks=1&newbks_redir=0&sa=X&ved=2ahUKEwi
qxJm7jYL1AhWlV98KHQTtD4oQ6AF6BAgJEA
l#v=onepage&q&f=false

» *French Cookery: comprising L'art de la cuisine française, Le Pâtissier royal, Le cuisinier parisien*
   William Hall (London 1836)

https://archive.org/details/b29338098

Works concerning Antonin Carême

» *19th Century France – La Cuisine Classique* (chapter 8 of "The Delectable past; the Joys of the Table")
   Esther Aresty (New York 1964)

https://archive.org/details/delectablep
ast00ares/page/126/mode/2up

» *The Century of Carême* (chapter 9 of "Culture and Cuisine: a Journey through the History of Food")
   Jean-François Ravel (Garden City, New York, 1982)

https://archive.org/details/culturecuisin
ej00reve/page/230/mode/2up

» *L'art culinaire au XIXe siècle Antonin Carême* (catalog of the
exhibit held by the City of Paris to celebrate the 200th birthyear
of Antonin Carême)
   Délégation à l'action artistique de la ville de Paris
   (Alençon, Normandie, 1984)

https://www.lefestindebabette.fr/produ
ct/collectif-lart-culinaire-au-xixe-siecle-
antonin-careme-1784-1984-
catalogue-de-lexposition-a-lorangerie-
de-bagatelle-a-paris-3e-
arrondissement-en-1984/

» *Antonin Carême, 1783-1833: la sensualité gourmande en
Europe*
   Georges Bernier (Paris 1989)

https://archive.org/details/antonincare
me1780000bern

» *Cooking for Kings: the Life of Antonin Carême, the First Celebrity Chef*
   Ian Kelly (New York 2004)

https://online.ucpress.edu/gastronomi
ca/article-
abstract/5/1/105/45931/Cooking-for-
Kings-The-Life-of-Antonin-Careeme-
the?redirectedFrom=fulltext

» *Le roi Carême* (a novel)
   Philippe Alexandre and Béatrix de l'Aulnoit (Paris 2005)

https://archive.org/details/leroicareme
0000alex/mode/2up

» *Talleyrand et Antonin Carême: la gastronomie au service de la diplomatie* (article in the September 23rd edition of the newspaper "Le Parisien")
    Charles de Saint-Sauveur (Paris 2018)

https://www.leparisien.fr/politique/talle
yrand-et-antonin-careme-la-
gastronomie-au-service-de-la-
diplomatie-23-09-2018-7899591.php

Works by Doctor William Kitchiner

» *Practical Observations on Telescopes*
first edition (London 1815)

https://archive.org/details/b30795680

» *Apicius Redivivus; or, The Cook's Oracle*
first edition (London 1817)

https://archive.org/details/b21533908/
page/n5/mode/2up

» *The Cook's Oracle*
third edition (London 1821)

https://archive.org/details/b21526357

» *The Art of Invigorating and Prolonging Life by Food,*
Clothes, Air, Exercise, Sleep, &c.; And Peptic Precepts
Pointing out Agreeable and Effectual Methods to Prevent and
Relieve Indigestion
    second edition (London 1821)

https://archive.org/details/artofinvigora
tin00kitciala

» *Observations on Vocal Music; and Rules for the Accent, and*
Emphasis of Poetry
    first edition (London 1821)

https://books.google.com/books?id=BntWDjGC
9SwC&pg=PP10&dq=kitchiner&hl=en&newbks
=1&newbks_redir=0&sa=X&ved=2ahUKEwi3-
6HphYL1AhXtUt8KHbWsA_44FBDoAXoECAY
QAg#v=onepage&q&f=false

» *The Economy of the Eyes: Precepts for the Improvement and*
Preservation of the Sight
    first edition (London 1824)

https://archive.org/details/economyey
es00kitc

Works concerning Doctor William Kitchiner

» *Obituary—Dr. Kitchiner* (entry in the May edition of "The Gentleman's Magazine")
   Sylvanus Urban, *pseudonym* (London 1827)

https://books.google.com/books?id=Y
H0dAQAAMAAJ&pg=PA470&dq=kitc
hiner&hl=en&newbks=1&newbks_redi
r=0&sa=X&ved=2ahUKEwj-
yoqfg4L1AhXsRzABHTWcAt04ChDo
AXoECAoQAg#v=onepage&q&f=false

» *Eccentricities of Dr* [sic] *Kitchiner* (satirical article in "The Book of Days: a Miscellany of Popular Antiquities," under the February 26th entry; the day of Kitchiner's birth)
   W. and R. Chambers Company (London 1863)

https://books.google.com/books?id=u
JILw50Xk14C&pg=PA298&dq=kitchin
er&hl=en&newbks=1&newbks_redir=0
&sa=X&ved=2ahUKEwiT1qmh_4H1A
hXblWoFHV_iD6QQ6AF6BAgLEAl#v
=onepage&q&f=false

» *Personal Reminiscences: Dr. William Kitchiner*
  Archibald Constable (New York 1876)

https://books.google.com/books?id=e
UYDAAAAYAAJ&pg=PA209&dq=kitc
hiner&hl=en&newbks=1&newbks_redi
r=0&sa=X&ved=2ahUKEwj-
yoqfg4L1AhXsRzABHTWcAt04ChDo
AXoECAcQAg#v=onepage&q&f=false

» *Some Old Cookery Books and Their Authors: Dr. Kitchiner
and the Cook's Oracle* (Printed in the September edition of
"Table Talk" magazine)
  Charles Cooper (Cooperstown, New York, 1914)

https://books.google.com/books?id=zQFBAQA
AMAAJ&pg=PA486&dq=kitchiner&hl=en&newb
ks=1&newbks_redir=0&sa=X&ved=2ahUKEwjy
xYmU-IH1AhV-
SzABHcIwAYs4ChDoAXoECAMQAg#v=onepa
ge&q&f=false

» *Dr. William Kitchiner and his Cook Book*
Betsy Copping Corner (New Haven, Connecticut, 1954)

https://www.worldcat.org/title/dr-william-
kitchiner-and-his-cook-book/oclc/1027018984

» *Dr. William Kitchiner, Regency Eccentric: Author of the
Cook's Oracle*
Tom Bridge and Colin Cooper English (Lews, East Sussex,
1992)

https://archive.org/details/drwilliamkitc
hin0000brid

Works concerning *la grande cuisine classique*
(a personal selection from the shelves of my library)

» *The Modern Cook*
   Vincent La Chapelle (London 1733)

https://archive.org/details/moderncook
01lach

» *The Physiology of Taste: or Meditations on Transcendental Gastronomy* (a full translation of the 1825 original)
   Jean-Anthelme Brillat-Savarin [J. C. Nimmo, Editor]
   (London 1884)

http://berkelouw.com.au/rare-book/a-
handbook-of-gastronomy-brillat-savarin-s-
physiologie/244314/buy-online

» *Les classiques de la table, à l'usage des praticiens et des gens du monde*
    M. F. Fayot [Editor] (Paris 1843)

https://archive.org/details/b21525869/
page/n9/mode/2up

» *The Modern Cook; A Practical Guide to the Culinary Arts and All its Branches*
    Charles Elmé Francatelli [one of Carême's latter protégés], 13th
    edition (London 1861)

https://archive.org/details/b21530245

» *The Escoffier Cookbook: A Guide to the Fine Art of French Cuisine* (a full translation of the original 1903 *Le guide culinaire)*
Auguste Escoffier (New York 1969)

https://www.goodreads.com/book/show/27366
9.The_Escoffier_Cookbook

» *Ma Cuisine* (a full translation of the 1934 original)
Auguste Escoffier (London 1984)

https://archive.org/details/macuisine0000esco

» *Larousse Gastronomique* (translation of the 1938 original)
Prosper Montagné (New York 1961)

https://archive.org/details/laroussegastrono000
0mont_w7s3

» *A Concise Encyclopaedia of Gastronomy*
André Simon (New York 1952)

https://books.google.com/books/about/A_Conci
se_Encyclopedia_of_Gastronomy.html?id=PJ8
sAAAAYAAJ

» *An Illustrated History of French Cuisine: from Charlemagne to Charles de Gaulle*
Christian Guy (New York 1962)

https://www.goodreads.com/book/show/21452
82.An_Illustrated_History_of_French_Cuisine_f
rom_Charlemagne_to_Charles_de_Gaulle

» *The Art of French Cooking by the Great Contemporary Masters of Cuisine: 3760 Recipes and Instructions for Masterpiece Cookery*
Bart Winer [Editor] (New York 1962)

https://www.secondwindvintage.com/p
roduct/1962-the-art-of-french-cooking-
by-the-great-contemporary-masters-
of-the-cuisine-new-revised-edition-
french-cookbook-french-cook-
book/?add-to-cart=23666

» *Modern French Culinary Art*
   Henri-Paul Pellaprat (Cleveland 1966)

https://archive.org/details/modernfrenchculi00p
ell

» *Gastronomy of France*
   Raymond Oliver (London 1967)

https://archive.org/details/gastronomyoffran00oliv

» *La Cuisine: Secrets of Modern French Cooking* (translation of the 1967 original)
    Raymond Oliver (New York 1969)

https://archive.org/details/lacuisinesecrets00oliv/page/2/mode/2up

» *Classic French Cooking*
    Craig Claiborne and Pierre Franey (New York 1971)

https://archive.org/details/classicfrenchcoo00time/mode/2up

» *The Hundred Glories of French Cooking*
    Robert Courtine (New York 1973)

https://www.deslegte.com/the-hundred-glories-
of-french-cooking-2774225/

» *La Technique: An Illustrated Guide to the Fundamental
Techniques of Cooking*
   Jacques Pépin (New York 1977)

https://www.splendidtable.org/story/2018/09/05
/jacques-pepins-la-technique-was-a-game-
changer-for-home-cooks

» *The Grand Masters of French Cuisine: Five Centuries of
Great Cooking*
   Céline Vence / Robert Courtine (New York 1978)

https://app.ckbk.com/book/0399122206/the-
grand-masters-of-french-cuisine-five-centuries-
of-great-cooking

» *Auguste Escoffier: Memories of my Life* (translation of the 1985 original)
    Laurance Escoffier [Editor] (New York 1997)

https://archive.org/details/augusteescoffier0000
esco

» *A Palate in Revolution: Grimod de La Reynière and the Almanach des Gourmands*
    Giles MacDonogh (London 1987)

https://www.worldcat.org/title/palate-in-revolution-grimond-de-la-reyniere-and-the-almanac-des-gourmands/oclc/16468441

» *Paris Boulangerie-Pâtisserie: Recipes from Thirteen Outstanding French Bakeries*
    Linda Dannenberg (New York 1994)

https://www.biblio.com/9780517592212

» *Great Cooks and their Recipes: from Taillevent to Escoffier*
Anne Willan (London 2000)

https://archive.org/details/greatcookstheirr0000
will/page/n3/mode/2up

Works by Lady Sydney Morgan

» *Saint Clair; or, The Heiress of Desmond*
first edition (London 1803)

https://books.google.com/books?id=bFjc2ZXVL
T0C&printsec=frontcover&dq=morgan&ei=3nv
HYfH5Gom-
2Qbs2LTlAw&cd=1#v=onepage&q&f=false

» *The Wild Irish Girl; A National Tale*
third edition (London 1807)

https://books.google.com/books?id=IPj5BgdS
UoC&printsec=frontcover&source=gbs_ge_su
mmary_r&cad=0#v=onepage&q&f=false

» *France*
first edition (London 1817)

https://books.google.com/books?id=jroBAAAA
YAAJ&printsec=frontcover&dq=lady+morgan+f
rance&hl=en&newbks=1&newbks_redir=0&sa=
X&ved=2ahUKEwjLka7s5_0AhW3SjABHfg_A
nwQ6AF6BAgLEAI#v=onepage&q&f=false

» *The Book of the Boudoir*
first edition (London 1829)

https://books.google.com/books?id=X3adV59l
wSsC&printsec=frontcover&dq=lady+morgan&
hl=en&newbks=1&newbks_redir=0&sa=X&ved
=2ahUKEwiB6Juv4_0AhUlTd8KHZp5BJM4F
BDoAXoECAQQAg#v=onepage&q&f=false

» *Lady Morgan's Memoirs: Autobiography, Diaries and Correspondence*
unknown edition (London 1862)

https://books.google.com/books?id=ql9AAAAA
YAAJ&printsec=frontcover&dq=lady+morgan&
hl=en&newbks=1&newbks_redir=0&sa=X&ved
=2ahUKEwih3JuQ5v_0AhXqV98KHfyvDWEQ6
AF6BAgDEAI#v=onepage&q&f=false

Works concerning Lady Sydney Morgan

» *Notable Irishwomen*
    C. J. Hamilton (Dublin 1900)

https://archive.org/details/notableirishwome000
0cjha/page/n5/mode/2up

» *Lady Morgan in France*
    Elizabeth Suddaby and P. E. Yarrow (London 1971)

https://www.biblio.com/book/lady-morgan-
france-suddaby-elizabeth-
yarrow/d/1287364232

» *Sydney Owenson, Lady Morgan and the Politics of Style*
    first edition (Palo Alto, California, 2009)

https://books.google.com/books?id=_hFUsDGe
8TYC&printsec=frontcover&dq=lady+morgan&
hl=en&newbks=1&newbks_redir=0&sa=X&ved
=2ahUKEwih3JuQ5v_0AhXqV98KHfyvDWEQ6
AF6BAgLEAI#v=onepage&q&f=false

Works concerning The Pavilion and John Nash

» *The Brighton Pavilion and its Royal and Municipal Associations*
John George Bishop (Brighton 1900)

https://books.google.com/books?id=LBQ5AQA
AMAAJ&printsec=frontcover&source=gbs_ge_
summary_r&cad=0#v=onepage&q&f=false

» *The Life and Work of John Nash, Architect*
John Summerson (London 1980)

https://archive.org/details/lifeworkofjohnna0000
summ/page/n7/mode/2up

» *Catalogue and Exhibit Guide to the Royal Pavilion, Brighton*
John Morley [Contributor] (Brighton 1984)

https://www.goodreads.com/book/show/55562
731-the-royal-pavilion-the-official-guide-to-the-
palace-of-king-george-iv

» *The Making of the Royal Pavilion, Brighton: Designs and
Drawings*
John Morley (New York 1984)

https://www.amazon.com/Making-Royal-Pavilion-Brighton-Drawings-dp-0879235284/dp/0879235284/ref=mt_other?_en coding=UTF8&me=&qid=

» *Views of the Royal Pavilion* (full-color reprint of the 1826 original)
  John Nash (London 1992)

https://www.goodreads.com/book/show/76927 18-views-of-the-royal-pavilion

APPENDICES

Acknowledgments

Carême in Brighton Appendices:
Acknowledgements

I warmly acknowledge the general support my work garners on the literary web-site *gayauthors.org,* but would like to thank the following site members for their individual help with this project.

First, to Parker Owens for editing and beta-reading *Carême in Brighton,* I owe tremendous thanks. His insight has been invaluable.

In addition, for their equally insightful beta-reading of the novel, my warm thanks go to Cole Matthews and Defiance19.

For their respective language and cultural skills, I extend my gratitude to Colochette (for French matters in the book) and to D. K. Daniels (for all things Irish). Both have been remarkably generous with me by sharing their time and knowledge.

Needless to say, any errors remaining in the novel are entirely mine. This includes the misstatement of time concerning when John Nash's masterplan of London was drawn up. I present the renovation of the city as not being under way by 1817, which it most certainly was. This is intentional, so I might have excuse to introduce how intimate a friend Philip Hardwick was to the Good Doctor. And the scene I wrote with this architect passing along the notion of how the development of the future Regent's Park, and its huge revenue stream to George, could have occurred in similar, private get-togethers.

I would also like to say that this project has been on my mind for a long time, re-visiting me from time to time with the possibilities of differing forms and content. In the shape it has assumed over the course of the nearly four years it has taken me to write it, two biographies offered important information.

Messrs. Bridge and Cooper English's *Dr. William Kitchiner, Regency Eccentric* (see *"for* Further Reading" above) provided the clues to follow up on what being a religious outcast in Regency England must have been like. I had never encountered reports of the religion-based mob murders known as "Gordon's Riot" before reading the authors' account of it. And they also show how this pro-Anglican Church violence touched the young William Kitchiner directly as a child. (Nowadays we'd call this a "race massacre," but in the centre of 1780s London, the looting and lynchings were directed at members of the oppressed and benighted Catholic minority.)

In addition, although the best biographical material on the life and times of Antonin Carême remain entirely French, Ian Kelley's 2004 *Cooking for Kings* (see *"for* Further Reading" above) offers something none of the French sources I've read do: a detailed review of the ledger books from the Pavilion for the time Carême was working there. Although seemingly dry, the numbers Kelly quotes – and the below-stairs goings-on hinted at in these authentic accounts – have provided the sure grounding from which my fiction was launched.

And, as for you, dear reader, as you come to the conclusion of *Carême in Brighton,* I express gratitude for your forbearance and look forward to your reading more of my work. Thank you.

www.ingramcontent.com/pod-product-compliance
Lightning Source LLC
Chambersburg PA
CBHW020226260626
47156CB00002B/550